THE COUP
BY
JOHN UPDIKE

"WHAT A RICH, SURPRISING AND OFTEN FUNNY NOVEL . . . one of Updike's strongest . . . a book that stands with the two *Rabbit* novels and *The Centaur* as an example of what this extraordinarily prolific novelist can do when his imagination, as well as his language, is strenuously engaged."

—*New York Times Book Review*

"A POWERFUL WORK, BEAUTIFULLY CALIBRATED, PERSUASIVE AND LUSTROUS . . . passionate and humorous in equal degrees. The novel itself is a coup. . . . Updike is a writer whose mastery of the novel is indisputable."

—*Bookviews*

Fawcett Crest and Premier Books
by John Updike:

THE POORHOUSE FAIR   23314-6 $1.50

RABBIT, RUN   24031-2 $2.25

PIGEON FEATHERS   23951-9 $1.95

THE CENTAUR   23974-8 $1.95

OF THE FARM   30822-7 $1.50

THE MUSIC SCHOOL   23279-4 $1.75

COUPLES   24023-1 $2.50

RABBIT REDUX   24087-8 $2.25

A MONTH OF SUNDAYS   C2701 $1.95

PICKED-UP PIECES   23363-4 $2.50

MARRY ME   23369-3 $1.95

TOO FAR TO GO   24002-9 $2.25

THE COUP   24259-5 $2.50

JOHN UPDIKE

The Coup

FAWCETT CREST • NEW YORK

THE COUP

THIS BOOK CONTAINS THE COMPLETE TEXT OF
THE ORIGINAL HARDCOVER EDITION.

Published by Fawcett Crest Books, a unit of CBS Publications,
the Consumer Publishing Division of CBS Inc., by arrange-
ment with Alfred A. Knopf, Inc.

Copyright © 1978 by John Updike

ALL RIGHTS RESERVED

ISBN: 0-449-24259-5

Excerpts from The Koran (fourth revised edition) are re-
printed by permission of Penguin Books Ltd. © 1956, 1959,
1966, 1968, 1974 N. J. Dawood.

Dual Selection of the Book-of-the-Month Club
Selection of the Quality Paperback Book Club

Printed in the United States of America

10 9 8 7 6 5 4 3 2 1

TO MY MOTHER

fellow writer & lover of far lands

ACKNOWLEDGMENTS

The Koran quotations are from the Penguin Classics translation by N. J. Dawood. The Melville lines at the head of Chapter IV come from "The House-top: A Night Piece," composed during the Draft Riots of July 1863 in New York City, when George Opdyke was mayor. The epigraph for Chapter VII is taken from an address given by Professor el-Calamawy at a conference on "Arab and American Cultures" that she and I attended in Washington in September of 1976. Professors George N. Atiyeh of The Library of Congress, G. Wesley Johnson of the University of California at Santa Barbara, and Carl R. Proffer of the University of Michigan have generously responded to requests for information. My African history derived from books by Basil Davidson, Robert W. July, E. Jefferson Murphy, Olivia Vlahos, J. W. Nyakatura, Alfred Guillaume, Paul Fordham, Colin Turnbull, Alan Moorehead, Leda Farrant, Jacques Berque, Roland Oliver, and J. D. Fage. For geography, I used the *National Geographic* magazine, children's books, *Beau Geste,* and travellers' accounts from Mungo Park to Evelyn Waugh, from René Caillié to John Gunther. Two out-of-the-way volumes of especial value were *The Politics of Natural Disaster: The Case of the Sahel Drought,* edited by Michael H. Glantz, and *Islam in West Africa,* by J. Spencer Trimingham. Thurston Clarke's *The Last Caravan,* a factual account of the Nigerien Tuareg during the 1968–74 drought, was published while I was retyping my manuscript, too late for me to benefit from more than a few details of its informational wealth. My wife, Martha, helped with the typing and, for the year in which she was this novel's sole reader, beautifully smiled upon it. Not that she, or any of the above, are responsible for irregularities in my engineering of *The Coup.*

J. U.

Does there not pass over man a space of time when his life is a blank?

THE KORAN, sura 76

The Coup

One

MY COUNTRY of Kush, landlocked between the mongrelized, neo-capitalist puppet states of Zanj and Sahel, is small for Africa, though larger than any two nations of Europe. Its northern half is Saharan; in the south, forming the one boundary not drawn by a Frenchman's ruler, a single river flows, the Grionde, making possible a meagre settled agriculture. Peanuts constitute the principal export crop: the doughty legumes are shelled by the ton and crushed by village women in immemorial mortars or else by antiquated presses manufactured in Lyons; then the barrelled oil is caravanned by camelback and treacherous truck to Dakar, where it is shipped to Marseilles to become the basis of heavily perfumed and erotically contoured soaps designed not for my naturally fragrant and affectionate countrymen but for the antiseptic lavatories of America—America, that fountainhead of obscenity and glut. Our peanut oil travels westward the same distance as eastward our ancestors plodded, their neck-shackles chafing down to the jugular, in the care of Arab traders, to find from the flesh-markets of Zanzibar eventual lodging in the harems and palace guards of Persia and Chinese Turkestan. Thus Kush spreads its transparent wings across the world. The ocean of desert between the northern border and the Mediterranean littoral once knew a trickling traffic in salt for gold, weight for weight; now this void is disturbed only be Swedish playboys fleeing cold boredom in Volvos that soon forfeit their seven coats of paint to the rasp of sand and the roar of their engines to the omnivorous howl of the harmattan. They are skeletons before their batteries die. Would that Allah had so disposed of all infidel intruders!

To the south, beyond the Grionde, there is forest, nakedness, animals, fever, chaos. It bears no looking into. Whenever a Kushite ventures into this region, he is stricken with *mal à l'estomac.*

Kush is a land of delicate, delectable emptiness, named for a vanished kingdom, the progeny of Kush, son of Ham, grandson of Noah. Their royalty, ousted from the upper Nile in the fourth century by the Christian hordes of Axum, retreated from Meroë, fabled home of iron, into the wastes of Kordofan and Darfur, and farther westward still, pursued by dust devils along the parched savanna, erecting red cities soon indistinguishable from the rocks, until their empty shattered name, a shard of grandeur, was salvaged by our revolutionary council in 1968 and, replacing the hated designation of Noire, was bestowed upon this hollow starving nation as many miles as years removed from the original Kush, itself an echo: Africa held up a black mirror to Pharaonic Egypt, and the image was Kush.

The capital is Istiqlal, renamed in 1960, upon independence, and on prior maps called Cailliéville, in honor of the trans-Saharan traveller of 1828, who daubed his face brown, learned pidgin Arabic, and achieved European celebrity by smuggling himself into a caravan from Timbuctoo to Fez and doing what hundreds of unsung Berbers had been doing for centuries, maligning them as brutes even while he basked in the loud afterglow of their gullible hospitality. Previous to French organization of the territory of Noire in 1905 (checking a British thrust arising in the Sudan), the area on both sides of the river had been known, vaguely, as Wanjiji. An Arab trading town, Al-Abid, much shrunken from its former glory, huddles behind the vast white-and-green Palais de l'Administration des Noirs, modelled on the Louvre and now used in its various wings as offices for the present government, a People's Museum of Imperialist Atrocities, a girls' high school dedicated to the extirpation of the influences of Christian mission education, and a prison for the politically aberrant.

In area Kush measures 126,912,180 hectares. The population density comes to .03 per hectare. In the vast north it is virtually immeasurable. The distant glimpsed figure blends with the land as the blue hawk blends with the sky. There are twenty-two miles of railroad and one hundred seven of paved highway. Our national airline, Air Kush, consists of two Boeing 727s, stunning as they glitter above the also glittering tin shacks by the airfield. In addition to peanuts are grown millet, sorghum, cotton, yams, dates, tobacco, and indigo. The acacia trees yield some marketable gum arabic. The natives extract ingenious benefits from the baobab tree, weaving mats from its fibrous heart, ropes from its inner bark, brewing porridge and glue and a diaphoretic for dysentery from the pulp of its fruit, turning the elongated shells into water scoops, sucking the acidic and refreshing seeds, and even boiling the leaves, in desperate times, into a kind of spinach. When are times not desperate? Goats eat the little baobab trees, so there are only old giants. The herds of livestock maintained by the tribes of pastoral nomads have been dreadfully depleted by the drought. The last elephant north of the Grionde gave up its life and its ivory in 1959, with a bellow that still reverberates. "The toubabs took the big ears with them," is the popular saying. Both Sahel and Zanj possess quantities of bauxite, manganese, and other exploitable minerals, but aside from a streak of sulphur high in the Bulub Mountains the only known mineral deposit in Kush is the laterite that renders great tracts of earth unarable. (I am copying these facts from an old *Statesman's Year-Book*, freely, here where I sit in sight of the sea, so some of them may be obsolete.) In the north there were once cities of salt populated by slaves, who bred and worshipped and died amid the incessant cruel glisten; these mining settlements, supervised by the blue-clad Tuareg, are mere memories now. But even memory thins in this land, which suggests, on the map, an angular skull whose cranium is the empty desert. Along the lower irregular line of the jaw, carved by the wandering brown river, there was a king, the Lord of Wanjiji, whose physical body was a facet of God so radiant that a curtain of gold flakes protected the eyes of those entertained in audience from his glory; and this king, restored to the throne as a constitutional monarch in the wake of the *loi-cadre* of 1956 and compelled to abdicate after the revolution of 1968, has been all but forgotten. Conquerors and governments pass before the people as dim rumors, as entertainment in a hospital ward. Truly, mercy is interwoven with misery in the world wherever we glance.

Among the natural resources of Kush perhaps should be listed our diseases—an ample treasury which includes, besides famine and its edema and kwashiorkor, malaria, typhus, yellow fever, sleeping sickness, leprosy, bilharziasis, onchocerciasis, measles, and yaws. As these are combatted by the genius of science, human life itself becomes a disease of the overworked, eroded earth. The average life expectancy in Kush is thirty-seven years, the per capita gross national product $79, the literacy rate 6%. The official currency is the *lu*. The flag is a plain green field. The form of government is a constitutional monarchy with the constitution suspended and the monarch deposed. An eleven-man Suprême Counseil Révolutionnaire et Militaire pour l'Émergence serves as the executive arm of the government and also functions as its legislature. The pure and final socialism envisioned by Marx, the theocratic populism of Islam's periodic reform movements: these transcendent models guide the council in all decisions. SCRME's chairman, and the Commander-in-Chief of the Armed Forces, Minister of National Defense, and President of Kush was (*is*, the *Statesman's Year-Book* has it) Colonel Hakim Félix Ellelloû—that is to say, myself.

Yet a soldier's disciplined self-effacement, my Cartesian schooling, and the African's traditional abjuration of ego all constrain this account to keep to the third person. There are two selves: the one who acts, and the "I" who experiences. This latter is passive even in a whirlwind of the former's making, passive and guiltless and astonished. The historical performer bearing the name of Ellelloû was no less mysterious to me than to the American press wherein he was never presented save snidely and wherein his fall was celebrated with a veritable minstrelsy of anti-Negro, anti-Arab cartoons; in the same spirit the beer-crazed mob of American boobs cheers on any autumnal Saturday or Sunday the crunched leg of the unhome-team left tackle as he is stretchered off the field. Ellelloû's body and career carried me here, there, and I never knew why, but submitted.

We know this much of him: he was short, prim, and

black. He was produced, in 1933, of the rape of a Salu
woman by a Nubian raider. The Salu are a sedentary tribe
in the peanut highlands of the west. His mother, a large,
oppressively vital woman of the clan Amazeg, became the
wife by inheritance of her husband's sister's husband, her
own husband having been slaughtered the same night of her
rape. The peanut lands are brown, the whispering feathery
brown of the uprooted bushes as they dry, precious pods
inward, in stacks two meters high, and Ellelloû from the
first, perhaps taking his clue from these strange fruits that
can mature only underground, showed a wish to merge
with his surroundings. In the public eye he always wore
brown, the tan of his military uniform, unadorned, as monotonous and uninsistent as the tan of the land itself, the
savanna merging into desert. Even the rivers in Kush are
brown, but for the blue moment when the torrents of a
rainstorm boil murderously down a wadi; and the sudden
verdure of the rainy season soon dons a cloak of dust. In
conformity with the prejudices of the Prophet, Ellelloû
resisted being photographed. Such tattered images, in
sepia tints, as gathered fly specks in the shop windows
and civic corridors of Istiqlal were hieratic and inex-
pressive. His one affectation of costume was the assumption, on some state occasions, of those particularly
excluding and protective sunglasses whose odd trade
name is NoIR. It was said that his anonymity was a
weapon, for armed with it he would venture out among
the populace as a spy and beggar, in the manner of the
fabled Caliph Haroun ar-Raschid. Colonel Ellelloû was a
devout Muslim. He had four wives, and left them all (it
was said) unsatisfied, so consuming was his love for the
arid land of Kush.

At the age of seventeen, to escape the constriction of
village life, in whose order his illegitimacy and his
mother's widowhood gave him a low place, he enlisted in

the *Troupes coloniales* and eventually saw service in French Indochina prior to Colonel de Castries' defeat at Dienbienphu in 1954, by which time he had risen to the rank of sergeant. In battle he found himself possessed of a dead calm that to his superiors appeared commmendable. In truth it was peanut behavior. Out of the tightest spot, even as when the hordes of General Giap outnumbered the defenders four to one and the Asiatic abhorrence of black skins was notoriously lethal to the *troupes noires,* Ellelloû had faith that the pull of fate would rescue him, if he be numb enough, and submit to being shelled. During the subsequent campaigns of his division, which was called into fratricidal struggle with the independence-seekers of Algeria, Ellelloû left no trace of himself on the military record. He re-emerges from the shadows around 1959, with the rank of major, as an attaché to King Edumu IV, Lord of Wanjiji. The Gallic imperialists' failure with Bao Dai had not totally soured their taste for puppet monarchs. The king was then in his sixties, and had spent a dozen years under house arrest by the colonial representatives of the Fourth Republic in retribution for his alleged collaboration with the Vichy government of Noire and their German sponsors, his shame doubled by the heroic example of resistance offered by Félix Eboué of French Equatorial Africa to the south. Ellelloû continued in close association with the king and with the liberal-bourgeois-elitist administration to which the king lent his tarnished authority, until the coup of 1968, in which Ellelloû, though secondary to the well-mourned people's hero Major-General Jean-François Yakubu Soba, played a decisive, if not conspicuous, part. He became Minister of Information in 1969, Minister of Defense later that year, and upon the successful assassination attempt upon General Soba on the twelfth day of Ramadan, President. According to the *Statesman's Year-Book,* he keeps an apartment within the grandiose government building erected by the French and another in the military barracks at Sobaville. His wives are scattered in four separate villas in the suburb still called, as it was in the days of imperialist enslavement, Les Jardins. His domicilic policy is apparently to be in no one place at any specific time. More than this, of the legendary national leader and Third-World spokesman, is difficult to discover.

Why did the king love me? I ask myself this in anguish, remembering his infinitely creased face surrounded by wiry white hair and in color the sunken black of a dried fig, his way of nodding and nodding as if his head were mounted on a tremulously balanced pivot, his cackle of mirth and greed like a fine box crushed underfoot, his preposterously bejewelled little hands, so little thickened by labor as to seem two-dimensional, so lightly gesturing, lifting in a wind of hopeless gaiety and sadness such as lifts puffs of dust on the street. His pallid eyes, not blue yet not brown either, a green, rather, blanched by his blindness to a cat's shallow-backed yellow, always reminded me that his royal line had come from the north, contemptuous and foreign, however darkened—arrogant assailants, themselves in flight, bringing with them, worse than their personal cruelties, the terrible idea of time, of history, of a revelation receding inexorably, leaving us to live and die to no purpose, in a state of nonsense. What did this blind man see when he looked at me? I can only speculate that, amid so many possessed by their personal causes, by schemes of aggrandizement for themselves and their clans and their wives' clans, I was a blur of a new color, patriotism. This arbitrary and amorphous land descended to him from the French, this slice of earth with its boundaries sketched by an anonymous cartographer at the infamous Berlin Conference of 1885 and redrawn more firmly as a military zone for occupation a decade later, its pacification not complete until 1917 and its assets to this day mortgaged to La Banque de France and its beautiful brown thin people invisible on every map— what was it? The historic kingdom of Wanjiji had expanded and contracted like the stomach of some creature that does not eat for centuries; by the time the Gauls, at de Gaulle's mystical bidding, abandoned colonial rule and cast about for an agency wherewith to rule covertly, Wanjiji had shrunk to a name and a notion of infinite privilege in the head of one ancient prisoner. He, casting about in turn, saw in me, an exile returned with re-educated passions, what he failed to discern within himself: an idea of Kush.

In the Year of the Prophet 1393, which the comic arithmetic of the infidels numbers as 1973, at the end of the wet season, which had been dry, the President went to visit the king. The people thought the Lord of Wanjiji dead, executed with his ministers and his cousins those first tonic months of the Revolution, in the inner Cour de Justice, where now the girls of the Anti-Christian High School played hockey and volleyball. In truth King Edumu was held a secret captive in the Palais de l'Administration des Noirs, along the wall of whose endless corridors, at the level of a walking man's knuckles, ran a painted green strip like an interior horizon. The floor was speckled with flakes of lime fallen from the ceiling above, where the frosted foliations of Art Nouveau were a few of them unbroken. In the perpetual dusk of these halls soldiers saluted the dictator as he passed, and their whores with a whimper and a swirl of their rags hid in the doorways of offices become barracks. At this hour the smell of scorching feathers wafted from chambers where once clerks whose very mustaches appeared thin as penstrokes had scribbled a web of imaginary order. From the king's guarded apartment came a perfume of cloves and a drone of the Koran. The old man to relieve the boredom of his captivity and perhaps to curry favor with his fanatic captor had converted to the True Faith and for the hour before evening azan had read to him those suras which body forth Paradise. *"For the unbelievers We have prepared fetters and chains, and a blazing Fire. But the righteous shall drink of a cup tempered at the Camphor Fountain, a gushing spring at which the servants of Allah will refresh themselves. . . ."* The enchanting old villain formerly had taken pride in a barbarous animism of blood and substitution, and in the interstices of French supervision had exercised the fructifying privilege of royal murderousness. Young female attendants especially had fallen victims to his whim. And though their screams under the ax and the smothering pillows had escaped from the palace windows, there was never a shortage of nubile, trembling, onyx-skinned, heavy-breasted replacements, thrust forward not only by the sycophancy of their families but by something suicidal and, beneath their moist terror, voracious within themselves. *"Reclining there upon soft couches, they shall feel neither the scorching heat nor the biting cold. Trees will spread their shade around them, and fruits will hang in clusters over them."* The king's cell was lit by a clay-colored slant of late sun. He knew Elleloû's tread, and with a divinely scant gesture signalled his reader, a young Fula wearing upon his shaved head a plum-red fez, to be silent.

Never large, the king had shrunken. His little hooked nose alone had resisted the reshaping of time and sat in the center of his face like a single tart fruit being served on an outworn platter. His shallow yellow eyes shifted rapidly and still appeared to see. Indeed, an examining physician had reported that they remained sensitive to violent movement, and to a candle held close enough to singe his eyebrows.

"Splendor of Splendors," Ellelloû began, "thy unworthy agent greets thee."

"A beggar salutes a rich man," the king responded. "Why have you honored me, Ellelloû, and when will I be free?"

"When Allah the Compassionate deems thy people strong enough to endure the glory of thy reign."

They spoke in Arabic, until a more urgent tempo drove them to French. All their languages were second languages, since Wanj for the one and Salu for the other were tongues of the hut and the village council, taught by mothers and lost as the world expanded. All the languages they used, therefore, felt to them as clumsy masks their thoughts must put on.

"I am not asking to rule again," the king replied, "but merely to set my face beneath the stars."

"The very stars would enlist as your soldiers and put their spears to our throats; the people are parched, and your resurrection would set them afire."

"I cannot see the smile on your lips, Ellelloû, but I hear mockery twist your voice. State your purpose, and leave irony to Allah, in Whose sight we are mice in the gaze of a lion. Have you some business worth the ruin of an old beggar's peace?" He returned his hand to his lap with a papery grace that belied its burden of garnets and emeralds and silver filigree; the king sat in a *lungi* of striped white silk in a nest of pillows and bolsters, his wrists resting symmetrically on the knees of his folded legs. Around his brow was tied a riband of spun gold in token of the curtain of the unsurpassable metal that formerly had shielded from his radiations the mortals who came grovelling to him in petition. His hair, long uncut, stood far out from his head in wiry rays, a halo of wool, as awesome as comical. Ellelloû was reminded disagreeably of murky photographs he had seen in the Istiqlal underground press, *Les Nouvelles en Noir et Blanc*, of American "hippies," young scions of corporation lawyers and professional rabbis who, to dramatize the absurd sexual spree their reactionary drug-addled hearts confused with the needed real revolution, affected headbands in presumptuous emulation of the red men their forefathers had unceremoniously exterminated.

Seen in this light, the king appeared so vulnerably displaced, so gallantly ridiculous, that Ellelloû was moved to confess, as a wayward son to drunken father: "I have been north. My adventures there trouble me."

"Why do you seek to be troubled? A leader must not be divided within himself. He is the unmoved pivot, the frozen sun."

"The people starve. The rains now have failed for the fifth year. The herdsmen steal millet from their wives and children to feed the cattle; still the animals drop, and are fallen upon for the little meat left on their bones. I have seen vultures come to the feast and be themselves stoned and consumed. The people eat bats and mice, they eat skinks and scorpions, gerbils and termites; they glean the carcasses that even jackals leave. The hair of the children turns orange. Their eyes and bellies bulge. Their heads are shaped like the skulls of mummies baked in the sand. When they grow too weak to whimper, their silence is the worst."

"It anticipates the silence of Paradise," smiled the king.

As their own silence widened, Ellelloû felt he had failed. He felt himself at the center of a cosmic failure, his failure to communicate the reality of suffering at one with the cosmic refusal to prevent this suffering. Held mute in a moment without a pose, a mask, Ellelloû felt the terror

of responsibility and looked about him for someone with
whom to share it. The attendant who had been reading
from the Book of Books sat cross-legged on a green satin
cushion, eyes downcast, his thumb curved to turn the
page. At a glance I saw in him a police officer, and knew
that my conversation with the king would be reported in
full to Michaelis Ezana, my Minister of the Interior. I
knew too that the king would eventually offer words of
wisdom to fill the void between us where his smile had
feathered. In the days when I had been his courtier his
words would overnight condense in my mind like dew on
the underside of a leaf. My eye continued about his cell.
Though it contained objects of pure gold and of the fanatic workmanship that only extreme poverty coupled
with faith in an afterlife produces, it also held much that
could be termed rubble—scraps of torn cloth, sticks of
wood bound together as by a playful idiot, small pouches
of spicy dust, visible bones and bits of once-living matter
dried and darkened out of recognition, and a certain
amount of sheer dirt, most conspicuous in the corners but
some of it apparently with deliberation sprinkled recently
on the inlaid lid of an ivory chest, on the head and
knobby shoulders of a pot-bellied ebony idol, and on the
carved saddle-seat of the sacred stool of Wanjiji. This last
had been tucked into a corner at a tilt, one lion-foot having been broken and not repaired. How repair, indeed, so
sacred an object? The workman's hands would uselessly
tremble in such close proximity to the holy. Amulets—
Koranic phrases, often inauthentic, in little bark or leather
cylinders—were littered here and there, and empty bowls
in which, before their liquid had evaporated, a soul had
been captured. My soul, perhaps. How often, I wondered,
had my death been rendered in mime, and the king's escape been effected via the fragile fabrications of *juju*? My
palms prickled to think there were prayers of which I was

the urgent object, prayers arising all over the land; like a massive transparent ball my terror, my responsibility, threatened to roll over me again. I flung my attention to the walls, where hung a number of framed portraits this king of eclectic sensibility had collected in the years of his constitutional reign, when he subscribed to Western magazines—de Gaulle, Nkrumah, Farouk, an etching of King Yohannes IV of Ethiopia, a poster of Elvis Presley in full sequinned regalia, Marilyn Monroe from a bed of polar bear skins making upward at the lens the crimson O of a kiss whose mock emotion led her to close her greasy eyelids, and a page torn from that magazine whose hearty name of *Life* did not save it from dying, torn roughly out but sumptuously framed, showing a female child dancer in patent-leather shoes poised in ·mid-step with bright camera-conscious eyes upon a flight of stairs leading nowhere. At her side stood a pair of long legs in checked trousers belonging, it was my growing belief, to a black man whose hands were muffled in white gloves and whose head was cut off by the top of the page. The king caught my mind in mid-flight.

"The white devils," he said, "give grain. And milk transmuted to powder. And medicine that by a different magic might turn the children's hair black again."

Disturbed by the decapitated black dancer, I exclaimed, "Food from filthy hands is filth! The integrity of Kush rejects the charity of imperialist exploiters!"

"*Der Spatz in der Hand,* my old friends used to say, *ist besser als die Taube auf dem Dach.*"

"Gifts bring men, men bring bullets, bullets bring oppression. Africa has undergone this cycle often enough."

The king performed the dainty pragmatic shrug with which, in the days before the Revolution, he would have a page boy mutilated for dozing in an anteroom. "Your friends the Russians," he said, "are generous exporters of spies and last year's rockets. They themselves buy wheat from the Americans."

"Only to advance the revolution. The peasantry of America, seeing itself swindled, seethes on the verge of riot."

"The world is splitting in two," said the king, "but not in the way we were promised, not between the Red and the free but between the fat and the lean. In one place, the food rots; in another, the people starve. Why emphasize the unkind work of nature that keeps these halves apart?"

"I am not the creator of this Revolution but its instrument," I told the king. "It is not I but the will of Kush that rejects offal. A sick man must vomit or grow sicker. When the Revolution occurred, the task of the Conseil— of General Soba, and Ezana, and myself—"

The king nodded wearily, anticipating, his head on that delicate pivot, nodding, nodding.

"—was not to inspire the people but to protect from their enthusiasm the capitalist intriguers who under your protection had infested Istiqlal; but for our intervention they would have been slaughtered ere they could be expelled."

"Enough were slaughtered. And their thin-lipped wives taken alive for the harems of the socialist elite."

"A phrase without meaning," I said.

The king said, "Let me tell you of an event without meaning: the hand of the giver is outstretched, and that of the beggar remains closed."

"Begging has its holy place on the streets, not in the corridors of government."

"Daily, I beg for my freedom."

"Your freedom consists of being hidden. I envy you that freedom."

"And well you might. The deaths in the north are on

your head." The king smiled, lifting those blind eyes which were like loci upon a plane of crazed crystal. "It is good. The people adore the Lord who asks them to die. Had I not been so tender a father to my children, had not my policies sheltered them from the rage of the absolute, they would not have turned their backs. Where there is poverty, there must be drama. Your rule will be long, Hakim Félix, if your heart does not soften."

I could not leave it like this. I pleaded, "The purity of Kush is its strength. In the lands of our oppressors the fat millions have forgotten how to live and look to the world's forsaken to remind them. The American crates piled at our borders stank of despair; I went there and ordered them burned."

"Reflections of so signal a deed have flickered even in this remotest of caves. I commend you, Colonel Ellelloû, ruler of lava and ash. Only Satan has a like domain."

"Spoken like one of his legions, like one whose eyes are still closed to the light of the Prophet. Though you have taken upon yourself a pretense of Islam, your faith is centered across the Grionde, where terror and torture still reign, where *juju* still clouds the minds of men, as the tsetse fly poisons their blood. Here, the sky shows its face. There is one God, unknowable, without feature. Praise be to Allah, Lord of the Worlds."

"The Beneficent, the Merciful," the king responded. "You do an injustice to the sincerity of my adherence. I find Islam a beautifully practical religion, streamlined even, the newest thing in this line. But as to cruelty, the rain forest beyond the river holds none as rigorous as the fury of a jihad. I am blind, but not so blind as those righteous whose eyes roll upward, who kill and are killed to gain a Paradise of shade trees, as I hear in the Book." He gestured toward the reader, who remained impassive, quiet as a machine waiting to be activated; this police spy was young and smooth, his oval face rather feminine in its stolid fineness beneath the plum-colored fez. "Your sky," the king told me," "shines all day like the flat of a sword. The sky-spirit has come to hate the earth-spirit. Your land is cursed, unhappy Félix. You have cursed this land with your hatred of the world."

"I hate only the evil that is in the world."

"You burn its food while your subjects starve. And it is said you brought death in the north."

"An American committed suicide. We stood by helpless."

"That was an error. In Africa, one white death shrieks louder than a thousand black lives."

"You hear much, in your cave. I too have my ears, and they hear the people murmur that the old king somewhere lives, and drags the land with him into senility."

The king returned his heavy hand, gently as an ash drifts back to the hearth, to its site on his knee. "Then show me to the people in my vigor."

"What they say is true. You are old. You were old when I was young."

"Young and helpless: who was it who plucked you from the shadows where you had been hiding, hiding in such fear you had almost forgotten the languages of Kush, and set you at his side, in a resplendent new uniform, and taught you statecraft?"

"The question answers itself, my lord. And the fact that you have breath to ask it testifies sufficiently to my gratitude. Even when I was young, you lied to minimize your age, and a generation has grown whiskers since."

"What concern is my physical state to anyone but myself, since I am no longer king?"

"The people, though we seek to educate them, believe as did their fathers that there is no way to leave the royal stool but through the gate of blood. The natural death of a king is an abomination unto the state."

"And you? What do you believe?"

"I believe—I believe the debts between us have been paid."

"Then kill me. Kill me in the square by the Mosque of the Day of Disaster and show the people my head. Water the land with my blood. I have no fear. My ancestors bubble in the earth like *pombe* brewing. The thought of death is sweeter to me than honey dipped from the tree."

"The people will ask, Why was this not done before, in the morning of L'Émergence? The king's ministers and lackeys were relieved of the misery of their lives, why was he spared? Why for these five years of blight has Ellelloû kept the heart of reaction alive?"

The king said swiftly, "The answer is plain: out of love. Inopportune love, and the unpolitic loyalty of the fearful. Tell them, their colonel is a man who holds within himself many possibilities. Tell them, it is not they the ignorant who hug to themselves the bloody madness of *juju* but their leader as well, the progressive and passionate embodiment of Islamic Marxism, who to mitigate their suffering proposes nothing better than the murder of the decrepit old prisoner who was once the alleged chief of benighted, mythical Wanjiji!" The king laughed, a frightening crackling of his crystal plane, which Ellelloû in his orb of numbness felt to be a plane of his fate. The king spoke on, his little silken figure agitated, lifted upwards, as if by strings of song. "Tell them, the madness of the divine anoints their leader, rendering Kush the beacon of the Third World, the marvel and scandal of the capitalist press, the kindling of glee in a billion breasts! But remember, Colonel Ellelloû, murder me once, the dice have been thrown. There will be no more magic among the souvenirs of Noire." His tongue rattled and fell away to a whisper within the prolonged *r* of this abhorrent old name. His eyes, shallow-backed, reflected the last light from the window, the scabbing green-painted frame of which admitted as well the muezzins' twanging call to first prayer, *salāt al-maghrib*; it echoed under the cloudless sky as under a darkening dome of tile. "The day has begun," the king said. "Go to the mosque. The President must display his faith."

As Ellelloû walked down the corridor, where the smell of scorched feathers had thickened, and the muttering of the soldiers and their whores had grown richer and more conspiratorial, the pretty young reader's voice picked up the dropped thread: *"They shall be attended by boys graced with eternal youth, who to the beholder's eyes will seem like scattered pearls. When you gaze upon that scene you will behold a kingdom blissful and glorious."*

They shall be arrayed in garments of fine green silk and rich brocade, and adorned with bracelets of silver. Their Lord will give them a pure beverage to drink. Indeed, it had been dry in the north. By noon of the first day's drive, our party of three having gathered in the Palais garage at dawn, the wideflung peanut fields broke up into scattered poor plantings of cassava and maize that scratched our eyes with their look of hopeless effort. The rarely glimpsed cultivator of those gravelly fields would lift a bony arm in greeting as our Mercedes poured past, trailing its illusory mountain of dust. The pisé rectangles of Istiqlal, their monotony of dried mud broken in the center of town by the wooden façades of Indian storefronts, a-swirl with Arabic and Hindi, and the concrete-and-glass abominations flauntingly imposed, before the Revolution, by the French and, since, by the East Germans, soon dissolved—once the tin shantytown of re-

settled nomads was behind us—into the low, somehow
liquid horizon, its stony dun slumber scarcely disturbed by
a distant cluster of thatched roofs encircled by euphorbia,
or by the sullen looming of a roadside hovel, a rusted can
on a stick advertising the poisonous and interdicted native
beer. More than once we had to detour around a giraffe
skeleton strung across the *piste*, the creature drawn there
on its last legs by the thin mane of grass that in this desolation sprang up in response to the liquid that boiling radiators spilled in passing. Yet all morning we saw not
another vehicle. As the heat of the high sun overpowered
even our splendid machine's air-conditioning, Mtesa, my
driver, pulled into a cluster of huts woven of thorn-
strands over an armature of acacia boughs and compacted
with mud; these shelters had hovered on the horizon for
half an hour. Opuku, my bodyguard, rummaged through
the napping inhabitants and found a withered crone who
mumblingly muddled together some raffia mats for our repose and brought us grudging portions of oversalted couscous. The water from her calabash tasted sweet and may
have been drugged, for we slept so soundly that we were
awakened well after the time of *salāt al-ʿasr*, and then
forcibly, by a young woman, naked but for her pointed
nosepiece and throat-rings of rhino hair, who evidently
wished to soothe us further with the gift of her charms,
which had been rubbed to a noxious gleam with rancid
butter. This sad and graceful slave received a kick from
Opuku, a sleepy curse from Mtesa, and words of enlightenment from me in regard to the Prophet's extollation
of chastity in women, and of his admonishments to men
that they not abuse female orphans. Our afternoon prayers hastily performed, we offered the old woman a handful of paper *lu*—so called, the malicious wit of the
departing French had it, because they were circulated *in
lieu* of hard currency. Upon being thunderously informed

by bull-necked Opuku that I was President of the nation, with power of life and death over all Kushites, while in sober proof Mtesa drove up in the Mercedes with its fluttering flag of stark green on the fender, our venerable hostess sank to her knees wailing, closed her eyes against our largesse, and begged instead for mercy. This she received, in the form of our departure. We drove into the night, a night of creamy blue, without lights, or one wherein the occasional far speck of a campfire shone with the unaccountable watery beauty of a star. By prearrangement we were to spend the night in the region called Hulūl, at the secret Soviet installation there.

No road marked the way to the buried bunkers, and no conspicuous ventilation shafts or entrance ports betrayed their presence. The occasional straggle of nomads with their camels and goats may have noticed that acres of the soil had been dislocated and reconstituted, or may even have stumbled across extrusions of cement and aluminum masked by plastic thornbushes and elephant grass; but when the nomad does not understand, he moves on, his mental narrowness complementing the width of his wandering life, which might derange more open minds. In a sense the land itself is forgetful, an evaporating pan out of which all things human rise into blue invisibility. Not far off, for instance, in the Hulūl Depression stood the red ruins of a structure called Hallāj, and no one remembered why it was so named, or what congregation had worshipped what god amid its now unroofed pillars.

Even the secret at hand had its inconsequential side. Three sets of MIRVed SS-9 ICBMs in their subterranean sheaths pointed north to the Mediterranean, west toward similar U.S. installations in the lackey territory of Sahel, and east to the remote Red Sea ports of Zanj, which in certain permutations of nuclear holocaust might become strategically significant enough to vaporize. Our Kushite

rockets were "third wave" weaponry; that is, by the time
they were utilized the major industrial and population
centers would be erased from the globe. Like the players
of a chess contest reduced to a few rooks, pawns, and the
emblematic kings, the major powers, yawning over their
brandy, would be pursuing a desultory end game, to determine which style of freedom—freedom from disorder,
freedom from inhibition—would suffuse the spherical
desert that remained. That world, amusing to contemplate, would not only be Saharan in aspect but would be
dominated by underdamaged Africa, in long-armed partnership with Polynesians, Eskimos, Himalayan Orientals,
and the descendants of British convicts in Australia. More
amusingly still, Michaelis Ezana, a nagging doubter of our
Soviet allies, maintained that the rockets were in truth
dummies, sacks of local sand where the warheads should
be, set here by solemn treaty merely to excite the opposite
superpower to install, at burdensome expense, authentic
missiles in neighboring Sahel. Whatever the case, a slab of
earth eight meters wide and two thick lifted at the pre-
arranged signal from our headlights (dim, undim, out,
dim), and the party of Russian soldiers below rejoiced,
amid the furious electricity of their vast bunker, at this
diversion. In preparation for our visit they had all become
drunk.

Mtesa and Opuku, blinking in amazement at this
bubble of sun captured underground, were swamped with
hairy embraces, Cyrillic barks, and splashing offers of
vodka, which Opuku did not initially refuse. I informed
them, in my loudest French, *"Pas d'alcool, s'il vous
plaît! Le Dieu de notre peuple nous l'interdit,"* and upon
many repetitions of this baffling negation won for myself
and my small party the right to respond in chalky Balkan
mineral water (fetched from the sub-cellar) to their inter-
minable toasts and to observe with sobriety this foreign

enclave. The Russians had been here since the secret SAND (Soviet-Allied Nuclear Deterrents) talks of 1971 and in the two years since had amply furnished the bunker in the stuffy tsarist style of Soviet supercomfort, from the lamps with fringed shades and soapstone bases carved in the shape of tussling bears resting on runners of Ukrainian lace to the obligatory oil paintings of Lenin exhorting workers against a slanted sunset and Brezhnev charming with the luxuriance of his eyebrows a flowery crowd of Eurasiatic children. The linguist among them, a frail steel-bespectacled second lieutenant whose Arabic was smeared with an Iraqi accent and whose French sloshed in the galoshes of Russian *zhushes*, fell dead drunk in the midst of the banquet; we carried on with minimal toasts to the heroes of our respective races. "Lumumba," they would say, and I would answer, as their glasses were refilled, "À Stakhanov." "Nasser, *da*, Sadat, *nyet*" was met, amid uproarious applause, with "*Vive* Sholokov, *écrasez* Solzhenitsyn," to applause yet more tumultuous. My opposite number, Colonel Sirin, who in this single installation commanded perhaps the equivalent in expenditure of the entire annual military budget of Kush, discovered that I comprehended English and, no doubt more coarsely than he intended, proposed honor to "all good niggers." I responded with the seventy-seventh sura of the Koran ("*Woe on that day to the disbelievers! Begone to that Hell which you deny!*") as translated into my native tongue of Salu, whose glottal rhythms enchanted the Reds in their dizziness. Our store of reciprocal heroes exhausted, the briefing blackboard was dragged forth and we matched toasts to the letters of our respective alphabets.

"Ш!" the colonel proposed, milking the explosive sound for its maximum richness.

I tactfully responded with the beautiful terminal form of " ‫ق‬ ."

" ‫ﺧ‬ ! !" he boasted, "*le plus belle* letter all over goddam world!"

I outdid him, I dare believe, gracefully proposing, " ‫ﺢ‬ ."

There was a presentation of medals, and a monumental picture-book of the treasures accumulated by the subterranean monks of Kiev, and then these strange men began to dance from a squatting position and in demonstration of manliness to chew their liquor glasses like so many biscuits. Since they were their own best audience for these feats, I persuaded a young and relatively sober aide to show us to our chambers. Several of the officers staggered along, and one especially burly Slav playfully planted a foot in Mtesa's backside as we knelt to our deferred *salāt al-ʿishā*.

Failing to fall asleep promptly within the smothering softness of the Soviet bed, with its brocaded canopy and its stony little packets for pillows, I reflected back upon the customs and the orgy we had been privileged to witness, and located along the borders of my memory an analogy that seemed clarifying: with their taut pallor, bristling hair devoid of a trace of a curl, oval eyes, short limbs, and tightly packed bodies whose muscular energy seemed drawn into a knot at the back of their necks, these Russians reminded me of nothing so much as the reckless, distasteful packs of wild swine that when I was a child would come north from the bogs by the river to despoil the vegetable plantings of our village. They had a bristling power and toughness, to be sure, but lacked both the weighty magic of the lion and the hippo and the weightless magic of the gazelle and the shrike, so that the slaughter of one with spears and stones, as he squealed and dodged—the boars were not easy to kill—took place in an incongruous hubbub of laughter. Even in death their eyes kept that rheumy glint whereby the hunted betray the pressures under which they live.

Once during the night the telephone in our overfurnished chamber rang. When I picked it up, there was no voice at the other end, nor was there a click. Through the long tunnel of silence I seemed to see into the center of the Kremlin, where terror never sleeps. And our hosts were up early to see us off. Their uniforms were fresh and correct, and their faces—those square semi-Asiatic faces that appear too big for their thin features—were shaved, betraying only in an abnormally keen sheen, a drained, thin-skinned look, their carousal of a few hours before. It was their rule never to stray aboveground, even when, before the famine became extreme, fresh milk and meat might have enhanced their diet of frozen and powdered provisions—as if even one slice of authentically rank native goat cheese would fatally contaminate this giant capsule, this hermetic offshoot of the insular motherland. In this they were unlike the Americans, who wandered everywhere like children, absurdly confident of being loved. Nor was the Soviet exclusiveness confident and inward, like that of the French. By the terms of their treaty—at their insistence, not ours—a soldier or technician found afoot in the open air was to be jailed and segregated from the populace. One's impression could only be of a power immensely timorous, a behemoth frightened of even such gaunt black mice as we poor citizens of Kush. We shook hands, the colonel and I. I thanked him for his hospitality, he thanked me for mine. He said Russia and Kush were brothers in progressivism and in the unanimous patriotism of their polyglot peoples. I responded to Colonel Sirin (his bespectacled interpreter being still abed comatose) as exactly as I could; our two peoples, I said, were possessed of an "*essence religieuse*" and our lands of "*les vacances magnifiques.*" Mtesa and Opuku witnessed this unintelligible exchange wonderingly, and the Mercedes, coughing on its heady swig of Siberian diesel fuel, took us up the ramp, to the slab of desert that lifted on pneumatic hinges to admit scalding floods of light and to reveal again the shimmering horizons of our journey.

The Hulūl Depression, its gravels and crusty sands ruddy in color, as if the rivers that had long ago emptied into this cracked lakebed had been tinged with blood, gave way, while the sun climbed toward its incandescent apogee, to the foothills of the Bulub Mountains. The *piste* diminished to a winding track, treacherously pitted and strewn with a flinty scrabble that well challenged the mettle of our Michelin steel-belted radials. The distances became bluish; as we rose higher, clots of vegetation, thorny and leafless, troubled the rocks with their grasping roots. In the declivities that interrupted our grinding, twisting ascent, there were signs of pasturage: clay trampled to a hardened slurry by hooves, excrement still distinguishable from mineral matter, some toppled skeletons of beehive huts, their thatch consumed as a desperate fodder. Aristada, which thrives on overgrazed lands, tinged with green this edge of desolation. Our route went not directly across the Bulubs, but along their shoulder; to the east the horizon was low, though undulating, and the smoke of a nomadic encampment, of Teda or the dreaded Tuareg, manifested itself to the keen eyes of my companions. I, in seeking to verify their glimpse of potentially sinister smoke, seemed to see an altogether different apparition: two golden parabolas showed above a distant deckled ridge and, as I gazed incredulously, slowly sank from sight, the motion of the car carrying us behind an escarpment. Neither Mtesa nor Opuku could confirm my sighting, though we halted the car and prowled the searing terrain for a vantage. The rocks here held iridescent streaks of strange sleek minerals. Having halted, we performed our *salāt az-zuhr* and fell asleep in the shade of a ledge, where lizards came to skitter across us as if our dozing bodies had joined the vast insensate chorus of changeless stone, the touch of their feet daintier than the first tingling drops of a rain.

The days of the journey merge in my memory after that poisonous glimpse of golden parabolas; a sort of delirium of distance overtook us. We traversed many sorts of naked soil—flinty orange gorges, black clay where slatelike slabs had been set with the regularity of a demented divine masonry, stretches of purple gravel varied by shifting hillocks of amber sand. In the wide belt of transition between withered sudan and stark desert, there were islands of what had been, before the drought, pasture land, whose inhabitants, human and animal, had been stranded by the rising sea of dearth. We saw strange sights; we saw naked women climbing mimosa trees to crop the twig-tips for cooking, we saw children gathering the wild nettle called *cram-cram*, we saw men attacking and pulverizing anthills to recover the crumbs of grain that had been stored there. Even the most brackish water holes had been drunk dry, and the trees rimming them reduced to stumps stripped of bark by savage hunger. My hand grows too heavy to write as I remember this misery. Most grotesquely, the sun each day beat upon these scenes with the serene fury of an orator who does not know he has made exactly the same points in a speech delivered the day before. As we neared our destination on the northwest border, and the population thickened in consequence of the rumored excitement there, I abandoned the Mercedes and assumed the wool rags of a Sufi, the better to mingle with my people in their suffering.

A party of itinerant well-diggers took me up, to bring them luck. In truth, they had need of it—a party of four, two male Moundangs, a Galla dwarf, and a Sara woman who cooked and serviced us all. The leader, Wadal, a tall morose man whose lassitudinous brown length seemed an enlarged analogue of his impotent penis, which he kept morosely displaying through the rents in his tattered *galabieh*, had no nose for water. Repeatedly his party had been greeted with rejoicing in the encampments, welcomed with a clattering of tambourines and the booming of the chief's great *tobol*, only to be, after a few days of digging, while they fed their futile exertions upon the herdsmen's precious morsels of seed grain and caked blood, called into solemn conference with the *caïd* and sent away beneath a hail of Tamahaq curses and flung pebbles. Wadal presented himself to me as a man of former property, whose plenteous herds of humped zebu had been turned to bones by the drought; but his woman whispered to me that he was a rascal without a tribe, who had never had so much as a pet pi-dog to his name. His father had been a *dibia* in a village to the south, and the son had been banished for blasphemy, for urinating on the fetishes in a fury of despair over his own impotence, which she assured me her lewdest wiles had proven intractable. Yet her fate had been cast with his when, a beautiful virgin asleep in her father's compound, this wretched outcast had crept into her hut and, as he had done to the fetishes, polluted her and rendered her forever unfit for marriage. She had nowhere to go but with him, though her father had owned herds that blanketed the hills, and her mother had been the granddaughter of an immortal leopard whose outline could now be traced in the stars in the sky. She may have told me these things to pass the night, for she slept little, and came to me even after she had ministered to another, during the days when we made our way north through the clustered encampments, begging and dancing and promising a deluge if our

lives were spared. Named Kutunda, she showed herself by
moonlight to be a wild and wakeful woman, lost in her
stories, adept at languages, bewitched by the running of
her tongue, which was as strong as her smell. I was sensitive to her tongue's strength, for my own mouth was tender; to prove my authenticity as a dervish I had, more
than once, held a hot coal from the campfire in my mouth
and mimed swallowing it. Such things are possible, when
the needful spirit transfixes the body, and fear does not
dry up the saliva. God is closer to a man than the vein in
his neck, the Koran says. A Salu proverb has it, A man's
fate follows him like the heel of his foot. Kutunda's rank
smell grew sweet to me, and her low sharp laugh in the
act of love lies within me like a bit of flint. We would
sleep, often, in the ditches of our unsuccessful wells. The
well we dug deepest—I was not precisely digging but
standing on the edge of the pit chanting sacred verses and
dodging clumps of dirt the dwarf tossed in my direction—yielded instead of water a Roman vase, banded
with the scrolling waves of the fabulous wine-dark sea im-
possibly far to the north; also, a corroded metal disc that
must once have served as a mirror. The Sahara long ago
was green, and men crossed its grasslands in chariots.
That was the meaning of our national flag, its field of
bright and rampant green. The soil here had become
gun-metal gray, with flickers of spar, and the people we
travelled among had turned that gray tint which, in a
black man, presages death. The blacks were slaves,
bouzous, for we were in the territory of the Tuareg,
whose pale eyes glittered above the indigo of the *tagilmust*—so wound, all six meters of it, as to cover their
mouths, which they regard as obscene, the hole that takes
in as obscene as the hole that expels. The camels were
humpless and dying with that strange soft suddenness of
camels, settling on their haunches and letting the spirit

depart without a sigh. Among the tents, when the murmur of the day's prayers had subsided, a silence descended worse than the silence of death, because willed; only the children whimpered, and these only below the age of eight, before they could receive the consolatory discipline of religion. In their reduced state, their bodies took on a sculptural beauty—the amorphous padding of flesh lifted to reveal the double chord of curved ribs, the arms and legs similarly demarcate, femurs and humeri wrapped tightly, the same tightness pulling the lips back against the teeth and covering the temple concavities of the skull with pulsing drumheads, while in contrast certain protuberances acquired a glossy bulging smoothness, the bloated bellies and those pop eyes magnetically alert beneath the children's brows like the stares of gods through ritual masks. The cattle had grown too emaciated to bleed, and in these steppes blood mixed with curdled milk into a coagulated, chewy porridge was a staple of the diet. From being fed, our party of well-diggers turned into feeders, sharers of the stores of goat cheese, peanut paste, and dried smelt that at night I received from the refrigerated hampers of the Mercedes, which followed us some miles behind, gray as a ghost, nearly invisible, but for the pillars of dust it raised and that stood motionless above the steppes for hours on end.

When I asked those around me, in my rusty Salu or my defective Berber, if they blamed Allah for their condition, they stared uncomprehendingly, asserting that God is great, God is beneficent. How could the proclaimed source of all compassion be blamed? And several, with burning eyes, with the last embers of their energy, picked up a stone to hurl, had I not turned my back.

And when I asked others if they blamed Colonel Ellelloû, the President of Kush and Chairman of SCRME, one man responded, "Who is Ellelloû? He is the wind, he is the air between mountains." And I felt sickened, hearing this, and lost in the center of that great transparent orb of responsibility which was mine. Another told me, "Colonel Ellelloû is expelling the *kafirs* who have stolen our clouds; when the last white devil has embraced Islam or his head has rolled in the dust, then Ellelloû will come and bleed the sky as the herder slits the neck-vein of his bullock." And I felt myself a deceiver, in my dirty disguise, my mouth still sore from last night's magic. A third shrugged and said, "What can he do? He is a little soldier who to secure his pension killed the Lord of Wanjiji. Since Edumu passed to his ancestors, the underworld has sucked happiness from the earth." And this vexed me with a question of policy: should I kill the king? Some had not heard of Ellelloû, some thought he was a mere slogan, some hated him for being a freed slave, one of the *harratin*, from the south. None seemed to look to him to lift the famine from the land. Only I expected this of Colonel Ellelloû, who should have been in Istiqlal, signing documents and reviewing parades, instead of making his way with a few outcasts through the cloud of nomads that had been drifted toward the border by rumors of an impending miracle.

The border of Kush in the northwest is nine-tenths imaginary. Through the colonial decades the border was ignored by the proud Reguibat, Teda, and Tuareg who drove their herds back and forth across it without formality or compunction; the vast departments of French West Africa were differentiated only in the mysterious accountancies of Paris. But since 1968, when our purged nation took on a political complexion so different from that of neighboring Sahel—Kush's geographical twin but ideological antithesis, a model of neocapitalist harlotry decked out in transparent pantaloons of anti-Israeli bluster—border outposts have been established to safeguard symbolically, in the ungovernable vastness, our Islamic-Marxist purity. As we approached the border station we could see, all the length of a day's travel, sometimes striated and inverted by the atmospheric mirrors of mirage, and unnatural mountain, made of tan boxes.

A crowd of thousands, a lake-sized distillation from the emptiness, had gathered about this apparition, which loomed a few meters over the border, at this place called Èfù. The station consisted of three low buildings of flint, flattened cans, and sun-baked mud: the barracks for the soldiers, the detention rooms where no one had ever been detained, and the customs office, its roof not flat like the other two but a pisé dome from whose pinnacle the beautiful Kushian flag fluttered as the day swiftly expired. A flash of green, indeed, signalled a phase of the sun's withdrawal—a kind of shout of expiration from just below the horizon, whose parched reaches were duplicated by a saffron strip at the base of the westward sky, slag residue of the day's furnace. Directly overhead, an advance scout of the starry armies trembled like a pearl suspended in a gigantic crystalline goblet of heavenly nectar. By these mingled lights, amid the lip-music of camels and the clack of camel-bells, through the fragrance of cooking-fires fed by dried dung and hacked tamarisk, I threaded my way among the Kushites toward a space of confrontation, where the four young border guards, in pith helmets and parade whites, none of them older to my eye than eighteen, rigid and luminous in their terror, faced the muttering horde drawn to this place by the hill of aid heaped on the edge of enemy Sahel. Ruled by a foppish Négritudinist whose impeccable alexandrines on brown beauties swaying under their laden calabashes followed the poems of Valéry in *Le Livre de Poche* anthologies and whose successive Parisian wives were kept svelte by lubrications of bribery from the toubab corporations and the overachieving Japanese, Sahel from the air presented a patchwork of tin roofs and hotel swimming pools, drenched golf courses and fields perforated like colanders by the patient mudholes of hand-dipped irrigation. Contempt inspired me, enlarged me, at the thought of my rival state and its economic inequities, so that by the time I had wormed to the front of the crowd, I had forgotten my mystic's rags and presented myself to the soldiers as if my authority were manifest.

The sergeant in command lifted his rifle and levelled it at my chest as I stepped forward too boldly. "I am Ellelloû," I announced. Kutunda, unasked, out of female curiosity or presumptuous loyalty, had followed me, and now embraced me from behind, lest I step into a bullet. "Ellelloû, Ellelloû," the crowd murmured at my back, in widening, receding waves. They did not doubt; skepticism is wonderfully sapped by hunger.

The youngest of the four soldiers stepped forward and with the butt of his rifle, deftly as if dislodging a scorpion, knocked my clinging protectoress loose. "He is a poor magician!" she shouted from the sand, through bloodied lips. "Forgive him his madness!"

The soldier nodded in bleak disinterest and lifted his rifle again—of Czech manufacture, and obtained at a unit cost that Michaelis Ezana had more than once cited in his mockery of Communist brotherhood—to give me a similar tap, when I produced from the folds of my rags the medal the Soviets had awarded me the week before. Its brass star and bas-relief Lenin made the young man blink. And the crowd behind me, having taken up my name, was now returning it to the fore with such a windy swollen chorusing that my claim to authority seemed divinely reinforced. "*Ellelloû, Ellelloû*": It was a whirlwind. To the sergeant who, having inspected the medal, now pressed it against his own breast with a smile from which the two lower incisors had been removed, I suggested, within our growing complicity, that he compare my face with the portrait of the President of Kush that must hang somewhere in his official quarters.

Slowly comprehending, he sent his corporal to fetch such an image. The boy returned, after what seemed a long search, with a framed oleograph half occluded by ingrained dust. The framed face was set beside mine. As the sergeant considered, I considered the medal he still held to his chest. I tried to compose my features into El-lelloû's calm, hieratic blur; at least our two faces were coated with the same dust. Kutunda meanwhile was kissing my feet in some paroxysm; whether she was adoring me as her leader, or bemoaning me as a madman about to be shot, was not clear from the quality of her kisses, which felt like the ticklings of a fountain at the base of a statue. From out of the anxious mob behind me, out of the stench of dung fires and stale sweat and the bad breath that goes with empty stomachs, there came, sharp as a honed sword, a sweet and vivid whiff, alcoholic and innocent, of hair tonic such as would blow from the open doorway of a barbershop in Wisconsin. It came, and went.

In my trance I was too sanguine. I had underestimated the mischievous streak in my sergeant. He wanted that medal. "No resemblance," he pronounced aloud, in several languages, and I was being dragged away, Kutunda still ardently offering herself as an impediment underfoot, when my fate was dramatically reversed—put into reverse gear, one should say. The Mercedes clove through the crowd like the breath of Allah, and Opuku and Mtesa in their livery and armory of pistols and leather strapping put an end to the debate over my identity. Their guns said, *He is Ellelloû.* In a matter of minutes my khaki uniform and NoIR sunglasses were upon me, the sergeant was prostrate before me, and the medal had been bestowed upon him in ironical pardon.

Let me record, however, before proceeding to the climax of this adventure (whose details are, as I write, confounded with the tumbling of sea-smoothed pebbles), for the consolation of the less easily redeemed, that at the very moment of seizure, when it appeared I might be taken off to a summary execution or at best a prolonged interrogation more entertaining to others than to myself, that a merciful numbness and detachment seized me as well, and I saw myself as negligently as a sated hawk sees a jerboa scuttling to its hole in the desert floor.

Vested in my dignity, I faced the apparition that loomed beyond the border: a pyramid of crates, sacks, and barbarically trademarked boxes. USA USA USA, they said, and *Kix Trix Chex Pops*. The twilight in our land is brief, after the flash of green, and I could not make out the legends on the topmost boxes; there seemed to be barrels of potato chips. Of how this mountain of fetchingly packaged pap had materialized in the desolate *aftouh* of Èfù there appeared little trace; stretching away into the heavily subsidized depths of Sahel, straight as a jet-trail, a beaten track testified to the passage of wheeled vehicles, none of which was visible. Nor was there any sign of human activity around the prefabricated fort that stood opposite to our outpost within the symmetrical vacancies of our unallied nations. Only one man, a white man in a buttondown shirt and a seersucker suit, showed himself, loping our way with that diffident, confident saunter that needs for setting an awninged main street during an American summer's lunch hour, when dozens of small businessmen, toothpicks between their lips, stroll, eye the competition, and glad-hand one another. This toubab had the tact, however, not to offer me his hand; days in the desert had wilted somewhat his certainty of being found lovable. His French was so haltingly and growlingly pronounced I switched our conversation into English.

His eyebrows lifted, under the boyish bangs with their obligatory touch of gray. "You have an American accent."

"We are well trained in the tongues of others," I told him, "since no one troubles to learn ours."

"Who'd you say you were again?"

I felt I knew this man well. As is common in his swollen country, he was monstrously tall, with hands of many knuckles and fingernails the width of five-*lu* pasteboards. His age was not easy to estimate; the premature gray and show-me squint of these Yankees is muddled in with their something eternally puerile, awkward, winning, and hopeful. They want, these sons of the simultaneously most expansionist and most avowedly idealistic of power aggregations, to have all things both ways: to eat both the chicken and the egg, to be both triumphant and coddled, to seem both shrewd and ingenuous. I saw him as a child, in his parents' well-padded, musty home on some curving suburban street, squinting into the fragile glued frame of a model airplane, or licking the sweetened mounts of his stamp collection, unaware that, opening beneath him, an abyss in the carpet, a chute of time would bring him to the respectable adventurism of the foreign service and this evening moment, amid a mob of Tuareg, while a strip of saffron still lingered above the westward safety of Sahel. A stir of pity, like the first unease that will lead to vomit, I bit down. He was young on the ladder of power, still assigned to the negligible nations, the licorice and caramel and chocolate people in their little trays at the front of the store; hard work and no filching would take him, as his gray hair whitened and his sleek wife wrinkled, deeper into the store, to the back room where the wholesalers grunted, amid the aromas of burlap and vinegar, their pennywise accommodations. Better for him to have become a professor of Government at a small snowy Midwestern college. My mind's eye held his wife, who would be freckled and fair and already watching her weight and slightly hardened in the role of foreign service helpmate, too ready to repack the constantly pruned possessions, to adjust her manner to a new race of servants, to learn a new smattering of shopping phrases, to cater gaily, adroitly, and appropriately to those couples above them, below them, and beside them in the dance of legations and overseas offices. I even knew how she would make love: with abashed aggression, tense in her alleged equality of body, primed like a jammed bazooka on the pornographic plastic fetishes and sexual cookbooks of her white tribe and yet, when all cultural discounts are entered, with something of graciousness, of helpless feeling, of an authentic twist at the end. . . . The squirm of nausea again. I pictured their flat in Dakar or Lagos, their "starter house" in a suburb of Maryland or Virginia, with its glass tables and incessant electricity, an island of light carved from our darkness, and my pity ceased. I told the tall intruder, "I am a citizen of Kush, delegated to ask why you are troubling our borders and what means this mountain of refuse?"

"This isn't refuse, pal—it's manna. Donated to your stricken area by the generosity of the American government and the American people acting in conjunction with the Food and Agriculture Organization of the United Nations. U.S. Air Force C-130s have been flying this stuff in to the emergency airfield in northern Sahel and I've been sent down here from the USAID office in Tangier at the urging of the FAO people in Rome to locate the bottleneck vis-à-vis distribution of the emergency aid to the needy areas of Kush and to expedite the matter. I've been sitting out here in the underside of nowhere frying my ass off for two weeks trying to contact somebody in authority. Whoever the hell you are, you're the best thing I've seen today."

"May I ask a few questions?"

"Shoot."

"Who was it, pray, who informed you of this supposed neediness?"

He touched his sunburned forehead and shoved back the sheaf of dry hair there. His suit, designed for cocktail parties on embassy lawns, had rumpled, out here in these badlands. His sweat had caked dark not only on his collar but along the hems of his pockets, wherever skin repeatedly touched cloth. "Who're you trying to kid?" he asked me. "These cats are *starving*. The whole world knows it, you can see 'em starve on the six o'clock news every night. The American people want to help. We know this country's socialist and xenophobic, we know El-lell(û)'s a schizoid paranoid; we don't give a fuck. This kind of humanitarian catastrophe cuts across the political lines, as far as my government's concerned."

"Are you aware," I asked him, "that your government's cattle vaccination project increased herd size even as the forage and water of this region were being exhausted?"

"I've read that in some report, but—"

"And that the deep wells drilled by foreign governments disrupted nomadic grazing patterns so that deserts have been created with the wells at their center? Are you aware, furthermore, that climatic conditions in this region have been the same for five years, that the 'humanitarian catastrophe' you speak of is to us the human condition?"

"O.K., O.K.—better late than never. We're here now, and what's the hang-up? I can't get anybody to talk to me."

At my back, the impatient murmur of the Tuareg intensified, and with it intensified, to fade quickly away, that misplaced barbershop sweetness. "I will talk to you," I said, raising my voice so that our audience might understand, at least, that I was on the attack. "I am Ellȯlloû. I speak for the people of Kush. The people of Kush reject capitalist intervention in all its guises. They have no place in their stomachs for the table scraps of a society both godless and oppressive. Offer your own blacks freedom before you pile boxes of carcinogenic trash on the holy soil of Kush!"

"Listen," he pleaded, "Zanj is taking tons of grain a day, and they have *Chinese advisers* over there. This thing cuts right through the political shit, and anyway don't yell at me, I marched for civil rights all through college."

"And have now been predictably co-opted," I said. "I am not as ignorant of your nation's methods as you may suppose. As to Zanj, I am told that you have favored its suffering citizens with tons of number two sorghum, a coarse grain grown for cattle fodder, which gives its human consumers violent diarrhea."

He shed some insolence at this information, and assumed a more confiding tone. "There've been some ball-ups, yeah, but don't forget these primitives are used to a high-protein diet of meat and milk. They eat better'n we do. We send what we have."

"I see," said I, gazing upward at the terrace of crates, fitfully illumined by some torches that had been lit in the throng of witnesses at my back. *Korn Kurls* had been stamped across one whole tier, and *Total* in letters of great momentum repeated itself over and over on the wall of cardboard that reached into darkness, toward the blazing desert stars.

"Listen," the American was trying to sell me, "these

breakfast cereals, with a little milk, sugar if you have it, are dynamite, don't knock 'em. You're chewing cactus roots, and we know it." In another tone, boyish and respectful, he asked, "You really Elleloû? I love some of the things you wrote in exile. They were assigned in a Poli Sci course I took at Yale."

So he knew of my exile. My privacy was invaded. Confusion was upon me. I took off my sunglasses. The brightness of the lights shed by the torches was surprising. Should I be getting royalties? At the back of my skull the horde was chanting, "Elleloû, Elleloû. . . ." As if to escape a lynch mob, I stepped forward, across the invisible Sahel-Kush border, toward the dark mountain of aid. Seeing this political barrier breached, my American confided, "They really want this stuff," in a voice that implied the battle was over; I would sign some papers, his starchy bounty could be abandoned, he would be received into his wife's freckled bed in Tangier, and his superiors would commend him all the way back to Washington. Alas, there was no safety for him in my heart, or in this night. His pallor, now that night was altogether upon us, appeared eerie, formless, or rather having the form of a parasite shaped to conform to the sunless innards of a nobler, more independent creature. The nomads and their rabble of slaves with a giant rustling crossed the border after me, pressing us with their flapping torches into a semi-circle of space against the cliff of cardboard—cardboard, giant letters of the Roman alphabet, and polypropylene, for our benefactors shipped their inferior sorghum in transparent sacks, whose transparency revealed wood chips and dead mice and whose slippery surfaces reflected the torches, torches that highlighted also with red sparks the rungs of an aluminum ladder set against the cliff, the drops of sweat on the American's parasite-gray neck, and the agitated eyeballs of the Tuareg. "Elleloû, Ellelloû. . . ." As their murmur had conjured me from the desert, so I must conjure from within myself a gesture of leadership, an action.

Our toubab's slavish, hard-breathing, panic-suppressing demeanor begged for cruelty. Scenting a "deal," a *détente*, he told me, "No kidding, there's a lot of real food value up there, I remember when they unloaded seeing Spam and powdered milk." He clambered up the ladder to look for these strata, while the Tuareg pressed closer, shaking their torches indignantly at such an act of levitation. I could scarcely hear his shouts ". . . here you go . . . Carnation . . . add three parts water . . ."

"But we have no water!" I called up to him, trying, it seems now in hindsight, to buy time for both of us. "In Kush, water is more precious than blood!"

He was swallowed by darkness, between the torches and the stars. "No problem," his voice drifted down. "We'll bring in teams . . . green revolution . . . systems of portable trenching . . . a lily pond right where you're standing . . . here we go . . . no, that's cream of celery soup. . . ." His voice, pattering down upon them like a nonsensical angel's, had become an intolerable irritation to the Tuareg masses. As their torches drew nearer, the source of the voice could be seen, a white blur disappearing and reappearing, even higher, among the escarpments and crevasses of combustible packaging.

Within my numbing orb of responsibility, my arm had become leaden; yet I lifted it high, and dropped it in solemn signal, so that the inevitable would appear to come from me.

Torches were touched to the base of the pyramid; it became a pyre. To his credit, the young American, when he saw the smoke and flames rising toward him, and all those slopes beneath him ringed by exultant Kushite patriots, did not cry out for mercy, or attempt to scramble and

leap to a safety that was not there, but, rather, climbed to
the pinnacle and, luridly illumined, awaited the martyr-
dom for which there must have been, in the training for
foreign service provided by his insidious empire, some
marginal expectation and religious preparation. We were
surprised, how silently he died. Or were his cries merely
drowned within the roar of the ballooning tent of flame
that engulfed the treasure-heap his writhing figure for a final minute ornamented like a dark star? When he had
stood beside me, I could smell on the victim, under the
sweat of his long stale wait and the bland, oysterish odor
of his earnestness, the house of his childhood, the musty
halls, the cozy bathroom soaps, the glue of his adolescent
hobbies, the aura of his alcoholic and sexually innocent
parents, the ashtray scent of dissatisfaction. What dim
wish to do right, hatched by the wavery blue light of the
television set with its curious international shadows, had
led him to the fatal edge of a safety that he imagined had
no limits? I checked my heart's tremor with some verses
from the Book, that foresees all and thereby encloses all:
*On that day men shall become like scattered moths and
the mountains like tufts of carded wool. On that day there
shall be downcast faces, of men broken and worn out,
burnt by a scorching fire, drinking from a seething fountain. On that day there shall be radiant faces, of men well-
pleased with their labors, in a lofty garden.*

The Tuareg and their slaves were in a joyful tumult.
Opuku and Mtesa came and guarded me from the confusion. There was a slithering in my palm of another, smaller hand. I saw that Kutunda, her broken lip scabbed, was
still with me, that I had replaced Wadal as her protector.

Now the fire had taken its first giant draught, and our
nostrils acknowledged the quantity of grain our triumphant gesture had consumed, for the scorched air was

bathed in the benevolent aroma of baking bread; the desert night, as flakes of corrugated-cardboard ash plenteously drifted downward, knew the unaccustomed wonder of snow.

Two

I N THE season the toubabs call fall, Colonel Ellelloû returned to Istiqlal, his recessive mood deepened by an incident on the straight road south of Hulūl, near the vanished city of Haïr. The trinity of himself, Mtesa, and Opuku had been squared by the addition of Kutunda, whose unwashed female body brought to the interior of the Mercedes an altogether new fragrance, overlaid upon the oily distant scent of German workmanship, the clinging understink of camel dung, and the haunting aroma of the dreadful bonfire, which had crept in the windows and permeated the gray velour inexpungably as an evil memory. They were silent for miles, as each brain whirred its own wheels: Mtesa intent upon steering his marvellous machine, Kutunda wondering what would become of her and putting out through her shabby coussabe pungent feelers of fright and compliance, and Opuku apparently asleep, his round skull scarcely lolling on his muscle-buttressed neck as his dreams revolved (Ellelloû surmised from the man's moans of unease) images of violence, of flame, of lust for the pale, straight-nosed, black-clad nomad women. In Kush we never cease dreaming of intercourse between dark and fair skin, between thick lips and thin lips, between wandering herdsman and sedentary farmer.

The Mercedes had driven all night, to erase the fire from the dark of our minds. Dawn had broken and passed. The landscape in the vicinity of Haïr is pink and flat, salty and shimmering; a dot in the distance dissolves or becomes a blood-colored boulder the spaces themselves seem to hurl. Ellelloû in his rumpled khaki was gazing forward through the windshield over the shoulder of his driver while the head of the oblivious Kutunda rested heavily on his shoulder. Then a dot placed at the unsteady apex of the triangle the road's breadth dwindled to—the horizon teetering upon its fulcrum, some bumpy paws of the Bulub foothills being retracted on the right, a thorn-mantled zareba just perceptible in the dusty depths to the left—this dot enlarged with a speed out of proportion to that of the Mercedes and declared itself, at a distance perhaps of two kilometers, to be another vehicle. Within a few seconds, of time stretched like rubber by the laws of relativity, the alien vehicle was by, quick as the shadow of the wing of a hawk. Ellelloû marvelled, for the thing had appeared to be, not an explicable peanut lorry or piece of military transport, but a vehicle such as could not possibly be roaring along in Kush—that is, a large open-backed truck to whose flatbed were chained twin stacks of mechanically flattened bodies of once-bulbous, candy-colored American automobiles. Their engines had been removed, the space had been crushed wherein children had quarrelled, adolescents had made love, and oldsters had blinked mileage-mad holidays away.

In jerking his head to follow the truck's swift disappearance into the trembling pink folds of the north,

Ellelloû awoke the fair Kutunda. For fairish, or merely dusky, she was, beneath the layers of dirt, with a moonish face and lips broad but not everted in form. Her lips as she attempted to respond to arousal seemed stuck by the mucilage of sleep to her small, rather inturned teeth. Her eyes widened, sensing Ellelloû's alarm. The colonel had grasped Mtesa's shoulder and, in the barking, shrill voice with which, over the state radio, he would announce some new austerity or reprisal, he was asking, "What was it? Did you see it?"

"Truck," the driver answered.

"What kind of truck?"

"Big. Fast. No speed limit out here."

"Did you ever see any other truck like it?"

The answer came after maddening deliberation. "No."

"Where do you think it came from?"

The driver shrugged. "Town."

"Istiqlal? Never. Where would it get those—those *things* it was carrying? Where was it taking them?"

"Maybe from Zanj going to Sahel. Or other way around."

"Who would let it through the border? Who would sell it fuel?"

Mtesa conceded, "Funny thing," but with no more concern than if he had seen an unusual bird at a water hole, or a bizarrely maimed beggar on the street. The ignorant see miracles every day.

It occurred to Ellelloû that Mtesa was bluffing, humoring him; he had seen nothing. He commanded, "Tell me what you saw. *What* funny thing?"

"Big truck toting squashed *voitures*."

"What kind of *voitures*?"

"Not Benzis."

Ellelloû slumped back defeated. He would have preferred that the truck have been his private hallucination.

Better his own insanity, he reasoned, than that of the nation. The vision, if actual, placed upon him an unwelcome necessity to act, to cope with a strange invasion, for he knew that the affronting apparition was a commonplace sight on the clangorous, poisonous, dangerous highways of the United States. Kutunda, who had been asleep, and to whom the thing had been invisible, felt to occupy the only undistorted quadrant of the car, and in his weariness Ellelloû toppled into the comfortable vacancy of her fragrance of musk and dung, of smoke and hunger, of Kush.

Evidently upon his return to Istiqlal Ellelloû established Kutunda in an apartment above a basket-weaving shop whose real dealings were in hashish and khat; her presence here, and his suspicion of a conspiracy whose headquarters were in the capital, reinforced his habit of venturing disguised into the city, especially the disreputable section known as Hurriyah, which rises, like heaps of mud boxes stacked for removal, against the eastern wall of the vast Palais de l'Administration des Noirs, with its sixteen pilasters representing the sixteen most common verbs that require *être* instead of *avoir* as auxiliary in all compound tenses. Its façade is topped with eight marble statues of an unreal whiteness, uneroded in this climate, that symbolize the eight bourgeois virtues—*Assiduité, Economie, Médiocrité, Conjugalité, Tempérance, Optimisme, Dynamisme,* and *Modernité.* Its blank side glows in the dawn like the flank of an eternal, voluptuous promise heaving itself free of the earth, above the little roofs of thatch, cracked tile, and rock-weighted tin.

So it loomed in Ellelloû's eyes, as he blinked from the pallet he shared with Kutunda. In sleep her stringy, lustreless hair—so different from the soft and wiry curls that adorned, cut close or braided in ornate patterns, the skulls of Ellelloû's Salu sisters, and three of his four wives—had drifted stickily across her face; her hair held red streaks amid the black, and the kohl with which she had beautified her eyes had smudged. The dusty brown of her cheeks showed in the slant light linear shadows of a single diagonal tribal cicatrice, one on each cheekbone. The noises about them in the slum, the banging of calabashes and scraping of warm ashes and the unwrapping of hashish packets concealed in fasces of rattan below and the buzzing of children's recitation from the Koran school across the steep ochre alley, made it hard to return to sleep, his *salāt as-subh* performed, and Ellelloû lay there beside her hard-breathing unconsciousness like a thirsty man lying on the lip of a well, conscious that the nation was dying, that the beginnings of its day were the leavings of the night, that the dry sounds he heard, of rattling, scraping, unwrapping, reciting, were hopeless sounds, scavenging sounds, of chickens too thin to slaughter pecking at stones that would never be seeds. Allah Himself was dried-up and old, and had wandered away.

When Kutunda awoke, he asked her, "Would it help, to kill the king?"

She performed her duties in a pot and went about the room naked, carelessly mingling her limbs with the swords and sentinels of sun the horizontally slatted windows admitted in impalpable ranks. Shafts of radiant dust swirled like barber poles. The room was irregular in shape, with rafters of twisted tamarisk. The walls of hardened clay mirrored her skin, flickeringly, as, with the quickness of greed, with the slowness of delight, my mistress assembled the decorations and ornaments—the dab of antimony on each eyelid, the manacles of gold about her wrists, the heaped necklaces of fine beads tightly strung on zebra-tail hairs—allowable to the dicta-

tor's concubine. As a perquisite of this position, my waif
set her jaw to give advice. Removed from the shadows of
the tents and ditches of the north, Kutunda appeared
older than when I had seduced her. Determined creases in
her brow and about her pursed mouth betrayed some previous years of taking thought; vexations had worn their
channels; perhaps a decade had passed since her first uncleanness. She had a squint; perhaps she needed glasses.
"Tell me about this king," she said.

"He is feeble but clever, my captive and yet my protector, in some sense that made me reluctant to order his execution when L'Émergence broke forth, and when his
violent death would have seemed unexceptional. All of
Edumu's political and cultural conditioning tended to es-
trange him from the working classes and the peasantry.
His regime was corrupt, in regard both to his personal
tyranny—he was carelessly cruel in the antique, sensuous
manner—and to the bourgeois ideology of his ministers,
who to maintain their own prosperity within the pathetically unrepresentative elite were selling to the Americans
what their fathers had sold to the French, who for that
matter thought they still owned it. Their only maneuver,
in the nation's war against misery, was to solicit, with
much incidental bribery, another foreign concession, to
build another glass hotel to function as a whorehouse for
the *kafirs*. The difficulty with government in Africa, my
dear Kutunda, is that in the absence of any considerable
mercantile or industrial development the government is
the only concentration of riches and therefore is monopol-
ized by men who seek riches. The private vices of Edumu
would have been trivial had his political orientation been
correct, that is, had he offered in any way to overthrow
the ancient patterns of adventurism and enlightened self-
interest which were tolerable when moderated by the
personal interplay of the small tribal unit but which are

sheerly brutalizing when that interplay is outgrown. His conservatism, which I would rather describe as a feckless impotence, was masked by considerable personal charm, even kindliness to his chosen intimates, and by the smiling obscurantism of the hopeless cynic."

"The king," Kutunda said, her squint drawing her cheek-scars up, underlining what I perceived as a recalling of me to the business at hand, away from the rhetoric of "Poli Sci," with a seriousness that made me shudder in fear for Edumu, for this wanton woman (her odorousness now enriched by the spices and perfumes of the black-market shops) had a hard head for men's affairs, "the king is old?"

"Older than anyone knows, but not likely, I fear, to do us the favor of dying."

"That would be no favor," Kutunda said. "It would deprive the government of whatever appearance of incentive might be gained by his execution as a sky-criminal."

She used here a technical Sara term referring to an offender not against his fellow men but against the overarching harmony of common presumptions: "political criminal" might be our modern translation. Naked but for the bangles and unguents of beautification, Kutunda began to strut with the importance my ears lent her words. Her heels firmly struck the floor; her toes seemed to prolong her grip; her stride, back and forth in the little room, gave me cause to remember that her grandmother had been a leopard. Her legs were thick and slightly bowed; her buttocks had that delicious wobble of maturity. I began vaguely to long for sex. It stretched my bones, to think how much of my life had been spent listening to naked women talk. "One must look for the center of unhealth," she explained. "This center lies not, I think, within the king, who cannot help being the type of man he is, but within your mercy toward him."

"He took me up when I was less than a grain of sand, a soldier with falsified papers, and set me at his side. He made me a son, when he had fifty sons already. I would sooner spill the blood of my true father, a Nubian raider whose face vanished with the wind, than this old tyrant who forgave me everything, and still forgives."

"What have you done to forgive?"

"I was born of a rape. And now I govern a starving land."

"Why were your papers falsified?"

"Because the truth would have done me no good, nor will it benefit you."

Her sable eyes, that seemed to strain for focus, slid toward me, seeing that she had presumed. Her tongue moved on, more humoringly. "We must locate the center of the evil that makes the sky avoid the earth. They are lovers, the earth and the sky, and in the strength of their passion fly apart as quickly as they come together. They are like one of the white men's mighty machines; a single speck of evil will bring it to a halt. Now a demon does not occupy the entire body, but a pinhead point within it, for a demon has no necessary size, and must be small to fly. It may enter by a nostril or the anus, and take up residence in the gizzard or the little toe. Have you tortured the king, to find a spot where there is no pain? There the demon likely resides, and a heated dagger, thrust smartly in, will drive him out. But the surgery must be exact. Fingers make favorite burrows for the bad spirits; a reasonable precaution would be to slice off the old king's hands. I see you do not like that plan."

I had said nothing, merely attempted to visualize the event—the wrist veins pumping like the mouth of a jug, the eerie *Dasein* of the severed hand, still bearing its fingerprints, and the life-lines of its palm, though lifeless as wax.

Kutunda's head disappeared in her new green coussabe, one of several that had replaced the rags in which I had found her. Golden stitching of ecstatic concentricity stiffened its sleeves. Clothed, she became flirtatious and slimmer, and her gravely politic air dissolved into suggestions that were plainly malicious and jealous; she was jealous of my love for the king. "Cut off his testicles," she suggested, "and display them in the scales of the statue of Justice above the main portal of the Palais. *Wanjiji*," she scornfully pronounced. "There has been no Wanjiji since my grandfather's time, and even then its men were famous for their cowardice and gluttony. In war they waited till the men of the other village were gone and then they came in and butchered the children. Tear out his eyes and stuff them up his rectum, so they can spy out where his demon lives."

"A demon has come to live in *you*," I observed, grabbing at the gaudy cloth as she swirled by. Her ankle-rings of bronze and silver tintinnabulated.

"God has nowhere to alight in Kush!" She dodged me, her lips snarled back from her inturned teeth. "On the highest peak there sits a wrinkled old man in a cell, guarded by a soldier in khaki who wishes to hide in the dust. So the Compassionate One flies on, His river flows on, the sky remains bright, and Kush remains barren. You need to make a show, Colonel Ellelloû, so Allah will notice us all. We are easy to forget. There must be blood. Blood is spirit, it draws down spirit. Dismember the king; tie his limbs to four stallions and give them the whip. His shrieks will dislodge the atom of evil and happiness will descend." She exposed her childish teeth in a grin, tilted her round head, and began to do up her greasy braids.

"Your plan has something to it," I heard myself concede, though at the thought of my patron's dismemberment my own limbs, their stir of lust ignored and dissipated, felt leaden.

Not that, at this stage of his disintegration, the colonel conspicuously neglected his official duties. He was generally at his desk, military green steel in his fanatically austere office on the corner of the Palais de l'Administration des Noirs overlooking Al-Abid—the rotting canopies of its dusty *souk*, its rickety wharves and pirogues slender as spears—for hours before Michaelis Ezana reported from his adjoining office, and the two drank together their morning chocolate and in their unending dialectical contention mapped the nation's path into the future.

Ezana was all facts and figures, a proponent of loans from the World Bank and grants from UNESCO, of schemes for dams and irrigation, of capital investments cleverly pried from the rivalry between the two superpowers (and that shadowy third, China, that has the size but not as it were the mass, the substance, to be called super), and more lately of hopes of financial rescue from their brethren in Islam, the oily, dollar-drunk sheiks of Kuwait and Qatar. At the outset of L'Émergence, Ellelloû had shared Ezana's enthusiasm for these manipulations of their sovereignty, as elaborate and phantasmal as the manipulations of the teeming spirit-world conducted by the witches and marabouts beyond the Grionde. But, seeing the plans come to nothing, or less than nothing— the expensive peanut-shelling equipment fall into disuse for want of repairmen, the wells drilled become the focus of a ravaged pasturage, the one dam constructed become the source of a plague of bilharzia-infested snails—Ellelloû had retreated from these impure involvements and watched with a sardonic detachment Ezana's energetic attempts to engage the world in the fortunes of Kush. The

Minister of the Interior's habitual dress, formerly the rude
khaki of a fighter for the people, now tended toward suits
tailored in London, Milanese loafers, Parisian socks with
rococo clocks, and, though silk was expressly forbidden to
men by all the accreted moral authority of Islam, Hong
Kong shirts of a suspicious suppleness; on his wrist he
wore a Swiss watch of which the face, black, lit up with
the hour and minute in Arabic numerals when a small
side button was pressed. This watch fascinated his subor-
dinates, who wondered where, in its scanty black depths,
the device coiled the many minutes it was not called upon
to display. So it was with Michaelis Ezana, who could
produce whatever facts and figures were asked for, yet
whose depths remained opaque. And scanty; for, however
able and ambitious, Ezana utterly lacked that inward dimension, of ethical, numinous brooding, whereby a leader
bulges outward from the uncertainties of his own ego and
impresses a people. An observer seeing the two leaders
bow their heads together in conference would have noticed that, though equally short and black, of the two
Ezana gave more blackness back; blackness irrepressibly
bounced and skidded off the spherical, luminous surfaces
of his face. Whereas Ellelloû's was a mat black, the product of a long soaking-in. He tolerated Ezana because it
was etched, on the crystal plane of things possible, that
Ezana would never succeed him. Ellelloû's popularity, as
reports drifted south of his flamboyant personal victory on
behalf of the people against capitalist subversion, had
surged to a height where suppositions of madness would
not disturb it; so he dared, this morning, as the chocolate
cooled at their elbows, to confide his visions to Ezana.

"Returning from the site of the repelled invasion," Ellelloû said, "in the region of Haïr, we saw a strange
thing."

"A strange truck," Ezana quickly clarified. "As Minister of the Interior, Comrade, I have taken this sinister matter firmly in hand. The Bureau of Transport is at a loss. Of the two hundred twenty-six motored vehicles registered in Kush, seventy-seven of them public taxis and one hundred and four at the disposal of members of the government, the remaining forty-five registrants have been investigated and none answers to the description of a flatbed four-axle carrier of compressed scrap chassis."

"Who gave you, Comrade Ezana, such a complete description?"

"There were four of you in the automobile, of whom two, I believe, were awake. Draw your own conclusions."

Mtesa, a traitor?

Ezana smiled reassuringly. His plump fingers, loaded with gems like especially bright droplets of an enveloping lubricity, slid descriptively through the air. "The air of Kush is transparent, there are no secrets, only reticences," he said. "The truck is the thing. I cannot account for it. It is unaccountable."

"Also," Ellelloû ventured, comforted by the other's thoroughness, which brought all things shadowy into the light of numerical investigation, and might dispel even the dictator's unconfessed lassitude, "on the way north, in a gap of the Bulub hills, I glimpsed far off a golden arc, perhaps two golden arcs, I am not certain."

Ezana's fluid manner stiffened. "Did anyone other than yourself, my President, observe this apparition?"

"Neither Mtesa nor Opuku could confirm my sighting, though we halted the car and prowled the terrain for a vantage. Opuku had just pointed out the smoke of an encampment, and thus had drawn my gaze in that direction. If they had . . . one would have said . . . I thought . . . the region is strange."

"This was, I believe, the morning after your fatiguing night in the ICBM crib with the Russians, an experience in itself rather conducive to the unwilling suspension of reality."

"It was. But I was not so tired, nor so susceptible to the fumes of the alcohol spilled by uproarious barbarians, as to mistake my own eyesight. Could there be, I wonder, an ancient ruin in the vicinity, or an accessory Soviet installation the Minister of the Interior has omitted to acknowledge?"

"You are the Minister of Defense, and you know my opinion of this paramilitary foolery between the superparanoids. No need exists to double dummy rockets; and if it were the case why advertise the site with shining spires?"

"Not spires, arches."

"Whatever. The shimmer of the sand and the heated layers of air play strange tricks. Roul the desert devil delights in *trompe-l'œil*. Rest your mind, my President; I think the rumors of famine have troubled your peace of mind unduly."

"Rumors? They are facts."

"Exaggerated, moot facts. The Western press delights in making us appear incompetent. The nomads have always dragged our statistics down. Their way of life is archaic, wasteful, and destructive. Their absurd coinage of cattle has become ruinously clumsy. We must seize this opportunity to urbanize them. Already, the displaced nomads, and the sedentary farmers whose crops have failed or been consumed by the lawless herds, crowd to the edges of Istiqlal, where the tents and shacks, adjacent to the airport in full view of incoming flights, breed misery unalloyed by any suggestion of the picturesque. Their ancient nations have failed them; they are the citizens of our new nation, no longer of the Tuareg or the Salu or the Fulani or the Moundang but of Kush; Kush must reach down and house them, educate them, enlist them. This famine that so troubles you in truth is L'Émergence, given a fortuitous climatic dimension."

Ellelloû, though moved by echoes of his own rhetoric, asked, "Who will supply the wealth to house, educate, enlist as you describe?"

Ezana contemplated an upper corner of the room. "In the Ippi Rift," he began, "there is some interesting geology."

Ellelloû didn't hear. He had stood, to declaim, "The rich blocs each have client states whose prosperity is of more strategic moment than ours. Our place at the table will be the nethermost chair; let us remain standing, and at least trouble the conscience of the feast."

Impatience cinched shut the shining curves of Ezana's visage. "This feast has never had a conscience," he said. "We *are* at the table, Comrade, there is no helping it. There is no way a nation cannot live in the world. A man, yes, can withdraw into sainthood; but a nation of its very collective essence strives to prosper. A nation is like a plant; it is a lower thing than a man, not a higher, as you would have it."

"Yet the people look up, and must see something. You speak of the fortuitous; this is blasphemy. The famine exists, and therefore must have a meaning, both Marxist and divine. I think it means our revolution was not thorough enough; it left a pocket of reaction here in the Palais de l'Administration, on the floor below us, in the far wing. I know you know the king still lives. What would you say to his public execution?"

Michaelis Ezana shrugged. "I think it would be as an event not non-trivial. The king is already one with his ancestors."

Ellelloû warned, "It would horrify the world bourgeoisie, who are sentimental about monarchs. Their offers to bring us the benefits of their eight virtues might slacken, and your office would have less paper to handle."

Ezana repeated his shrug, exactly. "It would sever a strand to the colonial past. He is your personal prisoner, deal with him as seems expedient." He reshuffled back into his briefcase the fanned papers—graphs, maps, computer print-outs—that again had failed to interest the President. Ellelloû sat down and sipped his chocolate, which had grown cool. But no mere tepidity had subverted its taste: there was something added and subtracted, something malty, ersatz, adulterate, mild, mellow, vitaminized. Ambushed by recognition, Ellelloû blurted out to Ezana the one word, "Ovaltine!"

Sittina, my third wife, lived in a villa among bushes of oleander, camel's-foot, and feathery bamboo, among children she no longer even pretended were mine and half-completed paintings, weavings abandoned in mid-stripe on the loom, and shimmering gowns which needed only to be hemmed to be finished. On the harpsichord, *The Well-Tempered Clavier* always stood open to the same fugue. She was too variously talented to push anything through to mastery. Soot-black, slender, the huge hoops of her earrings pierced through the tops of her cup-shaped ears rather than the lobes and touching one shoulder or another as she moved her lovely small tipped-back head, she was elevated and detached in her view of me, and I found this oddly confirming.

"So the Palais kitchen makes Ovaltine instead of pure Ghanaian chocolate for a change," she said. "What of it? You think you burned all the produce the Yankees are smuggling in? It's not that easy, they make tons more of junk every day. Don't worry about it, Félix. Face it, Africa is crazy about trading. Where else can you buy in the marketplace honest-to-God fingernail clippings? I mean, it's wild."

She said all this glancingly, over her shoulder, in her offhand American English. The daughter of a Tutsi chief, she had been sent in a time of Hutu massacre to a small all-black college in the state of Alabama, and indeed had set several sprint records there. The turn of her calves and the length of her thighs had won my heart, in the heyday of Edumu's restored rule, when she competed in the Noire Pan-African games of 1962. Though she had ever been in our marriage elusive, like the wind she raced with, I could never consider her a bad wife. Often in the bed of another, in my virile thirties, in the carefree Sixties, the thought of her pointed tits and trim bean-shaped buttocks had given me rise. Yet the reality of her was more mixed than the thought, the inner image of her. Sittina and I had not made love for four years, though the youngest of the glossy, long-skulled children that wobbled and prattled through the room, chased by parrots and pet patas monkeys, was under two. Sittina was wearing a loose-throated long-sleeved dashiki with rainbow-dyed culottes of crushed voile; they flapped and swayed with the movements of her wonderful impatient legs. She was engaged, in one of her abortive projects, with fashion design, and her outfit, so contemporary and timeless both, so Western and African, was one of her creations. But, she explained, between bursts of attention to the needful children—each of whom cast at me, in my unadorned khaki, the glance one gives a gardener or messenger boy who has come six steps too far into the house—that it was impossible nowadays to obtain cloth or even needles and thread, that there was nothing for sale in the markets but the cheapest sort of *merikani*, faded bolts the missionaries must have brought, and that since the Revolution had reduced the European community so drastically there

were no customers anyway, the wives of the Kuwaitis
never came out of their compounds, the Albanian women
were stringy-haired savages smelling of wet wool, and that
awful Mrs. Ezana—how can he stand her?, she's *such* a
bluestocking—went everywhere bare-breasted, as a sign
of political undeviation. *Pas chic*, Sittina said. Her words
had all the substance of a complaint but not, truly, the
tone. I felt I had come on the afternoon of a visit to or by
some lover; hence her benign, if abstracted and hurried,
manner. She continued, "What are you doing about the
drought? Even the price of a goat head is out of sight. A
single cassava brings two hundred *lu*. You put some millet
paste on the windowsill to curdle and in five minutes it's
stolen. The refugees from the north come into town and
rob—what else can the poor things do? My night guard
had his throat slit the other night and walked home in a
sulk. Don't ask me where *I* was, I forget. They took the
stainless steel flatware and two of my old trophies but
hadn't the sophistication to steal the Chagall." The
Chagall, of the customary upside-down Jew smiling at a
green moon, had been our wedding present from the king.
Now it hung on the far wall between an Ife harvest-drama
mask and a Somali saddle-cloth of an exceptionally elaborate pattern. Sittina, who bore the name of a Queen of
Shendy, had furnished the spacious living-room of the
villa in a scattered "artistic" style with sub-Saharan artifacts whose solemn blacks and browns, whose surfaces of
red-stained animal hide and hollowed gourd still redolent
of the organic matrix from which they had been gently
lifted by the last stage of manufacture consorted with the
glib rectilinearity and mechanically perfect surfaces of the
Danish armchairs and glass-and-aluminum coffee tables
that had been salvaged from the pillage of the European
quarters in 1968. The whole room, with its cracks and
gaps and air of casual assemblage and incompleted inten-
tions, seemed an insubstantial sham compared to a room I

could suddenly remember, of white-painted moldings and unchipped knickknacks, of impregnable snugness and immovable solidity, tight as the keel of a ship, carpeted wall to wall, crammed with upright, polished, nubbled, antimacassared furniture including a cabineted television set and a strange conical table of three platterlike shelves that held a gleaming trove of transparent paperweights containing in their centers crinkled paper or plastic flowers, evil eyes of all colors whose stare seemed a multiform sister to the grave gray-green Cyclops stare of the unlit television screen, all this furniture in this exotic far-off room sharing a feeling of breathless fumigated intrusion-proof cleanness that pressed on my chest as I waited for someone, love embodied, as perfect and white as the woodwork that embowered her, to descend the stairs; the varnished treads and slender balusters did a kind of pirouette at the foot of the stairs, a skillful cold whirl of carpentry that broke, by one of those irruptions to which my mind was lately prone, through the dusky mud tints of Sittina's villa, the tender fragility of things African, the friable dishes and idols and houses of earth moistened and shaped and dried again, of hides and reeds crumbling back to grass and dust, of the people themselves for their bright moment of laughter rising out of the clay and sinking again, into the featureless face of Allah, which it is the final bliss for believers to behold, through the seven veils of Paradise. My memory laid a cold curse on the present moment. Sittina's offhand beauty, the sense of suspension her mind spun, in the disarrayed room, as she waited for me to leave, so she could proceed with that life of uncompleted curves that amused her, underlined the desolation known only to those who live between two worlds.

But who, in the world, now, does not live between two worlds?

"I'm glad," I said to her, of the Chagall; and of the drought: "We are taking steps."

"God, Félix, the depression rolls off you like a stench."

"Sorry. Something about you touched me just then."

She made a swift movement, testing her hair, which was pulled back from her skull and intricately pinned by two dried fish spines. The women of Kush spare no pains to knit and knot their hair in extraordinary patterns. No doubt there is a Marxist explanation for this, having to do with a disproportion of available labor to available materials, all history testifying, with the tedious workmanship that crowds our museum cases, to a terrible excess of life, of time, that overruns all crannies as tropical tendrils embroider every inch of available light. Sittina's gesture had been flirtatious. She offered, haltingly, "I have an appointment to go out, but if my lord . . . has come in search of his . . . rights, I will stay. Cheerfully. It once . . . we . . . I am attempting to apologize for something I am not certain I caused. Until the Revolution, we were together enough. Is that not so?"

"It is so, Sittina. Your shadow in a dark room . . ." I could not finish, the memory slipped its sheath.

"Did I become an enemy of the people, that I had to be rebuffed?"

The recollection of her warm shadow, the sudden scissoring embrace of her long thighs, my hand underneath those taut buttocks, overlaid the stuffily immaculate living-room with its evil dance of balusters and staring glass *objets*, and I found myself too sliced, by successive waves of lost experience, to explain well what I did wish to share: "Under the old king, there was a kind of life possible, which we borrowed from him, his vitality and his unexamined assumption that he was right, right to demand and consume what so many strained to donate out of their poverty. When he was displaced, much that was let us say healthy and morally neutral went with him, inextricably involved as it was with the corruption, the bourgeois feudalism, the unpurged way of looking at things. You and I were among the innocent sweepings. I am sorry."

She said, "I had forsaken my father for you, at a time when he lived hunted in the mountains. When the tide of massacre reversed, he beckoned me to take my place among the Tutsi as a princess. I declined. And still I stay here with you, though all Africa says you are crazy."

"Is that so?"

"It is so that they say it. The truth of what they say, I cannot judge. Our traditions treat madness as sacred, and we look to the sacred to rule us."

"The appointment you are about to keep, does it excite you?"

"It did. Now you've confused me."

"Remember our trysts, under the stadium, when we were children of the king?"

"The king, the king. *You* are king now."

"Do you still make that cooing noise, when you spread your legs?"

"I have said, I will stay." She spat, a Tutsi courtesy. "Go. My blood is heavy in me."

"I must say, you're spreading a lot of guilt around."

"Some day, when the land is healthy again, it would please me to be enlisted among the men who serve you, Sittina."

"You deserted, when this army contained no body but yours. And I understand you brought back a Sara wench from the north, and have installed her above a basket shop."

"A matter of state, merely. The woman acts as my adviser."

"Ask me my advice"—her words kept rhythm with the

vigor of her circular motions as she wound a turban about her skull, and finished with a swash around her throat— "and it would be to give Kush back to old Edumu and the frogs and get some decent pâté back in the shops."

"I liked what you said about madness," I said. "Did you know," I went on, unwilling, somehow, to have this dishevelled visit terminate, "that the British once had a plan of flooding the entire Sahara, before they realized it was a plateau? They thought it would fill like a bathtub because it was under the Mediterranean on their maps!"

Sittina was setting off, swooping here and there to kiss her children like a black heron dipping her narrow head to catch fish; half-unthinkingly she finished by kissing her husband, the swoop and dip being minimal here, because the dictator of Kush was a mere six inches shorter than she. Her breath, snatched inwards in the exultation of her departure, smelled of anise. As she retreated, the cut of her culottes, and a lift given her figure by the addition of the turban, made her look high-assed.

"I love you," said Ellelloû, unheard.

The trial of the king proceeded smoothly. The revelation that he was still alive proved, surprisingly, to be no surprise. The populace had always sensed it. The monarch's health was still drunk in the palm-wine bars, in the narrow stalls where the faithful chew khat while the pagans swallow *barasa* and guinea-corn beer. Even in the public schools, in the lists of the Lords of Wanjiji, the reign of Edumu IV was learned with an open dash, without a date of termination.

For the sake of the foreign press, then, developments within the Palais de l'Administration des Noirs were staged through a successive lifting of veils of rumor. The first rumor was that the king had been living in exile across the river, among the loyal Wanj who continued their life of trading fish and hippo teeth for salt and juju beads under the remote rule of Captain Bokassa of former Oubangui-Shari. The next rumor was that the king had ill-advisedly crossed the Grionde to lead a revisionist, pro-monarchial coup; this preposterous attempt, founded on fantastical CIA intelligence that the people of Kush were disenchanted with L'Émergence and SCRME, of course failed, encountering on the north bank of the river the magnificent solidarity of the Kushite national conscience. The third rumor claimed that, amid terrific loss of life among his followers, the king was taken into custody, and (this was the fourth rumor) captured papers revealed that the severe food shortages of recent years had been caused not by the climate of Kush nor its bountiful soil but by royalist conspirators within the administration. According to the fifth rumor, Lieutenant-Colonel Michaelis Ezana was superbly extirpating these anti-people, pro-feudalist traitors from the Department of the Interior and the Bureau of Transport, which had been discovered exporting foodstuffs to neighboring Sahel, along whose border one massive illegal cache had been discovered and destroyed by the personal vigilance and action of Colonel Ellelloû himself, in response to information provided by a female patriot, Kutunda Traorē, a *griot* of the doughty Sara tribe.

Mentioning Kutunda had been Ezana's idea, not mine. He had met her at my office, where she would visit me during the heat of the mid-day to enjoy the air-conditioning and to bring me lunch of peppered raw mutton and honied manioc from the Hurriyah market, and to borrow some *lu*. The rustle and intricate engraving of paper money delighted her innocence; in the village of her girlhood there had been, apart from heads of cattle, only two types of currency, both rare—giant bars of iron impossible for a woman to lift, and tiny round mirrors that, if dropped, were hard to find. Ezana spoke a rusty dialect of Sara, and spent hours with Kutunda, giggling and yelping over his own grammatical errors.

For the people of Kush, a pronouncement was promulgated:

TO ALL CITIZENS OF KUSH

Le Suprême Conseil Révolutionnaire et Militaire pour l'Émergence announces that miserable *Edumu* formerly known as *Lord of Wanjiji* has been found *Guilty of High Crimes and Misdemeanors* against the *People* and *Physical Environment of Kush,* leading to *Widespread Shortages, Dislocations,* and *Suffering.* The *National Honor of Kush* and the *Will of Allah* demand that *Justice be Done* to this *Reactionary and Discredited Exploiter of the Many,* Who in the course of his *Mockery of a Reign* appropriated to Himself the *Means of Production* and the *Headwaters of Revenue,* as well as *Wantonly* and without *Mercy* ordering the *Deaths and Ignominies* of those who served Him, and privately doubting to his *Intimates* the *One True God,* the *Compassionate* and *Merciful,* Whose *Prophet* is *Mohamet. Aforesaid Edumu's Very Presence* in the *Land* dilutes and *Undermines* the *Scientific Socialism of Kush,* this *Blot* upon *Our Flag* will be *Joyously Removed* the twelfth *Day* of *Shawwāl* in this *Year* 1393 *A.H.,* in the Square of the *Mosque of the Day of Disaster,* within the *Holy Capital* of *Istiqlal.*

Colonel H. F. Ellelloû
President of Kush
Chairman of SCRME

This announcement, printed on green placards, was posted on the walls of the city, and was chanted, in Arabic, Berber, French, Tamahaq, Salu, Sara, Tshi, and Ga, from the minarets of the mosques, from the windows of the Palais de l'Administration des Noirs, from the weathered wooden balconies of the Indian shops and the reed roofs of the riverside *souk*. Word had even been posted in the panoramic revolving restaurant of the glass skyscraper the East Germans had erected to the glory of socialism.

Yet the crowd that came to the execution was small. By mid-morning the sun stood high and the clay of the square, packed by the passage of footsteps to the smoothness of ivory, was white to the eye and scalding to unsandalled feet. Several military trucks had been aligned and the sides removed, to make a platform for the ceremony. King Edumu, bobbing with the aftereffects of his interrogation, which had focussed on the soles of his feet, and blinking in this unaccustomed breadth of light, which penetrated even his crazed corneas, was led forth in white robes by some soldiers who, it was clear from their carriage and aura, had greeted this great day with tumblers of *kaikai*. The meagre throng, at least half of them children given a school holiday, attempted a cheer that ebbed into puzzled sullen silence as the king, his little body more than once having to be disentangled from his voluminous, luminous *lungi*, was lifted into position on the flatbed of the central truck, where Ellelloû, Ezana, and the nine other colonels were seated on folding chairs. A headblock had been hacked of blood-red camwood. The king stood awkwardly beside it, not knowing at first which way to face. Behind him, in a ragged arc doubled, as a rainbow is sometimes doubled, by an arc of parasols above it, wives and offspring and lesser government officials crowded the subsidiary trucks and even perched on the cab roofs. Of

Ellelloû's four wives, none had deigned to appear, but
Kutunda Traorē was present, resplendent in a cascading
emerald *boubou* and a turban that Sittina had designed.
Vivaciously speaking to one bureaucrat and then another,
tossing her head and switching her hips, she had appointed herself the hostess of the occasion. Ellelloû
searched her face vainly for traces of the smudged whore
he had found among the well-diggers. Why, he wondered,
generation after generation, century after century, must
vulgarity repossess all the energy? Still, Kutunda's childish
delight and stocky self-importance alone struck, in this atmosphere of embarrassed, underpopulated anti-climax,
the ringing bronze note of gleeful release and public complicity he had hoped for.

Not quite alone; for there was another who entered
unembarrassed into the occasion, and that was the king.
Though crippled by age and inquisition, and more inse-
cure in his gestures under the vacuous dome of sky than
in the close-walled cells of his confinement, the king had
the forms for his feelings. Beneath the glitter of his gold
headband and the cloud of his unshorn wool his fig-dark
features shone with formal courage. The little arc of his
nose aimed, amid the insolent hubbub, in the direction of
the citizenry. They, with the exception of a few children,
had tucked themselves well back from the trucks, in the
alley-mouths and beneath the café-awnings at the shady
rim of the square. So far from continuous, a blanket of
unified humanity as Ellelloû had imagined, it was a crowd
of clots, as recalcitrant-appearing perhaps as those clots
of blood from which Allah first fashioned men. The king
lifted his arms.

He spoke in no language that Ellelloû knew. A few of
the crowd, its drowsy buzzing ceased, stepped forward
from the alleys and the awnings onto the blazing clay,
better to hear; these were the ones who understood Wanj.

Thus the blackest and most stoic faces sifted forward, leaving behind the brown, the reddish-tan, the merely dusky. The king in his blindness stared directly into the sun, orating.

"People of Wanj, rejoice with me! Today I go to join our ancestors, who live below, who are our blood! These mad soldiers who attempt to govern us are puppets of the ancestors, who dangle them a moment before they toss them aside. If their rule is just, why has the sky-god withheld rain these five years? They say Edumu is the center of the sickness, but when I was the Lord of Wanj and had bewitched the French with their little round hats to be my policemen and scribes, rain fell in abundance, and the palms poured their wine upon the ground, and there were not enough camels in Noire to carry our peanuts to Dakar! Of what am I accused by these poor soldiers, those apostles of *'le socialisme scientifique'* [for Wanj had no words for this concept]? Of black magic, of being *'un élément indésirable'* within the fabled purity of Kush! I say Kush is a fiction, an evil dream the white man had, and that those who profess to govern her are twisted and bent double. They are in truth white men, though their faces wear black masks. Look at them as they sit behind me, with their fat wives and fatter children! What have these men to do with you? Nothing. They have come from afar, to steal and enslave. I challenge them by the ancient code of Wanjiji: let him who accuses me execute me! If a demon give his hand strength, then guilt shall travel up his arm and become his soul's burden. If he falter, then I will live, and those who speak Wanj will still have a Lord and a living connection with the gods of their ancestors!"

The crowd hissed and murmured in its desultory way; the sun, mounting higher, was draining purpose and clarity from the holiday. Colonel Wambutti, who spoke Wanj, crouched forward and murmured the gist of the king's words into Elleloû's ear. The President promptly nodded, comprehending the challenge. He stood and glanced about for the executioner's sword.

Credit the now (in some quarters) discredited Elleloû with the grandeur of his response in this hour. Squeamishly he had absented himself from the interrogations of the king, and upon the occasion when the old man, his feet so flogged their soles had become bubbles of livid flesh, had indeed confessed to conspiring with Roul the desert devil and with Jean-Paul Chrêmeau, the Christian, alexandrine-indicting premier of Sahel, to bring about drought and demoralization, Elleloû had been prowling the city disguised as an orange-seller; by the time the President could be located and brought to the dungeon, the king had recanted, and hurled at him an absurd litany of American trade-names—"Coca-Cola! Polaroid! Chevrolet! IBM!" Indeed, the scandalized marabouts and professional torturers agreed, devils were at work here. Elleloû had gone pale at the outburst, and turned on his heel.

Not so now. A power beyond him descended and gave him calm. He stepped lightly to the king's side.

The king said softly into the sun, "I know that step."

"Are you sure?"

The king did not turn his head, as if to avoid what glimmers of my face might come to him. He preferred to rest his gaze in blank radiance. "Another saying came to me after our conversation."

"What was it, my Lord?"

"*Wer andern eine Grube gräbt, fällt selbst hinein.* Who digs the pit for others, falls in himself. It was said of their Führer, by my old friends."

"A pit awaits all of us. Yours is no deeper than others. You are simply at its lip."

"I was not thinking of myself, but of Colonel Ellelloû." He laughed; it was like a small fine box being crushed underfoot. His body smelled, faintly, of cloves.

"It is not I who acts," I said, "but Kush."

"Then, there can be no talk of mercy?"

"It is not a lesson I was well taught."

"Your teacher perhaps had too much to teach."

"It would be an impiety to usurp the prerogative of the Most Merciful. Why talk of mercy among men, when justice can be achieved?"

"Can it?"

"See." Behind his back I extended my hand. Opuku was holding the giant scimitar, taken for this ceremony from its case in the People's Museum of Imperialist Atrocities, for in the name of ethnic integrity the French had permitted executions in this classic manner until the importation of the guillotine, now also in the Museum. The Suprême Conseil had rejected the idea of bringing forth the guillotine for this state occasion as savoring of neo-colonialism. All of the executions during the early Émergence had been by firing squad. Blue smoke had risen from the inner courtyard of the Palais in rectangular clouds, like cloudy cakes released from a mold. Think of it. My mind in its exalted, distended condition had time to entertain many irrelevant images. Think of the blade of that guillotine, wrapped in straw and burlap to protect its edge, but perhaps gaps worked loose in the wrapping causing glints of reflection to fly across the desert as the pack-camel swayed on its way as it brought humanitarian murder to this remotest and least profitable heart of Africa.

The handle of the scimitar, bronze worked to imitate wound cord, nearly fell from my hand, so unexpectedly ponderous was the blade. In this life woven of illusions and insubstantial impressions it is gratifying to encounter heft, to touch the leaden center of things, the *is* at the center of *be*, the rock in Plato's cave. I thought of an orange. I lifted the sword high, so that the reflection from its flashing blade hurtled around the square like a hawk of lethal brightness, slicing the eyes of the crowd and the hardened clay of the façades, the shuttered fearful windows, the blanched, pegged walls and squat aspiring minaret of the Mosque of the Day of Disaster. In the glare of the sky the swooping reflections were swallowed, disgorged again upon the earth as the scimitar was lowered and steadied. A speech in response to the king's seemed called for.

"People of Kush! Be deaf to this criminal's blasphemies! Gladly your President takes into his hand the instrument of God's rectitude! Praise Him Who abides! *The unbelievers love this fleeting life too well, and thus prepare for themselves a heavy day of doom!* The day of doom has come to the alleged Lord of Wanjiji! He is an empty gourd, a mask without a face! When Edumu ruled, he gathered to himself riches that your labor created. He took to himself your most lissome women, and called your best land his own. The toubabs levied their taxes through the maze beneath his throne; under cover of his kingship the riches God has hidden in our mountains and our river were ferried away. Infidel harlots in countries of fog and clouds are adorned with our jewels because of this betrayer. Sentimental elements within the Suprême Conseil have preserved his life to this moment! This was a mistake, an abomination! God has cursed this land accordingly! By the sword in my hand I shall cleanse the land! Sacredly is it written: *Idolatry is worse than carnage.* Those of you who moved forward to hear the words of Wanj, hear these words! The Lord of Wanjiji is a clot of blood, a speck upon the purity of Kush. His life has been long and odious. He is cunning. His wisdom is barren. He has mocked Ellelloû. He has mocked the Revolution. I act now as myself, not as Ellelloû, but as the breath of L'Émergence, blowing away a speck of dirt! God's will gives my arm strength! Behold, those who doubt!!"

Opuku meanwhile and one of the colonels—Colonel Batwa was my impression, an ex-prize fighter—attempted to bring the king to kneel and place his head on the saddle-shaped block of red camwood. The king in his blindness, or out of some notion of abused dignity, resisted; there was more kick in his old body than one would have thought; the crowd chuckled a bit. I could feel, through the pink mists my verbal frenzy had set to swirling in my skull, his sensations, his struggling stiff frailty; I entered in, was pushed and pulled among jostling shelves of muscular darkness, of dazzling not-seeing. My hair was gripped, a hardness knocked against my chin, sun-hot camwood scorched my throat. A smoky smell. The orange in my mind rolled away. The king's head had been arranged on the block. Looking down, I had become perilously tall. The path the scimitar must descend through air appeared a long flaw in crystal. A few drops of sweat glinted in the net of wrinkles on the nape of the old man's neck, bared as Opuku, perhaps rougher than need be (it crossed my mind), tugged forward for me the mass of Edumu's hair, matted and yellowish like a sheep's. I eyed my spot between two vertebrae. Incongruously, there entered my mind from afar the image of a candy apple, such as one buys at county fairs in Wisconsin—its tough glaze, its slender wooden stick, its little cap of coconut. The first bite is the most difficult. The king cleared his throat, as if to address one of us. But his thought went nowhere, a trickle in the hot sands of his terror, and an intense mechanical interest arose like a hiss of steam from the point between two cervical lumps where two wrinkles conveniently crossed. Opuku's hands gripped deeper into the wool, as if the king were tensing to struggle, and I saw that the moment I wanted with all my being behind me was still a fraction of a second ahead. The divine breath grunted into my chest and the scimitar descended. Though the blade struck through to the wood, the noise was clumsier, more multiple, than I had expected.

Sun. The clay of the square was accepting yet another day's merciless brilliance. An edge of green metal, unpainted where the paint had chipped—the flatbed's crimped lip—took my eye. I found I was waiting, in the pocket of sharp quiet before the crowd loosed an appalled, triumphant roar, for the king, as his throat-clearing had promised, to say another word.

The very ink in my pen coagulates at these memories. Robust Opuku held up the king's head at arm's length, as the center of an opposing basketball team demonstrates his intimidating one-handed grip. Relief at the thing accomplished flowed through me, so I was slow to notice how little blood flowed from the severed head. This medically explicable fact—the brain in its fury to live had drawn blood up into itself like a sponge—was to haunt the kingdom I had inherited. The king's eyes were blissfully closed, while his body in its silken white *lungi* flipped about with a hideous undirected strength, even the arms flailing. Opuku with a booted foot pressed the body flat, as the chopped throat, romantically rich in purples and blues, spilled blood sobbingly. There came uninvited into my mind the flat side of that candy apple, where it has rested while hardening, and where the sugary semi-elastic glaze was thickest. The taste of this glaze, bitten into, and its stubborn texture were as vivid to me as Kutunda's cry of joy, a thrilled female keening less voluntary than a dog's howl, cutting through the stunned air. A host of gnats had come to drink.

So it seemed from the truck—gnats, blood, a crimped edge of metal, and irrelevant fairgrounds memories all compressed by the sunlight into one unfeeling, unmeaning moment, through which there coursed nevertheless a palpable liquid relief. From the vantage of the crowd, it looked far otherwise: Ellelloû's neat brown figure, sunglassless, stepped forward and with a leverlike stroke altered the quality of the smallest of the puppets posed on a makeshift stage. The head was held up. Then other puppets, unpredicted, appeared: blue-clad Tuareg, the lower halves of their faces covered by *tagilmusts*, perhaps twenty of them, on fine Arabian horses rode in from the eastern side of the square, mingled with the khaki men on the green trucks, and after a tussle carried off the smaller of the king's two bodily remains.

Up close, Opuku received a slash on his arm, and Colonel Ezana's wife was the butt of an indecent suggestion; but the very speed of the attack (which had the crowd been as numerous as expected would have been disastrously impeded) and its apparently limited objective of carrying off the severed head enabled it to pass like a loud but harmless wind. Some of the crowd thought the episode merely a part of the governmental pageant that had been arranged.

Ellelloû with admirable presence of mind addressed those spectators that had not fled the scene. "Citizens of Kush! Fear not! The alleged Lord of Wanjiji is dead, his would-be rescuers have had to content themselves with the unspeakable refuse of his physical remains! His soul has gone to everlasting fire! The forces of imperialism and reaction have again been thwarted! There is no doubt that these brazen terrorists are hirelings of the American paper tiger, or perhaps fanatical capitalists disguised in the robes of the Tuareg! We of Le Suprême Conseil Révolutionnaire et Militaire pour l'Émergence laugh at their presumption and invite the socialized people of Kush to defecate upon their individualistic, entrepreneurial violence!! The loathsome theft shall be avenged, have no fear! Disperse to your homes, and prepare for the deluge! You have witnessed the enactment of a purgation profoundly pleasing to Allah, and deeply beneficial to our green and pleasant land!"

Ellelloû shouted all this, in a rapture of abandonment to the furious wind within him, that could be vented only into the imaginary ear of his nation, but in his private aspect knew that his accusations were problematical, for he had seen the eyes of the raider who had snatched the king's head from Opuku's slashed arm, and they were not the wolvish eyes of a Targui or a North American, frosted and blue, but amber and slant like the survival-minded eyes of wild swine. Also, Ellelloû, transfixed by his battle-calm, waiting through a microscopically lucid series of milliseconds to be tumbled like a rabbit by a lion, too tranquil to think of lifting his bloodied scimitar in self-defense, scented through the flurry of odors of unwashed flesh and Arabian horsehair, a subtle sweetness chiming with his memories of the banquet in the rocket bunker. Vodka.

While the capital still buzzed of these portentous events (which the majority of the indolent populace had lacked the civic conscience to witness, and which, in the recounting to the unpatriotically absent, became unreal), Ellelloû descended into the Hurriyah district in the disguise of an orange-seller, to visit Kutunda. Now that the effects of the drought and famine were felt even in the metropolis, there were no oranges to sell, and the peddler instead

offered to the echoing, anfractuous alleys the mere image
of oranges, put into song:

"*Round and firm as the breasts of one's beloved's*
      younger sister,
she who exposes her gums when she laughs,
and spies from her pallet wondering when her time
      will come;

to the touch delicately rough like one's own testicles,
stippled waxy hides tearable and acrid when torn,
staining one's fingers with the sharpest essence of the
      juice;

when the hide is scattered like thick rose petals,
the fruit is found partitioned in quarter-moons,
each in its papery baby skin dulcet as dust;

parted from its many brothers too greedily,
each segment will weep bright tears of juice,
foreshadowing the explosion in the consumer's mouth;

how sweet is the water of the juice! Our lips sting,
the rivers of our heart rush upward
to greet the miracle secreted in this symmetry!

And the color, what is the color? The color
is that strip of the heavens closest to the dunes
before the green flash announces the arrival of night."

For such a song, which the singer elaborated through
many variations—evoking in some versions the navel and
the crusty button at the poles of the orange, dwelling
rhapsodically in others upon the tasteless mossy inside of
the skin that holds the drops of nectar like jewels in a

felt-lined case, and in still others upon the joys of spitting out the seeds—coins or cowries would be cast from the windows, appearing in his path like a sudden spatter of the rains that had failed to come, or paper notes would be thrust at him by servants sent out by the wealthy; for with the drying-up of merchandise to buy, *lu* had become plentiful, and many were in a cash sense wealthy. People would attempt to bribe him to sing a song of bananas, or couscous, or spring lamb turned on a spit with peppers and onions, but he would say No, he was a seller of oranges, and could conjure up only *their* image amply enough to banish the reality of hunger.

Kutunda was finding her quarters above the basket shop insufficient. Her new possessions—billowing clothes, bulky jewelry, inlaid tables, throw pillows, cuddly stuffed Steiff animals, mechanical beauty aids, a hair-blower and a Water-Pik—were overwhelming the little pisé-walled room which a month ago had seemed such a grateful improvement over the exiguous spaces of a tent or a ditch. Ellelloû, removing the stained robes and net yoke of an orange-seller, noticed on her wrist a watch with a blank black face. "A gift," she admitted. "Look, you press here, and the numbers come up! It is what they call electronic wizardry."

"In exchange for what service to Ezana?"

"For my services to the state; my wisdom and counsel."

"In urging the murder of the helpless old king?"

"I merely urged what your heart had already decreed but lacked the courage to execute."

"Lacked the madness, I now think. What good has come of it? The sky is as blank as your watch-face, and horror clouds my heart. Since the day, Ezana is formal and correct with me; I feel he is standing clear of my ruin."

"Ezana will dodge as you turn. There is no leader left

in Kush but my colonel. Let me show you the clothes I bought; the shopgirl said they were designed by a Tutsi princess." As she walked back and forth to her bulging cedar wardrobe, her heels thumped in the manner specifically enjoined by the twenty-fourth sura, *And let them not stamp their feet in walking so as to reveal their hidden trinkets,* the same sura that says consolingly, *Unclean women are for unclean men, and unclean men for unclean women.* She hurled one width of rainbow-dyed cloth over her head, wriggled it smooth, gazed at herself in the mirror with pursed lips, held a bloodstone earring against the lobe of one ear, and rejected the outfit by baring her tiny teeth, bowing her head, swinging her hands to the nape of her neck, giving the garment a sharp forward pull, and becoming naked again, her stout legs first. Her buttocks in the seriousness of this ritual had a tightened tuck, a flattening of their outward curve that touched me with its sign of pliant aging.

Yet, in bed, in darkness, my manhood recoiled from her familiar maneuvers of hands and mouth, grown since our desert courtship to fit my predilections as closely as a worn saddle fits its camel's humps. Now her mouth, moist as it was, burned; whenever my stalk verged upon response, upon enlargement and erection, the picture entered my mind of the king's severed neck, its pulsing plumbing suddenly sliced across and emptying itself, by spurts that seemed sluggish, into the crystalline vacancy of that moment before the Tuareg, too late, galloped into the square. The blood of mine that had been flowing to produce the engorgement of potency fell back, alarmed. "You are angry with me," Kutunda at last observed, weary of wanton exertions.

"Why would I be?"

"You mourn the king."

"Had the whim ever seized him, he would have done

worse to me. He took me up, I think, because he was amused by my ambivalences. Even his mercies were sardonic. He sat on the world lightly, like the spider that is immune from the web's stickiness."

"Yet you found my hatred vulgar, and further bear against me the grudge men always bear against those women they have conquered. It is a puzzle: the men who need women hate them, and those who do not, like your comrade Ezana, do not."

"More your comrade than mine now. You have a magical timepiece to mirror his, and the two of you giggle in Sara, hatching my doom."

"*You* are hatching it," Kutunda said, as quickly as she had set an ornament to her ear and taken it away; yet she could not take this truth away, though from the pinch of her lips she wished she could. *Unclean*, we are all unclean, with our smudges of truth.

I said to her, in explanation of my impotence, "You have lost the good smell of dirt you had in the ditches of the north. Now you stink of French soap. I cannot make love through the fragrance of our exploiters."

"You are sad. Forgive me my fun with Ezana. He is an innocent man, but so full of words and ideas; his being practical gives us much to talk about. It is exciting. We talk of the refugee camps, of re-education, of irrigation, of eliciting capital investment from the superpowers and multi-national corporations, with low interest rates and twenty-year moratoriums."

"It is futile. We have nothing they need. We are no one's dominos. Tell me a story, Kutunda, to distract me from my shame, as you used to in the ditches, when you would come to me from poor limp Wadal." Remembering this man made me wonder, Could she be the source of impotence, driving her from man to man in an orgy of betrayal? These modern women have yet to evolve a modern male to service them.

She told me a strange tangled story, of intricate blasphemy, as once of Wadal urinating on the fetishes, only now of Michaelis Ezana, who beneath his buttery black outward form was Roul the desert devil, a creature of blanched bones and arbitrary flesh, who sets lakes all around us, yet renders the spot where we stand burningly dry. Men in their thirst bite their fingertips and suck the salty blood; they kill their camels and drink the mucoid fluid in the stomach of the carcass. In this guise Ezana rules Kush, driving the whirlwind of the Tuareg on before him, eroding the pious and egalitarian republic of his archenemy Colonel Ellelloû. In the remoteness of the Ippi Rift there is a city to rival Istiqlal; here men copulate with pangolins, and women allow hyraxes to enter their vaginas, and all the moisture that Allah had allotted for the land of Kush is kept in a giant transparent sack underground, entered through a cave mouth of golden arches, a wobbly sloshing bubble deeper than a gypsum mine, and descending into it Ezana takes the form of an octopus, and sucks screaming, drowning maidens into his beak, and awaits the maiden, a maiden dusky and fearless and virginal, with teeth dainty as seed-pearls, who with a scimitar of tourmaline will sever the octopus beak of Roul though he eject a cloud of ink; and then she will puncture the transparent sack so that water will flood the land, and the bones of her father's herds will come to life, lowing, and the tamarisk and *Mimosa ferruginea* will bloom, and camels will become intelligent dolphins, and what other turbulent nonsense Ellelloû was never to know, for he fell asleep, amid the sliding of Kutunda's solid limbs and the nightmare shapes her voice conjured up.

He was awoken at dawn by twin sharp needs: to urinate and to pray. His duties performed, he lay beside the woman; in her sleep her hair had made tentacles across her face and a trail of saliva from the corner of her lips gleamed indeed like some trace of a subaqueous struggle.

Through the slats at the foot of the pallet the white flank of the Palais de l'Administration des Noirs glowed pink and mute in the first flush of light. Thus, Ellelloû saw, loomed political power immemorially to the masses of men: a blank wall, a windowless palace that inscrutably shoulders us away.

Also he perceived that a new strange sound had come to mix with the scratching dry noises of the Hurriyah slum—ashes being scraped, calabashes clicking, the Koran being murmured. From somewhere under him music was arising, rasping muffled music of an alien rhythm, with words, repeated in the tireless ecstasy of religious chant, that seemed to say:

> *"Chuff, chuff,*
> *do it to me, baby,*
> *do it, do it.*
> *Momma don't mind what Daddy say,*
> *we're gonna rock the night away.*
> *Do it, do it,*
> *do it to me, baby,*
> *chuff, chuff, sho' enough,*
> *ohhhhh."*

Three

SOLDIERS at the command of the government systematically searched the hovels of Hurriyah for transistor radios, cassette players, four-track hi-fi rigs, and any musical instrument other than the traditional tambourine, *alghaita, kakaki, hu-hu,* hour-glass drum, end-blown reed flute, or that single-stringed instrument, whose sounding box is a goatskin-covered calabash, called the *anzad*. El-lelloû at this point in time vigorously prosecuted the cause of cultural, ethical, and political purity in Kush. Any man caught urinating in a standing position, instead of squatting in the manner of Mohamet and his followers, was detained and interrogated until the offender could prove he was a pagan and not a Christian. Overzealous enlistees from the swaddled north seized and flogged young girls on the banks of the Grionde, under the impression that their bare breasts imitated decadent French fashions. The flocks of secretaries working within the corridors and anterooms of the Palais de l'Administration des Noirs were enjoined from wearing tight skirts and blouses; the corridors and anterooms were obediently thronged with loose *boubous* and *kangas*. Yet underneath these traditional wrappings, Colonel Elleloû suspected, the women were wearing elastic Western underwear, spicy brands called Lollypop and Spanky.

Within the inner rooms of the Palais he and Ezana conferred not quite as usual; a new note, a post-coital irritability, had entered their discussions since the execution of the king. That had been Elleloû's trump; Ezana still held his cards. Though for state occasions he still appeared in the revolutionary uniform of khaki, taking his place in the row of SCRME sub-colonels as alike as the ten digits of two gloves on their balcony or viewing platform, in the privacy of his office he had taken to wearing powder-blue or even salmon-pink leisure suits, with a knit shirt open at the neck and cuffless trousers of tremendous flare. The Marxist explanation for this flare, Elleloû thought, would be the same as for a sultan's pantaloons, or a burgomaster's lace. He felt his own thin khaki tight on his back as he leaned forward, appearing to plead, in that tense voice which even when amplified by giant loudspeakers had something of the anxious, as of an impediment overcome, about it: "There is a conspiracy. The dreams of the people are being undermined."

Ezana smiled. "Or is it the dreams of the people that are doing the undermining?"

Elleloû said, "They would all acknowledge that we are on the right path, were it not for this cursèd, adventitious drought."

Ezana's smile contained one gold tooth, which seemed squarer than the others. "The drought cannot be adventitious and cursèd both. If we believe in curses, we do not believe in accidents. At any rate, my comrade, who in Kush denies that we are on the right path? Save for the paltry few imperialist quislings and extinct fossils enjoying re-education in what were once the wine cellars of the French? The security forces of the Department of the Interior, supplemented by anti-terrorist squads of the Kushite army, have found no radios, no trucks loaded with crushed Fords and Chevrolets. True, in a closet of a Koran school, the troops unearthed a cache of bubble gum. But we have always known that there is a black market dealing in Western luxuries smuggled in from our doctrinally unsympathetic neighboring states, or lingering from our own lamentable pre-revolutionary era.

"Let us not, however," Ezana continued, and Ellelloû marvelled at the inexhaustible smooth machinery of the man's mouth, that functioned within the resonating mellow hum of self-delight, "discuss trifles. Let us discuss peanuts. To natural disaster, my President, world geopolitics has added economic distress. The nub of it is, now that the Americans are no longer vexed by Vietnam and the Watergate imbroglio promises to remove from their chests the incubus of Nixon, they have woken to the fact, long patent to the rest of the world, that they as a race are morbidly fat. An orgy of dieting, jogging, tennis, and other narcissistic exercises has overtaken them, and—this is the *crux*—among the high-calorie casualties of their new regimen is the unsavory stuff called peanut butter. Apparently, spread on so-called 'crackers' and unappetizingly mixed with fruit-imitative chemical 'jellies' between slices of their deplorable rubbery bread, this paste formed a staple of the benighted masses' diet. Well, in the national lunge toward athletic slimness and eternal physical youth, less peanut butter is being consumed, and the peanut growers of their notoriously *apartheid* South are compelled to export.

"Nothing, Comrade Colonel," Ezana went on, with a louder and more urgent tone, seeing his auditor stir and threaten to interrupt, "more clearly advertises the Ameri-

can decline and coming collapse than this imperative
need, contrary to all imperialist principles, to export raw
materials. Nevertheless, for the time being, their surplus
peanuts are underselling our own in Marseilles, and those
farmers who at governmental urging devoted their land to
a cash crop now wish they had grown millet and yams to
feed their own children. Without the francs the peanuts
would have brought, we lack the hard currency with
which to procure replacement parts for the Czech dyna-
mos, and electricity will fail in Istiqlal."

"Not a bad thing, perhaps," Colonel Ellelloû offered,
caressing his cup of chocolate, which he had tasted war-
ily, and found unimpeachable. "Kush will revert to God's
light, and not turn the night to uses inveighed against by
Mohamet. *By the light of day, and by the fall of night,
your Lord has not forsaken you.* What has electricity
brought us, I ask, but godlessness and ever more dependence upon the Czech middlemen?"

Ezana's gold tooth flashed as he flipped a piece of yellow paper across his desk to the President. "Without the
mercy of electricity," he said, "we would be deprived of
communications such as this."

Ellelloû read: REPLY SOONEST ALL INFO RELATING DIS-
APPEARANCE DONALD GIBES OFFICER USAID ACTING CON-
JUNCTION W/FAO AND WFP NEAR NW BORDER KUSH SEP
1973. URGENTEST. KLIPSPRINGER UNDRSCTRY DEPT STATE
USA.

Ellelloû said, "They must have meant Gibbs. Nobody is
called Gibes in America."

"The probable," Ezana told him, "is not always the actual. In regard to this cable, what shall our government
do?"

"No answer is more eloquent," Ellelloû answered,
"than no answer."

"Men may follow this piece of paper. And after the

men, guns and airplanes. This Gibes was precious to somebody."

"Gibbs, it must be," Ellelloû said. "Gibes is an insult."

"Be that as it may, if his government make this man's fate a point of honor, the effects may be disproportionate, as so lamentably often proves true in affairs between nations. The Americans have not the Asian discretion of our friends the Soviets, who take such lasting pleasure in bullying the already subdued, and in surviving the incarceration of their own winters. The Americans have the chronic irritation of their incessant elections to goad them into false heroics, and if I understand them historically have reached that dangerous condition when a religion, to contradict its own sensation that it is dying, lashes out against others. Thus the Victorians flung their Christianity against the heathen of the world after Voltaire and Darwin had made its tenets ridiculous; thus the impoverished sultan of Morocco in 1591 hurled troops across the Sahara to occupy Gao and Timbuctoo, a conquest that profited him nothing and destroyed the Songhai empire forever."

"I do not know Americans," Ellelloû lied. "But I do not think that having just extricated themselves from the embrace of General Thieu they will risk themselves against the starvelings of Kush."

"Exactly not," Ezana agreed, with a pounce as jarring as disagreement. "Until the moralistic Vietnam misadventure fades, they will content themselves, like our ex-mentors the French, with selling hardware to all sides of local conflicts and keeping the peanut-oil supply lines open."

"In that matter of peanuts and electricity," Ellelloû ventured, "might the Banque de France consider another loan?"

"Interest on present loans, my good President, plus the

salaries of our civil service, account for a hundred and eleven per cent of the Kush national budget."

Ellelloû's heart sank at the statistic.

But Ezana said, "Not to worry. These debits are in fact credits, for they persuade the capital-holding countries to hold us upright. Meanwhile, all capital drifts to the oil-exporting nations. From there, however, it drifts back to the countries that produce machinery and luxury goods. Praise Allah, we need no longer, in a sense, concern ourselves with money at all, for it exists above us in a fluid aurosphere, that mixes with the atmosphere, the stratosphere, and the ionosphere, blanketing us all with its invisible circulations."

"By these as by other circulations, it never rains on Kush."

"You exaggerate. There was an exceptionally heavy dew just this morning. In the global aurosphere there can be transient lows and highs, but by the laws of the gases nothing like a complete vacuum. Our turn will come; perhaps it is already coming."

"In the form of Big Stick telegrams." Ellelloû found this conversation depressing, all the more deeply so because of Ezana's mental nimbleness. This man's twinkling joy in being among the elite was the opposite of infectious. To take pleasure in power seemed childish sacrilege. Power was reality, power was grief. Ellelloû felt his heart falling down through the veils of semblance into the utter vacuity upon which all things rested. Lives, millions of lives, hung on Ellelloû's will and dragged it down. The famine weighed upon him sickeningly. Energy had silted to the bottom of his soul. He had returned to this hypothetical slice of desert, steppe, and savanna grateful for its searing simplicity, on fire with the wish to seal off its perfection; but his will had not averted congestion—rather, had become an element within it, this confused, derivative congestion of the actual, of which Ezana, with his rapid fingers and shapely leisure suit, was the condensation, the gleaming dewdrop on the nettle of the nation.

"What if we respond," he was suggesting, tirelessly, of the cable, which in Ellelloû's mind had already been consumed, and turned into snow like the first dry biting flakes that announced the November beginnings of the Wisconsin winters, when a second, white continent was imposed upon the green, brown first, "with a cable protesting CIA interference in the internal affairs of Kush, that is, their clumsy and ghoulish, how can we say, *caput*napping of the king, who was executed with full legality, by the Koranic and Marxist codes? We would have no trouble producing evidence of culpability; even the footprints they left on the dust showed a tread-pattern peculiar to American sneakers."

"They were on horseback."

"Several dismounted, in the flurry. Abundant clues fell from their pockets. Jackknives, dental floss."

"Overabundant," Ellelloû said.

"We can send irrefutable wirephotos. Cheaper, we can leak glossies to *Les Nouvelles en Noir et Blanc*, to which every Western embassy subscribes."

"And yet," Ellelloû said, "the one Targui who passed close to me had Russian breath. Beets and vodka."

Ezana shrugged. "There is a sweet green tea the Tuareg drink that smells similarly."

"And yet you say this was not the Tuareg, but the CIA."

"I do. This CIA, did it not arrange for the assassination of its own President and his brother? There is no fathoming their devious designs. They are a cancer that grows of its own mad purposes."

"This fury of anti-Americanism," Ellelloû observed, "comes strangely from my Minister of the Interior."

Ezana spread his fingers, their nails manicured to a
lunar lustre, upon his glass desktop as if to confess "the
jig was up" and he would "level." He said, "I wish to
discredit in advance rumors that may distract my
President."

"Rumors of what?"

"Of a sad absurdity. Among the superstitious rabble of
our poor retrograde nation, some say that the king's head,
magically joined to its spiritual body, talks prophecies
from a cave deep in the mountains."

Ellelloû had not heard this rumor, and it lit his de-
pression like a splinter of moon in the depths of a well.
"Again," he pointed out, "something Russian in this. The
Bulubs are proximate to the missile crib."

Ezana sat back, and sipped his chocolate, contemplating his President much as the black face of his wristwatch
contemplated the turn of the heavens. Ellelloû, his heart
lightly racing at the possibility that the king had in some
sense survived and therefore his own responsibility was in
some sense mitigated, sipped his own chocolate. "Not the
Bulub Mountains," Ezana told him, "but the Balak."

"The Balak? In the Bad Quarter?"

Ezana nodded complacently. "Where not even the *National Geographic* has been."

The Bad Quarter: the trackless northeastern quadrant
that borders on Libya and Zanj. Neither scorpions nor
thorns thrive there, not even the hardy *Hedysarum alhagi*
eulogized by Caillié. Wide wadis remember ancient water,
weird mesas have been whipped into shape by wicked,
unwitnessed winds. By day the desert is so blindingly hot
and pure the sands in some declivities have turned to molten glass; by night the frost cracks rocks with a typewriter
staccato. Geometrically perfect alkali flats end as abruptly
as floors at the base of metamorphic walls soaring as by
reversed lava flow to crumpled crests where snow had

been sighted by Victorian explorers, in a century more humid than ours. "I must go there," Ellelloû said, the will to do so being born in him as airily as a dust devil on the Square by the Mosque of the Day of Disaster; Ezana's complacence evaporated.

"I cannot advise that, my President," he said. "You are putting yourself at the mercy of fate."

"Where all men are, at all times."

"Some in more dignified postures than others."

"My posture is always, simply, one of service to my country."

"How can you serve your country by chasing phantoms?"

"How else?" It may be, Ellelloû reflected [and I now, with greater distinctness, write], that in the attenuation, desiccation, and death of religions the world over, a new religion is being formed in the indistinct hearts of men, a religion without a God, without prohibitions and compensatory assurances, a religion whose antipodes are motion and stasis, whose one rite is the exercise of energy, and in which exhausted forms like the quest, the vow, the expiation, and the attainment through suffering of wisdom are, emptied of content, put in the service of a pervasive expenditure whose ultimate purpose is entropy, whose immediate reward is fatigue, a blameless confusion, and sleep. Millions now enact the trials of this religion, without giving it a name, or attributing to themselves any virtue. That rumored cave, undoubtedly a trap, which Ezana for some devious reason wished me to avoid, though he would enjoy the freedom of my being away from Istiqlal, beckoned to me; my whim as man, my duty as President, compelled me there. For have not African tyrants been traditionally strangers to their domains, and should not ideal rule attempt to harmonize not only the powers, forces, and factions within the boundaries but the vacancies as well, the hallucinations, the lost hopes, the dim peoples feeble as ropes of sand?

Yet Ellelloû was slow to depart, and remained in Istiqlal all the month of Shawwāl, which the Salu call the moon of hesitation. The Tuareg *iklān*, whom the Western press unfairly referred to as slaves, pried loose cakes of salt from the crusted bed of Lake Hulūl and brought them south to trade for smelt, yams, amulets, and the aphrodisiac powder whose principal ingredient was ground rhinoceros horn. Michaelis Ezana zealously watched the economic indicators for signs that this annual salt harvest might be reversing the long Kushite recession.

One day Ellelloû, in full panoply of state, the solid green national flag fluttering from the fender of his Mercedes, visited his first wife, Kadongolimi, at her overcrowded villa in Les Jardins.

He was met at the door by a bony bare-chested man with the slant eyes and taut coffee skin of the Hausa; though the hour was eleven in the morning, this fellow was already drunk on palm wine, and Ellelloû identified him as a son-in-law. Within the villa, the rooms had been so bestrewn with goat hides and raffia and the ceilings so blackened with the smoke of cooking-fires that the atmospheric tang duplicated that of the dictator's native village, where he had wed Kadongolimi at the age of sixteen. Children, some of them presumably his grandchildren, teemed and shrilled through the battered, notched, bedaubed doorways of the villa; the louvers and latches of the windows had been smashed and jammed so that a hut darkness reigned in rooms designed as if to admit the colorful kind light of southern France. The smells of rancid butter, roasted peanuts, pounded millet, salted fish, and human eliminations mixed in an airy porridge that

Ellelloû's nostrils, after a minute of adjustment, found delicious: the smell of being Salu. He unbuttoned the top button of his khaki shirt and wondered why he didn't visit Kadongolimi more often. Here was earth-strength.

A chastely and utterly naked young woman came and took his hand, with a naturalness that only a daughter could bring. He fished for her name and came up with only the memory of her face, with its arching little braids and slightly drooping Kadongolimi-like lips, mounted on a shorter, chubbier body, without this swaying adolescent slimness. She led him through the maze of clatter and clamor, the rooms alive with squatting groups and pairs mending, stirring, crying, feeding, scolding, crooning, loving, and breathing, all under the sanction of the fibrous, staring fetishes of hacked wood and stolen fur and feathers, supernatural presences not repugnant or ridiculous in their setting but one with the mats, the grinding stones, the wide bowls and tall pestles, not disposed decoratively as in Sittina's eclectic villa but here used as the furniture of daily life, brown and rough as a seed pod splitting to let new life through. His old tongue came back to him, spoken with that accent of overemphasis peculiar to his native stretch of the peanut lands, with the swallowed *l*'s and pop-eyed clacks of his mother's people. Nephews, daughters-in-law, totem brothers, sisters by second wives of half-uncles greeted Ellelloû, and all in that ironical jubilant voice implying what a fine rich joke he, a Salu, had imposed upon the alien tribes in becoming the chief of this nation imagined by the white men, and thereby potentially appropriating all its spoils to their family use. For there lay no doubt, in the faces of these his relatives, that through all the disguises a shifting world forced on him he remained one of them, that nothing the world could offer Ellelloû to drink, no nectar nor elixir, would compare with the love he had siphoned from their pool of

common blood. And it was true, at least, that since he
had taken office this villa had absorbed the villas to the
right and left of it and become a sprawling village compound in the heart of Les Jardins, lacking only the spherical granaries of whitened mud looped around the huts like
giant pearls.

His naked daughter led him across a courtyard where
the flagstones had been pried up to form baking ovens.
Across the way, through a cloister, Kadongolimi had established sedate quarters, darkened and fragrant, where
she held court to the hosts of her progeny. She had grown
fat as a queen termite, and spent hours propped in a
half-reclining position in an aluminum-and-airfoam chaise
longue the white occupiers of this villa, great sunners and
users of Bain de Soleil, had abandoned when one day the
servants no longer answered their clapping and instead a
boy of a soldier appeared and announced that they, being
the wrong color now, had been deposed from the Istiqlal
elite. Kadongolimi when she took possession had had the
chaise longue dragged indoors and made it her daybed.
Two docile tots fanned her bulk with palm fronds. Her
cheeks were marked with the semi-circular tattoos that,
until outlawed by SCRME, identified and beautified the
brides of the Salu. Her earlobes had been pierced and distended to receive fist-sized scrolls of gold on days of fes-
tivity and pomp; today, empty, her lobes hung like loops
of thick black shoestring to her shoulders. She lifted a
pink hand, a pulpy-petalled small flower put forth by a
swollen old limb. "Bini," she said. "You look like carrion.
What is eating at you?"

She called him "Bini," his Amazeg name, by which she
had known him since the age when he had squirmed
down from his mother's hip and begun to walk. Kadongolimi was four years older than he. When he was five, she
was a leggy screeching personage of nine, bossy as a

mother. A cousin, her hands had rattled on his skull in the courteous search for lice. When they married, she had been a woman for a third of her life, and the shuddering, rustling bushes of her experience interposed between them their first nights. Her superiority never left them but became enjoyable. Ellelloû in her presence floated as in an oily bath, underestimated, weightless, coy. To Kadongolimi he would always be a child who had just left his mother's hip. There being no chair in the room, he squatted down on his hams, plucked a twig from a bush poking through a hole in the wall, and began to clean his teeth.

"The gods," he answered diffidently, tasting the twig. Some substratum in the phloem or xylem savored smartly of those little glossy red American candies prevalent in wintertime, that relenting time of winter when the icicles crash from the eaves and the black streets shine with the melting of drifts.

"You should never have forsaken the gods of our fathers," Kadongolimi told him, gingerly shifting her pontifical weight in the precarious hammock of aluminum.

"What had they given our fathers," Ellelloû asked his wife, "but terror and torpor, so the slavers Arab and Christian alike did with us as we did with animals? They had the wheel, the gun; we had *juju*."

"Have you forgotten so soon? The gods gave life to every shadow, every leaf. Everywhere we looked, there was spirit. At every turn of our lives, spirit greeted us. We knew how to dance, awake or asleep. No misery could touch the music in us. Let other men die in chains; we lived. Bini, as a boy you were always active, always pretending to be something else. A bird, a snake. You went away to fight in the white man's wars and came back from across the sea colder than a white man, for at least he gets drunk and he fucks."

Ellelloû nodded and smiled and tasted the twig, moving

it from tooth to tooth. She had said these things before, and would say them again. His replies too had the predictability of song. He said, "I returned with the true God in my heart, the Lord of the Worlds, the Owner of the Day of Judgment. I brought back to Kush the God half of its souls already worshipped."

"The empty half, the cruel half. This God of Mohamet is a no-God, an eraser of gods; He cannot be believed in, for He has no attributes and is nowhere. What is believed in in our land, what gives consolation, is what remains of the old gods, the traces that have not been erased. They are around us everywhere, in pieces. What grows, grows because they are in the stem. Where a place is holy, it is holy because they live in the stones. They are like us, uncountable. The God who made us all made us and turned his back. He is out of the picture, he does not want to be bothered. It is the little gods that make the connections, that bring love and food and relief from pain. They are in the *gris-gris* the leper wears around his neck. They are in the scraps of cloth the widow ties to the fire bush. They are in the dust, they are so many." Her great black arm, with a gleaming wart in the crease of the elbow, dropped at her side; she flung a pinch of dust at her squatting husband.

Perhaps the twig he was chewing contained in the inner bark an hallucinogen, for the dust seemed to grow in the air, to become a jinni, a devil, with boneless hands and too many fingers: the spectre of the drought. Kadongo-limi laughed, exposing toothless gums.

"How are the children?" he asked.

"Bini, we had no children, they all sprouted from other men. You were a boy who had no idea where his *kiki* should go. Then you returned from the land of the tou-babs a twisted man and took younger wives. The long-legged Sittina, who has led you such a chase, and the One

Who Is Always Wrapped. Then the idiot child Sheba, and now I hear there is yet another, a slut from the desert."

"Kadongolimi, let not your grievances, which are somewhat real, destroy all other reality. The children born before the French conscripted me to defend their plantations in Asia surely were mine, though their names escape me."

"You were not conscripted, you enlisted. You fled."

"You had grown huge, in your flesh and in your demands."

"Bini, you always fantasized. You left me slender as a bamboo."

"And returned to find you big as a baobab."

"Seven years later, how could I be unchanged? You avoided me. You avoided me because you knew I would discover the secrets of your absence. I discovered them anyway."

"Spare me hearing them. Sell them to Michaelis Ezana. He has set up a talking head in the Bad Quarter to discredit my regime. I am going there to confront this marvel."

Pity leaped in her, as a frog disturbs a pool. "My poor Bini, why not stay in Istiqlal, and rule as other leaders do—give your cousins assistant ministerships, and conduct border disputes with other nations to distract us from our poverty?"

"Poverty is not the name of it. A barefoot man is not poor until he sees others wearing shoes. Then he feels shame. Shame is the name of it. Shame is being smuggled into Kush. A blow is needed, to reawaken our righteous austerity."

Kadongolimi said, "You killed the king."

"Imperfectly. Ezana manipulates the body."

"Why do you blame Ezana?"

"I feel him all about me, obstructing my dreams."

"Reality obstructs your dreams. Ezana wishes only to administer a reasonable state."

"A state such as Kush is too thin to be administered except by gestures. When we effected the Revolution, we discovered a strange thing. There was nothing to revolutionize. Our Minister of Industry looked for factories to nationalize, and there were none. The Minister of Agriculture sought out the large land holdings to seize and subdivide, and found that most of the land was in a legal sense unowned. There was poverty but no oppression; how could this be? There were fishing villages, peanut farmers, mammy markets, goats, elephant grass, camels and cattle and wells. We dug deeper wells, that we could do, and that proved a disaster, for the herds then did not move on but stayed until the grassland around the wells had been grazed to dust. We sought to restore autonomy to the people, in the form of citizens' councils and elections with pictographic ballots, but they had never surrendered autonomy in their minds. The French had been an apparition, a bright passing parade. The French had educated a few *assimilés*, given them jobs, paid them in francs, and taxed them. They were taxing themselves, to govern themselves. It was exquisitely circular, like their famous logic, like their villanelles. Ezana does not see this. He admired the French, he admires the polluting Americans and their new running dogs the Chinese. He mocks our allies the Russians, whose torpid monism throbs in tune with our own. He hired Russian double agents to impersonate Tuareg, so I would become confused. He has seduced my Sara protégée with promises of an office of her own, and typing lessons, and contact lenses! Forgive me, Kadongolimi, for troubling your repose with this tirade. I feel sore beset, infiltrated. I can appear thus disarmed only with you. Only you knew me as I was, hoeing the peanut fields, and playing *ohwari* by the hour. You remember my mother, her violence. My father, his absence. My brothers, their clamor and greed. My uncle Anu, his lopsided smile and lasciviousness, that extended even to she-goats, and the leg, its nerves severed by a Nubian bayonet, that compelled him to become a carver of masks. I came to ask after our seed, our children. That silent girl with budding breasts who led me in, was she ours? We last clasped a dozen years ago, and she would be not younger than that. Kadongolimi, remember the games we would play—I the lion, you the gazelle?"

"I remember less each year I lie here, forgotten by my husband. I remember a boy who didn't know where his *kiki* should go."

Ah, Ellelloû. He was stricken with the unsatisfiable desire to rescue this his first woman from the sarcophagus of fat into which she had been lowered and sealed, to have her come forth as again half of the young lithe couple they had been, amid curtains of green, the conical roofs and circular granaries of their village scattered like dewdrops along a web of paths that threaded outward into cassava patches and pastures yielding to the broad peanut fields with their elusive musky fragrance of starch. And when the wind blew, the grasslands beyond whitened in clusters of racing pallor like racing deer, white-throated, white-rumped waterbuck and the oryx with his slim slant horns. Giraffes would come into the peanut fields from the acacia plains and with splayed front legs and lowered necks feed from the tops of the drying stacks, and be chased away by the boys of the village clapping together bowls and pestles and rattling gourds. Drifting like clouds the giraffes would canter away, their distant mild faces unblaming, the orbs of their great eyes more luminous than the moon. In this village, where all was open and predetermined and contiguous and blessed, Kadongolimi had confided to him in the dappled shelter

of sun-soaked bushes the smell of her pleasure, the taste
of her sweat. In harvest season they would hollow caves
in the heaped mountains of uprooted, drying peanut
plants. The skin of her back took a hatched imprint. She
had been careless of herself, bestowing her body wherever
she was admired with the proper courtesies, the requisite
hours of dancing, heels stamping the earth, the ceremonial
sleeplessness. But when betrothed to Bini she drew upon
herself, with the shaved skull and crescent tattoos, the
dignity of a bespoken woman. He remembered the long
arc of cranium the shaving exposed, and the silver curve
of sun upon it when she came, still wet from her ritual
bathing, to be accepted by his mother as her daughter. By
the forms of the marriage, which lasted days, Kadongolimi curled on a mat like a newborn while her mother-in-
law touched her lips with milk symbolic of her own. Bini
watched this awestruck by its implication of a solemn
continuum of women, above him, around him, always.
And he remembered how the shaved skull thrust forward
Kadongolimi's face, the insolent long jaw, the heavy lips
like numb, dangerous fruit. He remembered her ears, then
delicate and perforated to receive only the smallest rods
of gold. And in their own hut her soft muffled salty smell,
and her genitals simple as a cowrie. While he slept, the
morning outside resounding to the blows of her pounding
millet to meal, for him, her husband. Sun shuddered in
the heaved fan of chaff. The depth of lost time made him
dizzy; he stood, spitting out the twig. His thighs ached,
their muscles stretched by the unaccustomed squat.

Kadongolimi, too, met resistance, seeking to arise. The
naked girl, who had been standing unnoticed in the
shadows, stepped forward; Ellelloû, startled by the motion, turned his head, and his gaze was splashed by the
sun-saturated bougainvillea the vanished colonists had
planted in the patio, now gone wild. He and the girl

raised Kadongolimi to her feet; the woman gasped, astonished to find her spirit wrapped in so much inertia, in the weight that sagged as if to crack his arms and shoulders and then swayed away onto the slender girl, whose breasts were the shape of freshly started anthills.

"Tell me," Ellelloû whispered to his wife, "is she not ours?"

"Oh, Bini," she grunted. The effort of standing nearly smothered her words. "You are the father of us all. What matters the paternity of this good child? You yourself were born of a whirlwind. She loves you. We love you. In this house you will be welcome when all else crumbles. Only be not too long. In your absence, weeds spring up. Even the earth forgets."

One bright day Ellelloû, walking the streets in the stiff blue disguise of a government messenger boy, saw, along one of the narrow sandy lanes that zigzagged down from Hurriyah, a Muslim woman wearing freaky sunglasses. Unlike his severe NoIRs, they were round-square in shape, oversized, attached to the temples below center, and more darkly tinted at the top of the lens than at the bottom. Otherwise she was wearing the traditional black *buibui* of Muslim women, thong sandals, and a veil. She disappeared into a doorway before Ellelloû could halt her and ask at what illegal and subversive market she had made her purchase. He would have cited to her the holy verse, *Unbelievers shield their eyes; the truth continues to blaze.*

In the void created by her vanishing there blossomed then the memory of a tree of sunglasses he had seen when new in the land of the devils, in 1954, he a young deserter enrolled as a special student at a liberal arts college in the optimistic city of Franchise, Wisconsin. He had wan-

dered on that September day, its slanting sunlight peppered
with sprinkles of scarlet in the ponderous green of these
North American trees, among a thousand white students,
through the questionnaires and queues of college en-
rollment, and across the wide main street, as a-whirl with
traffic as a dance of knives, to the awninged bookstore,
where in accordance with his course requirements he
loaded up with Tom Paine, the Federalist papers, the Ar-
thur Schlesingers, a typographically frenzied scrapbook of
masterly American prose, a lethally heavy economics text
in a falsely smiling cover of waxen blue, and empty notebooks that he himself was to scribble full of lectured wisdom, their covers mottled like long-rotten wood and their
pages suggesting fields of endless thin irrigation ditches.
His purchases left him thirsty. From under the awning
next to the bookstore he glimpsed through a wide pane of
reflection-shuffled glass, above a jumble of faded cardboard totems, a counter that promised some kind of
drink, perhaps a silvery *arak* or, in accordance with the
symbols advertising sun-tan lotion, palm wine. Ellelloû
was not then the devout and abstemious Muslim he became. He entered. The hazards and betrayals of military
service and his remarkable flight, which had taken him
from Dakar, where he was to have been reassigned to the
Algerian struggle, to Marseilles and then London and To-
ronto, where he was hidden in the French-speaking ghetto
behind Queen Street, had not prepared him for the interior of this American drugstore, these walls and racks
crowded with intensely captive spirits, passionate, bright,
and shrill, their cries for the release of purchase multiplied by the systematic madness of industrial plenty.
Boxes contained little jars, little jars contained capsules,
capsules contained powders and fluids that contained relief, catharsis, magic so potent, as advertised by their
packaging, that young Hakim feared they might explode

in his face. In another area there were intricate instruments, sealed upon cardboard with transparent bubbles, for the plucking and curling and indeed torturing of female hair, and next to these implements blunt-nosed scissors, children's crayons, paper punches and yo-yos and, farther on, rows of Mars Bars and Good 'n' Plenties and Milky Ways laid to bed in box after box proximate to a rack of toothbrushes, dental floss, and abrasive ointments phallically packaged and chemically fortified to resist the very decay that these celestial candies, marshalled inexorably as soldiers on a parade ground, were manufactured to generate. Hakim's instinct was to smash, to disarray this multifaceted machine, this drugstore, so unlike the chaste and arcane *pharmacies* of Caillièville, where the sallow Frenchman in his lime-green smock guarded his goods behind a chest-high counter showing only a few phials of colored water. This place was more like a witch's hut of murky oddments hurled to infinity by omnipresent mirrors, even mirrors overhead, circular suspended convex mirrors which foreshortened into dwarves the slack-faced toubab sons and daughters as they shuffled along these artificially cooled aisles like drugged worshippers selecting a pious trinket or potion from the garish variety of aids to self-worship. Sickly music flowed from invisible tubes in the walls. Hakim, in the loose brown suit of an overweight separatist who ran a bistro in colonized Ontario, paused before an upright rack of tall cards, vulgar and facetious, yet which these U.S. indigenes in their ancient freedom were apparently meant to mail to one another in ritualized insult; many of the cards had a tactile element, a piece of fuzz glued to a bit of cartoon clothing, a passage of cardboard raised in the manner of hammered trays from Baghdad, and even, in some of the cards, a hole that appeared to reveal something indecent (*un*

derrière), which, when one opened the card, was revealed
as something innocuous (a plate of pink ice cream).

"Don't touch."

"Pardon?"

He identified the voice as arising in the loose-skinned
throat of a scrawny besmocked oldster, prodigiously pallid, his forehead blotched by some evidently non-tropical
skin disease. "Hands off, young fella. Get those cards
dirty, they ain't worth nothin' to nobody."

"Je vois." Dirty? Moving away, he nearly bumped into
a tree of sunglasses. Less a tree, in truth, than a bush, the
height of a man, armored in many dark eyes. The whole
thing sluggishly, unsteadily rotated. Bini, the future Ellelloû, quickly put his dirty hands behind his back, to display to the querulous attendant that it was not he who
was touching this prodigious, fragile array, causing it to
tremble. It was, he saw, a young white woman on the
other side. With impatient authoritative jerks of her slender bare arms she was pushing at the rack to make it dis-
gorge the, for her, ideal pair of sunglasses. She plucked
out a pair with flared tinsel frames, set them deftly but
rather roughly on her thin-lipped, decisive face, and
sharply asked Hakim, "Whaddeya think?"

"Charmante," he brought out, when he realized she
was addressing him.

She replaced the frames, not in the slot where she had
found them, and seized a pair with rims of pale-blue plastic, the lenses also blue. These, blanketing the upper half
of her face, emphasized the chiselled prettiness of her
mouth and the angry-seeming spatter of freckles across
her nose. "Not so good," he said, remembering to speak
English this time. "Too much blue."

The girl put on a third pair, and this time smiled—a
fierce quick smile that pounced upon the space between
her pointed chin and bone-straight nose—for when I

solemnly looked to give my third verdict, the dark lenses were mirrors, and what I saw, my brown suit swallowed by the two receding drugstores packed into the girl's mocking sockets, was myself, badly shaven, badly dressed, bug-eyed with youth and fright. Her name was Candace. We were to meet often, as fellow freshmen, and became lovers. She was blond. When her summer's freckles faded, her whiteness was so powdery I imagined I could lick it off.

"Our parched lips sting / and the rivers of our heart rush upward / to greet the vivid juice of symmetry," El-lelloû sang, climbing the narrow brick stairs that ascended to the second floor from the panelled and bossed ancient doorway, so low even he had to stoop, that stood beside the doorway into the basketry-and-hashish shop like an overdressed child beside its preoccupied mother; the shop door stood ajar, yielding to the nameless itinerant seller of images of oranges a murky glimpse of the shop's proprietor leaning forward from beneath his overhanging wilderness of drying raffia and completed but unshaped weaves to exchange with a customer shrouded in rags an elongate packet for a sheaf of rustling, dust-colored *lu*. Beneath the customer's ragged hem Ellelloû glimpsed, or imagined he glimpsed, denim cuffs and the coarse arabesque of platform soles. A tourist, perhaps. Ezana's figures (the Ministry of the Interior had jurisdiction over the Bureau of Tourism) showed that tourists, against all discouragements, were arriving in ever greater numbers, to feast their eyes upon the disaster of the famine, to immerse themselves in the peace of a place on the crumbling edge of nothingness. *Eradicate tourism:* he made the mental note, and tapped the three syllables of his name, El/lel/loû, on Kutunda's door, beneath the brass anti-burglary lock she had recently installed. *Eradicate property*, he thought, *eradicate theft*.

Kutunda was dressed, for it was mid-morning, in the trim Dacron skirt and jacket, with secretarial upsweep and sensible dearth of bangles, in which she reported to her office in the Palais de l'Administration des Noirs. And Ellelloû had seen her flitting in and out of Ezana's office wearing reading glasses like two half-moons cradled on their backs; when she gazed level across their tops, her brown, nearly black eyes appeared startled, her brain beating time behind them and the inquisitive, interrupted arch of her eyebrows also offending him, for she had taken to plucking only the hairs between them, whereas in the desert, with a flint for a razor, she had for beauty's sake painfully scraped them to a thin line. When women cease to beautify, Marx warns, an economic threat is posed to men. "I have an appointment," she told him, as if in truth and not in disguise he was a seller of oranges, with none to sell.

"With your President. Now," Ellelloû told her. "Take off that absurd capitalist costume."

Her tone slipped to a more deferential notch as she offered, "I can put myself at your service any time after lunch, my lord."

"*Allah reprieves no soul when its term is ended,*" he quoted, and slipped from his own costume. A fearful reluctance, for she had been imbued with un-Kushite ideals of punctuality, dragged at her hand as together they undid the buttoned, zippered work of the past hour's dressing. The uncovering of her brassiere, and the prim clean underpants, excited him; in the America he had known, a lust had attached to these radiantly laundered undergarments greater than that assigned the naked body, which had confusing associations of aesthetic beauty and the inviolability of marble. Her eyes unaided by spectacles perceived the sign and sceptre of his having been stirred; the dictator bade her, still in her elastic underwear, to kneel to him. Amusement flavoring her indignation, Kutunda with her generous mouth, whose lips had the width but not the eversion of the blacker maidens of the Grionde, and whose little inturned teeth tingled like stars in the night of his nerves, rhythmically swallowed him; their silhouettes, as shallow in relief as figures on a Pharaoh's wall, were almost motionless in the full-length mirror she had installed, between two of the big armoires she had bought to hold her swelling wealth of clothes. In addition to these, silk-lined and papered outside with reproductions of *La Chasse à la Licorne* and other Flemish *menues verdures*, Swiss reproductions so fine one could see every thread of the tapestries, Kutunda had acquired a steel desk supporting what appeared to be a dictating machine, plus tiers of plastic in-out trays, and flanking this desk two new powder-gray four-drawer filing cabinets, so that when Elleloû elected to drive home the seed his skillful and by now inspired mistress had brought to the verge of light, it was not easy to find a space of floor in which to execute his decision; the dramatic tug whereby he removed her underpants also brought his elbow into sharp contact with an edge of metal and tears to his eyes. The red thought, *Sex is atrocity*, flashed into his mind, along with the holy text, *Impatience is the very stuff which man is made of*. He pushed on; down among the steel handles and jutting drawers he recovered the earthy closeness, if not the satisfactorily rank aromas, of their first love-bouts, in the gritty ditches of unsuccessful wells. He laughed as her guttural cries exactly fitted his recollections.

"My President," she said, when her breathing eased, "has found himself again."

"One finds many things thought to be lost, in the preparations for a trip."

"A trip again? It's just a few months since you went north to the border and repelled the American invasion."

"And rescued the lovely Kutunda."

"And rescued the lovely Kutunda," she repeated mechanically. She was throwing on clothes and glancing at her wristwatch, pinching it to redden its face with numbers.

"What appointment with Ezana and his underlings," Ellelloû asked, "can take such precedence over your adored?"

"You take everything so personally," the wench accused, retightening her chignon and snatching up her briefcase. "I adore you, but it's not much of a career, is it, sitting around above a hash shop waiting to turn on the adoration? Michaelis gives me things to do; I can't really read yet, but I can talk on the telephone, and almost every day now I have these fascinating conversations with a woman whose Sara is quite fluent but really so funnily accented, I have to control myself from laughing sometimes—she phones all the way from Washington nearly every morning, I forget what hour it is their time, I really can't see why the imperialists don't have the same time we do, they must be going to bed at dawn and having lunch under the stars. Michaelis has tried to explain a thousand times, he says the world is round like an orange, and spins, and the sun is another orange—"

"What do you talk about, with this woman from Washington?"

"Oh, anything, we just warm the line up. She tells me what the weather is like, and how long the lines are at the gas stations, and what a nice man Mr. Agnew was, always so well-spoken and well-groomed"—she glanced about wildly, looking for something she lost, and then found it, the alligator case containing her reading glasses—"and then Mr. Klipspringer comes on and talks to Michaelis."

"And what does this lackey of the oppressors say to Colonel Ezana?" I asked, my fury, which pressed inside my head like corked champagne, defizzed by the melancholy observation that she no longer moved like the great-granddaughter of a leopard, but more electrically, twitchily, like a modern woman connected to a variety of energy-sources. Her nobly stout legs, with their calloused, broadened heels and pantherlike thighs, had been slimmed, by some (I imagined) calibrated diet whose pseudo-medical niceties were catered to even in the depths of our famine.

"Oh, I don't know, they talk in English, I suppose about the reparations—"

"Reparations?"

My doxy was frightened, seeing that these matters, which had become commonplace in her bureaucratic life, were a scandal to me; feigning, this time, a search, she with her briefcase and Dacron suit and trim legs and taut shiny hair from which all sand and mutton grease had been rinsed, looking everywhere but into my face, backpedalled and dodged about the cluttered, compressed room, before whose door I stood guard, soldierly though naked, a small brown man not really weary of being deceived. The knot of guilt in my belly needed still more digestive acid.

"My President surely knows," Kutunda fluttered, "of the negotiations concerning the American, Gibbs, who immolated himself on the pile of contraband either in madness or in protest of his nation's continued efforts to subvert Southeast Asia, or of American complicity in the recent renewed Israeli assault upon Arab integrity. Apparently at college he had been radical. His widow wants his ashes. At the moment, if my understanding is accurate, and it may well not be, in exchange for the ashes and an apology to President Chrêmeau, whose territory was violated—"

"Never! He violated ours by giving the white devils free passage."

"And you know, of course, about the Koran in Braille."

"Braille?"

"A wonderful invention," Kutunda explained with innocent enthusiasm, "that enables the blind to read with their hands. As his part of the bargain Klipspringer is going to ship thousands—ten thousand, twenty thousand, he's waiting for Michaelis to pull together the 1970 census figures—and along with them twenty or thirty absolutely apolitical instructors in this alphabet, you tattoo it onto the paper, I've felt some, it tingles, you can't see it but you can feel it, for a study center they would be willing to put up in Istiqlal, on the site of the USIS library that got burned down in the coup five years ago. It's quite dramatic-looking, I've seen blueprints, concrete wings supported by polyurethaned nylon cables, and stainless steel letters all across the front, naming it for, they wondered if you'd object, the old king Edumu, because he was blind. You must know about it. Hasn't Klipspringer talked to you over the phone too? He talks to me, sometimes, before Michaelis comes on, only his Arabic is about as simple as mine, he gets me to giggling. Please don't frown. Klipspringer absolutely promises there won't be any CIA people among the Braille instructors, he hates the CIA more than we do, he says they've gone and preempted the policy-making powers of Congress, whatever that means, and nobody in Washington will have them to any parties. You did know all of this, didn't you? Tell me you're just teasing."

"I never tease my Kutunda, because she tells me such good stories. Take a message, if you will, to my old comrade Lieutenant-Colonel, once Corporal, Ezana. Tell him it has come to my attention that he verily *is* Roul, the desert devil."

"And I can go? That's super. I haven't missed too much of the meeting, it was going to be a slide show and those are always slow to set up. Klipspringer has sent us a whole crate of carousels showing agriculture and irrigation in the Negev. You could come too. You could give me a ride. Don't you have anything to do up at the Palais? We could make love after lunch if you wanted, I'm sorry if I seemed preoccupied this morning, you caught me at a bad time, but I didn't fake my climax, I swear it. It was a beautiful climax, really. Only my President can lead me so utterly to forget myself, I am led to the brink of another world, and grow terrified lest I fall in and be annihilated. It's neat."

It heartened me to see the desert child in her revived, wheedling and winsome, at the thought of a ride in my Mercedes.

"I'll drop you on the way," I said. "I still have my morning prayers to do."

The little Mosque of the Clots of Blood was obscurely placed in the east of Al-Abid, from which remote section the Palais showed its unfinished side, the unstuccoed mud bricks crumbling cariously. Here the land becomes flat and the space between the square earth houses, the *tembes*, widens, and tufts of dry grass where footsteps neglect to tread evoke the savanna that once flourished here, before goats and God killed it. The mosque has no minaret, and protruding support timbers stick from its sides like toothpicks from an olive. All civic prestige was a century ago transferred to the Mosque of the Day of Disaster; but within the vacant court a limestone fountain

whose worn lip was edged with a raised inscription that
could be made out to be the first verse of the ninety-sixth
sura, *Recite in the name of your Lord, the Creator, who
created man from clots of blood,* offered through all the
hours of the days and nights of our drought fresh water
for the ablutions of the pious. From what source?
Touching my hands to the reverently incised stone, then
to the startling running cool crystal of the liquid, then to
my lips and eyelids in the prescribed manner, I thought of
thirst, of its passion greater than any other save the passion for pain to cease, and of the unknown men, their
names and bones now lost as thoroughly as grains of sand
underfoot in Istiqlal, who had dug down to this undying
spring, where so few chose to come.

The interior of the Mosque of the Clots of Blood was
empty, always empty but for the senile imam at the five
appointed prayers of the day, between which appointments it stood open to the unpopulated peace of Allah.
Turn up your eyes: can you detect a single flaw? The
wall containing the mihrab had been covered with a pale-
blue tile, patternless. I knelt; prostrated myself; repeated
the *rak'a* thrice; then sat back on my heels, my hands at
rest on my thighs, and let the meditative backwash of
prayer move through me, purifying.

In America my friends, late at night, confidential and
searching on wine and beer, for hashish then was known
only to musicians, would inquire about my religion, proposing the possibility—to their minds, an empirical certainty—that God did not exist, as if this possibility
rendered futile the exercises of my piety, which to their
minds appeared a wasted enterprise, a bad investment.
My faith was not then beyond being troubled, and if in
those small inebriated hours I gazed down within myself I
saw many shifting transparencies and at the bottom of
them no distinct and certain God. Indeed on the rational

level many contra-indications could be espied. But then the God of our Koran is the last God to be born, a furious Last Gasp that set the tongue of the Prophet to whirling in terror and whose mystics have whirled ever since, a God Who cuts like a hot knife through the polyheaded pictorial absurdities of the Hindu and the Catholic, the Methodist and the fetishist, a God without qualities; so perhaps belief in Him also lacks qualities. Some of our Sufis have divulged that at the height of purity in which Godhead dwells existence and the lack of it are trivial quibbles; the distinction amid that radiance looms imperceptible. What can be purer than non-existence? What more soothing and scourging? Allah's option is to exist or not; mine, to worship or not. No fervor overtops that which arises from contact with the Absolute, though the contact be all one way. The wall of pale-blue tiles echoed the repose and equilibrium within me, a silence never heard in lands of doubt and mockery.

Blue tile. A single fly, whose motions showed supernatural intelligence in their avoidance of repetition and any curve that might be broken down as geometric. My mind flowed with this fly into emptiness. I saw what I must do. It was a step along transparent stairs. All praise be to Allah, the Magnificent, the Merciful. A single small window, the scallops of its arch half-crumbled into dazzling dust, showed the depth and strength of the blue day besieging in vain the little mosque's thick walls. My gaze drank these tiles.

Ezana looked up, surprised to see me, more surprised to see Opuku and Mtesa behind me. It was not our usual hour for consultation. In the hour of dusk, he had put on a sashed robe of paisley silk and was sipping from a tall glass in which a slice of lime floated, while the air conditioner purred at his ear. He was reading a book, an American novel, no doubt concerning the grotesque sexual misadventures of a Jewish intellectual or a self-liberated woman. Its contents were making him smile, and the smile was slow to leave his face. His manner remained mellow well into our conversation. He lifted his feet, slippered in Italian leather, from the Moroccan hassock where they rested and would have risen in greeting had I not signalled him to stay at ease. "I have come to be briefed," I said, "upon the negotiations with the Americans that I understand are proceeding."

"Not negotiations, conversations," he said. "This fellow Klipspringer is rather hard to cut short, he is so—what do you Americans say?—*giving*."

"You Americans?"

"Forgive me, my President, *the* Americans. You have just walked into this book I am reading, full of these poor benighted bourgeoisie struggling to psychoanalyze the universe. I am tasting this trash the better to understand our enemy. They are a strange lost race, poorer than they know. I wonder if we of the Third World might not have eventually to welcome them among us—they too have a deficient balance of trade, a high unemployment rate, an agricultural bias in the national temperament, and the need for a protectionist tariff if their struggling native industries are not to be overwhelmed by the superior efficiency and skill of the old Axis powers. Indeed, Comrade President, at a time when the Arabs have all the capital, the Siberians and the Brazilians all the undeveloped resources, and the Chinese all the ideological zeal, one wonders if in the interests of global stability a grant of aid to the United States might not be a prudent apportionment within our next year's national budget. I jest, of course."

"Of course. Yet it does sound as though this Klipspringer has all too amiably insinuated confusions into the mind of my chief minister. These people are pirates. Without the use of a single soldier their economy sucks wealth from the world, in the service of a rapacious, wholly trivial and wasteful consumerism. My order was, in answer to their overtures, no answer."

"But no answer is an answer, which goads the interrogator. By discussing, we are delaying, and dissolving. This wretched Gibbs has not been mentioned for days. We cannot pretend the Americans do not exist; they have leverage upon the French, and if the French cease to underwrite our peanuts we cease to exist in the world."

"Or begin to exist in a better world."

"Also, as my Colonel knows, some reactionary elements evaded our revolution and took refuge in Sahel; an infusion of American arms might turn these ridiculous dissidents into an invading force, which would find our borders permeable and our population, however loyal to the name of Ellelloû, desperately weakened by drought."

"Hungry men make good soldiers," I pointed out. "When it comes to battle, the poor retain a golden weapon: they have little to lose. Their lives are a shabby anteroom in the palace of the afterlife. The Prophet's vivid Paradise is our atomic bomb; under its blast the poor toubabs shrivel like insects clinging to soulless existence. *Of the life to come they are heedless.* As to the French, they are too busy stuffing their money down the throat of the Concorde to look up; the entire wealth of a nation of misers has been swallowed by this aeronautical goose. Forget the infidels, they are mired in materialism and its swinish extinction of spirit. Defiance is our safest as well as noblest policy."

"Even your shy friends the Soviets," Ezana pursued, "are not exempt from American influence, now that the unspoken standoff has been translated into *détente.*"

"What has driven you, Comrade, so low, into this slime of *Realpolitik?* I will save you from the demon you have inhaled. If another call from this Klipspringer is honored with courtesy, the cables to the Palais shall be cut on my order."

His face, all hemispheres and highlights, went dull with disappointment. His gold tooth winked out; his lower teeth showed in a grimace of grief. "But tomorrow we were to discuss the possibility of an addition to the Braille Library, a leprosarium dedicated to the memory of my father. Yours, I know, was a whirlwind, a pinch of fertilizing dust; my father I knew and loved. He had been a warrior, then, as the French pacification spread, a ferryman, at a bend of the Grionde where the banks draw close. Perhaps because of his ventures to the southern side, he contracted leprosy in mid-life, turned silver and perished limb by limb. His nose, his fingers. I watched it transpire. My present dignity and the indignation that enrolled me in the Revolution alike stem from a vow he extracted from me with his final breaths. I vowed that I would climb high into the order of things, that other citizens of Noire would never have to endure suffering and humiliation as unmitigated as his."

"Better, perhaps, to have vowed to face your own end with less complaining than, from the sound of it, your progenitor."

Ezana blinked away this insult to his father. He leaned forward from his easy chair, to confide his message urgently, to press its warmth into the sinuous channels of my ear. My comrade in his foppish accoutrements became more naked to me than since the fury and fear of L'Émergence, and that aftermath in which we conspired together to do away with the empty-headed Soba. Ezana said to me, "The world is not what it was. There is no longer any deep necessity to suffer. The only lesson suffering ever gave was how to endure more suffering. What gives men pain, with some lingering exceptions, can now be cured. Smallpox, even in our bedevilled land, is being encircled and exterminated. We know what children need in their bellies, even when we cannot put it there. The fading of an afterlife—for it has faded, my friend Ellelloû, however you churn your heart—has made this life more to be cherished. When all is said and done about the persisting violence on our planet, and the pronouncements of SCRME are set against the fulminations of *Les Nouvelles en Noir et Blanc*, the fact remains that the violence, relatively, is small, and deliberately kept small by the powers that could make it big. War has been reduced to the status of criminal activity—it is no longer the sport of gentlemen. This is a great thing, this loss of respectability. We feel it everywhere, even in the vacancies of Kush. Hatred on the national scale has become insincere. The self-righteousness has vanished, that justified great slaughter. The units of race and tribe, sect and nation, by which men identified themselves and organized their youth into armies no longer attract blind loyalty; the Cubans and Belgians, the Peruvians and Indonesians, all mingle at our Palais receptions, lusting after one another's wives and complaining alike about the tedium of the diplomatic service in this Allah-forsaken penalty post of a backwater. Such interplay betokens an increase of humane pragmatism and a decrease of demented energy that makes my vow to redeem my father's life inevitable of success."

"These units you disparage," I said, "were mankind's building blocks. If they dissolve, we have a heap of dust, of individual atoms. This is not peace, but entropy. Like all comfortable cowards, Comrade Ezana, you overvalue peace. Is it possible," I asked, "that some principle of contention is intrinsic to Nature, from the first contentious thrust of bare existence against the sublime, original void?

The serene heavens, as witnessed by astronomers, shine by grace of explosion and consumption on a scale unthinkable, and the glazed surface of marble or the demure velvet of a maiden's eyelid are by the dissections of particle physics a frenzy of whirling and a titanic tension of incompatible charges. You and I, for additional example, have long been at odds, and the government of Kush has been born of the dialectical space between us. Out of the useful war between us, a synthesis has emerged; a synthesis, for a while at least, does package the conflicting energies that met within it."

Ezana's fingers, forced apart by the thick rings upon them, spread wider, in careful thought, upon the glass of his desktop. "I sometimes wonder, my President, if even the fruitful diagrams of Marx do schematic justice to the topology of a world where the Soviet proletariat conducts a black market in blue jeans while the children of the capitalist middle class manfacture bombs and jovial posters of Mao."

"Or where," I added, "the chief minister of a radical junta holds subversive conversations with the American secret intelligence and attempts to infect his own President with the false, sentimental, atheistical pluralism acquired thereby."

Ezana's rejoinder was aborted, for Kutunda, her secretarial suit concealed, as per government regulations, in a flowing *boubou,* burst into Ezana's office accompanied by an oval-faced young man whom I recognized, through the veil of his formal blandness, as the young Fula policeman who had read the Koran to the king. He still wore his plum-colored fez, but the white vest and pantaloons of the high-servant caste had been exchanged for a tapered shirt of needle-fine stripes and taupe slacks of indecently close tailoring about his hips yet so wide at the cuff only the square enamelled-looking tips of his shoes were unenveloped. Both Kutunda and he were holding full glasses and returning to a species of party. She also held a box of those salty biscuits called HiHo, and her young escort a red-rimmed crescent of Edam cheese. They had returned, however, to witness their host's being taken into custody by Mtesa and Opuku, at my command, as a traitor to the state, and as a wearer of silk. Ezana was confined to the king's old rooms in the barracks wing of the Palais de l'Administration des Noirs, above the floor occupied by the People's Museum of Imperialist Atrocities and within earshot of the shrieks of the Istiqlal Anti-Christian High School for Girls volleyball team.

His protests, his pleas, would fatigue me to scribble. One of them was, "My President, if you incarcerate your Chief Minister, and simultaneously proceed with your individualistic, entrepreneurial pilgrimage to the rumored cave in the Balak Massif, you will leave Kush without a head of state!"

I doubted that Kush would notice, but to be on the safe side, and to demonstrate to Ezana my liberated, inspired powers of decision, I turned to the young fez-wearing spy and appointed him Acting Minister of the Interior, Chief of the Bureau of Transport, Co-ordinator of Forests and Fisheries, and Chairman of the Board of Tourism. Kutunda, I said, would instruct him in his duties.

Duties, duties. Before I could depart it was necessary that I visit my second wife, that I press my little thornbush to my bosom. She lived, the Muffled One, in a shuttered villa in the most venerable part of Les Jardins, where the plane and chestnut trees imported by the *colons* had grown tall in the fifty wet years prior to 1968, only to falter, droop, and die in the five years since. Their blanched skeletons, brutally cropped in the Gallic man-

ner, lined the curving avenues. Candace's villa had been
rankly overgrown, but the drought had done some work
of pruning where the hand of man had been idle; a
sapless, leafless *Petrea volubilis* made its desiccated way
along cracks in the stucco façade, clutching the shutters
with splintering fingers and spiralling up the little Ionic
pillars of the front portico. The vine had been prying
loose the tiles from the portico roof when its life had been
arrested. My ring of chimes produced a strange rustling
noise within, but Candace was at the door quickly, as if
she had been watching my approach through the blind
walls.

Or perhaps she had been about to go out, for she was
muffled head to toe in a dull black *buibui* with the addition of a face-veil that covered even her brow. A scatter-
ing of holes smaller than the holes in a cabbage-grater
permitted her to see, in speckled fashion. Perhaps some
retrograde corner of Afghanistan or Yemen still holds a
crazed old spice merchant, sheik, or bandit who keeps his
concubines thus; but in Istiqlal, where socialist progressivism had reinforced the traditional insouciance of
African womanhood, such a costume had to be taken as
an irony, a sour joke upon me.

"Holy Christ, look who it isn't," her voice exclaimed
through the layers of muslin.

Behind her stood a big Songhai maid with a basket on
her arm. This girl's face showed alarm at my visit; to her
I was the ghost of authority, and her ultimate employer.
Candy had no other servant, and not because of any penu-
riousness of mine. In the early years of our marriage,
when I had lived with her half, then a third, of my time,
the household was appropriately staffed. As my visits
dwindled, she bade the attendants drop away, racing
through the housework once a month, even poking in the
vegetable patch, until the sun nearly smothered her. Now

she and her girl were going out shopping; but since Candy
almost never purchased anything, preferring to order all
non-perishable goods from the United States by mail-or-
der, I could only conclude that the purpose of these expe-
ditions was to display herself, muffled, as a mystery and,
among rumormongers, a national scandal. People said
that Ellell#û had mutilated his wife in a passion, or to sat-
isfy a perverse sexual need had married a monster of
deformity.

"You have your fucking nerve," she continued,
"showing up here in your little soldier outfit as if I owe
you anything but a—a good kick in the balls."

Her native inhibitions had given pause to the phrase
that her native freedom of speech and, now, her feminist
consciousness of genital oppression had suggested. But
Candace was not a ball-kicker, she was a heart-stabber.

"My adored," I said, "I have come to bid thee good-
bye. I am about to walk the edge of my fate, and may fall
off."

My Islamic courtesies of course infuriated her. "Don't
give me any of this Kismet crap," she said. "I knew you
when you couldn't tell the Koran from the Sears, Roebuck
catalogue." As if in recoil from this stab, she angrily
turned, my pillar of cloth, and it was alarming, how
closely her back resembled her front. In full purdah she
seemed less a person than a growth, a kind of gray aspar-
agus. Candace waved the frightened Songhai away, with
that jerky embarrassed roughness of those who think their
servants should be their friends, and let herself drop
wearily into an imitation Chippendale armchair ordered
from Grand Rapids. She had tried to reconstitute, in this
French villa spun of sub-Saharan materials, the rectilinear
waterproof comfort of a Wisconsin living-room. But the
tile floor, the *banco* walls, the rattan furniture betrayed
the illusion, which termites and the breakage occasioned

by our terrible dryness had further undermined. Without
removing any of her wrappings, Candace put her san-
dalled feet up on a curly-maple butler's tray table whose
leaves had warped and loosened in the weather. Where
her parents might have had a pair of painted-porcelain
mallards with their hollow backs bedding narcissus bulbs
rooted in pebbles, she had set an earthen dish holding
some unshelled peanuts. I took one, cracked it, and ate it.
There is a sweetness, a docile pithy soul-quality of taste,
to our Kushian goobers that I have never met elsewhere.
"Well, chief," my wife said, "how's top-level tricks?
Chopping old Edumu's noggin off didn't seem to raise the
humidity any."

"These spiritual balances are not easy to strike. I have
put Michaelis Ezana into the king's old cell, which might
make the difference. He has been compromising the honor
of our country with your ex-compatriots."

"Poor guy, probably just trying to bring a little rationale into Elleloû's heaven on earth."

"Tell me," I countered, "the rationale of the Universe,
and I will order my heaven accordingly."

"Don't go undergraduate on me," Candace said.
"That's how you got me into this hellhole, being all winsome and philosophical, building the no-nations up from
scratch. Scratch is the word. Scratch is where you start,
and scratch is where you end. God, it's hot in this damn
bag."

"Take off the veil," I suggested. "Your joke is wasted
on your forbearing husband."

"Joke, my ass," she said, and my own nervousness
eased at the hardening of her voice, certain as daybreak
to go harder and higher. "Who was it who smuggled me
in in wraps in the first place? Who was it used to tell re-
porters I was a *zawiya* Berber too pious to be seen? And
then after those rotten Pan-African games leaked it

around that Sittina was his second wife instead of his
third? Who was it, Mr. Double-*l* double-*l oo*, who put me
deeper into wraps when came the Revolution and every
Yank in Istiqlal was shipped back to Ellis Island? Christ,
if you don't think I wouldn't have been over-goddam-
joyed to go back with the rest of them where you can
have a drink of water without lifting out the centipedes
first and bowing toward smelly Mecca five times a day
and having to kick starving kids out of your way every
time you walk the goat, you have another think coming.
But oh no, not me, crazy old Candy, all A's in Poli Sci
but loyal as a mutt out of class, crazy, conditioned to be
some man's slave, sitting here watching my fucking life
melt away, and you call it a joke. You *would*," Candace
said, and undid her head wraps with furious counter-
clockwise motions. A trembling white hand unclasped her
veil.

Her face. Much as I had first seen it, without the mir-
roring sunglasses, the receding aisles of evil goods, her
cheeks still round and firm, her chin pointed, her nose
bone-white, bone-straight. She even smiled, her fierce
quick smile, in relief at her head's being free. "Christ, I
can breathe," she said. Flaxen wisps looped in damp des-
habille onto her flushed brow; from the corners of her
blue eyes, the milky blue-green of beryl, fanned vexed
wrinkles that could have been produced, in another life,
by laughter. Her powder-pale skin was still young; it had
not suffered in my country as it would have in her own,
had not been baked and whipped by the sun of golf courses
and poolside patios and glaring shopping center parking lots in these years when, as the Wrapped One, she
had sheltered herself amid the mysteries of Istiqlal. I was
glad of this. Watching her unwind her headshawl, and
then unveil, I remembered how I had seen her naked, and
the memory of her body moving pale, loose, and lithe in

the neon-tinged darkness of an off-campus room numbed
me so that had all the world's sorrow been at this moment
funnelled into my poor narrow being I would not have
felt an iota more: I was full.

With the air she could now breathe she had launched a
bitchy monologue. "How *is* dear Sittina? Still chasing
cock and playing Bach? And my big momma Kadongolimi? You still mosey round to your old *awa* for your fix
of tribal juice? And that other idiot, little Sheba—has she
learned to chew with her mouth shut yet? But you like
that, don't you? You like these dyed-in-the-wool down-
home Kushy types, don't you? Hakim Happy Ellelloû, de
mon ob de *pee*ple. De mon what om, right? Well here's
one cunt that hates your guts, buster. You better stick a
stamp on me and send me home."

"You belong here."

"Divorce me. It's easy. All you have to do is say '*Tallaqtukī*' three times. Come on, say it. One, two—
Divorce me and you'll have a slot for this new twat,
what's her name."

"Kutunda. Our connection is entirely official. As to
you, my beloved Candace, my personal attachment aside,
you serve a purpose for the nation. There is pressure on
our borders. When the Day of Disaster comes, I can point
to you as proof that the President of Kush is anti-imperi-
alist but by no means anti-American."

"You don't know what you are, you poor little spook.
You are the most narcissistic, chauvinistic, megalomania-
cal, catatonic schizoid creep this creepy continent ever
conjured up. And that's saying a lot."

Her clinical epithets reminded me of her book-club
books—the warping, fading, termite-riddled stacks and
rows of volumes imported from her native land, popular
psychology and sociology mostly. How to succeed, how to
be saved, how to survive the mid-life crisis, how to find

fulfillment within femininity, how to be free, how to love, how to face death, how to harness your fantasies, how to make dollars in your spare time—the endless self-help and self-exploration of a performance-oriented race that has never settled within itself the fundamental question of what a man *is*. A man is a clot of blood. Hopeful books, they disintegrated rapidly in this climate; she had run out of shelf space and stacked this literary foreign aid on the floor, where our great sub-continent of insects hollowed out the covers from underneath, their invisible chewing a rerun of the chewing of her eyes as she read away the monotonous succession of her days, weeks, and years.

Candace was on her feet and speechifying. "I hate you. I hate this place. I hate the heat, the bugs, the mud. Nothing *lasts* here, and nothing changes. The clothes when you wash them dry like cardboard. A dead rat on the floor is a skeleton by noon. I'm thirsty all the time, aren't *you?* Happy"—the nickname she gave me in college—"I'm *sink*ing, and I can't *do* anything about it. I'm seeing the only shrink in Istiqlal and he shrugs and says, 'Why don't you just *leave?*' I tell him, 'I *can't*, I'm married to the *Pres*ident!' "

Her straw-blond, straw-bright hair fell forward as if to veil her sobbing; my impulse to reach and offer comfort was checked only by my certain knowledge that this offer would fail, that my loving touch would feed her anger as the books on how to be happy fed her unhappiness.

She lifted her head, her eyes red-rimmed but abruptly dry. In the simple bold style with which she had once asked me, "How do I look?", she asked, "Can't you get me out of this?"

"*This*, as perhaps your friend the Freudian marabout has already suggested, is you. You have chosen. I am powerless to alter your choices. When we were in your land, not mine, it was you who courted me, and I in my poverty, my strangeness, my blackness, was slow to respond. I was afraid of the consequences. You were heedless. Your heart demanded. So be it. Here you are. Had you allowed me, fifteen years ago, to give you the children I then wanted, your son would be taller than you now, and your daughters would be cheerful company."

"Shit on that," Candace mumbled. "I wasn't sure. You weren't either. We didn't want to take on that responsibility, everything was difficult enough, we knew what we were doing might not work."

"You didn't wish," Ellellloû told her, "to become the mother of Africans."

"It's not that simple, and you know it. You were different once we got here, you didn't make me feel secure. Big Momma had you half the time, and then you got so thick with the king. Anyway, I didn't always use the diaphragm, either, and nothing happened. Maybe one of us is sterile. Your other wives, are those children yours? We should have discussed things like this years ago. Where were you?"

"Tending to duty." The primness of Ellelloû's answer indicated that the conversation had exhausted its usefulness for him. He had suffered enough recrimination to fuel his departure.

Sensing him about to slip away, Candace clung and asked, "If I tried to go home, would you stop me?"

"As your husband, I would indulge you in all things. As father, however, of all the citizens of Kush, I would feel obliged to discourage defection. In this time of crisis and dearth, our human resources must be conserved. Border patrols have been instituted to confine the nomads. Every peanut caravan as it departs includes a quota of spies and enforcers. I wish the imperialist press, which describes our socialist order as a squalid police state, to receive no malicious hint confirming rumors of maladmin-

istration within Kush. Your presence," Ellelloû told his
wife, "is especially cherished here. Let me add that
Opuku's brother, whom you have not met, nor would I
wish it, has in his patriotic love of order developed a
number of interesting ways to inflict discomfort without
leaving any mark upon the body. I confide this to you in a
spirit of tenderness and affection."

The white woman's eyes blazed; the rims of her lips
wrinkled with tension. "You sadistic little turd. When I
think of what I wanted to give you. You know what everybody at college used to say to me? They said I was
crazy to put myself at the mercy of a Negro."

"You needed to prove them right," Ellelloû said, bothered by a certain poignant twist in her body, as in some
late-Hellenic robed statues, implying the erotic axis of the
body within, and within that an ambivalent torque of the
soul—in Candace's case, between taunting and plea, a re-
gret that even in her extremity of rage she should taunt
her husband with the blackness that had made him fascinating and herself noble and the two of them together undergraduate stars at McCarthy College, in that distant city
of Franchise.

"I shouldn't tell you this, but you know what Professor
Craven used to say to me? I won't say it."

"Say it, if it will help you."

"He said, Today's slave, tomorrow's tyrant."

"Excellent. By the same token, Today's liberal, tomorrow's bigot. You could have had Professor Craven, you
could have been for a time his reigning student concubine,
but you chose to slight him."

"He was married."

"So was I."

"I couldn't believe it. When I met Kadongolimi here,
when I saw she really existed, I nearly died. How could
you *do* that to me?—have such a big fat wife. I thought

you were making her up. We were in America. You were
so touching, such a ragamuffin."

Ellelloû slapped her, so little did he like being reminded of the pathetic figure he had cut in those days. Lest she
think the blow had been unconsidered, he repeated it; the
pink stain on her cheek glowed wider than his hand as it
deepened to red. She would have twisted quite away had
he not held her shoulders. Her pose reminded him now of
those thin-lipped, supernaturally cool Flemish Virgins impassive, with averted eyes, beside a pointed arch giving
upon a tiny crowded turquoise landscape. The rift of sorrow in him widened. Terrible, he thought, that rebuke
had come upon her not for any of her insults but for a
moment of innocent openness, remembering a ragamuffin.
"Believe this then," Ellelloû told her harshly, in apology.
"For your safety: you are my wife. For your comfort: this
will pass. I will not always be President."

Colonel Ellelloû finally departed from Istiqlal in the
last month, Dhū ʾl-Hijja, of that troubled year. The afternoon temperature in the square of the Mosque of the Day
of Disaster was 112°F., 44.4°C. The dictator took with
him, along with the faithful Opuku and Mtesa, his fourth
wife, Sheba.

Four

Beneath the stars the roofy desert spreads
Vacant as Libya.

—HERMAN MELVILLE, 1863

THE REGION called the Balak is the size of France,
if Alsace-Lorraine had been permanently conceded to
Germany and by the same treaty Belgium had been an-
nexed. Arab traders as early as the year 400 A.H. noted a
peculiarity of these barren heights which European adven-
turers of the nineteenth century A.D., such as Heinrich
Barth and Gustav Nachtigal, confirmed: a local absence
of color. The sky here is white, and the earth, in contrast
to the vivid ochres, reds, and mauves of the northwest
quadrant of Kush, shows in its rocks and dunes, its playas
and wadis, its *reg, erg,* and *hammada,* only dreary varieties of gray. The valleys of molten glass have already
been mentioned; the low xerophytic growth has, by the
process of natural selection, subdued its natural green to a
tint fainter than that of the palm leaves in a faded oleograph of the Holy Land. Here bloom, famously, the
world's dullest flowers; here white scorpions and black
snakes live off one another's eggs. Travellers have provoked skepticism by reporting how even the gaudiest

goods and garb are gradually drained to monochrome in the slow climb through the Massif; dear Sheba, laden with gold and coral, copper and jasper, lapis lazuli and chrysoprase, her eyelids daubed with antimony and her fingernails with henna, her exquisite *chocolat-sans-lait* body wrapped in silver-embroidered indigo, scarlet, and turquoise, even her feet clad in sandals whose parrot green chimed with the parrot-belly pink of her toenails, day by day was overlaid with deeper and deeper layers of the dust of colorlessness. Her skin, glossy as coal, shed its purple highlights; the palms of her hands no longer lifted to release glimpses of lilac; even her tongue seemed no longer red, lolling in the velvet orifice her careless jaw revealed as she incessantly chewed kola nuts. Her teeth and the whites of her eyes in this atmosphere gleamed more brilliant than ever, and the flaring edges of her lips and nostrils were emphasized as by an ink-laden fine quill. The stem of her neck, the virtuoso arabesques of her sullen profile, and the perfect, burnished crimpings of her ears all looked limned and shaded by an artist whose effects the addition of color would have muddied. Sheba was petite, the only one of my wives smaller than I, and her beauty was sharpened to a blueprint precision, the immaculate mechanics of a butterfly husk, with this removal of the rainbow.

Four hundred kilometers from Al-Abid the *piste* dwindled to an impassable trail between ashen rocks. We left the grayer-than-ever Mercedes to Opuku and Mtesa and joined, in the guise of a detribalized *anzad* player and her protector, a caravan carrying (we gathered) from Ouagadougou or Niamey to a contraband depot on the Zanj border a medley of sinister goods. The caravan leader was a hirsute, jittery brute of the Kel-ulli tribe; Sidi Mukhtar was his name and his person abundantly mixed what the intrepid Barth called the three traditional Arab qualities of *rejela* (valor), *sirge* (thievishness), and *dhiyafa* (hospitality). Sheba—who was kittenish at first—and I peeked whenever we could into the camel-bags, where we found such contraband as hallucinogenic khat, firearms of Czech and Mexican manufacture, plastic sandals from Japan, transistor radios assembled on such low-wage platforms as Singapore and Hong Kong, and boxes and boxes of Bic pens, Venus pencils, and Eberhard Faber typewriter erasers. There were also wooden crates of what Sheba thought would be bullets and grenades but when we pried a slat loose proved to be black ribbons on metal spools, white correction cartridges, and steely, spherical, UFOish IBM type elements for not only the Arabic alphabet but for the 276 characters of Amharic and the antique squiggles of Geez. Had Sidi Mukhtar known of our prowlings he would have staked us to an anthill and left us to shrivel like banana skins cast aside. Or so he said. Actually, the caravan was a loose, good-natured federation of like-minded individual mercantile entrepreneurs, in the best traditions of African humanism; the sole severity came in the distribution of the water, which was done with an iron hand.

Our days began at night. We were awakened beneath the stars—the stars! in the midnight absolute that arched above the Balak the constellations hung inflamed like chandeliers—and made our way, tinkling and sighing and snorting, toward the pearl dawn whose blush was as delicate as the pink tinge in nacre, to that point in mid-morning when the camels began to squat down simply of despair. The camel is an engaging creature spiritually: he proceeds steadily to the breaking-point beyond which he cannot go at all, and then, like as not, he is apt to squat down, blink, take one more breath through his rubbery nostrils, and die. We were supposed to sleep in our tents through the torrid mid-day, but in fact it was difficult,

with the whistle of the wind in the peg-ropes, and a sense
of restless activity outside (presences of sand that yet
muttered and cast man-shaped shadows on the translucent
tent-sides), and our thirsty anticipation of the water that
would be dispensed at dusk. The water skins, the *zemzimayas*, were brought around by an evil-smelling hench-
man of Sidi Mukhtar's; he determined our quotas by
counting the bobs of our Adam's apples, and never failed
to jostle Sheba's succulent breasts in tearing the leather
canteen from her hands.

To pass the dazed, insomniac afternoons Sheba and I
would attempt to make love, but grains of sand interposed
and abraded our venereal membranes. The sand here was
strange, black and white like salt and pepper, and at moments seemed an immense page of print too tiny to read.
She would lie with her head on my belly, gently blowing
me, or else play the *anzad* and sing, while I softly beat
time on the hollows of my abdomen:

> *"Do it to me, baby,*
> *do it if you can.*
> *If I can't have a drink of water,*
> *I'd as soon suck off a man."*

The sun beat upon the squares of camel hide above us so
hard as to render them thin as oiled paper held up to candlelight; in our writhings we sought the shadow of each
other's bodies. There would enter my mind those streams
and shady gardens old, harried Mohamet conjured up in
the after-hours babble of his mid-life crisis to lead the
mulish Meccans away from their stony idols and female
deities, and, more persistently still, of the soda fountain of
the Franchise drugstore, named if I remembered correctly
Oasis Pharmaceuticals and Sundries, where I had first met
Candace, amid that frightful hectoring of brightly pack-

aged newnesses, beside the baleful tree of sunglasses. And while Sheba's dear head, the lustrous hair of which she braided no two days with the same intricacy, rested stickily on my stomach and her ash-colored, thirst-swollen tongue loyally teased my absent-minded penis, my thoughts would swim through rivers of lemonade rickeys, lime phosphates that dripped their fizzing overflow into the chrome grate below the taps, Coca-Cola brewed out of syrup upon chips of ice, 7-Ups paler than water itself, and that mysterious dark challenger to the imperial Coke, the swarthy, enigmatic Pepsi, with whom I felt an underdog's empathy. Milkshakes were in those days of plenty so lavishly prepared that the counter-boy, ingloriously dubbed the "soda jerk," served them in two containers, one of cloudy, hefty glass and the other of the chill futuristic metal in which the sudsy marvel had been churned. These "soda jerks," I came to understand, were recruited from the adolescent ranks of the "townies"—that is, the permanent residents of Franchise, refugees from subsistence farming in the main, every last one of them white and Gentile, as opposed to those of us smuggled in academic gowns into the community as students at McCarthy College, whose brick pinnacles and massy treetops hovered above the gravelly flat roofs of the "towny" business section like the upper levels of a ziggurat, where only gods and priests feeding dead kings dare venture. Emerging, blinking, from Oasis Pharmaceuticals, my mind's eye confronted, between me and that ivy-shaggy campus corner opposite, the breadth of Commerce Street, with its dangling traffic light and surging traffic of opulent automobiles. Everything in America, through that middle bulge of the Fifties, seemed to this interloper fat, abundant, and bubble-like, from the fenders of the cars to the cranium of the President. Franchise was a middle-sized city of 35,000. Its main street ran straight as an arrow, disused trolley tracks still embedded in its center. Its few factories, mostly devoted to paper manufacture, were out of sight down by the lake, whose breezes they tainted with the chemical overflow of the pulping process. The lake had been left, with that romantic *douceur* the Americans trail in the wake of their rapacities, its Indian name, Timmebago, though the bestowers of that name had been long since scourged from its shores by gunfire, firewater, and smallpox.

In the summer, the brightness of which lasted into October, the merchants of Franchise lowered awnings above their store-fronts, and the virtually continuous strip of scalloped shadow laid along the dazzling wide sidewalk now merged with the stifling shade of the tent as I lay there flooded in my thirst by remembrance; my mind's eye, hesitantly, fearfully, looking both ways twice, crossed the dangerous street and hustled into the deep green closures of the college. Beneath the stately arches of the elms and the more horizontal branches of the oaks and copper beeches the spaces appeared subaqueous and we students, elongated as by refraction, silent swimmers. In this aquarium light the academic buildings seemed plaster temples lowered into our element as ornaments, with solid insides and painted-on windows; the pillared Classics building looked especially fake. Then the wheel of North American weather turned and there came an elemental change: the roof of elm-leaves was golden, and falling, and letting in sky, and the leaves were burning in great piles tended by the college grounds crew, grizzled old townies who ogled our girls; the autumnal fragrance of leaf-smoke overpowered the caustic emissions of the paper mills and recalled to young Félix the patches of brush that were cleared for cassava and maize by the women of his village. They would sing, chopping, uprooting, bending from the waist in unison beneath that African sky

whose vastness was so subtly distant a brother to the
vastness of the farm-country sky the straight main street
dissolved into, past the hedges, the lawns, the Victorian-
Gothic faculty housing. Above silver silos and corn rows
and rolling meadows studded with fat cows, the platinum
clouds piled one on top of another in a triumphant, va-
porous wealth. In Africa, the clouds ran like herds of wil-
debeest, strung-out and gray, hastening, always, to get
somewhere else, in this savanna that had to be vast, for in
any one place it was poor. Then, the carousel of seasons
turning again, fire became air, the leaves blew all away;
all was black and white, black twigs on white sky, black
men on white earth, and Candy was waiting, waiting for
her Happy, at the dark cave mouth of Livingstone Hall,
her snow-bright bangs set off by a knitted scarf the red of
Christmas ribbon. Her mother had knitted this scarf, and
the matching red mittens with which Candy was hugging
her mold-colored notebooks and big Ec text with its slick
cover of smiling blue tighter to her chest as if for warmth.
Snow was all about like a mirage, a liftingness in the bottom of Happy's vision that made the automobiles sing in
chains and lowered windowsills to the level of the ground.
This was truly another world, that had bred another race
of men to make their way, barking joyously, through this
illusory element, this starry mud. One handful of those
tiny ice-feathers would bite into his face now, would dissolve his lips and open his throat again, so he could croak
a word of love to Sheba. Kissed, Candy would hurry him
into the cave, where the radiators were hurling heat reck-
lessly against the cold that entered with them through the
double doors, the linoleum floors dirty with melted footprints and tracked-in fragments—matches, gum wrappers,
the little red strip that pulled open a cigarette pack—of
the culture of paper and radiant waste around them.

I must have dozed. When I awoke, Sheba's head was

heavy on my sandy belly or my Ec textbook was open in my lap to the dour visage of Adam Smith or a chart of the decline in the purchasing power of the guilder since 1450. A few more minutes, the lecture would end, and I could have my noon beer in the Badger Cafe. There were luncheonettes, ice-cream parlors, and bars in the city blocks around the campus; in these we would gather, these islands of warmth in the ocean of cold, and talk, Candy and I and her friends. A number of her friends were American Negroes, then beginning to be called Afro-Americans; she was one of those white women who cannot leave black men alone. No mark of Cain or Ham identifies such a female, but some questing chromosome within holds her sexually fast to the tarbaby. Candy's parents in her childhood had had colored cooks and maids, and at the side of these corpulent, didactic, floury-handed mammies the child had felt a cherishing and security absent from the hysterically neat rooms of the house beyond the kitchen. This had been in Chicago; at about the time of what in Africa they call a woman's first uncleanness her father moved his insurance agency to Oshkosh. Chicago's black circumambience thinned to an off-center pocket of paperworkers, ex-slaves whose escape had stopped short of Canada. And in all-white Franchise any dark faces must belong to McCarthy students: flip, coffee-colored Barry Little from Kalamazoo; Muslimized, bitter-black Oscar X from Chicago's South Side; quiet, cinnamon-and-ginger Turnip Schwarz up the river from East St. Louis. Med Jhabvala, with his pointed beard and fluting, female voice, and myopic, beautiful Wendy Miyamoto, from San Francisco, who got 99s on all her exams and rarely said a word, completed our shadowy circle. There was even an Indian on campus, a Dakota called Charlie Crippled Steer, who stalked along in fur-lined ear-flaps and threw things at track meets; he sat at our table once in a while, but did not like us. He did not like anybody, striding the snowy diagonals of our walks with a frozen grimace, his mouth a sad slash, his eyes small as currants. These marginal Americans fascinated me. But amid the maddening slapping of the tent flaps in the mindless wind, the overheard snuffling of stoic camels and the clangorous harangues of desperately bored cameldrivers, my flickering memories of that exotic Wisconsin seemed bits of a Fifties movie, with its studiously recruited cross-section meant to emblemize the melting pot, the fertile and level moral prairie of American goodness. This prairie's harvest celebration came at McCarthy each November, in the Thanksgiving football game against our arch-rival, Pusey Baptist, an even more northerly academic village of virgins and bruisers that, for the four years of my undergraduate career, was four times narrowly defeated—in 1954 by an intercepted pass, in 1955 by a goal-line stand, in 1956 by a heroic, dodging, arhythmical, incredible end run by a sandy-haired instant legend who next year died uncomplainingly of leukemia, and in 1957, most thrillingly for us non-gringos, by a field goal kicked sideways, soccer style, from the forty-three-yard line by a Peruvian general's degenerate son, who had gone out for the team as a way of making homosexual contacts. Memory, enough! Never-to-be-entered-again spaces the mind has hollowed out! The pom-poms! The beer kegs! The single-throated roaring in the concrete bowl, named Kellogg Stadium for its benefactor corporation and irreverently nicknamed the Breakfast Dish. And seen from high above through the vapor of tens of thousands of breaths, those synchronized American cheerleaders, a row of M's ("Give me an M," they would implore), yelling in the zero weather for victory as nakedly as Zulus ("Give me a $C!$"), their cheeks flaming ("Give me a C,

A, R!"), their breasts pouncing as in rapid succession each dropped to one knee and shot forth an arm. *Rah!*

I licked my lips, remembering the beer in the frats afterward, where the Pusey Baptists were invited to drown their annual sorrow, and the rugs stank like swamps of hops, and the exceptional co-ed, liberated without a restraining philosophy of liberation, liquidly consigned herself, in a ratty upstairs chamber, with hip-hoisted skirt and discarded underpants, to a line-up of groggy, beefy ejaculators. Sheba shifted her head, and our skins where melted together threatened to tear. She lay her head beside my arm, her jaw ajar, and with a gray tongue licked the sweat from my pores.

Was I happy? They called me so, but in truth the studies were hard. I had been granted a scholarship from some nefarious reserve of laundered and retitled government money, and had to keep up my grades, and in addition worked as waiter and short-order cook in various eating establishments within a walk of the McCarthy campus, including a Howard Johnson's, with its dummy minaret, on the thru-traffic edge of Franchise. I did not work in any of the places where my circle of friends gathered. I did not want them embarrassed by having me serve them. I did not want them to hear the towny waitresses and kitchen goons call me, not entirely without affection, Grease, Sambo, or Flapjack.

Where was I? The Off-Campus Luncheonette was foggy with cigarette smoke and thermal-interface steam, with the plinging of pinball and the twanging of Patti Page; the Pure Dairy Products Ice Cream Parlor had twirled-wire chairs and round marbletop tables whose butter-pecan-streaked-with-blueberry surfaces camouflaged the slopped excess of our gooey sundaes and viscid, frothy sodas; the Badger Cafe offered sawdust on the floor and high-backed booths of dark-stained plywood.

Here we would badger Oscar X about his remarkable faith. "You mean to say," Turnip Schwarz would insist in that Southern accent of gently prolonged incredulity, "that this Mr. Yacub *really* persuaded *exactly* fifty-nine thousand nine hundred and ninety-nine black people to this Isle of Patmos in order to breed some obnoxious race of white devils that none of these participants would ever live to see and that none of them would want to *be* anyway?"

Oscar X usually wore brown suits and a white shirt with tie, and spoke in a diction of acquired precision, neatly baring his teeth at the close of each rebuttal. "It did not happen all at once. It took, according to the Prophet Mr. Farrad Muhammad, two hundred years of regulated eugenics to create a brown race from the black, two hundred more to produce from that a red race, two hundred more to produce a race of yellow folk"—a crisp little nod here to Wendy, silent on her side of the booth—"and from this a final deuce of centuries to the ultimate generation and supreme insult to Allah, the blond, blue-eyed, hairy-assed devils, who went nude on all fours and lived in trees, as all the textbooks tell us."

"Friend," Barry Little told Oscar X, "that is the pathetic sort of horseshit with which the common nigger has been scrambling his brains in this land all along. You can't breed a race in a couple generations, you need a million years; and what the textbooks tell us for that matter is that the black man isn't the oldest thing, he is the newest thing in *Homo sapiens*, the latest improved model. This here Muhammad Fraud of yours had read a little *Reader's Digest* anthropology and had the Bible shouted at him by his momma and that was all the information plus his misery that he *had*."

Esmeralda Miller was the only black woman at McCarthy. Her father was a dentist in a small city in upstate

New York and she claimed she was a Marxist, in these days when that was a deadly serious thing to do. She was flat-chested and ash-colored and spoke in a level lustreless way, inflexible and indifferent, bored by arguing, the possessor of the flat truth. "You're both talking about alienation, man's alienation from his species being, and you can't talk about that without talking about the self-estrangement induced by forced labor. These racial categories are archaic, they have nothing to do with the class struggle; the black bourgeoisie, where it exists, is as oppressive, and in the last analysis as inevitably self-destructive, as the white, and now we have to add the yellow. Look at Liberia."

Wendy unexpectedly spoke. "Yet didn't Lenin point out that Western capitalism has forestalled its doom by the exploitation, through colonial imperialism, of the natural resources and cheap labor of the non-white peoples?"

"The white man is the devil," Oscar X broke back in. "He is a deliberately manufactured synthetic devil who is so disgusting the black man had to herd him across the Arabian desert and put him in those cold dark European Ice Age caves so he wouldn't destroy the world with his devilish mischief, and that is the proven historical truth, because that is where the white man came from; he was filling those caves full of gnawed-over bones while the black man down south was putting up those Pyramids easy as pie. These are *facts*."

The door of the café opened, admitting cold air and Candy. "Here comes pinktoes," Barry Little muttered. She fetched her own chair and sat at a corner of the already crowded table. The faint flurry of greetings died to a silence until Hakim Félix al-Bini cleared his throat and continued the conversation.

"It seems to me," he said, "the truth of a mythology

should not be judged evidentially piece by piece but by its *gestalt* result. This Mr. Yacub, with his big head and his resemblance to Frankenstein, seems more than we need, from the standpoint of plausibility; but then so do Hitler, and Joan of Arc, and Jesus. They existed. Many things exist, and our dreams tell us many more exist, or exist elsewhere. What matters in a myth, a belief, is, Does it fit the facts, as it were, backwards? Does it enable us to live, to keep going? Yacub seems implausible but it does seem true, as we look around, that the white man is, as Oscar says, a devil."

Candy blushed, right to the neck of her sweater. "I should resent this," she said, "except you're all so nice."

"We are not nice," Barry Little said. "We are rapist apes."

"White people don't mean to be devils."

"No devil does," Hakim Félix told her. "But that is your tragedy, not ours." He took pity. "I was thinking less of lovely American co-eds than of my French commanding officers. They wear stiff dark uniforms and boxes on their heads and they shriek and slap their African soldiers as if they are possessed. Even the way they move, in angry little jerks, suggests dead men animated by devils. What we call a *zombi*." He was annoyed at her, for she had distracted him, with her complicated human situation of a white woman compelled to mingle with blacks, from some urgent general truth his mind had almost framed.

Barry Little had turned to Oscar X again. "The U.S. Negro has peddled horseshit to Ol' Massah so long he can't stop peddling it to himself. Until he gets up off his shiny ass and starts playing the game he can keep squatting right at the bottom of the heap. The game is, grab. That's why we've come to school, to learn to grab. There's only one way up, and that's worm your way. Sister Esmeralda of the Communist Storefront Evangelical

Association and I agree about one thing at least: forget your color, colored man. Your dollar's as green as the next."

Turnip Schwarz said, "Willy Mays hit that ball over the fence, that's four bases for him too."

"You are one thousand percent off your greedy heads," replied Oscar X. "Without the Brotherhood of Islam or some such, the single black man in any Northern city is less than nobody. He is not there, he is a *hole*. When a brother of ours in Temple Two is pulled in by the devil police, we go show up at the station in our nice quiet suits and that brother gets legal attention. He is not bopped. Those devils tuck their clubs away and put on smiles, because they see *power*."

"You can have power without superstition," Esmeralda said.

"*No*," the future Ellellôu said; the word "suits" had reminded him of what he had wanted to say. "It takes a mountain of myth to make even a grain of difference. It takes Mr. Yacub and the Isle of Patmos to make a man in the ghetto put on a suit. Oscar, you say Allah showed up in Detroit in 1930 in the person of a raincoat peddler called W. D. Fard and then disappeared in 1934; the Christians say He showed up in Jerusalem in the year 30 and then disappeared in the year 33. What is the result of these incredible rumors? Slaves lift their heads a fraction of an inch higher. Is this enough result? It is. Nothing less will produce any result at all. The dictatorship of the proletariat, the divinity of this or that itinerant—the crucial question isn't Can you prove it? but Does it give us a handle on the reality that otherwise would overwhelm us?" His voice sounded strained, reaching. But he discovered in the faces in the booth that his high-pitched oratory was not absurd, or not only absurd. Of course he had in his mind not the parochial concerns of these Americans—even the poorest of them rich by African standards—but the dim idea, stirring, of distant Kush. Candy placed her pale hand upon his and patted it, in consolation for an impossible future, or to recall him to this moment, these foreign accents, these abundant beverages, this cozy bar, this "bull session."

Shots rang out beyond the tent, barking and then whining, spanking the sand in spurts. The rifles of the caravan guards, old M-16s bought at discount, were not slow to answer, through a thatch of grunts and scuffling. Men raced by. Shadows flickered on the tent sides. The silent comedy of men fighting for their lives. Ellelloû pressed Sheba beneath him, rolling her off the mat into a sandy corner where an assassin would not be likely to aim. His brain moved in the lazy logical notches that crisis activated in him, the synapses huge as lightning. He saw with microscopic clarity the glistening impasto of sweat and sand on Sheba's neck, noted that a necklace of fine lapis lazuli beads had been broken by the violence of his protective action. He calculated the odds that his identity had been detected, decided they were 50–50 (Mtesa, who had told Ezana of the mysterious truck, was the negative binary pole), and, given a prevalent co-efficient of danger, decided to stay in the tent, in his opaque, bullet-permeable prism of anonymity, rather than make a break into the wind, the dust, the shouts, the colorlessness. He amused himself, in the space between volleys of bullets, with searching amid the sand granules for the tiny lapis lazuli beads Sheba had shed, which would have been easier to find had their sparkling blue not ebbed from them. He sifted in his inner ear the friendly gunshots from those of the raiders, and heard the latter describing an arc that was coming no closer, that indeed was receding, into the desert reaches of the level truth that nothing matters in our human scale, for Allah truly is great. *Takbīr!*

This phrase had dawned in its grandeur for Ellelloû not in his animist village but far from home, where the clubby minority students of McCarthy College had in the cheerful, smoky, bibulous flush of youthful egoism and sexual undercurrent forged the personal armament that would hold off the white man's encircling, sniping world. Through Oscar X young Hakim rediscovered Islam, travelling with the black American to the mother shrine, Elijah Muhammad's Temple Two in Chicago, or to the nearer, less majestic Temple Three in Milwaukee. Amid these conservatively suited brothers and reserved, chastely gowned and turbanned sisters, the future Ellelloû, welcomed and yet set apart as an African, found reminiscence of his deserted continent's dignity, its empty skies and savannas, its beautiful browns.

Subsequent palavering in the stirred-up caravan failed to discover any purpose to the raid. Nothing was taken, not so much as a camel-bag. A number of empty bottles— Московская, they said, Особая Водка — dropped by the shouting, shooting camel-riders muffled in *tagilmusts* had the hollow glitter of a deliberate clue. "Either," the President confided to Sheba, "they were Tuareg drunk on CIA bribes, or CIA operatives wishing to seem to be disguised Russians, or Russians who with the clumsy effrontery of these telltale leavings wish to suggest that they are CIA operatives."

Sidi Mukhtar had another thought. "You know," he said, "still slave-raiders in Balak."

Ellelloû scoffed. "That all died out with Tippu Tib."

"Not all," the caravan leader said, some hidden cause for humor creasing the withered rascal's features. "More selective now. Quality market instead of quantity."

"But who would they be after?" Ellelloû asked, feign-

ing innocence of the knowledge that he himself, the
President, was the caravan's prize.

Sidi Mukhtar winked toward the disguised dictator's
tent. "Fine woman," he said simply.

Shadows, angels, dangers, trucks on the road, radio
waves in the air slip by us. The incident had the quality,
an impalpable slithering-by, of those Wisconsin nights
when, outside in the snow no whiter than Candy's hips
and flanks as they gleamed within the erotic turmoil of
bedsheets, a siren went by, bleating and beating blue upon
the bricks, the ivy, the windowsills, the steeples and silos
of sleeping Franchise. In their senior year Candy had received permission to rent a room off-campus, with another girl, who for erotic reasons of her own was much in
Green Bay. The room, above a realtor's office, was until
this intrusion of blue black and white. The black lover
would lift himself on an arm, the white beloved would lift
her head, to recall him to their act, their intimacy, which
had nothing to do with the tumult of which a fragment
had poured past, and of which other fragments—the pulsing red lights of fire engines or of an ambulance—would
in a minute follow. In this minute the frames of the prints,
the mirrors, the wallpaper pattern in this room showed
gray, gray on gray, the brightest gray the rectangles of the
windowpanes that sealed them off from the world outside,
whose murderous confusions swept by like the giant wings
of a snowstorm. Their love, their mingled moistures, their
breathing was suspended while the sirens passed. Were
the police coming for him? He was aware that in some of
these States skins of different colors rubbing was a crime.
For his penis in her vagina there could be a rope around
his neck. Nor did the Black Muslims condone copulating
out of the faith, let alone with a blue-eyed she-devil. It
was a conflict-making delight of his years here, being
driven by Oscar X through the white man's fat landscape

in a battered but capacious and powerful '49 Oldsmobile, while the radio poured forth Dinah Washington and Kay Starr, heading toward a temple of Islam in the slums of some Midwestern metropolis, where they might be frisked by grim Irish police or held up at knifepoint by unconverted juvenile delinquents of their own color. Dangers everywhere, slipping and sliding by.

Félix had perceived through the shadows a stain of blood on the bedsheet. Indeed, she had felt different tonight, not her usual just-tight-enough lubricity, but her wetness somehow rougher than usual, clotted. Unclean. Involuntarily he had grimaced, and had been told, "You should thank God. Up to this morning I was afraid I was pregnant."

"Wow," he said, Americanized.

She wanted to squeeze even more intimacy out of the revelation, to win more praise, for a fear endured. "Is that all you can say? You know, it's a rotten thing, to be a woman. You can't run away from your body. And the worst thing—"

"The worst thing, dear Candy?"

"Never mind."

"The worst thing was, you didn't want to be carrying a black baby?"

"No, I'd rather like that, as a matter of fact."

"Then what was this worst thing?"

"I won't tell you." She left the bed to get a cigarette. In the room whose dimness seemed a cubic volume of smoke, her body, crossing to the bureau, was pale, loose, lithe. She struck a match. A red glow formed the center of her voice. "I wasn't sure who the father was."

A police car bleated in the white night, more distantly. It did not take very many minutes of verbal struggle, as he remembered the incident, for him to elicit from her that the other possible father had been Craven.

•

Sheba had been too stoned to feel much alarm during the raid. As the spanking, whining sound of rifle fire receded, and violent silhouettes ceased to be projected through the dim prism-shaped volume of the tent, she bit my shoulder to suggest that I could withdraw the protective mass of my body from on top of hers. She shook some of the sand from her elaborate coiffure of tiny braids pinned into parabolas, and to revive herself for the night's trek popped a kola nut. With slack-jawed rapture she chewed, dying the inside of her mouth a deeper shade of gray. Along with her supply of Liberian kola nuts she had a bundle of Ethiopian khat and, for back-up, some Iranian bhang. Her gentle spirit rarely descended to earth.

Her robes hanging loose, her squat showed me between the parted roundnesses of the thighs her exquisite genitals, underparts profiled in two bulges, the cleft barely masked by the gauze of a thousand perfect circlets. Seeing me stare, Sheba laughed and, without abandoning the rapture of kola-chewing, urinated on the desert sand. In my madness of thirst, of love, I reached forward with cupped hands to rescue some of the liquid, though I knew from tales of other travellers that urine was as acid as lemon juice. It haunted my mouth for a burning hour. I went outside to discuss the raid. Sidi Mukhtar showed me the vodka bottles in the sun, their highlights hot as laser beams. I returned to the tent, where sweet Sheba, mellower, sang to the melancholy creak of her *anzad:*

> "Do it to me, baby,
> do it, do it.
> Take that cold knife from its sheath,
> stick it in me underneath,
> backwards, frontwards,
> down my throat,

> *this trip has gone on*
> *too long."*

My responsive song, to which I kept time by tapping the pummel of my camel-saddle, concerned oranges, an orange imagined this time as shrivelled, and so infested by insects it hums like a spherical transistor radio, until its substance is consumed and the shell, brittle and stippled, shatters, like a clay myrrh-holder from ancient Meroë. Our fellows in the caravan, wearying of cursing the raiders and vowing highly anatomical revenge, gathered at the tent-flap, and tossed in to us fistfuls of obsolete coinage, cowrie shells and tiny mirrors, and pre-devaluation *lu* with its Swiss-tooled profile of King Edumu, his head as bodiless on these coins as it was in reality. The caravan drivers, porters, guards, navigators, blacksmiths, leather-workers, translators, accountants, and quality-controllers all lusted growlingly after my Sheba, who contrived while laying double- and triple-stopped fingerings upon the neck of the *anzad* simultaneously to expose one bare foot and braceleted ankle. These men, their faces mere slivers of baked skin and decayed teeth showing through the folds of their *galabiehs* and *keffiyehs*, crowded too close, and, feeling challenged, I pushed one. He fell like a stick lightly stuck in the sand, and fainted; so weakened were we all by the hardships of the Balak. Then came at last the water bag, the swallowed streams of paradise, the rogue's lascivious nudge of my wife's pendulous breasts, the sunset prayers, the saddling up, the by now automatically deft repacking of our armful of effects into capacious *khoorgs*, the tying fast of the rolled tent-hides. Our camels suffered their cinched burdens with a thirupping of their lips and a batting of their Disneyesque eyelashes. From afar Sidi Mukhtar hallooed. The moon showed its silver crescent. The night's advance had begun.

These details are not easy to reconstruct, as I write where I do, with its distractions of traffic, its *parasols* and promenading protégés, its tall drinks of orange Fanta and seltzer water braced with a squid-squirt of anisette. But in the listening half of my brain a certain jointed, clanking rhythm of our days remains, a succession of ordained small concussions, refastenings, bucklings, and halloos as they passed down the line, avowing our readiness to march, with certain death the penalty for falling out of our musical chain of snorting, swaying camels and cajoling, whirling guides.

But O the desert stars! What propinquous glories! Tremulous globes overseeing our shadowy progress with their utter silence. More than chandeliers, chandeliers of chandeliers. *Um al-Nujūm,* the Mother of Stars, ran as a central vein, a luminous rift, within a sky, black as a jeweller's display velvet, that everywhere yielded, to the patient, astounded eye, more stars, so that the smallest interval between two luminaries was subdivided, and subdivided again, by the appearance of new points, leading awed scrutiny inward to a scale by which the blur in Andromeda became an oval immensity whose particle suns could be numbered. Under such a filigree our papery line of silhouettes passed, camel-bells softly chuckling, through the nocturnal escarpments and craters, wearily disturbing the undisturbed sand. Sheets of lava rose around us like apparitions, eruptions through a crystalline mantle whose splinters had lain for aeons where they fell. Abundant sandstone testified to a Paleozoic ocean; deeply cut dry canyons proved that once in some ghostly humid time great rivers had watered the Massif. Scaley defiles, of shale a-gleam as if wet, suddenly gave way to giddying views, immense gray bowls of emptiness sweeping to the next jagged, starlit range. What meant so much inhuman splendor? *But when the earth is crushed to fine dust, and your Lord comes down with the angels in their ranks, and Hell is brought near—on that day man will remember his deeds.* My life by those lunar perspectives became a focus of terror, an infinitely small point nevertheless enormously hollow, a precipitous intrusion of some substance totally alien and unwelcome, into these rocks, these fantastic orbs of fire, this treacherous ground of sand. I could not have withstood the solitude, the monotony, the huge idiocy of this barren earth, had not Sheba been by my side, sullen and warm. I loved in her what the others, the cruel illiterates of the desert, scented—her vacancy. Where another woman had an interior, a political space that sent its emissaries out to bargain for her body and her honor, Sheba had a space that asked no tending, that supported a nomadic traffic of music and drugs. Such a woman is an orphan of Allah, a sacred object. Sheba never questioned, never reflected. I said to her, "The stars. Are they not terrible?"

"No. Why?"

"So vast, so distant. Each is a sun, so distant that its light, travelling faster than the fastest jinni, takes years to reach our eyes."

"Even if such a lie were true, how would it affect us?"

"It means we are less than dust in the scheme of things."

She shrugged. "What can be done, then?"

"Nothing, but to pray that it not be so."

"So that is why you pray."

"For that, and to reassure the people of Kush."

"But you do not believe?"

"For a Muslim, unbelief is like a third eye. Impossible."

We swayed in silence. Our fatigue was a tower to which each night added another tier. I said, "And do you know, there are laws all about us? Laws of energy and light, laws that set these rocks here, and determined their shape, and their slant. Once an ocean lay down many grains of sand; once the bodies of more small creatures than there are stars above us laid down their skeletons to form islands, great shoals, which volcanoes lifted up, and then the wind wore down again, and water that rained, and flowed, and vanished. Once all this was green, and men hunted elephants and antelope, and drew pictures of themselves on the rocks."

"Show me such a picture."

"They are hard to find. I have seen them in books."

"Things can be made up and put into books. I want to see a picture on a rock."

"I will hope to show you one. But what I am saying is more than that once men hunted and even fished here. I am saying that perhaps again this will be true, and we will be forgotten, all of us forgotten, of less account than the camels whose hides make up our tents. Past and future are immense around us, they are part of the laws I speak of, that are more exact than anything you know, they are like those rocks that when you split them come away exactly flat. Everything obeys these laws. Things grow by these laws, and things die by them. They are what make us die. We are caught inside them, like birds in a cage— no, like insects in a cage that is all bars, that has no space inside, like a piece of rotten wood, only not rotten but hard, harder than the hardest rock. And the rock, one single rock, stretches out to those stars, and beyond, for in truth they seem very close, and there is a blackness beyond, where those same laws continue, and continue to crush us, finer than the finest dust, finer than the antimony you use to make your eyelids gray. Help me, Sheba. I am sinking."

"I do what I can. But you make what I do seem very little."

"No, it is much."

After a pause, while the feet of our steeds slithered on the cold sand, she asked me, "When do you think we will reach our destination?"

"We will reach it," I told her, "when there is no farther to go."

"And how will we know when that is?"

"The drought," I told her, "will have ended."

In the home of Candace's parents, where she took me late in our freshman year, the white woodwork was like a cage also. I marvelled at the tightness, the finish. Her father came toward me from rooms away, a big man with Candy's beryl eyes and gray hair so thin and light it wandered across his skull as he gestured. I had the impression that his bigness was composed of many soft places, bubbles in his flesh where alcohol had fermented and expanded; he shook my hand with too much force, overcarrying. "So you're the young man my daughter has been raving about," he said.

Raving? I looked at Candy's pointed polite face, whose straight fine nose had come from her mother; I had just met the lady, who seemed afraid. Maybe the something bloated and patchy about the Dad was fear too. We were all afraid. I was alarmed, as the house opened to me—its woodwork interlocked like the lattice of an elaborate trap; its pale, splashy, furtively scintillating wallpaper; its deep, fruit-colored, step-squelching carpets; its astonishing living-room, long and white, two white sofas flanking a white marble coffee table bearing porcelain ashtrays and a set of brass scales holding white lilies whose never-wilt lustre was too good to be true. And what were these little saucers, with tiny straight sides and bottoms of cork, scattered everywhere, on broad sofa arms and circular end tables, as if some giant had bestowed on the room the largesse of his intricate, oversize coinage?

"Daddy, I wouldn't say 'raving,'" Candy corrected,

embarrassed, her face, that I now perceived as a clash of genes, blushing.

"Rave is what she does, Mr.— I don't want to mispronounce."

"Call me Felix," I said, Anglicizing the *é*. I wondered if I should sit, and would the sofa swallow me like some clothy crocodile? Often in America, in drugstores and traffic jams, I had the sensation of being within a bright, voracious, many-toothed maw. The Cunninghams' living-room had puddles of cosmetic odor here and there. As in the old cinema palace on Commerce Street, a heroic stagnation had overtaken decor. Seating myself on the edge of the bottomlessly spongy sofa, I touched the brass scales and, sure enough, discovered a refusal to tip. Once an honest artifact, it had been polished, welded, and loaded with plastic lilies. Fixed forever, like that strange Christian heaven, where nothing happened, not even the courtship of houris.

"*Asseyez-vous,*" Mrs. Cunningham had suggested, with a smile touchingly like her daughter's, only somehow uneven, as if Candy's quick smile had been crumpled up and then retrieved and smoothed and pasted over a basic frown.

But when I responded, in textbook French, complimenting my hostess on the beauty of her room and its florid and cinematic appointments, her visage went as blank as that of the enamelled shepherdess on the mantel, frozen in a pose of alert unheeding vis-à-vis the fluting shepherd in the exactly corresponding mantel position. Between them stood an impressive clock with a pendulum of mercury rods, and its action may have been interfering, on their chilly elfin plane, with the call of the shepherd's piping. The fireplace itself, the hearth whose symbolic domestic centrality was so primitive that even I might have found here a familiar resonance, was swept as clean as a

shower stall and ornamented with unscathed brass andi-
rons supporting three perfect birch logs that would never
be burned.

Mr. Cunningham restored the conversation to solid English. "Feelicks, if I'm not being too personal, what's
your major going to be at McCarthy?"

"Freshmen are not required to declare, but I had
thought Government, with a minor in French Literature."

"French Literature, what the hell use would that be to
your people? Government, I can see. Good luck with it."

"In the strange climate of my native land, Mr. Cunningham, the literature the French brought us may trans-
plant better than the political institutions. There is a
dryness in Racine, a harshness in Villon, that suits our
case. In French Indochina, not many years ago, I had the
experience of trading memorized sonnets by Ronsard with
a prisoner of war, a terrorist who was later executed. In
the less developed quarters of the world, the power politics of the West can be brushed aside, but its culture is
pernicious."

"*Candy*," Mrs. Cunningham began with the overemphasis of the shy, having seated herself in a wing chair
patterned in cabbage-sized roses, her lean shins laid
gracefully, diagonally together with a dainty self-conscious
"sexiness" that reminded me of her daughter . . . who
had vanished! *Horreur!* Where? I could hear her voice
dimly giggling in some far reach of the house. She had
gone upstairs, it later transpired, to talk with her "kid"
brother; or was it into the kitchen, to renew acquaintance
with the Cunninghams' colored cook? At any rate, she
had left me alone with her terrifying pale parents, the female of whom was posed in mid-sentence, and who now
settled on the verb she had paused to locate among her
treasury of "nice" things—"al*lud*ed to your romantic
adventures."

"Not romantic, Madame; dreary, truly. The French in exchange for their poems asked that we fight in other poor countries. I obliged them in Indochina, for it took me out of my native village; when it came to Algeria, where the rebels were fellow Africans, I became a rebel myself, and deserted."

"Oh dear," Mrs. Cunningham said. "Can you ever go back?"

"Not until the colonial power departs. But this may happen within the decade. All it needs is a politician in Paris who is willing to act as a mortician. In the meantime, I enjoy your amazing country as a dream from which I will some day wake miraculously refreshed."

"There's a question I'm rarin' to ask you," Mr. Cunningham said, rising ominously, but not to throttle me, as his growling tone for a second implied to my alert nerves, but to move to a tall cabinet and get himself another drink, from a square bottle whose first name was Jack, or was it Jim? The riddle of my own name he informally solved with, "How about *you*, fella?"

My mouth was indeed dry, from unease. "A glass of water, if it's no trouble."

He threatened to balk. "Plain water?" Then his mind embraced my response, as something he might have expected, from an underprivileged delegate from the childlike underworld. "Wouldn't you rather have a 7-Up? Or a Schlitz?"

I would have, and brushed from my own mind the mirage of a beer sitting golden on a dark table of the Badger Cafe; but I felt the family dinner ahead of me stretch like a long trek through a bristling wilderness of glass and silver and brittle remarks, and had resolved upon sobriety as my safeguard. Also there was some silent satisfaction in impeding this big white devil's determination to be hospitable. "Just water, if you please," I insisted.

"Your religion, I suppose?"

"Several of them."

"Some ice in it?" he asked.

"No ice," I said, again against my desires, but in conformity with an ideal austerity I had grown like a carapace, in which to weather this occasion.

"Alice," he said, with unexpected euphony; his obedient wife arose—the shepherdess *did* hear the shepherd—and went into the kitchen, which seemed to be, by one of those inscrutable jurisdictions whereby American couples order the apparent anarchy of their marriages, her province. Mr. Cunningham, freshly reinforced by his bottled cohort, pursued his interesting question, which was, "What do you make of our American colored people?"

I had already enough converse with the disciples of Elijah Muhammad to hear the word "colored" as strange, but this strangeness was swallowed by the expanding strangeness of the preceding "our." I looked at my feet, for I was travelling in treacherous territory. My search for an answer was needless, for Mr. Cunningham was providing it.

"What can we do," he was asking me, "to help these people? They move into a nice neighborhood and turn it into a jungle. You pour millions of state money in and it goes up in smoke. Our American cities are being absolutely destroyed. Detroit used to be a great town. They've turned it into a hellhole, you get mugged by these kids right in Hudson's, the downtown is a wasteland. Chicago's going the same way. Hyde Park, all around the university, these lovely homes, a white girl can't walk her dog after supper without a knife in her stocking. The Near North Side's a little better, but two blocks in from the Lake you're taking your life in your hands. Why do you think I moved the family up to Oshkosh? I lost forty grand a year by leaving the city. But hell, the rates on real estate were going out of sight, the only way to get your money out of some of those neighborhoods was burn 'em down. Cars, anybody who keeps a car on the street should have his head examined. They wouldn't just steal 'em, they'd smash 'em up—pure spite. What's *eating* the bastards? You'd love to know."

Mrs. Cunningham returned with the water in a glass with a silver rim, and I thought of desert water holes, the brackishness, the camel prints in the mud, the bacterial slime that somehow even across the burning sands manages to find its live way.

Mr. Cunningham's tone tightened a little, with his wife's return. There was this flattering about his tirade: that he was addressing me as a fellow sufferer, that the heat of his grievance had burned away my visible color. He went on, "I've had my knocks up here, trying to make a name coming in cold in the middle of life; but at least I'm not afraid my daughter's going to be raped and don't have to lock the car every time I stop to take a piss at a gas station."

"Frank," Alice said.

"Sorry, there, but I guess even over in the Sahara you know what a piss is."

"*Nous buvons le pissat,*" I said, smiling.

"Exactly," he said, slipping a glance of small triumph into his wife. "Anyway, where was I? Yeah, my question: What's the solution for these people?"

"Provide them useful work?"

Made in all timidity, this suggestion seemed to tip him toward fury. His patchy look intensified, his hair fluffed straight up. "Christ, they won't take the jobs there are, they'd rather rake in welfare. Your average Chicago jiga-boo, he's too smart to dirty his paws; if he can't pimp or hustle drugs, or land some desk job with dingbat Daley, he'll just get his woman pregnant and watch the cash roll in."

"That is—what do you call it?—American individualism, is it not? And enterprise, of an unforeseen sort."

He stared at me. He was beginning to see me. "Christ, if that's enterprise, let's give it all over to the Russians. They've got the answer. Concentration camps."

"Daddy, you promised you wouldn't," Candy cried; for she had come down the stairs, freshly brushed, her face alight with the happiness of "home," her crimson lips renewed, her rounded slim body bouncy as a cheer-leader's, in a cashmere sweater and a pleated wool skirt, which swirled as she swung herself around the newel post whose carpentered pirouette I had admired upon entering.

"Wouldn't what, dear?" her mother asked, as if straining to hear, in this room of silent clocks and chiming resemblances.

"Wouldn't bother Happy about the Chicago blacks."

"Not just Chicago," her father protested, "it's lousy everywhere. Even L.A., they're pulling it under. Hell, Chicago at least has a political machine, to make payoffs and keep some kind of lid on. In a city like Newark, they've just taken over. They've done to Newark what we did to Hiroshima. Grass doesn't even grow where they are. They are the curse of this country, I tell you, no offense to our friend here."

"Daddy, you are so ignorant and prejudiced I just can't even cry about it anymore. I didn't want to bring Happy here but Mother said I must. You make me *very* ashamed in front of him."

"Happy, hell, he's out of it. He's an African, at least they got some pride over there. As he says, they have their own culture. The poor colored in this country, they got nothing but what they steal." And he not quite drunkenly winked at me. It crossed my mind that I, as an African, was being thanked because I had not come over here to stay and raise the automotive insurance rates with my thievery; more, he saw me as the embodiment of the mother continent that yearned, he hoped, to take the Afro-Americans back into a friendly, oozy chaos.

"Exactly," I said, and stood. "Nothing but what they steal." In the rebellious act of standing I changed my perspective on the room, and was freshly overwhelmed by its *exotisme*, its fantasy, the false flowers and fires, the melting-iceberg shapes of its furniture, its whiteness and coldness and magnificent sterility; the emptiness, in short, of its lavish fullness, besprinkled with those inexplicable cork coins.

[I express this badly. The wet ring from a glass of Fanta has blurred my manuscript. I long to get back to the Bad Quarter of Kush, and the spaces of my dear doomed Sheba.]

The "kid" brother had followed Candy downstairs. Frank Jr. was a furtive, semi-obese child of fourteen—old enough, in my village, for the long house—whose complexion showed the ravages of sleeping alone, night after night, in an overheated room with teddy bears, felt pennants, and dotted Swiss curtains. The smile he grudged me displayed a barbarous, no doubt painful tooth-armor of silver and steel. His limp dank handshake savored of masturbatory rites. His eyes were fishy with boredom, and he tried to talk to me about basketball, of which I knew, despite my color, nothing. For this family occasion the child had put on a shirt and tie; the collar and knot cut cruelly into the doughy flesh of his neck. I thought, Here is the inheritor of capitalism and imperialism, of the Crusades and the spinning jenny. Yet he did not so much seem Mr. Cunningham in embryo as Mr. Cunningham, with his quirky bravado, desperate wish to be liked, and somehow innocently thinned and scattered hair, seemed a decaying, jerry-built expansion of his son. I perceived that a man, in America, is a failed boy.

Then a black woman came into the alabaster archway of the living-room. For all the frills of her uniform, she looked familiar, with her heavy lower lip and fattening charms. Her uncanny resemblance to Kadongolimi was reinforced by her manner, which implied that she had had many opportunities in life and might well, with equal contentment, be elsewhere. "Dinner, ma'am." We all stood, in obedience to our queenly servant.

But before we went in, Mrs. Cunningham, with a predatory deftness that showed a whole new piece of her equipment for survival, had silently as a pickpocket knifed behind me and placed my empty water glass, which I had set down in the center of an end table beside a sofa arm, securely within one of the little cork-and-silver saucers. Of course. They were "coasters," which in the friendly bars of Franchise took the form of simple discs of advertisement-imprinted blotting paper. By such sudden darts into the henceforth obvious, anthropology proceeds.

Oscar X took the future Ellelloû to meetings of the Nation of Islam; they disliked the term Black Muslims, though both "black" and "Muslim" seemed canonical. Temple Three, in Milwaukee, was two hours to the south, but another rushing, radio-flooded hour, in that many-knobbed, much-rusted, lavishly chromate guzzler of *essence* called, I thought oddly in a nation obsessed with the new, an Olds, took us to Temple Two, in Chicago, where the Messenger of Allah himself could be heard. He spoke in a murmur, a small delicate man with some resemblance, I was to notice when I awoke in Noire, to

Edumu IV, Lord of Wanjiji. The Messenger wore an embroidered gold fez. He was a frail little filament who burned with a pure hatred when he thought of white men and lit up our hearts. He spoke of the white man's "tricknology." He told us that the black man in America had been so brainwashed by the blue-eyed devils he was mentally, morally, and spiritually dead. He spoke of a nation of black men, carved from the side of America like a blood-warm steak from the side of an Ethiopian steer, that would exist on a par with the other nations of the world. He rehearsed the services the black man had performed for his slavemasters in the United States, from cooking their meals and suckling their babies (yes) to building their levees and fighting their wars (yes indeed). He mocked the civil-rights movements, the "sitting-in," "lying-in," "sliding-in," "begging-in," to unite with a slavemaster who on the one hand demands separate schools, beaches, and toilets and on the other hand through the agency of rape had so mongrelized the American black man that not a member of this audience was the true ebony color of his African fathers. "Little Lamb!" souls in our crowd would cry out, and "*Teach,* Messenger!" The litany of wrongs never wearied him, this shambling gold-fezzed foreshadow of my king. At his mention of rape, I would find myself crying. At his mention of the tribe of Shabazz, for which the word "Negro" was a false and malicious label, I would find myself exultant. At his amazed soft recounting of some newly arisen marvel of devilish hypocrisy, such as the then recent Supreme Court decision which told black men they were integrated and thus opened them up to the sheriff's dogs when they were such fools as to take their little scrubbed and pigtailed daughters to school, or such ancient marvels of Christian tricknology as the mixing of slaves in the lots as they were sold so that no two spoke the same language or remembered the same gods, so that no idol remained to these slaves but the white devil's blue-eyed, yellow-haired, historically grotesque Jesus, I would find myself wild with visions of what must be done, of sleeping millions to be awakened from their brainwashing, of new nations founded on the rock of vengeance and led by such quiet brown hate-inspired men as this, our Messenger.

And on Tuesday nights (Unity Nights) or Friday nights (Civilization Nights) it was pleasant to mingle, and even to be cossetted as an African with a smattering of Arabic, among the beige-gowned women and dark-suited men who had redeemed themselves from the flash and ruin of the ghetto. Ex-criminals, many of them, they moved with the severity of *sous-officiers*, and I realized that, in this era when the magic wand is hollow and all wizards, chiefs, and Pharaohs went tumbling under the gun's miraculous bark, the army is the sole serious institution left—all others are low comedy and vacuous costumery. The army must rule. The United States takes noisy pride in its sack-suited government of lawyers and fixers, but the bulky blue army of police is what the citizen confronts. Their patrol cars bleat past every lulled couple's fornication nest. Their baby-faced officers waddle across Commerce Street with waistfuls of leather-swaddled armaments. Beyond these blue men, for my black friends, the government was a gossamer of headlines spun like fresh cobwebs each morning, and brushed away by noon. I perceived this then: government is mythological in nature. These step-children of Islam were seeking to concoct a counter-myth. *"Al-salāmu ʿalaykum!"* The Messenger's greeting rolled back: *"Wa-ʿalaykum al-salām!"* I had never heard Arabic, which in Africa stings like a whip wielded by slavers and schoolteachers, spoken so sweetly as here, in America, in the flat rote accents of children of janitors and sharecroppers, who had memorized their few phrases as the passwords into self-reliance and dignity. *Takbīr!* God is great! *Mā shā' allah:* it is as God wills.

If our non-alcoholic fruit punches, and the porkless delicacies prepared by the ankle-weary work-day kitchen slaves of white homes, all had a flavor of charade, it was a purposeful earnest charade, and with altogether another taste too, a sacred spicy something that prickled in my nostrils and made me, enacting my own charade as an authentic Child of the Book, feel more exalted, more serenely myself, than I did, in this treacherous land of *kafīrs,* anywhere else.

Although Oscar X, I years later learned, gave up the Faith in disgust at the Messenger's well-authenticated sexual lapses, and some of my chaste sisters have put on again the white robes of the Christian choir, and my earnest lean-faced brothers (their eyes glittering above their cheekbones like snipers levelling their sights, their dangerous nervousness sheathed in the quiet devil-garb of corporation lawyers and FBI men) have re-enlisted in the guerrilla war of the streets—though the Nation of Islam took a mortal wound when it became Malcolm's killer, and the Afro-American's misery moved on in its search for the revolutionary instrument, those ghetto temples were for me a birthplace. The Messenger disclosed to me riches that were, unbeknownst, mine. He taught me that the evils I had witnessed were not accidental but intrinsic. He showed me that the world is our enslaver, and that the path to freedom is the path of abnegation. He taught me nationhood, purity, and hatred: for hatred is the source of all strengths, and its fruit is change, as love is the source of debility, and its fruit is passive replication of what already too numerously exists.

At temple meetings, on vacation from Candy Cunningham and McCarthy College with their noble schemes for my transformation into a white-headed, lily-livered

black man, I was free to imagine myself in an absolutist
form. Crystals of dreaming erected within me, and the nation of Kush as it exists is the residue of those crystals.

The terrain became more mountainous; the patches of
thornbush, the scant tufts of the world's dullest flowers,
no longer could draw the least excuse for life from the
gray rocks, the black air. At night the sound of dry ice
shattering rocks gave staccato echo to the scrabble of the
camels trying to keep their footing on millennial accumulations of scree. We rattled as we went, and Sheba's *anzad*
(varied now and then by an end-blown flute that doubled
as a dildo in the face of my impotence) eerily harmonized
with the stony music our passage struck from the resonant
minerals and crystals jutting around us. Haematite, mag-
netite, kassiterite, wolframite, muscovite, mispickel, and
feldspars cast their glints by moonlight. I recalled Ezana's
dark geological allusions, and wondered how my old Minister of the Interior was faring in captivity. We had shared
the same *caserne,* heard together the call, "*Aux armes!
Aux armes! Les diables jaunes!*" Sentimental reflections
of all sorts coursed through my weary soul. The moons
waxed and waned; Dhū 'l-Hijja became Muharram,
Muharram became Safar, or else I had lost count.
The waterhole scouts ranged away from the caravan for
days, and some never returned. The moment was ap-
proaching when Sheba and I must leave the caravan and
seek out the cave where the head of Edumu IV reportedly
babbled oracles.

In the vicinity of the cave, Sidi Mukhtar told us, European rock doves had gathered, and now one or two of
these birds, gray, but with points of lustre on the head
and throat that bubbled up, in this monochromatic climate, to the verge of iridescence, could be seen at dusk

and dawn, dotting a distant slope of speckled asphalt-colored shale like pigeons in the lee of chimneys on city roofs. Up and down we wound our way through alleylike passes so narrow the sky was reduced to the width of a river above our heads. The ordeal was aging Sheba: the baby fat of trust had fallen from her cheeks; some of the looks she darted at me sideways, through the asynchronous heaving of our camels' humps, were positively dubious.

"Do you love me?" Candy would ask.

"Tell me what you mean by love," young Hakim would counter, his emotional defenses well fortified by the years of arid book-learning: from Plato to Einstein, a steady explosion, the sheltering gods all shattered.

"What do you mean, what do I mean?"

Follow-up emergency vehicles wailed by on the street below. Their spinning red lights dyed the icicles at the window a bloody red: fangs of a deep-throated growl. "To what extent," he pursued, "is your so-called love for me love of yourself, yourself in the Promethean stance of doing the forbidden, that is, of loving me?"

"To what extent, I could ask in turn, is your fucking me revenging yourself on the white world?"

"Is that what your parents suggest?"

"They don't know. They don't ask. After a certain age it's easier for them to forget you have a body. Marriage would be the only crunch."

"Indeed."

"What do you mean, 'Indeed'?"

"I mean, indeed, marriage would be a crunch." He changed the subject, so firmly she would know it was being changed. "This fucking to avenge oneself, I think that is an American style. I do not have, that I can detect, the sexual sense of outrage that our friends Oscar and Turnip and Barry bear toward the white man, whom they call, simply, the Man. The brown-faced Arabs were butchering and carrying off my people while the French were innocently constructing Chartres. The Tuareg have been more ruthless still. They are white, beneath their blue robes. In my land the black man is the Man, who performs generation after generation the super stunt of continuing to exist, to multiply among the pain and the heat. Noire is a river where others come to fish, but they do not swim with us."

"Touch me while you talk. Please, Happy."

He touched her white flank, from which the reflected red pulsing had ebbed. "In the village," he said, in his weariness surrendering to the first words that came, "we were always touching one another, uncles and sisters and friends, and then at thirteen the boys earn the right to sleep as an age-set, in the long house. I often think of your brother, the sadness of him sleeping alone, in a room all his. To emerge from such solitude into sexuality must be a great arrival, greater than in other nations, too poor to have so many rooms. And then the middle-aged of America do not touch either. At the end, the nurses and doctors handle you. It is a sign the darkness of the womb is being approached again."

She turned her back and her skin felt cold as a snake's. She had wanted to talk about marriage.

Pyrolusite, goethite, antimonite, quartz: Sidi Mukhtar named the crystals, winking. "Much treasure." He tapped the cliff. He had once fallen in with Rommel's armies and been trained in geology, in *Erdwissenschaft*. He had grown fond of the *anzad* player and her little protector. He was sorry to see them leave the caravan. But the dread time had come.

At the same moment, Ellelloû later learned from reliable sources, Michaelis Ezana was making his way through the midnight corridors of the Palais de l'Administration des Noirs. He had persuaded his guards, two Golo simpletons who had been shifted from the rat-killing detail at one of the surplus-peanut mounds on the plains near Al-Abid, that a six o'clock martini was a kind of internal ablution which should, for ultimate purity, be taken with the *salāt al-maghrib*. Day by day he increased the proportion of gin to vermouth to the point where the stout fellows, hardened imbibers of honey beer, toppled. His way was clear. As once before in these pages, as perceived from this same window, the muezzins' twanging call echoed under the cloudless sky as under a darkening dome of tile. Rather than risk confrontation with the soldiers and their doxies quartered in the fourth-floor corridor, who, if not fully alerted to the *nuancé* shifts of inner-circle leadership in Kush, certainly had caught the smoky whiff of *tabu* that now attached to Ezana, he, by a series of ripping, knotting, and measuring actions that like certain of these sentences were maddeningly distended by seemingly imperative refinements and elaborations in the middle, constructed a rope of caftans and agals and descended, through the silver kiss of the last moon of Safar, down the wall, in his terrified descent accompanied by his indifferent shadow, a faint large bat-shape whose feet touched his abrasively. Ezana attained, without the makeshift rope's breaking, a window of the third floor, which housed the People's Museum of Imperialist Atrocities. As he had in descending prayed, the window was unfastened; or, rather, the catch had long since come loose from the wood, baked by the daily heat to the friability of clay. He pushed it open with a crackle and, trembling, dropped to the floor inside.

Few visited the Museum but nostalgic reactionaries. The leather trappings on the French parade harness had been nibbled and consumed by the starving. The little model, meant to scandalize with its penury, of the typical servants' hut *circa* 1910 had been carefully dismantled and smuggled outside to serve as shelter for a family of Istiqlal's urban homeless. The torturing apparatus, dominated by a gaunt dental drill, and the guillotine, Gothic pinnacle of Gallic justice, cast the longest shadows as the Minister of the Interior stole barefoot among the dusty museum cases. The cases contained lumps of rubber and gypsum and other raw materials gouged from Noire by naked workers (shown in a miniature tableau, balsawood bodies expiring of exhaustion at the mouth of a papier-mâché mine) paid a few centimes a day. An entire case was filled with centimes. Another case held only imperialist mustaches and monocles; these latter winked as Ezana's shadow soundlessly passed. The next case held emptied bottles of the colons' ungodly poisons—absinthe, cognac, champagne, Perrier water; their glimmer was doused and rekindled again as Ezana, his heart thumping, slid by. In other cases, more darkly, lurked Bibles and missals in their pernicious range of sizes and languages; displayed with them, wittily, were the ledgers of the army of the profiteers, the plantation managers, the concessionnaires, the export-import agencies, the factors of European cloth and cutlery in the remote villages, the shipping lines that creakily plied the Grionde. Ezana had once made a study of these ledgers, and after some consultation with Ellelloû had suppressed this curious finding: none showed a profit. On paper, colonialism was a distinctly losing venture. The cost of the armies, the administrators, the flags, the forts, the bullets, the roads, the quinine, the imported knives, forks, and spoons, quite outweighed the grudging haul of raw materials and taxes elicited from the unprincipled, evasive chiefs and stubbornly inefficient populace. The most rapacious exploiter

of them all, King Leopold, who permitted appalling atrocities in an attempt to balance his books, had to be rescued
from bankruptcy. As the colonies were jettisoned into independence, the ledgers of the metropolitan capitals registered distinct relief. Noire, the most *outrée* region of *La
France d'Outre-Mer*, had been, in Paris, a minor statisti-
cal nuisance.

Why, then, had the oppressors come? As Ezana moved
barefoot through the deserted museum, the nagging question merged with the discomfort in his feet—their soles,
for too many years cradled in Italian leather, made tender
by the daring descent down the rough inner face of the
Palais. The Europeans had come, it seemed, out of simple
jealousy; the Portuguese had a fort or two, so the Danes
and Dutch had to have forts. Egypt fell to the British, so
the French had to have the Sahara; because the British
had Nigeria, the Germans had to have Tanganyika. But
what, then, was there to do with these vast tracts? Drain
swamps, shoot elephants, plant cocoa, clear the way for
missionaries. In Noire these activities had been carried
forward in the most attenuated way: there were few
swamps, and fewer elephants. Nevertheless the Gauls had
gone through the motions, and a handful of Frenchmen
who at home would have been outcasts here established,
on the backs of blacks little more aware of their presence
than of flies on their skins, a precarious, shrill self-importance. A case in the museum held whips, ranging from the
brutal *cicotte*, a length of hippo hide for flogging plantation workers into line, to the dainty silken *fouet* with
which a regional administrator's wife could chastise one of
her maidservants, knots having been artfully braided into
the ends of the threads. The next case contained obscene
accessories of a brothel in Hurriyah maintained for white
militia and laborers by the dusky *autochtones*. Contact, of
a sort, had been made. Civilization like an avalanche of

sludge had collapsed into the blank clean places of the maps. Skins rubbed as among sleepers with shut lids, thrashing and tugging at the covers. Along one dark wall there were great maps of the sub-Saharan empires, Songhai and Mali and Kanem-Bornu; these too had been imposed from beyond and their rise and fall punctuated by the severing of many an ear, hand, and head. On this same wall hung daguerreotypes gone coppery and quaint, of frilly picnics in the bush, of military parades aligning multitudinous buttons, of a painter in the goatee and slack white shirt of the *fin de siècle* scrupulously loading his easel with an Impressionist rendering of a beehive hut and a baobab tree. Stealthily past these images of an out-of-date intermingling Ezana crept, pondering the meaning of colonialism, the impossibility that a nation with the sublime literature and cuisine of France would subdue a scruffy sixth of an ungrateful continent in order to create flattering jobs for a few adventurous dregs, and the concomitant possibility that now this great land of Kush existed solely to give employment to a few revolutionary elitists like himself. The memorials of imperial atrocities stretched out their shadows as if not to let him go as he eased back the massive hexagonal bolt on a door beneath an oil portrait of Governor Faidherbe, action shots of the Hourst expedition, and photostats of especially atrocious pages from Colonel Toutée's famous diary. Ezana let himself stealthily into the corridor. It was empty. The flaking white ceiling, the green molding at the level of his hand, diminished toward infinity. Ghostly in his dirty prisoner's robe, his eyes bugging in his curvilinear face, his wristwatch holding the exact time to the second behind its own black face, Ezana moved close to the wall, pondering Ellelloû, his leader's far journey, the unlikelihood that he would reach his destination. He pondered his own survival, weighed the odds against a Palais coup.

But Ezana had no wish to lead. To advise, to raise quiet objections while chocolate quietly cooled, to train typists, sign directives, pull rafts of allied statistics from the consoles of filing cabinets, to see a nation and all its nebulous load of baffled human consciousness reduced to rigorous alignments of nouns and numbers, and furthermore to dress like a dignitary, to appear on an odd denomination of postage stamp, and to have an embezzled fortune banked against the Day of Disaster in a numbered Swiss account—all this he liked, but not to lead. A leader is one who, out of madness or goodness, volunteers to take upon himself the woe of a people. There are few men so foolish; hence the erratic quality of leadership in the world. Ezana furthermore didn't see that leadership was very productive or progressive; the results that truly changed the condition of mankind were achieved by anonymous men, accumulators of correct facts and minute improvements, men of unspectacular gifts who add the culminating touch and arrive at the nearly obvious conclusion while the charismatic sloganeers and lightning rods of the media go through their symbolic motions—paper gods consumed by the primeval conflagration of human curiosity. They could be scrapped in a minute, but there would always be a place for a man like him.

He crept along the corridor, and came at last to a stairway. Day-Glo-orange arrows pointed down and signs in six languages said DOWN ONLY. Ezana had reason to ask himself if indeed he did have a place. In his cheap robe of old *merikani*, its folds tapping his shaking knees and spherical buttocks, he felt transposed into that spatially vague afterlife so monotonously guaranteed by the rambling Mohamet. Did the stairway go down to the girls' high school or to the prison where dissident rural chiefs and adolescents addicted to contraband comic books underwent laborious courses of political re-education, with seminars on the Thousand Uses of the Peanut and the Thought of Josef Stalin thrown in for second offenders? Ezana had no business in either of these places; his education felt complete. Against all official indications he took the stairway up, to the floor where his old offices were. The image of his old suite—the shag carpet, the glass-topped desk, the In basket, the Out basket, and the little tree of rubber stamps beside the postage scales—burned in his mind like an oasis in the imagination of a desert traveller. Once seated in that place, he could regrasp the levers of government. Elleloû, however far away, would feel the nation rumble under his feet, the gears of progress re-engaged. The contretemps concerning Gibbs and Klipspringer would pass like a woman's petulance. He and Elleloû needed one another as the earth needs the sky, as the traveller needs the camel. One determines, the other implements. Already Ezana was beginning to feel snug, nestled back into place and reconnected to the power terminals.

The first thing he must implement, he saw with sudden executive clarity, was the cooling of Klipspringer. These Americans, they talk in billions, but turn out to have been "brainstorming." No matter: the quick winds of Washington would blow him away, and another bargainer would take his place. As for the Russians, he would work to rid Kush of their boisterous mischief. Obstructionists and familiars of confusion, profiteers of all disarray, they were behind this melancholy distraction of the President, Ezana had no doubt. The superparanoids, he had once amusingly called the world's present subdividers. He found them both gross, compared to the old imperialist powers, who in their chilly country houses and baroque chancelleries at least had partitioned the outgunned continents while being served delicacies beside which borscht and hamburger were so much dogfood. He was hungry, Ezana realized.

He wound his way through three echoing turns of the cast-iron spiral stairs and came to a door of riveted plates, each stamped with Art Nouveau efflorations. These noodly motifs the French had brought, along with military science, the metric system, and punctilio. This door swung open at a touch. Why? Ezana wondered if his guards might have awoken from their comas and alerted the authorities. But what authorities? The carpeted corridors, with their water-coolers and framed citations for bureaucratic excellence, their cork bulletin boards shingled with yellowing, curling inter-office memos and facetiously annotated clippings from *Les Nouvelles en Noir et Blanc,* were empty at this hour, like a valley whose inhabitants have fled before the rumored invader could materialize. The narrow door of Ellelloû's ascetic office was shut, its frosted glass inscrutable, intact, dark.

But behind the larger glass of Ezana's own office door, two dozen steps along the corridor, past a circular table holding copies of Cuban and Bulgarian magazines whose covers featured tawny beauties beaded with water on the beaches of the Black and Caribbean seas, a light burned. A guttural laugh, as from a ditch, arose within. He put his ear—abnormally small and infolded, even for a black man—against the glass. He heard beneath Kutunda's laugh another voice, male, loudly at ease. They were waiting for him, a party was in progress. Delicately Ezana opened the door and moved through his old anteroom to the inner office. There he was greeted by the dazzling sight of Kutunda in lacy red underwear, her hair bleached platinum and teased to a bouffant mass, bringing a wire basket of papers, like a cocktail waitress bringing hors d'œuvres, to the man behind the desk. This was the oval-faced young man who had once read the Koran to the king; he still wore his plum-colored fez and his expression of dense ebony calm, though in his hand was held, black and white and faintly blue, a gun.

"We need each other," he told Michaelis Ezana.

Five

E SMERALDA MILLER was an interesting color, a gray as of iron filings so fine the eye could not detect the individual grains. In Hakim's fancy the tint, which savored of manufacture, was a by-product of her beliefs, her economic determinism. At the same time she was an attractive, ectomorphic young woman, with a lean prognathous face, almond-shaped eyes framed in pink plastic spectacles, and a bewitching way of thoughtfully swaying her jaw, as if testing molar crowns her father had made for her. "What are you trying to achieve?" she would ask the young deserter from Noire, across the table in the Off-Campus Luncheonette, or later in the Pure Dairy Products Ice Cream Parlor, or later still in the Badger Cafe, with its beer-soaked sawdust on the floor, and its bubbling, phosphorescent advertisements. "Messing around with this deluded bitch Candy."

"Achieve? That's a rather other-directed way of putting it. What did Freud say? Pleasure is the removal of tension. There is a tension that screwing her relieves. No doubt the sex has a component of vengeance, of tasting evil, of stealing Charlie's prize, et cetera. From her side, kindred craziness. Still, we get along."

"She's no prize, is what you can't see. She put the move on you in the first place. You just took it. You've been taking it for years, now, and she's got marriage in her eye. What happens when you graduate?"

"I have told her, more than once, that I am married."

"To some old black cow in the heart of nowhere? This white girl no more cares about that woman than a bug under a rock. She doesn't believe she exists, and neither do I. Anyway, who says you're ever going back? Let's face it, Haps, you're American as apple pandowdy. I try to talk sense to you friend to friend, and you give me back David Riesman and overheard Freud. I love ya."

This last was said as lightly as these words can be said, as Bob Hope or Clark Gable says them, but Félix took them in, and understood her advice now as propaganda. He began to play with her. "As a Muslim, I am entitled to four wives."

"Shit. You're about as Muslim as I am Daddy Warbucks. I hope that stuff hasn't taken you in; it's just our usual native storefront I'm-comin'-home-Jesus routine, with a few funny phrases thrown in. *Inshallah*, Walla-Walla."

"I don't mock your faith," he said stiffly. "Anyway, you're wrong about my never going back. You don't follow the African news in the back pages. The British have given in to Nkrumah, and de Gaulle has been brought to power to end the Algerian war. Only de Gaulle can face down the military."

"God, you're impossible when you get on your great men kick. De Gaulle is just Ike with a bigger nose; they are bal*loons*. History is happening under*neath*. When the oppressed peoples rise *up*, they will just *take*. Meanwhile, nobody is giving them anything. France can bleed all it wants, international capital won't *let* it let go."

"International capital, I believe, has decided colonies are obsolete. The companies themselves, and their insidious products, are the new armies."

"The proletariat—"

"The proletariat, there is no proletariat. Show me the proletariat here. You have the blacks, kept in ghettos because of a superstitious horror of their skins, their rolling eyes, their whiplike penises—"

"Some are stubby," Esmeralda said.

"You have the Indians," Félix went on, "who never knew what hit 'em. And you have the white workers, who Marx to the contrary are thoroughly enrolled in consumerism, making junk and buying junk, drinking junk and driving junk. That is the revolution, surely—the triumph of the unnecessary. If Marx could see his English proletariat now, he wouldn't recognize such softness, such silliness, soaked through and through with ale and the telly. He thought the proletariat was a sponge that would have to be squeezed until a revolution ran out. What happened instead is it sopped up some of the surplus its labor had created and bloated, in a spongy way. There is a kind of poisonous mush abroad in the planet, Esmeralda, and the Muslims aren't quite wrong about its being devilish. It crowds out the good, it makes goodness impossible. Great fanatics can no longer arise; they are swamped by distractions."

"There you go, into obscurantism again. Ideas go back to basics. Food and shelter and clothing, medicine and transportation and the rest of it. Everybody has the same needs, but ninety per cent of the world's wealth is in the hands of ten per cent of the world's people. A revolution has to come."

"Movements have to come. Marx was right, the world

is a machine; but he thought some parts, the parts he named, moved while the rest held still. I see two major motions in the world now. There is this seeping down and outwards of Euro-American consumerism. And there is this groping upwards of the dusky underdog. But a third motion encompasses both. As the poor man reaches upwards, the ground is sinking beneath his feet, he is sinking in the spreading poverty, the muchness of humanity divided into the same weary constant, the overused, overpopulated world." He sipped his beer; its bubbles reminded him: "In my boyhood the giraffes, the elephants, the lions were familiar deities, come to play on the horizon of our world. Soon there will be no animals left bigger than men. Then, only cockroaches, rats, and men. So these gestures of economics are like the reaching gestures on Géricault's painting of the raft of the *Medusa,* gestures that will never grasp their objects, because the raft is sinking. Your Communism is such a failed gesture. In the industrialized countries of Western Europe, where Marx reasoned the uprising must come, the Communist party officials wear suits with vests, and sidle forward for their share, as you Americans say, of the pie."

Her silence, during which she appeared to be focusing closely upon his lips, emboldened him to continue, in what he fancied a Dostoevskian vein: "The age of any revolution is five years. After that, either its participants have wandered off, dismayed by failure, or else have succeeded and become an establishment, generally more tyrannous than the one they displaced. We Africans like de Gaulle. He reminds us of the giraffe, of the gods that no longer visit us. He will make a revolution, not from underneath but from above; give him five years. Algeria will get its independence, and with it, because the French are imperious and demand absolute logic of themselves, all the vast lesser bits of French West Africa, even my empty, unloved Noire. That is how history happens, in fits of impatience. Then de Gaulle will be thrown aside, like Robespierre; or else become a fussy old man losing quarrels with his Parliament. No matter; by then I will have returned. *Au revoir, les États-Unis!* Farewell, Esmeralda!"

The future Ellelloû had a strange sensation, sometimes, in talking to these Americans, black or white: their faces were units in a foreign language, they inhabited a stratum of reality, a slant of thought, so remote from his own that in the effort to be understood he grew dizzy. Esmeralda's solemn gray face, with that touch of languid sexuality working at the rounded points of her jaws, seemed across the table a chasm or a well he was looking straight down into, where his own head was distantly, waveringly mirrored.

She said, "You should write some of that up and send it to *The Journal of Underdeveloped Political Thought*."

The journal was really called *Political Thought in the Underdeveloped Nations*, and was published by a group of suspect liberals and malcontented expatriates in an adjacent Midwestern state, one also shaped like a mitten. Hakim took her advice, spinning out in a few long caffeine-crazed nights between terms that little string of articles mentioned sixteen years later, with unintended provocative effect, by the unfortunate Gibbs. They comprised in Hakim's mind the third triumph of his undergraduate career. The second had been his near-election, missing by four votes (his four black friends, he suspected), as Campus Organizer of Pep. His first had been his seduction of Candy.

"You really taking that bitch back with you?" Esmeralda asked.

He toyed with his empty beer glass, wondering if he should have another. "I had not thought so."

"Good luck, black boy, losing her. These white chicks

like to call the tune; leave off the loving, they holler rape."

"My native land would seem a barren place to Candace." The balusters of her staircase, the claustrophobic comfort of her father's living-room, swirled through his mind, as he exposed his lower teeth in reflection, conscious of Esmeralda's abnormally intent focus upon his lips. Her stare was numbing his gums.

"Somebody that strong-headed and spoiled thinks she could melt the North Pole if she went there. That's the weakness of a ruling class, they can't take in adverse information. How do you feel about Craven?"

He flipped the little cardboard coaster, idly, to the side without an advertisement. "Unhappy. I believe there have been tender passages between them."

"You can bet your ass on that. She'll fuck anything as long as it's not a boy her own age, race, and income bracket. That's *her* revolution. Haps, she's bad news. She's tough, and she's cold. What *is* the magic? You've been making yourself conspicuous with that girl since you set foot on free soil."

He thought of Candy, her pink cheeks, her red knitted headscarf, her neurotic sharp smile, and of how, coming up to her along a diagonal path, standing next to her in the cold, he felt airy and towering. He told Esmeralda, "It's like eating snow." Even this seemed too much a confession, a betrayal; he became angry with his interrogator. "Why should I come to this country to sleep with a black woman?" he asked her explosively. "My country is nothing but black women." Still in that squeezed voice of anger, he said, "How about another beer?"

"Beer back at the YCC," Esmeralda mumbled, submissively. The Young Communist Club kept two rooms in an asbestos-shingled tenement house on a back street of Franchise, for a rent that, though beyond the means of the meagre membership, was somehow met. Esmeralda could count, this night as on most nights, on having the place to herself. They walked along pavements packed with snow, only the heads of the parking meters protruding from the drifts, the whiteness hardened to ice and tinted by neon signs and the half-lit display windows of closed shops, ungrated in those safe days, even the windows of jewelry stores. Back from Commerce Street the pavements were erratically shovelled, so for some stretches, where a widow lived, or a family that had fallen below the social norms, glossy mounds had to be traversed on little paths, worn by the boots of schoolchildren. Candy for this weekend had gone away with her family, skiing in the Laurentians. The YCC quarters were identified only by the initials. No hammer and sickle, no red star. There had been problems with broken windows. Esmeralda turned up the heat. A mattress on the floor did for a bed. The term "crash pad" had not yet been invented. Esmeralda's body, naked on the sheetless ticking, was the same slate hue her face was, an even soft gray that moved him, taken with her stringy hips and underdeveloped breasts; the slaver's sperm, it seemed, had entered her blood line to steal shine from her skin, and joyful African protuberance from her body. When she left the bed, instead of glimmering in the darkened room like a candle, she vanished. What Félix liked best about these American seductions was not the exchange of salivas and juices but the post-coitus, the ritual cigarettes and the standing around in the kitchen rummaging up something to eat, their exploited genitals lit up by the sudden glow of the refrigerator, its polychrome wealth of beer cans, yogurt cups, frozen vegetables, packets of cheese and luncheon meats and other good bottled, wrapped, and encapsulated things. The young Communists, like any frat, kept a sweet, starchy, and spotty larder. To Hakim,

reared on nuts and porridges, this gentle, naked pecking
after food—Esmeralda concocted herself a sandwich of
peanut butter and marshmallow fluff—savored of home
and soothed the acerb aftereffects of the tragic act of love.
She had had no climax, and he had been distracted by the
giant red poster of Lenin, goateed and pince-nezed, staring upwards with the prophetic fury of a scholar who has
just found his name misspelled in a footnote. "She ain't
even taught you how to screw," Esmeralda said, pleased
to have an additional score on Candy, and depressing her
lover with the hint that their fornication, in such romantic
surroundings, had been merely an extension of a propaganda campaign. To an extent, it worked; he looked more
kindly upon Marx thereafter, as Marx, from a poster on
the other wall, grandfatherly and unfoolable, had looked
kindly down upon the heaving buttocks of the future
Ellelloû.

The time had come for them to leave the caravan. The
flinty passes had widened and the Massif now tipped
downwards toward the highlands of Zanj and, weeks to
the northeast, the southwest corner of Egypt. We thanked
Sidi Mukhtar with a purse of hundred-*lu* pieces. Feeling
that our relationship, though extended in time, had been
less close emotionally than it might have been, I confided
that I and my beautiful bride (as amorous, I further confided in coarse Berber, as she was shapely) had peeked
into some of the caravan's cases and discovered their
unexpected contents. His grin displaying the rift between
his front teeth, and lifting a pearl-sized wart nestled in the
flange of one nostril, our leader explained the eventual
destination of the office supplies: Iran. "The Shahanshah,"
he said, "has much wish to modernize. In his hurry he
buy typewriters from West Germans and paper from

Swedes and then discover only one type spool fit type-writer, only one type eraser not smudge paper. American know-how meanwhile achieve obsolescence such that only fitting spool stockpiled in Accra as aid-in-goods when cocoa market collapse. Formula of typewriter eraser held secret and cunning capitalists double, redouble price when Shah push up oil price to finance purchase of jet fighters, computer software, and moon rocks. French however operating through puppet corporations in Daho-mey have secured formula as part of multi-billion-franc deferred-interest somatic-collateral package and erect eraser factory near gum arabic plantations. Much borax also in deal, smuggled by way of Ouagadougou. Now Sadat has agreed to let goods across Nile if Shahanshah agrees to make anti-Israeli statement and buy ten thousand tickets to *son-et-lumière* show at Sphinx."

I did not believe the rogue's garbled story, but deemed it prudent to suppress my doubts. Instead, I repeated our appreciation of his *rejela* (valor) and *dhiyafa* (hospitality), said that his skill at navigating through the perils of the Balak argued a pious intimacy with the purposes of Allah, and, by way of parting compliment, confided, "Unbeknownst to you, you have been transporting, in the guise of two mendicant musicians, the President of Kush and one of his First Ladies. *Je suis Ellelloû.*"

"*Je sais, je sais,*" Sidi Mukhtar responded out of his bag of tongues, his face in merriment twitching like the skin of a sand lizard just emerging from his hole. "Otherwise, I kill. We see Benzi following us before mountains become too bad. Super car, gives ride free of sway."

"Why would you have killed me?" It is perhaps part of my inheritance from the communally tender, multi-generational, intra-supportive village of my upbringing to be always astonished that any real harm lurks in the world.

The third component of Sidi Mukhtar's personality, his

sirge (thievishness), shuffled cheerfully to the fore. He answered me, "To sell Madame to the Yemenis. Good posh black girls, with correct long neck and hollow back, very hard to come by. Only shoddy slaves come on market now. Mostly drug addicts from bourgeois European families, decadent riff-raff looking for security. Yemenis, Saudis need intelligent slaves, to operate electrical appliances."

Here, too, I doubted the mercantile tall tale, and distrusted the note of socialist snobbery he had injected, presumably to please me. His men loaded our camels with sacks of dried dates and sloshing skins of water. We exchanged farewells: my *"Allah Ma'ak"* for his *"Aghrub 'Anni."* The caravan, our home for these moons, shuffled, clanked, and sighed its way out of sight, as the tepid dawn washed away the shadows of the night and, with them, the stars. An hour later, we discovered that the villain had given us not water in our *zemzimayas* but wine, which our religion forbade us to drink, though from its bouquet it was a fair vintage; a lot of sturdy Bordeaux found its way into our trade routes, brought back to Dakar in the peanut-oil tankers as ballast.

Glimpses of rock doves led us upwards and leftwards, into a porous region of caves. At this height color crept back, first by way of iridescent hints in the birds' feathers, next in the rainbow-shimmer on the oil-smooth face of an overhanging rock. We passed through pastel moments much as Esmeralda and I had paced a gallery of neon auras on the way to our betrayal of pale Candace. Sheba rode a camel of the coveted *azrem* shade—a pinkish eggshell, dun toward the tail and white in the huge eyelashes that fringed the iris of glacial blue. My own steed was a mud-brown gelding with a worrisomely depressed hump and a nagging habit of clearing his throat. The pads of their feet, evolved for the *erg*'s slipping sands, split on the

rocky trails, and as the days wore on we often dismounted
and walked beside them, winding our way upwards, led
by the bubbling coo of coral-footed doves. The geology
was strange. Certain summits appeared to have been
molded by a giant, ill-tempered child, finger-furrows distinct and some petrified depressions holding the whirling
ridges of what seemed a thumbprint. The terrain felt
formed by play, of an idiotic sort that left no clues to the
logic of the game. A frozen bulbousness—double-dip,
Reddi-Whip accumulations of weathered lava topped by
such gravitational anomalies as natural arches and big
boulders balanced on smaller—gave way to cleavages and
scree as geometrically finicking as the debris of a machin-
ist's shop. Amid these splits and frolicsome tumblings,
caves abounded; where the caves multiplied, so did the
paintings left by the mysterious happy herdsmen and
hunters of the Green Sahara. Centuries of calm sunlight
had not faded their sheltered ochres and indigos. Wild
buffalo bore between their horns little round marks like
shrunken halos; their hunters were depicted with skins the
color of oranges and enlarged heads round as the helmets
of space travellers. In a deep cave a galloping goddess,
daintily horned, a shower of grain between her antennae
like static, rose to the domed ceiling, carrying up with her
the steatopygial silhouettes of naked mortals, running
also, overlaid and scattered like leaves in agitation slipping
from a tree. Brown, gray, custard, pepper, cinnamon: the
colors of our African cookery depicted, with the primitive
painter's numinous, nervous precision, the varieties of
cattle, as the herding culture replaced the hunting. These
very herds, no doubt, had helped turn the grassland from
green to tan, to dust, to nothing.

Sheba, gaunt now as a ballerina, her sumptuous costume in tatters from which color had forever fled, her intricate necklaces of lapis lazuli and jasper and of coral

from a shore where milk-warm waves lapped life into
quivery barnacles fallen bit by bit along our way, wanted
to stay in a cool dim cave, and die. We had drunk the
sardonic wine on the second day, blaspheming against our
bodies, and had vomited accordingly. The dried fruit
stuck in our throats like ash; her dear tongue was swollen
like the body of a frog in the dried mud of an exhausted
water hole; she spoke indistinctly, but I understood her to
say that she was dizzy, and that her skull had a sun of
pain in it. Begging her to rise and stumble another kilom-
eter forward with me, stooping down and with my own
depleted strength tugging at her resistless limbs, I thought
of all the women I had led into such a wilderness, a
promised green land of love that then had turned infertile,
beneath the monomaniacal eye of my ambition, my wish
to create a nation, to create a nation as a pedestal for myself, my pathetic self. The whites of her eyes, rolling upwards in a delirious faint, had become an astonishing
golden color, as in the hollow head with which a mummi-
fied Pharaoh is helmeted for *his* space-flight, the golden
eyes inset with onyx irises that have been stolen.

"Do it to me, baby, do it, do it," I crooned, to tease
her back to life, to bring her back from mummification
into the moist full skin of the girl I had met strolling the
alleys of Istiqlal, her svelte jaws methodically chewing up-
pers and downers, kola and khat, her ear pressed to a
transistor radio turned to the perfidious pop-rock stations
of Brazzaville, the same *Plus Haute Quarantaine* over and
over. I had been in the disguise of a gum-seller, little
packets of Chiclets that sold two for a *lu,* or for a kiss in
lieu of that. At the first touch of her lips I knew Sheba
had the mouth for me. Now those satin cushions, the upper even more generously stuffed than the lower, were
split, the skin at the edges of the split blackened as if de-

liberately singed, and the pale inner lining, next to her gums, blued by the onset of cyanosis.

"My . . . Lord," she pronounced. "Divorce . . . me."

"Never," I said, and managed to work her limp body onto my shoulders. I carried her from the cave to the camels, who were waiting with that impeccable poise of their species, conserving their inner resources. But as I dropped her diminished weight across the embroidered saddle cloth of her beautiful *azrem* mount, the creature died. It did not even keel over, but held in death its sitting position; the head on its long neck simply rested on the rocky trail, and twisted gently as the muscles relaxed. Its albino lashes lowered like drawgates.

Was this the end? *Never,* I repeated to myself. All of the nubile women in our land of Kush, above the lowest social stratum, carry a dagger with which to stab their own hearts if their honor is compromised, ere the rapist can work his will. My mother, alas, had had no such implement, but Sheba did. I plucked it, its blade of Damascus steel and handle of polished chalcedony, from the bindings of her bosom and cut open the dead camel's stomach, so we could drink the brackish green water secreted there. With this liquid I called Sheba back to life; she shuddered and wept, and as her strength returned cursed me in the astonishingly vile language which flows so easily from the lips of even the prettiest of the younger generation. As she gave out these signs of restored vitality, I loaded our baggage onto our surviving camel, my mud-colored mount, with his housemaid's knees and smoker's hack. He accepted Sheba's weight—*Takbīr!*—and I shuffled beside them on foot.

Vistas loomed, through clefts and apertures worn by wind erosion, of a hazed sea of sand so far below us as to be another planet; the prospect was westward, to the Ippi Rift Valley that runs north and south through the center of my great land. Closer to our eyes, petrophagous lichen silvered the relative damp of some shadows, and an inverted dwarf species of thornbush (*Alhagi inversum*) adorned the underside of ledges. The quality of the rock-paintings, too, was subtly changing; daubed ground ochre and charcoal paste gave way to a furry, swirling technique of primary colors sprayed from a can. Swastikas, stylized genitals, and curious forms involving circles attached to crosses or arrows or circumscribing a kind of airplane replaced the magical representations of Green Sahara's vanished animists. Some of the hieroglyphs could be read: ROCKETS, CLASS OF '55, GAY IS GOOD, REVOLUCIÓN AHORA, QUÉBEC LIBRE, HELTER SKELTER, FAT CITY. The letters of this last were themselves fat; this style was prevalent. Many of the inscriptions had been overlaid: the simple sign STOP had been amended to STOP WAR and then an anti-pacifist had scratched out the S. Some inviting surfaces were muddy with a mad tangle of colors, defying all decipherment, even if Sheba and I had had the stomach for it, which we did not. For our drink of camel bile had turned our bowels queasy. She had become the gray of the cardboard that stiffens a fresh ream of paper. I too, at this oxygen-scant altitude, under the vertical gaze of noon, on this leaden planet, could go on no farther. We half-toppled, half-crawled into the scribbled mouth of a cave, that seemed to be the entrance, a kind of kiosk, to a subterranean system in whose depths, unless my senses of smell and hearing betrayed me, cold flowers were being sold and pinball was being played.

The camel accompanied us inside, and was the first to fall asleep. Then Sheba succumbed to oblivion, her head, that little snug sack of loyalty, resting on my arm. The green demon of nausea churning within kept me from sleeping instantly; as my eyes adjusted to the gloom I saw that our shelter and, it seemed likely, tomb had once been a bower of love, and still was love's memorial. TEX LOVES RITA, a wall opposite proclaimed, and from this same wall, and those adjacent, the names of many more thronged like clouds of the damned to my attention, not all of them written in the flatfooted alphabet Roman imperialism marched through Europe, but many in our own incomparably dancing Arabic script, and some in the chunky formations of St. Cyril, the flowerets of lower-case Greek, Asia's busy bamboolike brushstrokes, and the staring, rectilinear symbols of Tiffinagh, that traces Tamachek onto the sand. So many names, so much love, so many cries uttered on the verge of *la petite mort,* so much sperm; my stomach sickened, and the blood ebbed from my head. But before I lapsed, in tune with Sheba's breathing, into the sleep that might be our last, I noticed, on a rock above her head this indelible legend: HAPPY LOVES CANDY.

"*What* did your father say?"

"It's not as if he talks about you a lot, he doesn't. He used to ask a lot of questions, he was very interested in you. He thought you could tell him the secret, of how the blacks can be the way they are, of why they don't love this country the way he does."

"His and theirs aren't the same country. They're as different as Heaven and Hell."

"I *know* that, Happy, don't argue with *me.* I'm just trying to be *him* for a minute. My goodness, you're touchy these days."

"Pre-partum blues," he suggested, in his lover's weary voice. The snow had melted, refroze, and finally receded for the last of the four times he would witness this beauti-

ful North American relenting; their graduation approached.

"And *carp*ing," Candy continued, unmollified. "At
times you sound exactly like Esmeralda. Fucked her
lately?"

He said nothing. He realized that to assure her that he
had not slept with Esmeralda after the occasion that
Candy had, with the astonishing nose that white women
have for infractions of their property rights, sniffed out
and goaded him to confess, would be to repaint in newly
vivid colors this baleful lapse, and to renew Candy's hy-
perbolic anger and grief. Her overreaction had baffled and
then frightened him. He had trapped, all innocently, a
source of passion, of human power, unknown to Africa.
In the village, the bushes had every night quivered with
casual pairings. He had taken Kadongolimi's many previous lovers into his arms along with her tattoos. The episode with Esmeralda had been painless, instructive, more
healthful than another beer, and on the whole less intimate, in terms of penetration of his nervous system, than
would have been a trip to her father the dentist. Really,
Candy had punished him too severely for this walk
through the snow; her copious tears over the event had
dried to an unending sarcasm, a baring of fangs in her
voice. These toubabs were indeed poison; he had less
trouble believing, as W. D. Fard has proclaimed, that
these blue-eyed animals, once engendered, had to be banished, a race of snarling, howling wolves, to the icy caves
of Europe. Candy would get a wolvish look at the thought
of his infidelity. Her lips would go parched; her eyes
would turn lifeless, cold, and small. She would begin to
talk about the sacrifices she had made for him. Her whole
life had been ruined, it seemed, by the injection of his
sperm. Yet, paradoxically, not a drop of that sperm must

be spilled out of her body. She had rights. She had put herself in great social peril. She, she.

She told him, "I can't trust you at all anymore. You two can sneak off into the bushes any time. You have such wonderful things in common. You both hate whites. You both have rhythm. I bet you talk about me, don't you? You call me pinktoes."

"*Please*," he said, embarrassed for her.

She did not notice this, in her zeal to embarrass him. "Don't you find her bony?" she asked. "And pedantic? And—well, *dreary*? So just barely middle-class? Think of her father, drilling all those teeth."

"As opposed to glorious yours, selling all those policies."

"Sneer at Daddy if you must, he'd do anything in the world for Mother and me. He'd kill for us, if he had to."

"Or just for the pleasure of killing."

Tears turned her eyelids pink. She set her arms stickily around his neck, proud of those tears, of her hot close breath. "Happy, this isn't us. What's gone wrong?"

You have gone wrong. You must let go. He suppressed these words, patiently asking once more, "What did your father say, exactly?"

"He was horrible," she sobbed. "Just horrible." Holding her, he was reminded of how, in an intermission of soldiering, he, a young husband not out of his teens, had held one of Kadongolimi's babies, that had been born while he was a year away, against his chest, and patted it to ease its colic, its inner demons, and this infant wished upon him had burped air; the women gathered around like a single-bodied black continuum had praised this little hiccup. So Candy now wanted to be praised for her sobs. "He said," she forced out, "he'd kill you if you tried to marry me."

"Marry you? And what did you say to that, darling?"

"I said"—a shudder, a big gulp, a sob, and then—"he couldn't stop us, we'd elope."

In his sleep with Sheba, Ellelloû rotated, his robes entangled beneath him and enfolding lumpy pockets of the white dust of the cave floor. He was aware through his dreams of these lumps and of her body, sunk in forgetfulness but now and then roused to rotate like his own, two carcasses turned on parallel spits, touching with a rustle, their hunger and thirst borne by shrivelled organs submerged beneath the reach of pain. Yet no submergence quite concealed from that mass of sporadic lights, colors, and linkages that was his immortal consciousness the fact of this proximate woman, her scent and sadness and the warm skin beneath her own robes, that had come through the Balak faded as by too scalding a wash. His sleeping brain acknowledged the certain graciousness of her accompanying him, though from the Marxist standpoint it could be maintained that she had no choice, it was accompany him or wander the streets as a waif of poverty. But what was this, this trek through silicon and starlight and now this death in a cavern strewn with condoms and Kleenexes and other sedimented evidences of love, but poverty? In Ellelloû's sleep an arch of pity and sorrowful gratitude built itself from his beating heart to this his rib, his mate, enclosing as in a crypt Sheba's body, her yielding lips, her blue-black brow smooth and round as a dome of tile. Then a scent of vodka was at his nostrils, and water was at his lips.

"*Prosnis', chernozhopyi!*" a Targui was shouting in my ear; and my first waking thought was that of course it must have been the Russians who stole the head of the king, for only they would have been so anthropologically obtuse within their own passionate, isolate culture and prodigious territories as not to know that the Tuareg were the traditional enemies of Wanjiji, holding the riverine kingdom in thrall when they were strong, retreating back into the desert when they were weaker. The Tuareg could not help but regard us as slaves, and we them as devils, devils from the desert, howling like the harmattan, their mouths masked because they had no jaws, just gaping throats that spewed vile yells and cruelty. These Tuareg succoring me had their mouths and noses swaddled; nothing showed but their wolvish pale eyes, and their muffled voices.

"*Eta chernaya pizda nichevo zhivchik, a?*"

"*Spokoino, u nikh u vsekh sifilis.*"

They muttered as if I had no ears. One of them wore steel-rimmed spectacles; when his comrades noticed I was awake, he began to address me in his slurred Iraqi Arabic and, his vocabulary failing, his sloshy French. "Rise up, Mr. President!" he cried through the haze of languages. "You are near the end of your journey! The path has been made easier! *Vive* Kush! *Vive le peuple et la fraternité socialiste et islamique! Écrasez l'infâme capitaliste, monopolisé, et très, très décadent!*"

Several Tuareg women, their naked faces impassive, the wrists and ankles dyed blue, were laving Sheba's feet and rebraiding her hair; though my dear girl flickered toward me a feeble smile, her eyes, under a helpless pressure, kept closing, the lids freshly anointed with antimony.

It was true, the upward path had been made easier. The steepness declined, as the summit neared, and an asphalt strip, wide enough for a golf cart, with green-painted pipe railings on the side of a precipitous falling-off, had been engineered where the natural trail might have seemed impassably rugged. Yellow signs advised FALLING

Rock and Oryx Crossing, and others advertised our growing closeness to the Oracle's Cave, to La Tête Qui Parle, to Мавзолей Эдуму Четвертого. My old brown baggage camel, who had been fed a barrel of Ukrainian millet (or could it have been Nebraska sorghum?), fairly danced on his threadbare legs as he bouncingly bore along the sumptuous little body of Sheba, who had been slipped a few kola nuts and was chewing through a high. I felt, as one does after too deep a sleep, uncaught-up with myself: the physical half hurried along to expectancy's accelerated heartbeat, while the spiritual man loitered behind in a fog, groping for the reason for his shadowy, guilty sensation of something undone, of something disastrous due. The path, briskly engineered through the rose-colored cliffs and abysses, was crossed by a newly built funicular railway; the crossing-marking, X, reminded me of something unpleasant I have always wanted to forget.

"You are crazy," Oscar X firmly, patiently stated, as if reciting a memorized speech. "You are what the Messenger terms a black man with a white man's head. Man, you are sad. You are evil and you are sad. I wash my hands of you. I wish to wipe you from my mind. *Anā lā aʿrifuka.* The Nation of Islam is one thousand per cent opposed to what you are undertaking. The mixture of the races is a crime against purity. The Word of God unambiguously proclaims, sooner a black man mate with a lazy shit-smeared sow or the female of the alligator species than entrust his ebony penis to the snatch of a white devil mare."

Félix imagined in the floridity of this indictment a simultaneous undercutting, a self-mocking. But he detected no humor or mercy in Oscar's face. People when they go behind the curtain of a creed become unknown. He said, "You know Candy. You like her."

"I have tolerated her," Oscar said. "But I have not liked her. She is the offspring of the stock that has enslaved us, that spits on us whenever it chooses. This woman has spit upon you, and you don't have the mother wit to wipe your fucking face." He sipped his Ovaltine and came up with a scummy lip.

Barry Little tried to help, telling Félix, "She was raised too clean. She needs to get down into it, but doesn't want to get real dirt on herself. So she tells herself a story in the dark. In her mind, you are the pimp and the customers both. That's a way these upper-class sheltered girls get their kicks, it's nothing personal in regards to you. Make it personal and permanent, that would be a big mistake. I'm not saying white and black can't live together, they *got* to, this separate black nation old Elijah Poole keeps plugging is fantastical purely. But in this particular case, of you and little Miss Cunningham, I'm saying that would be one fantasy on top of another. You don't know America, and she don't know Africa."

"Perhaps we know each other."

"You know each other in the dark," Barry said. "Out in the light, what do you see? Her momma's a washrag and her daddy's a redneck who'd fry your ass if he could find the button. Kiss her good-bye, you'd be doing her a favor as well as yourself. I'm not talking black or brown, I'm trying to talk to you straight. If you and she were both green in color, I'd have my doubts about the personalities."

"No such thing as color blind," Turnip Schwarz interposed. "No such thing."

Esmeralda said indignantly, "You're all talking to this boy as though he had a choice. Any choice he ever had

he threw away. He's been hustled. He's in over his head
and can't say No now."

"Just get on the plane to Timbuctoo, the way to say
No," Turnip said.

Félix felt hemmed in, shoved, in the businesslike
American manner. He resented their attempt to pry him
open and meddle in the fate he was nurturing within; he
could not explain to them how delicately all the truths
they advanced were built into his plan, were included in
the sprawling, devious budget that in the end would balance. It was true, Candy had come upon him and was
sweeping him along; but we can propel ourselves only a
little way out of ourselves and for the rest must play with
the forces beyond us that impinge. He gazed steadily at
Oscar and said, "I have been reading the Book of Books,
as the Messenger advises. *Women are your fields: go,
then, into your fields as you please.*"

Oscar blinked, and quoted back: "*You shall not wed
pagan women, unless they embrace the faith. A believing
slave-girl is better than an idolatress, although she may
please you.*"

"Jesus preserve us," Esmeralda breathed. Candy had
come in at the door of the luncheonette; even at a distance, through the smoke and jangle, the future Ellelloû
could see she had been crying. More trouble with her
parents, or Craven, or some other white spokesman. She
came toward their black table timidly now, sensing that
here too she was abhorred. Yet in honor of spring she
had put on a forsythia-yellow sweater and a pleated white
skirt. Félix lifted from his chair as a tide toward the
moon.

Oscar X stood up angrily. "I will not contaminate myself any longer," he stated so all could hear, "by consort-
ing with mongrel clowns and lackeys of the doomed
devil-race." To Félix he said, again with the precision

of something rehearsed, *"L'anatu Allāhi 'alayka."* He walked out, taking with him Temple Two and Temple Three, the joyful car rides together, the Brotherhood. His curse Félix felt as a blast of heat upon his face, the heat whose first wave had been, in infancy, the absence of his father. He felt this heat as Allah. Allah is the essential seriousness of things, their irreversibility. Our friends all die to us, some before we are born.

Let us step back a moment, onto the spongy turf of psychohistorical speculation. There was in our young hero (not so young as he appeared to his clamorous advisers; by 1958 he was going on twenty-six) an adsorptive chemical will that made him adhere to just those surfaces that would have repelled him: he took away from the United States not only the frightened body of Candy Cunningham in a blue linen suit but the Nation of Islam, internalized as a certain shade of beige idealism mixed of severity, xenophobia, decency, and isolation. As New World immigrants preserve in their ethnic neighborhoods folk dances and items of cuisine that in the old country have become obsolete, so Ellelloû held to a desiccated, stylized version of the faith that meanwhile failed for Oscar X, who fell away in the mid-Sixties, when the scandals of the Messenger's sexual strayings (not one but two secretaries pregnant!) unfolded to a bloody climax in the gunning-down of his schismatic Chief Minister Malcolm in New York City, on West 166th Street. So the Nation of Islam was just another gangland after all. In the strength of his disillusion Oscar became a trainee with the Chicago police, and with unfeigned enthusiasm helped bop long-haired protester heads at the 1968 Democratic Convention, at the same time as his repudiated brother was fomenting the revolution that overthrew Edumu IV and brought Islamic socialism to Noire, renamed Kush.

●

Now the path was continuously paved, and littered with bits of paper—torn tickets and Popsicle wrappers. The pigeons were thick about us, throbbling and strutting in their street-wise self-importance, too full of crushed Fritos and dropped popcorn to flutter away. The first people we saw were Chinese—a small close flock of official visitors, in their blue-gray many-pocketed pajamas, their mass-produced wire-frame spectacles (no doubt of identical prescription) resting on the fat of their cheeks as they smilingly squinted up from their guidebooks toward something on high we could not yet see. We had come upon them around a corner and, as if the dusty spectacle of the disguised President and his delectable, stoned consort on foot and camelback respectively had been organized for them as an additional local wonder, they obligingly switched, in a unified motion, their twinkling attention full upon us. These tourists appeared amazed when the weary camel plodded straight toward them, rippling his upper lip contemptuously, forcing them to break formation and crowd to the sides of the path. They joked among themselves in their curious pitch-chirping.

How had these Confucians come here? The question was answered by the next turn in the path, which revealed a parking lot blasted from the outcroppings and holding six or seven large tourist buses, some striped like zebras and others spotted like giraffes. Emblazoned on their sides was the name of a Zanj tourist agency, the same which in other directions exposed to the stupefied gaze of aliens, through smoky-blue windows that bathed our Africa in perpetual twilight, the oceanic herds of the Tanzanian grasslands, Lalibela's cathedrals carved from solid rock, the inexhaustible salt quarries of the Danakil Depression, and what other bleak marvels were exploitable in this continent whose most majestic feature is the relative absence of Man. To such buses the Zanj border was not far away, and evidently the entrepreneurs found no insurmountable obstacle there. I must create one. "I will close the border," I confided to Sheba. "This is an atrocity."

"I think it's an improvement," she said languidly, from within her trip. "Can I have another lemonade?"

We had patronized a refreshment stand manned by a detribalized Djerma, offering beverages in all bubbling colors. "The delicate ecology of the Balak," I told her, "is being devastated."

"There's lots left," she pointed out.

"One germ can kill a giant," I explained to her, vowing, "I'll have old Komomo's hide for this."

Wamphumel Komomo, President-for-Life of Zanj: height six foot six, weight three hundred seventy pounds. He wore (and still wears, but for my own peace of mind let this description be consigned to the past tense) garish robes so intricately worked each sleeve cost a seamstress her sight and a crown that consisted of a cheetah's snarling skull, gilded. Worse, he was a flirt. The British had taught him this. They had flirted with him by capturing him when he was a guerrilla leader, placing him in prison, scheduling his execution, and then, when the rising tides of freedom forced them to decamp, suddenly installing him as President, in return for his promise not to expel the white settler community from the fertile highlands and along the little seacoast. The shape of Zanj reached out to include its miserable Red Sea port like a child touching wet paint while looking the other way. The bulk of Zanj was as infertile, unprofitable, and stately as Kush. But old Komomo, with his picturesque regalia of catskins, ornamental welts, and medals from the lesser European armies, tirelessly flirted with the international community, inviting the Americans in to build him a desalination plant and then expelling them, inviting the Russians in to train his air force and then expelling them, milking even the

Australians and the post-Sukarno Indonesians for their
dollop of aid, their stretch of highway, their phosphate re-
finery, or mile-high broadcasting antenna. Now his pets
were the Chinese, who were building him a railway from
his nasty little port to the preposterous new capital he had
ordained in the interior, Komomo-glorifying Zanjomo, its
street-plan cribbed from Baron Haussmann, its government buildings based on photos of forgotten World Fairs,
its central adornment a mock-heroic bronze stalagmite
bearing Komomo's shifty features in imitation of Rodin's
Balzac and likely to survive the model's death for one
week, by which time the old nepotist's competing sons-
in-law will have melted it down for bullets. Not a tuck in
his patriarchal robes ungarnished by private gain, which
he extracted from the toubab corporations as blithely as
his forebears the cannibal chiefs extracted *hongo* from the
Arab slavers, Komomo flirted moreover with all the elements within his country, appearing in ostrich feathers in
a veldt village and a hardhat in a magnesium mine, placating the Africa Firsters by taxing the Indian shopkeepers
and placating the Asian community with public readings
from the Upanishads, balancing his denunciations of Ian
Smith and the still-exclusivist Zanj Athletic Club with frequent photographs of himself embracing some visiting
devil or local "landowner" and "business leader," touting
with scrupulously equal decibels the "tribal integrity" of
"our great African masses" and the "total impartiality" of
"our color-blind Constitution." The American press loved
this artful clown; in their rotogravures he looked like a
negative print of Santa Claus. Now he was flooding my
purified, penniless but proud country with animalistic
buses stuffed full of third-echelon Chou Shmoes, German
shutterbugs, British spinsters, bargain-seeking Bulgarians,
curious Danes, Italian archaeologists, and trip-crazed
American collegians bribed by their soused and adulter-

ous parents to get out of the house and let capitalism collapse in peace—all to see a dead head in the dead center of the Bad Quarter.

At the next turn of the path, as the bridle burned in my hands, so hard was it being tugged by my pack camel in the frisky throes of restored vitality, I could see a polychrome, polyglot little mob gathered at the mouth of what must be the cave. It looked artificial, but badly made, like a department-store window display, besprinkled with greenish glitter-dust. It is said that God, as he created these mountains of the Balak, worked in haste. It is also said that the royalty of Kush, chased from Meroë by the Christian hordes of Axum, may have come this way, constructing as they went cities scarcely distinguishable from the rocks. Or perhaps—a third possibility—the unsubtle Soviets, having selected this as the site from which to broadcast slander against the incorruptible President of Kush, had with their usual heavy hand engineered the locale to resemble one of those concrete medleys of domes and parapets that speak to their huddling hearts.

One of Dr. Frederic (without the *k*, yes) Craven's courses in the Government Department of McCarthy College was "U.S. *vs.* USSR: Two Wayward Children of the Enlightenment." Another course was "Plato to Pound: Totalitarianism as the Refuge of Superior Minds." There was a sardonic touch, too, to his seminars: "Bureaucratic Continuity During Political Crises" studied, with use of original documents, phenomena such as the adjudication of misdemeanors and traffic fines during the French Revolution and mail delivery during the American War Between the States. "Weak or Strong?: The Presidency from Fillmore to the Second Harrison" took the paradoxical position that American history would have been much the

same if the opponents of these Chief Executives had been
elected instead, and that the average man fared better under Pierce and Grant than under Lincoln. He also taught
the only course that touched upon the darkest continent:
"The Persistence of the Pharaonic Ideal in the Sudanic
Kingdoms from 600 to 1600 A.D." Félix and Candace
took this course together; their shoulder-rubbing proximity during lectures gave the lecturer pain. Candy was one
of Craven's "pets." In that sinister way of American intellectual men, he had grown handsomer with age, his boy-
ishly gaunt figure filling out without ceasing to be
essentially youthful; kept tendony by tennis and tan by
sailing through September on the cerulean, polluted surface of Lake Timmebago, he had created in time a kind
of vertical harem of undergraduate mistresses, whom
graduation disposed of without his even having to provide
a dismissive dowry. Candy, apparently, in some interstice
or worn spot of her harassed liaison with the future Ellelloû, had placed herself among Craven's concubines,
and had renewed the relationship when the young African—understandably, to all but her—had waffled or responded sluggishly to her female call for a "commitment"
that translated into elopement, bigamy, and for all he
knew, American arrest and incarceration. One warm day
deep in the reign of Dwight Eisenhower, Craven invited
the black student to his office, a cozy cave lined with
leaning gray government manuals and smelling of the
peculiarly sweet pipe smoke it was one of Craven's vani-
ties to emit. He offered Félix a low seat on his Naugahyde
seducer's couch but the youth, his manner stiff with a
wary dignity, took instead a hard straight chair whose
seat, all but the edge, was loaded with blue exam
booklets. End of term was at hand.

"Hakim Félix," the professor began, evidently imagining this mode of address was swankily parallel to use, in

Russian, of the patronymic, "let me begin by confessing some slight disappointment in your exam. You had the facts down pat, but, if I may say so, you seemed to show less gut feeling for the African ethos than some of the middle-class white kids in the course. Miss Cunningham, for instance, wrote an essay on kinship that damn near made me cry."

The student perched still farther forward on the over-burdened chair. "Africa is large," was the best excuse he could offer for his curious failure. "Also, the French did not encourage our ethos, they were intent upon inculcating their own."

"Well," Craven briskly conceded, sucking lip-smackingly upon his pipestem, releasing a blue wraith of saccharine alter-ego, "far be it from me to out-African an African. There was nothing strictly wrong, just my nebulous sense of something missing."

"Perhaps that is the very African ingredient."

Craven closed his pale, rather too mobile lips upon the amber of his pipestem. He did not relish fancy thinking not his own. "I asked you in, though, not to talk about that but to wish you well, really. Can you tell me your plans, Félix?"

"I plan to return, sir. The U.S. immigration officials have never been happy with my status here, though the college has been most liberal and supportive. In Noire, King Edumu, placed back on his throne—placed, I should say strictly, on a throne he never before occupied—in the wake of Guy Mollet's *loi-cadre* proclamation two years ago, has instituted a policy of amnesty toward political criminals under colonialism. And now that de Gaulle has offered the territories either internal autonomy with assistance or complete autonomy without, I think a new era is even more decisively under way, and I will be able to rejoin the military, and serve the new nation, without fear."

"There is no politics without fear," Craven said, "as there is no organization without coercion. However, I wish you well. Have *you* no fear, may I ask, of having lost touch, these four years, with the realities of your own people?"

"As your examination suggests I have. I do not know. My guess is, America will fade for me as even the most intense dreams fade, and in any case the realities of my people are not static, but in the process of transformation. Perhaps I can help create new realities."

"Perhaps." The pipe came into even more elaborate play, the amber stem pointing this way and that as Craven knocked, blew into, and rapidly reamed this little instrument of pleasure. "Will America fade, I wonder, so rapidly if you take a piece of it with you? A living piece. You know to whom I refer."

"I do, and assume your concern is for my political future. Rest easy, I beg you. The new President of Sahel, a poet of sorts, has for wife a *minette* from Lyons. The mighty Suleiman, as you well know, made his queen Roxelana, a consort of Russian blood paler than even the lovely strawberry-blond Mrs. Craven, to whom I hope you will forward my parting regards."

"I will," he said, in unwilled echo of his broken wedding vows.

"Surely," the student meekly persisted, "distinctions in tint of skin have no priority in the world that my professors, you foremost, have taught me must be welded into one, lest the nuclear holocaust transpire. I have come here in innocence, anxious to learn, and part of my American experience has been to fall in love; how could it have been otherwise? This is the land where love is broadcast with the free hand of Johnny Appleseed."

"Be that as it may"—one of Craven's favorite phrases, while he searched for his place in the lecture—"in the instance I have in mind, sentimental exogamist though I am bound to be, I can see, frankly, little good. The female is spoiled, neurotic, headstrong, and too young to know her own mind. You are older, a man of some experience, though I sometimes wonder if your experiences as you describe them do not partake of the fabulous. Why could you not be, for example, an American from say, Detroit, who affects a French accent and the prissy African manner? That would explain why, in your examination, you showed so little feel for the, shall we say, heart of the matter."

"Might it be the instructor who lacks the feel? Africa is not only log drums and sand dunes; we have cities, we have history, which you proposed to teach. We have languages, more than any other continent. We are a melting pot that will not boil over with the addition of one more female Caucasian. I think in your intelligence you have made an idea of blackness; when you look at me, you see an idea, and ideas do not talk back, ideas do not lust for the unlikely, ideas do not carry away the professor's—what do they say, in comic books?—'date bait.' "

"You speak as though you are the abductor. The impression I gather from your friends, *mon bon Félix,* is that you are the abducted."

"If by my friends you mean Esmeralda and Oscar, they have their own points of view, their own reasons for jealousy and malice. I cannot really see why you are bothering to hector a student on the subject of his personal life. If you have a claim to exert over Miss Cunningham, or a proposal to make to her alternative to mine, then do so; otherwise, let her join in silence the ranks of your lovely one-time students."

"Your welfare concerns me as well as Candy's."

"Let me ask you this: were I a Swiss or a Swede or even a pale-skinned Tibetan, would you be so concerned? Would you, even if you were, presume to call me in, like some shoeshine boy who has applied the wrong color polish?"

"I resent your implication. I have friends of every race; I was a vocal supporter of the civil rights movement long before it became fashionable. I am a charter member of the Franchise Fair Housing Committee. The fact that you and she are black and white is not the issue. Your education here has been an utter waste if you imagine that it is."

"My education here has been strange," Félix told Craven, contemplating with loathing the toubab's dry, prematurely gray hair; his soft broad lips like two worms bloodless and bloated; his complacent, ever youthful eyes. This man, the African thought, sails on the black waters of the world's suffering; the future Elleloû announced, "Your warnings about myself and Candy are not altogether foolish. Nevertheless, I will take her with me."

"Why on earth?"

"Two reasons at least. Because she wishes it, and because you do not. She has asked to be rescued, to be lifted from the sickly sweetness of her life in this sickening-rich country and replanted in an environment less damaged. Though you would all, black and white, deny her this, I will grant it. I will grant her freedom, in the style of your heroes, with their powdered hair and rouged faces, the Founding Fathers; Liberty or Death is the slogan you fling from your ivied fortress, your so-called Department of Government; I fling it back, demonstrating that your instruction has not been entirely wasted upon me. I thank you, Professor Craven. Good luck in your Cold War, your battle against Sputnik. Good luck in your magnificent campaign of seduction of ignorant virgins, so as to avoid looking into the ravishing eyes of the loyal, sorrowing Mrs. Craven."

Craven's white face had gone whiter, realizing through the sweetish pipesmoke that he was closeted with a demagogue. The dictator, remembering the incident, one of a number of better-forgotten run-ins obstructing his departure with Candy from America, realized that Craven (who had given him, in petty retaliation for this interview, on a postcard that took seven months to arrive in the then Cailliéville, a B- for the course) had somewhat resembled the martyred Gibbs.

The Kush International Airport, a single runway east of Al-Abid, shimmers like a mirage amid the whistling-thorn. The tires of planes touching down frequently explode from the heat. Zebu, before the drought reduced the herds to hides and bones, were a sometime hazard. Now, the government has erected a two-meter aluminum fence to protect incoming visitors from the squalid, disease-infested emergency camps of refugee pastoralists from the deserted savanna. The glinting fence and the riveted wings of the Air Kush 727 and the great metallic sheet of cloudless sky contracted to pained pinpricks the pupils of the two Americans disembarking and exchanging greetings with the three-person welcoming committee: an oval-faced young Fula wearing a fez; a shorter plumper older African affecting Italian shoes, an English suit in the flared mod cut, and a wristwatch without a face; and a fetching if slightly stocky Sara woman accoutered in seersucker and secretarial half-glasses resting on her bosom, hung from a wildebeest-hair cord about her neck. Had the encounter been witnessed by an interested observer (instead of by the indifferent, wraithlike mechanics in sagging gray coveralls drifting through the

haze of hunger, heat, and jet fuel fumes) he might have
deduced that a reunion among long-separated kin had
been effected. In truth, there was a similarity between the
effusive welcomers and the greedily welcomed, though the
former were solid black and the latter all-American. There
were two, a man and a woman. The woman was blond,
not in the flaxen way of Candy but brassily, glintingly,
with a tinge of tangerine; her peach-colored suit was too
hot for this climate and a rose flush overspread her face
in the first minute, before she was completely down the
shimmering metal stairs. Shadows below her eyes, emphasized by dents near the bridge of her nose, testified to
the fatigue of her just-endured journey and perhaps to her
recently suffered grief.

This was Angelica Gibbs, whom I had widowed. For
all her fatigue, she gave off, in my vision of this encounter
where I was absent, that American freshness which never
ceased to delight my eyes on the McCarthy campus, that
air of headlong progress, the uptilted chin cleaving gaily
through the subarboreal shade, a freshness born of fear-
lessness born in turn of inner certainty of being justly
blessed with health and love. She winced but would not
wilt in the brightness of Kush—a constant lightning, an
incessant noon. She shook hands with Ezana, Kutunda,
and the (among his other titles) Acting Chairman of the
Board of Tourism. Her manner was polite, timid, tired,
tentative. Not so the manner of the man with her, a short
plump man with heavy lids, liquid and lively brown eyes,
a hairline mustache waxed to two thornlike points, and
graying hair parted as centrally as his mustache. His limbs
were short and his center of gravity seemed low, so that
nothing could topple him, not even the uproarious embraces of Michaelis Ezana as the two joked like spiritual
brothers at last corporally united, Klipspringer (for it was
he) egging the hilarity on with his farcical Arabic and

worse Sara. Kutunda was enchanted into guttural giggles by the apparition, out of the tinny-voiced telephone, of this magical man who had libraries in his pocket and who pretended the world was round as an orange. Mrs. Gibbs, her youthful face prematurely consigned to a widow's watchful sobriety, and the young Acting (among other responsibilities) Minister of the Interior, were the most reserved, but were willing, even they, to pin the enthusiasm of hope to this sun-swept intermingling, as the giant turbines of the 727 died, whined to a silence, and the less prestigious passengers—shabby Moroccan merchants carrying carpetbags, black chieftains as languidly scornful as rock stars, waxen-faced alcoholic Belgian mercenaries on their furtive way south, Japanese salesmen of telecommunication components, nationless agents of the hydrocarbon cartels, plump disaster bureaucrats from the UN, Jehovah's Witness missionaries from New Zealand, and other motes of the mercantile and messianic riffraff that has always drifted across the monotonously unanswered question our continent poses—poked their heads from the plane, squinted, and tumbled down the stairs.

"Welcome to the People's Republic of Kush," said Ezana in his Oxonian English accent.

"Looks like the country north of Vegas," Klipspringer told him. "My sinuses feel better already. Washington's a freezing swamp this time of year." He spoke with the pith of memos. "God!" He rapturously inhaled. "Heaven!"

He smoothed back his already smooth hair and beamed toward the aluminum fence, behind which children fought rats for morsels. There was no such thing as garbage in refugee camps.

Klipspringer's black counterpart, as if dancing for his life, which in a way he was, for he had arranged this meeting on sufferance of my interim appointees, made expansive ushering gestures toward the black official Cadillac which had been specially borrowed from the running dogs of Sahel for the occasion. The Mercedes was shadowing me, and the old official Citroën had ceased to go up and down on its pneumatic springs and rattled worse than a Dahomey taxi.

"In my country," Ezana told him, "there once were two seasons, dry and rainy. Now there is one."

"Where is the poverty?" Mrs. Gibbs asked Kutunda.

Kutunda looked toward Ezana to decipher the gibberish. "Nowhere," he prompted her in Sara. Presiding above this friendly confusion was the serene oval face and sleek fez of the Acting Co-ordinator of Forests and Fisheries, who now, having been rehearsed in some ceremonial English, bowed above the short, pink, hopeful, jet-lagged Americans and said with exquisite intonation, "Goodbye."

"Hello, he means," Ezana interjected. "A greatly gifted administrator, a superb student of the Koran, but untrained in your language, which is an exotic one to most of our people."

Hearing the word "Koran," this Chief of the Bureau of Transport amended his greeting, *"Al-Salāmu ʿAlaykum,"* and at the touch of these satin syllables Angelica Gibbs thrilled.

Dear lady, why are you one of this quintet gathered, in the haze of my mind's eye, to make alliance against Colonel Ellelloû, who wanders more kilometers away than there are footprints on the moon, seeking to isolate the germ of the curse on his land? *Can he who follows the guidance of his Lord be compared to him who is led by his appetites and whose foul deeds seem fair to him?* I "zero in" on your face, dear Mrs. Gibbs, you mother of fatherless sons, you trekker through endless supermarket aisles and gargantuan consumer of milk and gasoline. How can you hate me—me, a fatherless son? I am so little. Your face is vast; powder has silted into the pores; years have gently webbed your beauty; disillusion has subtly dimmed the once-blue lakes of your eye-whites, the sensitive black of your pupils; there is a girlish, anxious tousle to your hair. I want to hide amid its ruddy roots, from shame at having caused you distress, at having displaced your far-flung arrangements with the world, all the filaments of your careful socio-economic compromise at a blow wiped away. Your great face, conjured from afar by the mystery of your unctuous, scrambling husband's death, turns a moment, before eclipse within the shadows of the Cadillac, toward the miraculously blank Kushite sky; your face is then blanched by solar fury as well as fatigue, and I, your invisible enemy, see, beneath your lifted upper lip, halfway down one of your splendid American incisors, a tooth bared by a vagary of thought and incandescent in the sun, a speck, no bigger than a *bi,* no bigger than a dot on a *bi,* a speck of lipstick, a clot of blood.

As, both on foot now, amid the lengthening shadows of the hour of sunset prayer, we moved upwards to the domed cave, Sheba surprised me by talking. "My lord, my husband: must this be?"

"My dear Sheba, we have travelled to the verge of death so we may arrive at this point."

"So you say; but perhaps the travelling, our hardships and our survival of them, was what was necessary for my lord's purpose: to purify his life and redeem his land."

"If that were so, then rain would be falling."

"Rain in the Balak would be empty noise on stone: perhaps beyond the southern horizon, where the savanna waits to be green again, rain falls."

"When rain falls in Kush, my blood will know it."

"My blood, too, talks. It tells me to be afraid."

"What could my Sheba fear? Her President is with her, and the Mercedes follows always behind, with Mtesa and Opuku and their machine guns."

"My President, I think," the girl said, her coiffure restored and her necklace resplendent yet the normal elastic sway of her walk still hobbled, as she made her way with bent, reluctant steps, "has no cause to fear. He does not love his life, and such men travel enchanted through the adventures they bring upon others. But I, I have not lived two decades, and am a woman, and my life is of the earth; though I have given my blood to the earth, it has not yet given me a child, and such peace as I have must come in the chewing of kola nuts and khat, and in the music which lifts one's soul a little free of sadness."

"I am sorry you are sad. A thousand girls in Istiqlal would exult in the honor of your position."

"The honor has been empty, but I embrace it still. My lord is the touch of Allah to me. Even when my tongue was so swollen I feared I would choke, I adored him. But here, amid these strangers, at the mouth of this artificial wonder, we enter an area of transgression. I wish I were back on the streets of Hurriyah, digging the scene and thinking of nothing."

"You sense this is a trap. But I have no choice but to enter it. I am the key that must dare to lose itself in the lock."

"Forgive me, but I do not fear for you, but for myself. That raid by the Tuareg, I was not so dazed I did not wonder if it was not for me they had come. And then those Tuareg that gave us water, I felt their lust. Our caravan driver said, the Yemenis are starving for slaves. I have value, else my lord would not have stolen me from the streets."

Her shoulders gave a limp doleful shrug as I hugged her. "How foolish and conceited my little queen has become! Always thinking of herself! Anyway, the Yemenis keep their slaves now in little air-conditioned ranch houses, with kitchenettes, door chimes, and a rumpus room with a dartboard!"

Yet, though I tried to tease her fear to nothing, her fresh self-expressiveness—her attempt to become an independently anxious and defensive individual—sexually excited me, so that, that night, my member, adamant as an adolescent's, penetrated the gently resistant darkness of a woman, troubled and palpable in her fear. My explosion of seed felt engendering, as her hips heaved to receive me deeper, on the oversoft, antiseptic motel bed, and then rolled, instantly, into sleep. For an hour, I caressed Sheba's shoulders, sheathed shoulder blades, and relaxed buttocks as if tenderly to seal a pledge into her body. Of the events that followed none more enduringly torments me than my never knowing if my instinct was correct, and whether or not a little Elleloû, wrinkled, innocent, and indignant, nine months later bubbled into this world's scorching atmosphere out of my fourth wife's beautiful blue-black loins.

We had to spend the night because the cave was closed. Indeed we were lucky to find a room in the shabbily constructed tourists' lodge, with its paper-thin partitions and dubious desk clerk. As we had made the last turn on the golfcart path through the lengthening lavender shadows, the matching frocks and mocking glances of a pack of Northern European schoolgirls poured past us on either side, and beyond them we saw a green steel grate inarguably drawn across the cave-mouth, saying FERMÉE, مغلق, Θ, Закрит. In smaller type beneath, we read, OUVERT de 9h à 12h et de 14h à 17h30. *Billets d'entrée 50 lu.* At nine the next morning, therefore, having breakfasted at one of the concessionaire stands that had sprung up like fungi on the spot, vending croissants and caviar, teriyaki and chili, kebab and hot dogs from beneath a chorus of umbrellas, Sheba and I joined the polyglot, vacuously titillated crowd waiting for admission. Among its members I noticed Mtesa and Opuku, standing slightly apart in their uniforms, which appeared fresh. Under cover of the bustle as the green shutter-gate was slowly cranked upwards, and a clammy waft of cold air breathed from the mysteries within, I sidled up to Mtesa and asked, "How did you get the Mercedes up those gorges?"

He stared at me almost impudently; he was growing a little mustache. "No need," he said. "Broad road up from plains. Well-marked, all tourist services. You came scenic way."

A bell rang, and the crowd pushed forward. Sheba clung to my side in the jostling, sudden darkness. Concrete stairs and ramps alleviated but did not entirely eliminate the treacherous unevenness of the cavern floor. Small spotlights illuminated noteworthy graffiti and, at one spot, a cluster of Silurian mollusc fossils whose sea bed had been gradually lifted into this arid altitude. The oracle was situated in an artfully framed recess; chains held back the curious from close inspection. *La tête du roi,* which as we stared slowly gathered to itself a greenish glow derived (I surmised) from the illuminatory expressionism of the Moscow Arts Theatre, seemed at first one more rough, cracked rocky protuberance among the many others that filled the recess like buds of subaqueous coral, like the polyps the electron microscope reveals in the smoothest matter. Then its details dawned.

Edumu's head, so small in life, had grown larger in death. Its eyes were closed, its lips lax and drooping on one side, perhaps deformed by the force of its severance. I had never chopped off a head before, and one of the disappointments of the Tuareg capture had been my subsequent inability to check my craftsmanship. I had kept my wrists firm and paused at the top. The blow had felt smooth and well-angled, considering my state of nervous tension and the muscular inhibition it induces.

A wreath of white cloth, reminiscent of the old king's *lungi,* enwrapped the sliced throat, and a kind of altar of Plexiglas demonstrated with its transparence that no body existed beneath the head. The head's expression was, well, drab. I was reminded of the dusty relics of grandeur in his cell, though the symbolic riband of gold on his forehead took glitter from the rheostatted spotlight. His foolish ecstatic halo of wiry white wool had been tidied and diminished; undertakers never get the hair quite right. When Edumu's eyelids lifted, the crowd gasped and Sheba grasped my hand so hard I felt a metacarpal snap. The pain lost itself, however, in my wonder at the old king's shallow-backed eyes. The crazed pallor of the irises was unmistakably his, *but these eyes saw.* Rather than drifting skywards as they used to in our interviews, they focused out upon us—upon *me,* it seemed—levelly. Fighting down the vomitus of superstitious terror rising in my craw, I reasoned that in this detail the enemies of my state had forfeited credibility.

The head's lips moved with the slight stiffness of an engine starting in the morning. "Patriotic citizens of Kush," it creakily addressed the rapt crowd, "there is great evil among you. A greatly evil man, whose name is known to you all, and whose face is known to few."

He and I had chosen my name together, laughing, on an evening in the Palais when he thought the Revolution was a joke, and he would be released from detention when its first wave of bluster was by.

"This man," the head continued, the mechanical action of its lips now uncannily corresponding to the drifting way Edumu had talked, as if a kind of wind blew in and out of his heart, "pretends to unite the multitudinous races and religions of Kush against the capitalist toubabs, the fascist Americans who carry forward the cause of international capitalism on behalf of the world's rapacious minority of blue-eyed white devils." Yes, his voice had slightly shifted, in the drafty chambers of my associations, to that of the Messenger, droning on softly in Chicago's Temple Two, a little brown precipitate of centuries of wrong, a gentle concentration of hate.

The head kept talking, with a sudden shrill jump in the amperage of the electrical system that, I realized, was picking up and broadcasting the vibrations of the lungless voice-box. "This man, while proclaiming hatred of the Americans, is in fact American at heart, having been poisoned by four years spent there after deserting the *Troupes coloniales*. He is profoundly unclean. One of his wives is American, the wife who is called the All Wrapped Up. Because of his black skin, he was subjected to discrimination and confusing emotional experiences in the land of the devils, and his political war, which causes him to burn gifts of food and assassinate those functionaries who bring these gifts, is in truth a war within himself, for which the innocent multitudes suffer. He has projected upon the artificial nation of Kush his own furious though ambivalent will; the citizens of this poor nation are prisoners of his imagination, and the barren landscape, where children and cattle starve, mirrors his exhausted spirit. He has grown weary of seeming to hate what he loves. Just as nostalgia leaks into his reverie, while he dozes above the drawing-board of the People's Revolution so vividly blueprinted by our heroic Soviet allies, so traces of decadent, doomed capitalist consumerism creep into the life-fabric of the noble, beautiful, and intrinsically pure Kushite peasants and workers."

I felt the hand of a hack writer had intruded these phrases into the tape and exclaimed aloud the Berber

word for still-fresh camel dung. My neighbors in the
throng shushed me angrily, having been thus far held fascinated by the head's analysis of our internal difficulties.

"Wrongly," the head continued, with a new decibel
shift, dropping the voice into a more plaintive timbre,
"was I, a harmless and cynical figurehead at worst, sacri-
ficed to the welfare of the state. The head that should
have rolled belongs to Colonel Hakim Félix Ellelloû.
Even as his public self puts on a wrathful show of extirpating traces of foreign contamination, his private self,
operating upon the innocent vacancy of our sublime but
susceptible territory, engenders new outbreaks of the disease. Even now an entire American boom town, with false
fronts, brazen bubble-gum-blowing whores, and *pombe*-
dispensing saloons has materialized within the Ippi Rift,
above a reservoir of water stored in porous sandstone
since the beginning of time against the coming of the
Mahdi. Destroy this evil city, citizens of Kush! But unless
you destroy its source, the repressed affections and idle
dreaming of your shadowy leader, other excrescences will
spring up instead, and your children will continue to
harken to rock music, your wives will secretly desire to
expose their ankles, and your brother, with whom you
have shared your last curd of goat cheese, will succumb to
the profit motive and become a soulless robot of greed
and usury, a cog in a machine driven by economic forces
beyond all human appeal! Citizens of Kush: Overthrow
Ellelloû! Overthrow Ellelloû, and rain will fall!"

I looked about me to see a citizen of Kush, and of
course there were none to be seen, only foreigners, adven-
turers, curiosity-seekers whose minds had already darted
ahead to the next sight, the return to the bus, the proba-
bility of finding a rest room without a long line. The head
was concluding, its lips clearly out of sync, "This has
been a vision vouchsafed to me in Paradise, where the

veil is lifted from the eyes of men. It comes to you courtesy of Soviet technology. Thank you for your attention.
Feel free to wander about the cave, only do not touch the
prehistoric Saharan art work, which the moisture of your
breath is gradually eroding. For your further entertainment a slide show depicting the Kush national heritage
will be shown on the wall behind me."

Six

THE PRESIDENT, all later accounts agree, had endured the diatribe with dignity. Only when the slide show began did he forcefully intervene. Clad, remember, in the tattered *galabieh* of a desert wanderer—an assistant musician, a sideman—Ellelloû stepped over the chain while the first slides exploded from the projector: Kodachrome fixations of dunes, of peanut pyramids, of the hydroelectric dam beloved of Michaelis Ezana, of feathery tribal dances along the muddy Grionde, of pirogues, of shambas, of a camel ruminating and a muffled Targui glowering before the unexpected background of Istiqlal's East German skyscraper. Taking abruptly distorted fragments of these images on his back and writhing shoulders, he ripped the head by its fleece from its roots of color-coded wiring cleverly threaded through the top sheet of Plexiglas, which was perforated two-ply. Sparks—green, orange—flew. Fear and astonishment made a momentary circle of peace around the desecrator.

Edumu's head shocked Ellelloû's haptic sense with its

weight, far less than when filled with watery brains and
blood, and its texture, which combined those of paper and
wax, dead in such different ways. The skull had been enlarged, to receive so much mechanical and electronic apparatus: another Sovietism, the dictator reasoned—for
with their superior miniaturization techniques the Americans could have fitted all this into the skull of a mole.
Yet, despite the small distortion of scale, Ellelloû, hugging
the head to his chest to break the last stubborn connections, found tears smarting in his eyes, for in life this
head, mounted atop the closest approximation to a father
the barren world had allowed him, had never been held
by him thus, and the act discovered the desire. They had
been two of a kind, small cool men more sensitive than
was efficient to the split between body and mind, between
thought and deed. The king had prepared him to rule,
though it had meant his own ouster. "A king must be a
stranger," he had told his ambitious attaché. "His function is to take upon himself the resentment of his people
for their misery." *A king must be a stranger:* this truth,
peculiarly African, rustled in Ellelloû's own skull while
the desecrated other pressed its little fig of a nose, rubbery in reconstruction, against his hushed heart. Then the
affronted electronic engineers, and a motley guard clad in
indigo Tuareg robes and green soldiers' uniforms, burst
from their hidden places and encircled him with intent to
kill.

Russian, Wanj, Arabic, Tamachek were shouted; Ellelloû's *galabieh* was rudely tugged and Edumu's head
was torn from his arms, though the riband of gold, the
dwindled veil of a sacred presence, remained in his fist.
His captors, pressing close about him, had terrible
breaths: not only vodka but the spoiled yeast of native
beer and the sourness of millet porridge licked from dusty

fingers mingled fiercely in the captive's face, along with an unaccountable distant sweet tang, of barbershop hair-oil.

"*Je suis Ellelloû*," he said, repeatedly, for his first assertion was not heard, or else his accent was not understood. He was struck beside the ear; a scarlet numbness overspread his face from that portion; he was spat upon, mistily; his arms were pinioned and his wrists twisted as an unseen other struggled with his fingers for the golden headband.

The pressure ceased, the uproar was quelled. Opuku and Mtesa had stepped forward, gleaming in the nakedness of power, Opuku's machine gun a beautiful *mitrailleuse* after a design by Berthier, oiled like a Nubian whore, and Mtesa's .44 magnum scarcely less enchanting. A patriotic poster was unfurled beside Ellelloû's face; the crowd of tourists, comprehending little and cowering back from the violence, applauded as if this comparison were part of the show, of the Kush national heritage. Indeed, the slide show had automatically continued throughout, planting a Berber grin squarely upon the grimace of a furious technician, and the next instant projecting upon our struggle the pastoral peace of a herd of sheep overgrazing the Hulūl Depression. Due to the poor photogravure of the poster, my identity was unsettled until one of the Soviets came forward and shook my hand; I recognized, amid the cocoa-paste of his absurd disguise as a nomad, the shallow, tilted, alert, hunted yellowish eyes of his race. "Colonel Ellelloû," he said, "*je présume.*"

"Colonel Sirin," I remembered.

"Death to the people's enemies and revisionist counter-revolutionaries wherever they may be found," he said, through his translator, who had appeared at his side in the baggy costume of a bespectacled Maoist sightseer.

"Just so," I said, and nodded toward the dreary relic of Edumu IV where it lay on the cavern floor, one more piece of debris, debunked, inoperative, a prop at the back of the stage. "Have you asked yourself," I asked the colonel, "if your perpetration of this charade does not constitute a serious breach of the treaties between our two great democratic nations?"

The colonel shrugged and talked at Russian length, words that were translated as, "It is very boring, in the bunker. As part of *détente,* our government has instructed us to mingle more freely with the local populations."

"There was no population here, until your contraption attracted it. Even so, the audience is composed of daytrippers from Zanj, with whom our border will be henceforth closed. Your plot has served to put a little profit into old Komomo's pocket, but has left the loyal citizens of Kush unmoved."

"Not quite unmoved, Comrade; for the First Citizen of Kush has personally come far to attend to the oracle, as we knew he would." The colonel was shedding his shamed face and costumed unease, and his affectation of omniscience rankled in conjunction with the recalled ordeal of his bunker hospitality—his drunken toastmaking, his materialist clichés, his atheistical mockery. The Koran says, *Woe to those who debar others from the path of Allah and seek to make it crooked.* And the king had once advised me, *Enemies are a spiritual treasure, allies a practical burden.* In his swinish Slavic fashion my ally, confident that the joke of his devious interferences was now shared, debonairly lit a Космос cigarette, that went ill with his rags and his paint. It came to me that in addition to closing the Zanj border I should abrogate the missile treaty, as Ezana had often advised: thus I was thinking fondly of Ezana at the very moment, give or take a minute, when he was falling in love, over cocktails and freeze-dried peanuts, with Mrs. Gibbs, her brassy hair playing Ping-Pong with points of light in Mr.

Klipspringer's freely administered bourbon. The wires leading into my head were as many as those into the dismantled king's.

I told the smirking colonel opposite, "And the oracle spoke a great deal of facile, impudent, and traitorous nonsense, in the style of that messiah of bourgeois self-seeking, the Zionist Sigmund Freud."

"The oracle spouted not only psychology, but geography as well—did you not notice?"

"The rumor of the metropolis in the Ippi Rift I take to be as phantasmal as the gadget's analysis of the President's neurotic sublimations."

"Not a metropolis, but a small industrial city, of the type you call—" Consultation with his translator finally produced the word, "upstate."

"With variegated housing and charming recreational sites," the translator added.

"Not an encampment of beggars could exist there," I told them, "but that the Minister of my Interior would have informed me. In our sublime vacancy even the birth of a camel makes vibrations."

The colonel smiled, and flakes of cocoa-paste fell from his cheeks. "The Minister of your Interior you have judged, correctly, to be a traitor. Also he is a man who dislikes friction. Your Soviet friends, however, remain true to the Revolution. In alerting you to danger, we have gone to some lengths to avoid your official channels, which are rotten with revisionist spies."

Ellellôu saw that truly he must travel on, westward to the Ippi Rift; but as this new leaf of adventure unfolded before him he felt only an exhaustion, the weariness of the destined, who must run a long track to arrive at what should have been theirs from the start: an identity, a fate. His trip to the Balak had been, in its wantonness, its simplifying hardships, freedom; his trip down from the Massif, by the unscenic highway, in the air-conditioned Mercedes, without his beloved Sheba, heartsick duty. Sheba had vanished in the tumult that had surrounded his uprooting of the head; in what shadows and by what hands she had been seized remained mysteries. The Russians, anxious to dispel the suddenly hysterical President's threats of abrogation and anarchy, had assisted in the furious search. Every cranny of the cave was probed; the apparatus of audio-visual illusion was overturned; the technicians' lockers were ransacked, even the refrigerators in the cafeteria, even the caviar barrels. She was not in the cave.

She had been taken outside, then. The clefts of the rocks were searched, while pigeons wheeled overhead and Ellelloû in an agony of remembrance relived running his fingers along the clefts of her body, recalled amid the mineral wilderness the wistful thin melody of her *anzad,* the rounded perfection of her glossy shoulders and blue-black thighs, the velvet caress of her lips on his indifferent member, her stoned docility and soft intermittent plea that there must be a better life than this. The *taste* of her, Ellelloû remembered, the kola in her kisses and the salt of her female secretions that mixed with the alkaline dryness of borax when, on the dirt beneath the stars, he would perform cunnilingus. The fast food and soft drink stands were one by one overturned and smashed as at Ellelloû's command the Kushite soldiers the Soviets with usurped authority had enlisted joined the frantic search. *Divorce me,* she had begged, after telling him, *You make what I do seem very little.* The tourist buses, wheeling in the parking lots with their squealing loads of curiosity-seekers from Dorset and Canton, were halted, and the passengers made to stand with their arms above their heads in the now-vicious noonward sun, as small in the sky as a pea, as a white-hot bullet. "Beat them," Elelloû commanded.

"Rape them!" The soldiers, bewildered teen-agers fresh from the peanut fields and the fishing villages, attempted in their innocence to obey, but the beatings were feeble and the objects of rape, withered and twittery in their long-sleeved English gardening dresses and floppy rose-gathering hats, were unappetizing. Russian engineers, galvanized by Ellelloû's fury, went through the buses with measuring tapes and hand computers, hoping to deduce a space where the priceless bride might be concealed. Tires were slashed, windshields smashed. The drivers, detribalized Zanjians preening hitherto on their trousered power to steer machines bigger than elephants, were pummelled for the fun of it. "Destroy!" the dictator cried, to the consternation of the Soviet colonel. "Destroy everything in this vicinity not created by the hand of God!"

"But the concrete walkways—"

"Shall be reduced to rubble. All this was imposed without my authority; by my authority all traces of desecration shall be removed."

"We obtained permits," the Russian sputtered. "The new head of the Department of Forests and Fisheries—all forms in order—a boon to future travellers—Eurodollars." His translator was struggling to keep up.

"Travellers," Ellelloû sweepingly replied, "were never meant to trivialize these peaks. But find me my Sheba unharmed, Colonel Sirin, and we will let this amusement park endure as a memorial to the happy event. Otherwise by my decree its desolation shall forever objectify the desolation of my heart."

"I offer a theory," the translator said in his own words, whether couched in sloshy French or muddy Arabic, I forget. "There were among us some authentic Tuareg, acting as advisers, scouts, and regional experts." In the exhilaration of speaking his own thoughts he went on, "Do you know, some say—it is very interesting—the

Tuareg are descended from Christian medieval crusaders who strayed; hence their frequent use of the cross as decoration, and their chivalric refusal to work with their hands?"

"That is interesting," Ellelloû agreed. "Where are these *kafirs?*"

It was soon discovered, amidst the swirling dust of poured concrete being pulverized and immobilized buses being overturned, that there were only false Tuareg, that the true had fled.

"They will sell her to the Yemenis!" Ellelloû cried.

"If so," the translator offered, "that too is not without historical interest, for Yemen was, in Biblical times, the land of Sheba. Perhaps she will feel at home there."

She would have a kitchenette, a frozen food locker, a little ranch house with chimes for a doorbell and Muzak piped into the den. She would wear an apron and house slippers, she would learn to push a vacuum cleaner. She would forget him; he would shrink to the size of a *bi* in her mind. The strong man wept. Ellelloû ordered Opuku to line up all the tourists and machine-gun them.

His child, like himself, would have a rumor, a gust of wind, for a father. This fantasy, that he had impregnated the *disparue* Sheba, hardened to a conviction as, having left the contrite Soviets in charge of restoring their developed hectare of the Balak to its pristine condition, Ellelloû descended in the Mercedes westward toward the Ippi Rift. The hum of the highway dulled his ears. His mind was carried back to the times when he and Oscar X and some one or two others (such as John 46X, who had kicked the heroin habit with the aid of Allah, had tried out for defensive lineman with the Packers, and had shoulders as broad as Opuku's, so when he came along Félix had to sit in the back seat) would descend south from Franchise to worship at the temple in Milwaukee or, an hour farther to the south, the Holy of Holies in Chicago. The green fields of Wisconsin would swing past like the swells of a soft sea. The white barns and silver silos bespoke an America where they in their gas-guzzling, mufflerless Olds were a devilish impurity, black corpuscles cruising along America's veins, past heaves of soil that, though casual as the shrugs of an ocean, had been memorized by farmers' footsteps, generation after generation. Over the car radio came Doris Day and twanging country plaints and, as the city neared, Dinah Washington and the rickety, jolly, hot-from-the-cozy-dark black man's jazz. Those tinkling notes never failed to catch the edge of the wave. Set on a ridge with the pride of a castle, a gaunt gabled farmhouse kept company with its one big tree. Poverty had roofed a house here and there with a patchwork of discounted shingles six different colors. Félix was fascinated by the power-line towers, steel skeletons whose shape suggested giants daintily holding threads of pure force in tiny arms hanging straight down, insulators. The delicate grandeur of their latticed forms repeated to the rolling horizon, and in moments the swiftly altering perspective from the back seat stamped one upon the other; such moments, like those of *déjà vu,* were thrilling, with a resonance beyond their visual proof that the towers diminished along a perfectly straight line. And Félix felt a meaning too in the backs of billboards, visible on the left, slatted structures solemnly designed, cut, trussed, and nailed to carry a commercial message fleetingly; one billboard had a curved silhouette which a backwards glance revealed to be that of a pickle, and another the outline, ominous when seen from afar, of a steer advertising his own demise through the channels of a local steakhouse. In the occasional distance a water-tower stood on its long legs like a Martian invader puzzling what to do next. In winter these fields turned white, white sprinkled with the

black calligraphy of snow fences and leafless trees, a landscape as void of growth as the one his gray car was end-
lessly speeding through, gobbling one horizon only to be
faced with an identical other. At times the dictator
wanted to flog his country for being so senselessly vast.
The day arched like a blinding headache above their
endless meal of kilometers.

Ellelloû, alone in the back seat, his motionlessness a
mask for his suffocating struggle with the resurging, un-
downable fact of Sheba's absence, was slow to sense the
constraint in the car, a tension and disapproval emanating
from the back of Opuku's round bald skull, connected to
the mass of his shoulders by a glistening pyramidal neck.
Ellelloû recalled that he had never heard machine-gun
fire, though he had ordered some. He leaned forward and
asked, "The tourists—did they die well?"

Opuku held silent.

Ellelloû persisted, "Or did they die ignobly, begging
and cackling for mercy? Pigs." He quoted, *"When the
Hour of Doom overtakes them, the wrongdoers will swear
that they had stayed away but one hour."*

Opuku confessed, "I didn't shoot them. I told them,
Run away into the rocks. Those too frightened and feeble
hid behind buses."

Ellelloû, his heart engulfed by rhythmic waves of grief,
asked his bodyguard why he had thus betrayed
L'Émergence. The motions of his heart, when he focused
upon them, were like the attempts of a man with clumsy
mechanical hands to drown in a bucket of bendable, skid-
ding plastic a cat crazy to live.

"No betrayal," Opuku said. "Those poor toubabs just
dragged in by Zanj tourist package. Old ladies. Gentlemen
marabouts."

"Capitalist vermin," Ellelloû replied apathetically, gazing out the window at the streaming void. "Warmongers and exploiters."

"Slant-eyes too," Mtesa pointed out.

"Nixon-lovers," was the reply, still lacking in spirit. But he did not like Mtesa's siding with Opuku. Their little counter-revolution must be quelled. The President took his eyes from the congenial dun vacancy visible and sought to ignite with a spark of his old fervor the predictable kindling of his rhetoric. "You had the gun in your hands and their faces before you," he told Opuku, "and pity intervened. Pity is our African vice. We pitied Mungo Park, we pitied Livingstone, we pitied the Portuguese and let them all live to enslave us." A sickening clothy memory, of Sheba mounted on her pink camel in full regalia, squeezed his body down, so his discourse continued in a higher pitch. "Imagine yourself a statistic on a toubab's accounting sheet, and further imagine that by inking you out, you and a thousand others, he can save a dollar, a shilling, a franc or even a *lu* on the so-called bottom line. Do you imagine, Lieutenant Opuku, that *his* finger will hesitate to pull *that* particular trigger? No, the ink will flow. You will be Xed out by Exxon, engulfed by Gulf, crushed by the U.S., disenfranchised by France, not only you but your entire loving nation of succulent wives, loyal brothers, righteous fathers, and agèd but still amusing mothers. All inked out, absolutely, without the merest flourish of compunction. In the vocabulary of profit there is no word for 'pity.' So your squeamish refusal to follow my distinct orders was a laughable freak, a butterfly from the moon, speaking an incomprehensible language to these deaf and dumb earthlings, who have no hearts, whose bodies are compounded of minerals utterly foreign to your own elastic arteries and stalwart bones. These people consist entirely of numbers; pulling the trigger of your government-financed—I am obliged to point

out—machine gun, your superb Berthier *mitrailleuse,*
would have constituted an act of erasure impeccable in its
innocence, as well as being a gift of obedience pleasing to
your President, and a polite enough message that even old
addle-pated Komomo, the king clown of pan-African confusion, might have comprehended. Opuku, remember the
Book: *Mohamet is Allah's apostle. Those who follow him
are ruthless to the unbelievers but merciful to one another."*

Ellelloû sank back into the velour, exhausted. He
tucked little remembered bits of Sheba—her earrings, the
fleshy bump in the center of her upper lip—around himself like ends and corners of a blanket. But he could not
doze; the tension in the car remained. Opuku smoked a
plastic-tipped cigarillo, having sulkily removed the highly
crinkly wrapper, and Mtesa steered unswervingly through
the flatnesses of the Ihoö, a plain of hardened talcum
hammered to its present form by millennia of the sun's
stagnant fury. In such a world Ellelloû's mind could fashion no shelter for itself, though his eyelids closed. He saw
green fields, the slatted backs of billboards, and heard
Mtesa suddenly grunt.

"Another truck?" Ellelloû asked. He was resigned,
now, to such wonders multiplying.

"No truck, sir. Look to the left."

Perhaps seven kilometers to the south, a lost city shim-
mered—one of the red cities that, some archaeologists believe, the refugee royalty of conquered Kush erected in
what was then grassland. Others thought they were Christian monasteries, whose cells were later used to house the
harems of wilderness sheiks expatriate from Darfur. The
stones of the walls, blue-speckled bricks it takes two modern men to lift, are silent, and for all their solidity have
crumbled, so that at this distance, to Ellelloû's eyes,
which also were not what they once were, they suggested

that ring of fragile shred which remains when a wasps' nest is knocked down. Out of this ragged papery rim rose, still intact and scarcely weathered, hewn from imperishable indigenous stone, a monolithic stairway leading nowhere.

Meanwhile (to extrapolate), at a choice table of the Afrikafreiheitswursthaus the East Germans had installed on the top story of their skyscraper, Mrs. Gibbs, Mr. Klipspringer, Michaelis Ezana, Kutunda Traorē, and the young police spy in the plum-colored fez were enjoying a glittering luncheon. Ezana was happy, in his element among the twinkling imported cutlery and crystal steins, talkative, giddy on Liebfraumilch, and in love with the brassy-haired American widow, whose natural grief was underlined by stomach troubles and an ear problem originating in the imperfectly pressurized Air Kush 727. Ezana was showing off his African cynicism and gift of tongues, and though his coquetry was wasted upon its object, it was enjoyed by her benignly smiling, heavy-lidded, delicately mustachioed escort, the professionally patient Mr. Klipspringer.

"Your Mr. Nixon," Ezana prattled in his musical, trippingly accented English, "I do not think this Watergate matter should do him any harm. How could such a puny *contretemps* offset his stirring accomplishments of the last six months? He has ceased to bomb Cambodia, renewed relations with Egypt, created trustworthy governments in Chile and in Greece, provided himself with a new Vice-President as tall and handsome if not as eloquent as the old, and enhanced the American economy by arranging with the Arabs to double the price of oil. Truly, a charismatic dynamo, who has fascinated the American people again in the workings of their own democracy."

Klipspringer chuckled. This man, what good nature, what tireless tact! "Maybe so, Mike," he allowed. "But from where I sit he looks like a loser."

"Indeed, a loser in a narrow sense; but reflect upon the purgative value of a leader who unravels before a nation's riveted eyes. If he falls, he will carry your nation's woes with him into the abyss. Twice recently, if I mistake not, your federation has been humiliated, by the North Vietnamese with their mortars, by the Arabs with their embargo. What more poetic and profoundly satisfying"— here he bestowed a dazzling, ignored smile upon the American widow, who was studying her plate wondering what, exactly, had gone into this sausage—"psychotherapy, if my term is correct, than the evisceration of a President, out of whom tumble in majestic abundance tapes, forgeries, falsified income taxes, and mealy-mouthed lies? This is theatre in the best African tradition, wherein the actor is actually slain!"

"Your own President, where is he?" asked Angelica Gibbs, prodding herself out of absorption with her own, obscurely troubled interior.

Ezana translated the inquiry into Sara for Kutunda and Fula for the man in the fez, who both laughed, that wicked bubbling African laughter connecting directly with the underworld; it rang in Ezana's ears as a permutation of his own intoxication with this tired-looking, diarrhetic angel who had come from afar to sit opposite him across the Afrikafreiheitswursthaus's laundered linen.

Instead of answering her, he lifted a fork before his face and said through its thoughtfully twirled tines, "The channels of the mind, it may be, like those of our nostrils, have small hairs—cilia, is that the word? If we think always one way, these lie down and grow stiff and cease to perform their cleansing function. The essence of sanity, it has often been my reflection, is the entertainment of opposite possibilities: to think the contrary of what has been customarily thought, and thus to raise these little—cilia, am I wrong?—on end, so they can perform again in unimpeachable fashion their cleansing function. You want examples. If we believe that Allah is almighty, let us suppose that Allah is non-existent. If we have been assured that America is a nasty place, let us consider that it is a happy place."

"It's the place for me," Mr. Klipspringer cheerfully interposed, "and I've been to Hell and gone. When I see that old soapy-looking Capitol dome from the window of the jet, I think, *This is it. This is me.*"

Ezana would not cease his flirting with the poor fatigued Mrs. Gibbs. "Now your President," he informed her, "is a master of such alternations of assumption. Let us suppose, he says, that China is not a bad place but a good place, a friendly place. We have many pleasant Chinese restaurants in the United States, he reasons, perhaps China is equally pleasant. Or let us suppose, he says, that the way to rule is not to lead and inspire the people but to hide from them, to absent oneself increasingly, like the ancient Tiberius, who frolicked upon his island while Jesus Christ was spreading subversion—are my facts correct?"

"I never heard it put quite that way, Mike," Klipspringer said, closing his lips then upon the wetted end of a Cuban cigar, which had cost him twenty *lu* in a basket shop where stacks of them were rotting, and crossing his eyes to ignite the other end with a propane-flame lighter. The man in the red fez noticed the lighter with admiration, and Klipspringer passed it to him. "It's yours," he said, with a soft chop of his manicured plump hand. And, with further delightful gratuity, blew a perfect smoke ring, that came spinning from beneath his pert mustache like a new-fangled missile.

"Our President also," Ezana continued to the pallid American beauty, "rules by mystical dissociation of sensibility, if I understand the phrase. Leaving the development of a plausible pragmaticism to those of us that stay behind in fallible Istiqlal, he explores the wider land for omens, to discover the religious source of the drought."

The man in the red fez, who was growing to understand more English than the others expected, interrupted with a spate of local language to which Ezana listened at first amusedly, then with some gravity. By a smart soft chop of his hand the speaker indicated he wished Ezana to translate.

"He says," Ezana told Klipspringer, "there is no drought. The nomads have survived many worse, by loaning their cattle to sedentary farmers in the south and reclaiming them when the dry sahel recovers again. The introduction of the cash-crop economy at the behest of the French has made this system difficult. The farmers no longer traffic with nomads, they need paper money to buy their wives' Japanese sandals and transistor radios. And he says furthermore the well-meaning white men drilled wells and vaccinated against rinderpest, and this increased herd size to the point where desert was formed by the livestock. He says there is no drought, just bad ecology."

Klipspringer's eyebrows were elegant silvery structures, trimmed but not overtrimmed, riding up and down on the emotions behind his brow like the vessels of Ra on eddies of spirit. They had arched high, lifting his heavy careful lids; in the space thus cleared his liquid brown eyes poured forth to the faces at the table all their luminous gift of caring. His baritone trembled with emotion. "Mike," he said, "you tell the man for me, No problem. Our technical boys can mop up any mess technology creates. All you need here is a little developmental input, some dams in the wadis and some extensive replanting with the high-energy pampas grass the guys in the green revolution have come up with. You have a beautiful country here, basically, and we're prepared to make a sizeable commitment to its future. You tell the man we're very sensitive to the ecological end of things, not to worry. They were worried in Alaska and now they've stopped worrying. The caribou've never been better off. Miracles are an everyday business for our boys."

"I want this murderer brought to justice!" Mrs. Gibbs suddenly cried from the depths of her sorrow and impatience, her queasiness and interrupted sexuality. "I want Don avenged." Baring her teeth, she exposed a fleck of lipstick on one incisor.

Klipspringer put his hand adroitly over hers. "Angelica, revenge isn't part of the international picture. Internationally speaking, revenge is a no-no. What we have instead are realignments."

"Madame is a guest of the state," Ezana reassured her. "It pains me to think she should be denied anything she desires in Kush."

Kutunda, jealous of her former patron's infatuation with this freckled she-devil from the land where ice grows downward, launched into a long story of how she had been taken captive by Ellelloû; he had broken into her hut where she slept, the chaste daughter of a widely respected *dibia,* and had desecrated her body with his urine so that, unmarriageable, she had no choice but to become his concubine. He kept her in a closet, illiterate, and compelled her to perform unclean acts; he even refused to give her typing lessons. The young man in the fez, whose Sara was nearly as good as his Fula, expressed rapture at her telling; he choked back his laughter, lest he miss a word. Ezana's Sara was not fluent enough to follow the torrent of vigorous and redolent idioms, and he contented himself with saying brusquely, at the tale's end, to the white widow, "This lady, a cultural attaché, also has grievances against our President. It is regrettably true, he has committed many unpopular actions in the last half-year. His inspirations are not always happy. He put to death our old king, whom many of the river-folk superstitiously venerated."

"Where is he? Where *is* he?" Angelica all but screamed.

"He has ventured, you might say, upon a good-will mission," Ezana said, glancing at the black face of his wristwatch, as if space as well as time were packed into its shallow depths, like life in a coil of DNA. "It is hard to say where."

"Where—iss—*ee?*" the Acting Minister of the Interior suddenly enunciated, in halting but vivid English. "Ee—iss—*here!*"

Everyone laughed, except Mrs. Gibbs, and Ezana turned to Klipspringer. "Let us discuss what you call our expanding relations. If the Braille Institute is to be built, it must be by local laborers, enlisted from our new masses of the urban unemployed, and following an indigenous design, in conformity with African humanism."

The American diplomat lowered his eyelids and rounded his cigar ash on the rim of the plate holding a few discreet shreds of sauerkraut and the rubbery tied ends of his consumed knackwurst. "You bet," he said. "Maybe with a little *souk*like string of shops, boutiques and travel agencies, nothing noisy, along the ground-level mall. We want to help you become yourselves. A settled identity is the foundation of freedom. An unsettled nation is an enemy of freedom. A nation hates America because it hates itself. A progressive, thriving nation, whatever its racial balance and political persuasion, loves America because, frankly, in my not so unprejudiced opinion, but the facts pretty well bear me out, America is downright lovable.

America loves all peoples and wants them to be happy, because America loves happiness. Mr. Ezana, you and the boss-man here"—his hand chopped toward the wearer of the plum-colored fez, who obligingly smiled and underneath the table squeezed Kutunda's knee so hard her own smile widened with pain—"may wonder why the American revolution has lasted nearly two hundred years, and yours is limping after only five. The answer is, All our Founding Fathers promised was the pursuit of happiness. Our people are still pursuing it, they'll never catch up to it; if they did, they'd turn right around and blame the Revolution. That's the secret, if you follow me."

"Ed, cut it out," Mrs. Gibbs said. "What are you doing about Don?"

"We're working on that," he assured her. "First you said you wanted his ashes, now you want revenge."

"There is a city," Ezana offered, "perhaps prematurely named, we might instead call Gibbsville."

"Where is this city?" she asked.

A spark of communication ran around the ring of faces, and Ezana sadly confessed, "We are not at liberty to divulge."

She looked at her companions at the table and saw through her tears black faces smilingly sealed upon secrets, secrets.

Ezana looked at her and saw beyond the brassy toss of her hair, through the tilted plate glass set there to make a panorama around the restaurant, at such a height the city no odor or peep of misery could arise, Istiqlal to the southeast: the bristling rectilinear business section directly underneath the skyscraper, narrow polychrome boxes whose sides were scrawled with lettering in many languages including even the native Hindi of the shopowners; the rows of camels and bicycles tethered and parked in the clay square of the Mosque of the Day of

Disaster; the mosque itself, its minaret a dusky phallus, its
dome a blue-tiled breast; the boulevards the French had
diagonally cut through the maze of mud rhomboids and
irregular alleyways; the dead chestnuts and poplars lining
the boulevards and resting like a tenebrous cloud upon
the pastel villas of Les Jardins; the scrappy glinting quilt
of the shantytown at Al-Abid; to the left, the airport and
the slender road to Sobaville; to the right, the venerable jumbled hump of Hurriyah lifted like a coy shoulder
into the rosy cliff of the west wing of the Palais de
l'Administration des Noirs; beyond, the *souk* and the
rickety dock and the pirogues; and farther beyond, a
black curve of the blue Grionde. *I love you, I love you*
ran through Michaelis Ezana's mind dizzily, and the white
woman's weary queasy face, the merriment arising between the red fez and Kutunda's bleached hair, the American's blanketing gray confidence that all would be taken
care of—all merged in this embracing, spiralling, panoramic feeling. In Kush, the politics of love was being
born.

The Ippi Rift is a global curiosity that hides itself
among the valleys of Northern Europe, belches forth its
tensions at Mount Etna and the Valle del Bove, slips
beneath the Mediterranean, and continues south to the vicinity of Johannesburg. Astronauts in their orbits see it
plainer than China's Great Wall. Those who live in it do
not see it at all. According to the theory of continental
drift, the Rift marks the line along which Africa will
eventually break in two—not, as would seem from a human standpoint sensible, along an east-west axis, so that
the Islamic/Caucasoid third would separate from the predominantly Negroid area south of the fifteenth parallel,
but longitudinally, with all our latitudinal diversity of race

and climate not only preserved but duplicated. The lengthy fault, whose incidents include the Øresund, the political division of the Germanies, Lake Tanganyika, and the Kimberly diamond fields, excites geological aberrations, and there have long been rumors of oddities— oases, rumblings, auroras—in its vicinity as it cleaves the otherwise featureless desolation of central Kush.

Nevertheless, the President of the nation was surprised, on the second day of his droning, mournful ride with the sulky Opuku and the evasive Mtesa, by the bulge of emerald that jumped through their windshield at a turning of their descent, in second gear, down the steep, pink-gray slope of the Rift's eastern bank.

In some parts of the world this green would have been a simple suburban lawn; here it appeared with an evil intensity, as a sudden face of Roul. Back upon the lawn crouched a menacing fabrication, a low "ranch" house, a façade of bricks gratuitously whitened in splotches and of aluminum siding that feigned the wooden condition of clapboards. Similar, though not quite identical, houses were arrayed along both sides of this road, which had become one of those curbed asphalt curves real-estate developers dub "crescents." Lawn sprinklers hurled rainbows against the crystalline aridity of the air. Otherwise there was no sign of life, not even a lone postman. The children must be at school, the housewives at the supermarket. Or else the whole development was a mock-up constructed to torment him. Ellelloû felt a skimpiness, a threadbare nameless something as of those towns that come and go while the passenger dozes above the road map in his lap and the driver fiddles with the radio, seeking a non-religious station. *As for the unbelievers, their works are like a mirage in a desert. The thirsty traveller thinks it is water, but when he comes nearer he finds that it is nothing. He finds Allah there, who pays him back in full.* Too soon, considering the spaces the city-builders had at their disposal, the crescents yielded to an unlovely straightaway with supermarkets and trash dumps and low windowless go-go dives. In the front seat, Mtesa and Opuku were becoming noisy; they had never before seen gasoline stations with plastic twirlers, or ice-cream stands in the shape of a sundae cup, with a painted cherry on top doubling as an air-conditioner vent. Or the golden parabolas of a MacDonald's, a meagre hutch of an eatery dwarfed by both its monumental self-advertisement and its striped lake of a parking lot. The sight of these wonders at first caused them to mutter and then to jubilate aloud, hilariously, as people will laugh with terrified exhilaration when immersed in the mist and tumult of a waterfall.

The straightaway thickened into a drab little "downtown," with pavements and traffic lights. Here, the sight of their countrymen wearing cowboy hats, blue jeans, tie-dyed T-shirts, and summer-weight business suits provoked even louder delight, infuriatingly, for Ellelloû was trying to plan his attack, to screen out the superfluous, to concentrate. He put on his NoIR sunglasses. The Mercedes had slowed to a stop-and-go crawl. A young girl, younger and coarser than Sheba, but with a touch of the ruminating insouciance Ellelloû painfully remembered, strolled past beneath the awnings, beside the parking meters, wearing an apricot halter tied high, tattered denim cut-offs the buttocks of which were patched with two faded cotton heart-shapes, and shiny-green platforms ten centimeters thick at the heels. She was chewing bubble gum with all of her brain.

Opuku leaned out and called to her in demotic Arabic, "Where you goin', little girl?"

"Wherever you ain't, fat man," was her answer, capped

by a popped bubble, which sprung forth fresh hilarity from the two soldiers.

The girl, who had delivered her rebuff with yet that languid provocative sideways tug of the eyes that Kushite women affect in potentially compromising social intercourse, was strolling past the window of a *cinq et dix,* and the ill-assorted muchness of its windows—the gimmicky, plasticky, ball-and-jacky, tacky, distinctly dusty abundance of these toys, tools, hobby helps, and cardboard games—agitated Ellelloû's breast with the passion to destroy, to simplify, *to make riddance of.* His hands trembled. He tried to reason. This excrescence in the heart of Kush was not lava, it was an artifact, a plurality of artifacts, that had been called here by money. Where money exists, there must have been pillage: Marx proves this much. There must be capital, exploitation, transmutation of raw materials. In a word, industry. Where there is industry, there is machinery, delicately poised and precariously adjusted. This poise, this adjustment, can be destroyed, and the whole devilish fabric with it. There was a blue-collar stink to this town. Franchise had been cleaner, with its breezy lake, its ivied sanctuary. Many of the men on this street wore oily coveralls, and some affected aluminum hardhats.

Ellelloû bid Mtesa stop the Mercedes before the entryway to an Army and Navy store, which, he discovered within, catered principally to the proletarian fads of youth, and was so far, here in the Ippi Rift, from the centers of distribution that its stock, especially for a man of Ellelloû's precise and wiry stature, was absurdly limited. In exchange for his khaki uniform—the Galla trader behind the counter was happy to have it, for the sheen and softness acquired during natural wear cannot be machine-imitated, and is much prized by the young—and several thousand *lu* Ellelloû obtained a pair, not of the greasy gray coveralls conspicuous on the streets but of blue bib overalls stiff with newness and double-stitching, an antique pith helmet in lieu of a hardhat, and a lemon-yellow T-shirt upon which were stencilled the words *Left Handers Are Easy to Love*. Thus attired, the dictator commenced, as was his way, to mingle with his people, leaving Mtesa and Opuku illegally parked in a loading zone.

The Saharan sun beat down dryly upon the twinkling conveniences of this doomed suburb of nothingness. Ellelloû felt this doom blazing within him. Thirsty, he entered a corner drugstore. It was cool within. Tall phials of colored water symbolized the healing magic of pharmaceutics. A rack of sunglasses stood dim with dust, untouched. The commercial contents of the shelves were a mere scattered shadow of the merchandise of the drugstore in Franchise. Lest the reader imagine that the disembodied head's facile diagnosis of the dictator's supposed psychotic condition was here being borne out by an hallucinatory echo of Franchise, Wisconsin, he should understand that this city was in every respect inferior to that prosperous lakeside paper-town; it was a Third-World stab at an industrial settlement, scarcely a block deep on either side of the main "drag," thin of soil and devoid of history and shade trees, its citizens transparently African, its commercialism sketchy and even, one could say, humorously half-hearted. Franchise was to this place as a fondly pruned and deeply rooted hydrangea bush would be to a tumbleweed.

The druggist, a tall black Hassouna in the traditional high-buttoned antiseptic jacket, glanced at the disguised tyrant's pith helmet with amusement. "Allah is good," he said. "How can I serve you, sir?"

"I am thirsty," Ellelloû explained. "Do you have a soda fountain?"

"Such frills went out of modern use years ago," the druggist explained, "when the minimum wage for soda jerks went skyhigh. You are living in the past, it seems. A machine that vends cans of soft drinks purrs in the rear of the store, next to the rack of plastic eggs holding gossamer panty hose. Take care, my friend, not to drop the pull-tab, once removed, back into the can. Several customers of mine have choked to death in that manner. We call it the Death of the Last Drop."

"I also, effendi, need advice," Ellelloû told him, less timorous now that he had caught something of the man's accent and style. For all its brave show of consumer-goods, the shop seemed infrequently visited, and its keeper had not lost the desert love of conversation. Words will bloom where nothing else does. Ellelloû confided, "I am looking for useful work."

The druggist lifted his elbows and polished the top of his case with his hands, which were long and limp as rags. "What sort of work might the gentleman be able to perform?"

The dictator was at a sudden loss. Fakir, digger, orange-peddler—his costume corresponded to none of his priorly assumed professions. He thought of Mr. Cunningham, his patchy florid face, his starched white shirts. He said, "I am in the insurance racket. I am a claims adjuster."

"I have heard of such men," the druggist admitted. He straightened up with startling briskness, as if suddenly awakened to the possibility that this stranger might be a hold-up man. His voice took on a solemn hollow threatening tone. "Well, sir, around here, the only work is to be had at the wells. Without the wells, and the toubab know-how, this would still be wilderness. You have heard, I dare say, of the wells?"

"Of course," Ellelloû lied.

"A tremendous natural resource," the other solemnly affirmed, having relaxed again, and replaced his tattered elbows upon the glass case, which his dusting had revealed to contain packets of candy-colored condoms and a fan of cream-colored vibrators, like smooth flashlights searching in all directions. "Hydrocarbons," the druggist intoned. "That is the future in a word, sir. The path away from poverty, the redemption of the nation. Gross national product, balance of trade, you know all these terms, I am sure. They might well have need for a man of your experience, sir. I have heard tell of accidents amid the machinery, of near-explosions. I recommend that you apply, and my *baraka* go with you. Would you like to freshen up on your way to the personnel offices? Some deodorant, a swig of mouthwash? Personal hygiene counts for a lot with these infidels. God sees the soul; men smell the flesh."

A wearisome fellow, really. A nation of shopkeepers is a morass of pleasantries. Woe to the economy that puts its goods on the rack of petty mark-ups. *Nationalize,* Ellelloû thought furiously. *Nationalize.* He asked, "How do I find these wells?"

"You follow your nose, man. Where have you been living, beneath the ground?"

"I have come from the Balak," the traveller apologized. "I have been a long time tracking down a claim. Permit me one more question, of a simplicity that may astonish you. Pray, what is the name of this town in which I find myself?"

The druggist indeed looked astonished. "Ellelloû," he said. He straightened again to his height before the banked Latinate myriads of his medicine-shelves, his dried herbs, his poisons distilled from convolute carnivorous flowers, his love-potions, sleeping potions, antihistamines, and diuretics. *"Ellelloû,"* he boomed, with the volume of a muezzin calling. "Our national independence leader, a god descended to us to fight for our freedom, a great man whose iron will is matched by his penis of steel." The druggist leaned far over the counter and whispered, "I trust you are not among those who with the archtraitor Michaelis Ezana conspired against the purposes and teachings of our inspired head."

"I am a simple apolitical professional man," the disguised dictator replied, with dignity, "seeking employment in the midst of a drought."

"No drought here, my good man. Our peerless leader, whose enemies foreign and domestic gnash their teeth in vain, perceived that the Rift, in its geological contradictions, would trap all life-enhancing fluids—water and petroleum, to name the foremost two."

Ellelloû had the irritating impression, from the discontinuous vigor with which the druggist adopted one manner after another, of a systematic insincerity that might relate (it occurred to him) to his failure to make a purchase. Still thirsty, but embarrassed and anxious to be off, he said in farewell, "God is good."

"God is great," was the disappointed answer.

Outside, the Saharan sun pounded down upon the faded awnings, unlit neon signs, and brick false fronts of the Avenue, a sign proclaimed, of the End of Woe. Ellelloû entered a luncheonette, narrow as a running man's stride and every surface of it coated with a film of wiped-away thumbprints and spillings. He ordered a lime phosphate, which he drank up with a single long lunge through the straw. The short-skirted waitress read his T-shirt and giggled. Her face was ugly—her teeth stuck straight out—but her legs were firm and smooth and the color of good healthy shit. He ordered a second lime phosphate and took it to a booth. Each booth had a mock-ivory selector for the jukebox at the back of the luncheonette, and he was surprised, flipping its yellowed leaves, to recognize some of the songs: "Sixteen Tons," by Tennessee Ernie Ford; "The Rock and Roll Waltz," by Kay Starr; "Blueberry Hill," by Fats Domino; "My Prayer," by the Platters. This last he could almost hum, as green fields and silver silos skimmed by. He began to feel bloated with flavored carbonation. And the Formica tabletop depressed him, its oft-wiped smoothness too much like the blankness of the sky. Ellelloû got up, paid, tipped the waitress a *lu,* and left. As he went out the door, the jukebox began to play, very scratchily, "Love Letters in the Sand."

A siesta emptiness possessed the streets. At the intersection where the Avenue of the End of Woe met another, an oblong traffic island held a statue of himself in bronze—even his sunglasses and bootlaces in oversize bronze, his face deep in shadow, his *képi* and epaulettes whitened by guano—within a fountain, whose rhythmic surges of water tossed upwards veils and ghosts of spray that evaporated before the droplets could fall back into the stone bowl from which these patient explosions were fed. Around the rim of this great bowl the nation's twelve languages spelled their word for Freedom. In Wanj there was no word, all of life was a form of slavery, and this gap in the circle of words children had worn smooth, clambering to frolic in the water. There were no children now. They were captive in school, he imagined, thinking of how aptly this fountain symbolized the universe, that so dazzlingly and continuously pours forth something into nothing. Sinuous green growth of a Venezuelan density flourished in the lee of the fountain, whose wafted breath licked him like a tongue as he crossed the shimmering intersection. Alone on the pavements with his sharp small shadow, helmeted and baggy, Ellelloû followed his nose. The shopping district thinned to barbershops and grimy-

windowed printing emporia with cases of their alphabets
gathering dust beside the quiet presses. Low cafés and
pombe bars awaited the after-hours wave of worker clien-
tele. Single-bladed ceiling fans desultorily turned within;
there was sawdust on the floors, and big green bottles
keeping cool under soaked burlap. An odor met his nostrils as sulphuric even, as caustic and complex, as the
scent of the lakeside paper mills in Franchise. There, too,
there had been, along the approaches to the industrial
heart of the place, its satanic *raison d'être,* this multiplica-
tion of trailer-homes with bravely set-out windowboxes
and birdbaths, ever more overwhelmingly mingled with
low cinder-block buildings enigmatically named or in
naked anonymity serving the central complex, which was
enclosed in apparent miles of link fence hung with scarlet
signs warning of high voltage, explosive materials, and
steep fines for even loitering on the fringes.

Ellellou approached this fence and looked in. Across a
large margin of macadamized desert that made absolute
dimensions difficult to grasp, a dark heap of slant-roofed
sheds, inscrutable chutes, black-windowed barracks, tapered chimneys, towers with flaming tips, and rigs for
pounding pumps belched forth a many-faceted clatter and
the oceanic chemical stench of hydrocarbon refining. The
ball-topped fractionating towers, the squat storage tanks
were linked to their underworld source of supply by a silver spaghetti of parallel piping. Little pennants of burn-off
flame adorned the construct like a castle. Though Ellellou's eyes spotted few human figures, which perhaps in
this uncertain scale would have been invisible, the whole
monstrous thing was delicately in motion, eating something from the soil and digesting it into a layered excrement palatable to the white devils worlds away. Beyond
and above the stinking, smoking, churning, throbbing
emissary of consumerism, the lavender western wall of the

Rift, too precipitous for any road, too barren for any life, hung like a diaphanous curtain behind which waited like a neglected concubine the idea of Kush. But Ellelloû could not smell the desert. Everything in the land his heart knew had been erased, save the blank sky, its blue so intense it verged on purple, overhead.

He moved along the fence, through the litter of drained cans and discarded brown pay-envelopes, until he came to a guard post, a plywood shack no wider than a telephone booth, and asked the man slumped in there for admission.

"Show me your pass."

"I have no pass, but I have business inside."

"Those at the main gate will determine that. What sort of business? You are dressed like a fool."

"I have a claim to adjust. I am a claims adjuster. There has been an accident inside."

This guard, a long limp Moundang in an unclean burnoose, studied him suspiciously. "There's been no accident here."

"From my mother I inherited the gift of foresight, maybe the accident is soon to occur," Ellelloû replied, and was about to improvise an ingratiating fable when he recognized the other man. "Wadal!" he cried. "Wadal the well-digger—have you forgotten your servant? We met north of the Hulūl, in Ramadan, and together we repelled the American infiltration."

From within the hood of his burnoose Wadal studied me with deepened suspicion, and placed his hand on the rifle in the sentry box. "I remember much confusion and smoke," he said. "And my Kutunda being taken from me."

"Kutunda for whom you had no use, and whom you had taken from another, and who in turn has been taken from me, by one who will not keep her long. You exploited her because you have been exploited. Let me in,

Wadal, and we will bring these desecrators and exploiters of the poor to justice. There is fuel for much smoke here."

He was still trying to fix me in his mind, as, emerging from the shadows of his tent, a traveller squints to distinguish mirage from mountain. "You claimed to be Ellelloû," he said, "and were clumsy with a shovel."

"I was clumsy because you chose unworthy places to dig. But now your nose has led you nobly. How did you come to this place? How long has it been here? How is it capitalized, and who provides the expertise? Who is its manager, its president?"

"We never see him, and we never ask," Wadal said, still unfriendly, the gun brought in close to his body. Through a rent in his burnoose I glimpsed his penis, languid. "He feeds us and pays us, and that is enough. He generates employment and boosts the gross national product. A few more wells, and we will be another Libya, another Oman."

"Another Bayonne, another Galveston," Ellelloû replied. He commanded, "Admit me to this inferno."

Instead of obeying, Wadal lifted his rifle as if to strike with the butt. A happy spark, the prospect of righting an old imagined wrong, lit his morose face from within; but at that moment a gray Mercedes in the silence of its perfect workings slid by on the crackling, littered gravel alley that ran beside the fence, and Wadal lowered his weapon. Ellelloû waved the car on, and turned his back upon the guard, having formed a more visionary plan than brute coercion wherewith to secure admission.

He went back through the streets of this new world named for him, into the barbershops and drugstores, the economy furniture outlets and the *cinq et dix* stores, the *pombe* bars and real-estate offices, the dens where men labored to repair electrical appliances engineered to be irreparable and the cinemas where numb heads pondered giant pink genitals laboring to symphonic music, and El-lelloû asked the citizens of Kush he found in these places, "Are you happy?" When their embarrassment produced a silence, or a grunted "What's it to you?" or a defiant "Yes" or an equally defiant "No" or an evasive measured response, he pursued the issue, saying, "Those who are not perfectly happy, follow me." And some did, though many did not, and some others were drawn along with the crowd, attracted by its promise of excitement, its air of destination, for they led lives of relative prosperity yet were kept by the very nature of the economy, its need to justify production by exciting consumption, in a low fever of dissatisfaction and ill-defined hopefulness. This little brown man, with his attractively fanatic military bearing in his crisp and absurd costume, fed that hopefulness, as does a comet, a mass murderer, a state lottery, an albino camel, or any other such remission from the hunger pains of the ordinary. With a mob at his back Ellelloû de-manded admission at the main gate.

Wadal must have alerted his employers of impending trouble, for a number of armed, uniformed guards were assembled behind the padlocked pipe-and-wire gates, and a toubab had been produced from within the insidious al-chemy of the oil works. He was short and pink and flus-tered; he wore a button-down shirt with rolled-up sleeves and had several pens clipped to the pocket. In the past, some had leaked, leaving blue spots. This was a mere desk-worker, a timid engineer, an agent of agencies in dis-tant cities of glass. He was no taller than I, and his eyes peered levelly into mine through his rimless spectacles and the electrified mesh. "You want work?" he asked.

"I want justice. We want reparations."

"Uh—think you've come to the wrong place. Hasn't he?" He made this inquiry of a tall black Nuer who had appeared beside him, clad in a three-piece checked suit of some slithery synthetic summer stuff, his shoulders wide as a buzzard's wings, a clipboard in his hand.

"You bet the punk has," this black man said, and told me, "I'm in P-R here. What's the story, buddy?" His brow bore the Nuer scars but his American English was smooth.

"I am Ellelloû," I told him.

"Sure, and I'm O. J. Simpson. You don't look so easy to love to me."

"The shirt is not my message. My message is, Justice, or Destruction."

"How about that? What sort of justice you have in mind? Big justice, little justice, or justice of the peace?"

"Justice for all. These citizens of Kush behind me claim to be imperfectly happy."

"So that's news? They sure as hell busted their asses to get here. Look, I don't know how well you know the local situation, but it's not exactly a hotbed of alternatives. We don't ask 'em to come to us, we fight 'em off. This is a pilot project, we're trying to keep it low-profile."

Ellelloû wearied of looking upwards at this slangy front man; he spoke to the plump white devil. "By whose authority was this project established?"

"Everybody's, as I understand it. We deal with the Ministry of the Interior, mostly. The President's a canny type who's lent his name but keeps his distance otherwise. The initial contacts were finalized before my time; they only keep us here a year, it's considered hardship duty. My company's cut of this operation is peanuts, but the top brass back in Texas has a soft spot for the Third World. The chairman of the board came up from a turnip farm."

"This isn't business," the P-R man interposed, a bit

stiffly, in unspoken rebuke of his superior's garrulity, "this is phil*ant*hropy."

Ellelloû asked the toubab, "You are yourself not top brass? What is your title?"

"Engineer's my title; recovery's my racket. A new strike like this is an oddball at this late date, better recovery in the established fields is the name of the game. Hydraulics and fluids have been my life. It's a miracle, what you can squeeze out of a rock if you know where to pinch it. There's enough water down there in domes to flood the Hulûl."

"And the oil? Is it O.K.?"

"Beautiful," said the engineer, chattery with the relief these infidels feel when discussing their work in avoidance of emotional or ideological issues. "It comes up so sweet you could gargle it. Prettiest sludge I've seen outside of Oklahoma. You know oil? When you crack most crude by the Burton process—"

The P-R man interrupted. "You are wasting your time with this man. He is a terrorist. He has no interest in real information."

"Anyway," the toubab lamely concluded, reluctant to leave his specialty, "your Mr. Ezana, he's pleased as punch, and he's got reason to be."

The crowd, bored by a technical conversation they could not hear, was beginning to chant, "Ellelloû, Ellelloû. . . ." The P-R man with his winglike shoulders and Nuer brow scars correctly scented danger in the situation, though he pretended not to recognize his President. At his command a small army of harried, bearded boys had appeared bearing a tangle of wires and an assortment of electronic boxes—loudspeakers, transformers, tuners. This system was set up on the parched earth. When the connections had all been made, he took up a hand mike of the phallic type, with a glans of soft black rubber, *whoofed* into it experimentally, and, satisfied, spoke:

"Ladies and gentlemen, workers and independent tradesmen, all citizens of Kush irregardless of tribe and tint: return to your homes and places of business. This madman, no doubt inspired by religious impulses he deems genuine, has misled you with a vision of unreal happiness. Your hopes of real happiness, that is to say, a relative absence of tension and deprivation, lie not with absolutists and charismatics but with an orderly balance of capitalist incentives and socialist mediations. Joyously allow foreign capital and expertise to combine with your native resources and ingrained cultural patterns." He consulted his clipboard, and continued: "The African humanism of your forefathers, as over against the antlike societies of Asia and the neurotic sublimations of the Christian West, urges upon you the ideals of patient cheerful labor, intuitive common sense, and a many-stranded web of kinship ties that reinforces rather than dilutes individuality. Do not, ladies and gentlemen, yield your priceless personhood to destructive gestures by alleged saviors. There is no God, though you are free to worship as you wish, as you are free to indulge in bizarre sexual practices with another consenting adult."

The speech went on too long, not so much for the crowd, which, ceasing to chant "Elleloû," had fallen under the spell exerted by oratory in our still predominantly oral culture, as for the American, who, natively impatient, of short attention span, and anxious to make an impression of himself as a genial and forceful fellow not prone to "stand on ceremony" and permeated with a sense of "fair play," took the microphone from his eloquent assistant and awkwardly boomed into it:

"Open the gates, we're not afraid of these good folks.

Industry's been a fine friend to this oasis, and by golly we intend to continue to be!"

The gates were swung open, the mob laughingly pushed through. The young technical crew hastily relocated their equipment and unsnarled the wires, and in the confusion Ellelloû—gently, as if lifting a little burden from the pink hand, a flower or libation proffered in homage—took up the microphone himself. It was as if he had seized a gun; he became potent; the crowd halted, conceding him a little stage of bare earth. His heart was pounding; his hand, holding the instrument, looked to his own eyes small and magically withered. He was beset by variable mental winds. The thought of Sheba returned to him—her dull betrayed eyes sought his from within a crush of cloth and coral—and with it a weary soft awareness of his lack of a woman, a woman who would lull him out of anger and put him to bed. But then he began to talk, and the breath of his throat as it leaped the inch between his lips and the spongy tip of the microphone was in his ears taken up by an amplified echo that seemed to blanket the world and impose a hush upon all its multitudinous contra-indications, and his heart was at peace in the center of the storm of his voice:

"Citizens of Kush! You have been grievously betrayed! You have been led by the atmospheric machinations of Roul the desert devil, in league with the dead hand of Edumu the Fourth and the living perfidy of Michaelis Ezana, to dwell in this pestilential hellhole called Ellelloû! *I* am Ellelloû! *I* am freedom!" He took off his pith helmet, to show his visage. The cheering was less than he expected. The P-R man had made a move to grab the mike, but now stood idly by, close, checking the integrity of his manicure, whistling through his teeth in an impudent attempt at distraction.

"What is freedom?" Ellelloû went on. "Can you put it

on with chains, can you hold it within stone walls, behind steel doors, in the circumference of electrified fences?"

"The fences are electrified for the safety of juveniles and stray dogs," the P-R man swiftly whispered.

Ellelloû spurned the clarification, urging into the amplifying system the swollen self-answer, *"No.* These heavy material things do not bestow freedom, they bestow its opposite, bondage. Freedom is spirit. Freedom is peace within the skull. Freedom is righteous disdain of that world which Allah has cast forth as a vapor, a dream. The Koran says, *The mountains, for all their firmness, will pass away like clouds.* The Koran asks, *Have you heard of the Event, which will overwhelm Mankind?* Freedom is foreknowledge of that Event, whose blazing light is the only true light, whose fire melts our chains and evaporates the walls of our impoverished lives!"

The P-R man muttered at his side, "Make your pitch. We can give you five more minutes."

Ellelloû said, and the microphone turned his words into clouds, scudding above the choppy black sea of the faces of the crowd, "You see at my side a bought black man, dressed in a white man's suit and taught to mouth the white man's glib tricknology. You see at my left an authentic pink devil, as apparently mild as the first suck of milk a baby lamb takes from its mother in the misted dawn pasture, but in truth as poisonous as the sting the scorpion saves for the adder. You see at my back a monstrous pyramid, foul in its smell and foul in its purpose, a parasite upon the soil of Kush and a corrupter of its people. As your President I command you, as your servant I beg you, to destroy this unclean interloper. A few well-aimed bullets should do it. The conflagration will lighten your hearts forever, and become the subject of a song you can sing your grandchildren!"

"He's advocating violence," the white man said, behind Ellelloû's back.

"He's got to be kidding," the P-R man reassured him. He held up three fingers where Ellelloû could see them, to indicate to the orator that, by some arcane rigor of technology, only three minutes were left to him.

"The beast behind me, drinking the sacred black blood of our earth, belching smoke and blue flame, and defecating the green by-products of petroleum," Ellelloû enunciated into the microphone, "is a mortal creature like any other, and I advise that my soldiers direct their first bullets into its jugular vein—that is, the exposed conduit removing the volatile gasoline vapors from the top of the fractionating tower, below the condenser ball." He wondered at himself, that he could spout all this; it was like holding live coals in the mouth, all it took was saliva and faith.

Yet the soldiers did not shoot. They stood in their green uniforms within the motley crowd, innocent bemused boys from herders' tents and grass huts, waiting for an apparition they could take an order from.

Ellelloû strove to become that apparition, with only his voice and two more minutes of electricity to lift him above the mass. The crowd, in its still good-humored bafflement and wishing perhaps to touch the fabulous electronic equipment, which in flaking gilt bore the name of a now-dismantled, drugs-scuttled rock group called Le Fuzz, crowded closer, menacingly close. As he tried to gather his inner forces to speak, he was aware at his back of the P-R man and the white engineer scratching quick memos—contingency plans, "scenarios"—to one another and also of, high in his nasal passages, an incongruous odor overriding the chemical stenches of industry. The smell had a penetrating sweetness, it carried with it woolen clothes and falling leaves and rosy Caucasian cheeks, it was, yes, the fresh glazed doughnuts the Off-Campus Luncheonette peddled to students as they sought a refuge from the sub-zero Wisconsin cold on mornings between classes. The doughnuts were laid out on waxpaper, still warm from the baking, their dough so cunningly fluffed it melted to a sugary nothing in the mouth, leaving flakes of glaze on the lips—how could that scent, forerunner of the taste, be present here, so vividly that Ellelloû, in this pause of his oration, salivated? No snack-cart for the workers was visible; yet the scent lived in his nostrils. And in his ears the scratching pencils of his enemies. These distractions joggled the fragile chalice holding the distillate of his message, his cosmic indignation, and prevented, perhaps, from being as good as it should have been this, the last speech of his public career.

He returned, in a low-pitched, factual voice, to the theme of petroleum by-products. "What does the capitalist infidel make, you may ask, of the priceless black blood of Kush? He extracts from it, of course, a fuel that propels him and his overweight, quarrelsome family—so full of sugar and starch their faces fester—back and forth on purposeless errands and ungratefully received visits. Rather than live as we do in the same village with our kin and our labor, the Americans have flung themselves wide across the land, which they have buried under tar and stone. They consume our blood also in their factories and skyscrapers, which are ablaze with light throughout the night and as hot as noon in the Depression of Hulûl! My people: in my travels, undertaken only for love of you, that I may better bear your burdens, I have visited this country of devils and can report that they make from your sacred blood slippery green bags in which they place their garbage and even the leaves that fall from their trees! They make of petroleum toys that break in their children's hands, and hair curlers in which their obese brides fatuously think to beautify themselves while they parade in supermarkets buying food wrapped in transparent petroleum and grown from fertilizers based upon your blood! Of your blood they make deodorants to mask their God-given body scents and wax for the matches to ignite their death-dealing cigarettes and more wax to shine their shoes while the people of Kush tread upon the burning sands barefoot!"

A new scent, also sweet but astringent, had arisen; he groped to identify it, while returning to larger, more spiritual themes:

"Such are the follies of a race that scorns both Marx and Allah. The world groans beneath the voracious vulgarity of these unbelievers. They suck dry vast delicate nations in the service of the superfluous and the perverse. The earth, misconstrued as a provider of petty comforts and artificial excitements, cannot but collapse into a cinder, into a gnawed bone whirling in space. Hasten that Day of Disaster, blessed soldiers of our patriotic army, and shoot the giant slave of grease mercifully in the throat, and restore this ancient Rift to its pristine desolation, beloved of Allah, the wise and all-knowing!"

Ellelloû identified the odor that had intruded: it was of the pink, "sanitizing" cake of soaplike substance that reposed within the bottom lip of urinals in the men's "rest" rooms of some American service stations and restaurants, and which had puzzled young Félix until he had been acclimated enough to understand it intuitively.

"You may say these wells have brought water. I say the Almighty could have made a river flow in this Rift. You say grass grows here now, where sheep can feed, and date palms, and orange trees, and what cannot be grown is purchased. I say, the Sahara once was altogether green, and the Merciful bestowed upon it a superior beauty, the beauty of the minimal, the changeless, the unpolluted, the necessary. The battle now in the world lies between the armies of necessity and those of superfluity. Join that battle. God has placed in your hands today the power to pulverize and incinerate this evil visitation, this malodorous eruption!"

But had he, intuitively or otherwise, understood its essence? The pink cake of strange substance, no doubt petroleum-derived, had sat across the porcelain slots meant to carry urine away; what purpose did this obstruction serve? A spiritual purpose, that of a talisman, a *juju*, an offering to the idea of purity.

"You say," he called into the microphone, which now seemed the narrow neck of a great echoing calabash trumpet, "that life here is hard and the drought has made it harder. I say, the unclouded sky mirrors the unclouded heart of Kush, the heart released from the tyranny of matter. *Magnify your Lord, cleanse your garments, and keep away from all pollution.*"

The devils behind him were still consulting. The crowd, whose depths and reaches he could not see, felt to his sense like a sail on far-off Lake Timmebago, at that instant when either the wind would catch, bellying the sail out taut, or else, the wind's drift having been misjudged, the sail would luff.

"My people: your President has carried our drought in his heart heavily, it has nearly dragged me down, until I made this recognition: the drought is a form of the Manifest Radiance, and our unhappiness within it is blasphemy. The Book accuses: *Your hearts are taken up with worldly gain from the cradle to the grave.* The Book promises: *You shall before long come to know. Indeed, if you know the truth with certainty, you would see the fire of Hell: you would see it with your very eyes.* Come, my people, let us build a great pyre. The white devils and their machinery have entered by the gate of our weakness, our wandering and unsteady dedication to the ideals of Islamic Marxism, the beauty of L'Émergence, the glory of Kush that was the envy of the Pharaohs and anathema to the Christians of Axum! Redeem your wandering, my people! Destroy this vile temple to Mammon! Soldiers, shoot! Ellelloû orders you to shoot!!"

In the answering, teetering silence, the P-R man's voice muttered, "O.K., that's plenty." The microphone was pulled from the dictator's hand. The P-R man said into it, "The management has a question I'm sure everybody here would like to hear your response to. The question is, What makes you think you're Colonel Ellelloû?"

"It shall now be proven," he said serenely, and waited for the crowd to give way before the irresistible certification, the Presidential Mercedes.

But the crowd failed to move as a single thing, as a sea pushed aside; instead, each head oscillated expectantly, amusedly, while the minute yielded no unifying phenomenon. Ellelloû stood on tiptoe, then attempted to jump himself higher by placing a hand on the P-R man's winglike shoulder. He saw neither Mtesa nor Opuku—no, on the third leap, there was Opuku, standing as a passive spectator just outside the fence with, the fourth jump revealed, the gum-chewing girl in the apricot halter. Of Mtesa and his Mercedes there was no sign, except possibly the scarlet letters, quickly faded to salmon in the Sahara sunshine, atop a ramp-riddled concrete structure, spelling PARK.

Beyond this sign, the sky was blank.

The crowd, as no omen materialized, began to rumble, cheated. The white engineer—his face glazed with perspiration and the parallel harrow-marks of a comb fresh in his thin pale hair, hair the color of the dung of a sick goat—said into the indispensable microphone, "Whaddeya think, good people? I think we've given this fella his chance. Any of you folks thirsty, you can have one free beer each at the commissary, to the right of the front door as you enter. Don't push, there's plenty for everybody."

"This is treason," Ellellôû managed to shout, his last official utterance, before the crowd with murderous jubilation rolled over him. He became a beanbag, a toy. The wells continued to pump, and on the other side of town the lawn sprinklers continued to twirl. A little cloud covered the sun.

Seven

*The struggle between man and fate is
a totally alien concept to Arab culture.*
—SAHAIR EL-CALAMAWY, 1976

I LIVE. Perhaps the white devil's offer of free beer saved
my life, for the crowd was in too much of a thirsty hurry
to halt and pummel me with the annihilatory zeal my
address had attempted to instill. One cracked rib, a fat
lip, the removal of my shoes, the bestowal of a quantity of
derisive spittle, and they were through with my body. The
life of a charismatic national leader cannot be all roses.
My wallet, with its rainbow of *lu,* its snapshots of my four
wives clothed and my mistress Kutunda in the nude, its
credit cards and plastic perpetual calendar and embossed
national air alert codes and Brezhnev's unlisted telephone
number, had also been lifted, and no doubt this semeiotic
treasure-lode enriches the arcana of some light-fingered
ex-nomad secure in his niche in the burgeoning oil industry. A little picturesque behanding would set the rascal
straight, I think—but then my judicial opinion is no longer solicited.

To be barefoot and walletless in Kush, in even this
modernized pocket of it, is to be at no very striking disad-

vantage. A few days and nights of soggy mendicancy, while the monsoon rains pattered down with their pre-Émergence verve, and during which I was kicked from more than one melting doorway by the property-proud burghers of Ellelloû, served to adjust me to the fact that I had indeed been abandoned by my bodyguard among the masses with whom it had once pleased me whimsically to mingle. After the loss of Sheba, such a fall followed as one segment of a telescope brings with it another, slightly smaller. No one to blow me, no one to bow to me. *Takbīr!* I was driven to look for work and shelter amid the happy mud. In my student need across the seas I had held a variety of lowly jobs—"nigger work," in the friendly phrase of the lily-white elite of Franchise.

The very luncheonette where, in the twilit last hours of my Presidency, I had treated myself to not one but two lime phosphates, hired me as a counterman, once I had demonstrated sufficient mastery of the junk cuisine with which the iron-stomached Satans of North America are poisoning the world. Cheeseburgers, baconburgers, pepperburgers; fried eggs in all their slangy permutations of ups and downs and overs; hash browns, onion rings, and hot pastrami were all within my repertoire at the sizzling, curdling grill. Egg rolls and pizza arrived frozen from the poles of Marco Polo's travels, needing only to be warmed. "Hero" sandwiches were cannibalized by my customers, who still believed, primitively, we become what we eat. From six to two, or from two to ten, I chopped, flipped, served. I juggled the orders in a rolling sea of music, for if the customers did not feed the ivory tune-selectors, Rose, as the toothy leggy waitress was called, did. She was a maddening hummer-along, and yet disappointingly unco-operative in other respects: my attempts to seduce her fell on barren soil—her hard-packed determination to achieve, with her husband Bud, upward mobility. They

lived in an aluminum box on the edge of town, equipped
with a chemical toilet and a fold-away kitchen sink. Once
this domicile was mortgage-free they planned to sell and
move onwards to a two-and-a-half-bedroom ranch house,
with one-and-a-half children. The next stage of escalation
would be a two-and-a-half-story fake-beam mock-Tudor
overlooking the sixth green of the golf course, while Bud
squirmed upwards through the greased tubing of the refin-
ery. Such progress in husbanded half-steps was freedom
to Rose, and my sidling attempts to drag her off the band-
wagon into my anarchic arms were as idle as an attempt
to seduce a locomotive from its tracks. No virtue as iron
as that forged on the edge of poverty. When he came into
the luncheonette, Bud, a big Moubi with arms that could
have hurled a spear seventy meters, sat with those mighty
arms meekly folded on the godless Formica as he stared
up into the spectral works of a hierarchical machine, his
lips pinched in unconscious imitation of the white man's
scolding visage. They shared, as she slaved, one dream.
Her only straying was in her head, as the lukewarm melo-
dies bathed our ears in their moony ache day after day.
Kush was the last stop on a long descent through levels of
national development; these records, their grooves
scoured of all but hoarse ghosts of song, had taken twenty
years to reach the Ippi Rift from their source in the
America of the Fifties. Over and over, hearty, hollowly
healthy voices blended with violins toward an uplifted climax of pre-rock wail, a ululant submission to the patriotic, economic call to sublimate. "Love Me Tender," the
youthful Presley requested; "Cry Me a River," Johnny
Ray begged; "Que Sera, Sera," Doris Day philosophized,
her voice snagging each time on some thorn in my soul.
The regal voices of Grace Kelly and Bing Crosby lightly
entwined in the drifting waltz of "True Love," and Deb-
bie Reynolds as delicately lisped of her clinging attach-

ment to "Tammy." There was, too, in counterpoint to these feminine trailings-off, a choral, masculine voice: "The Yellow Rose of Texas," "The Happy Wanderer": when these rousing tunes surged from the well of time, Rose and I slapped the plates down harder and shuffled more swiftly behind the counter (never failing, it seemed to me, to brush hips tantalizingly—was this altogether my doing?). "A Whole Lotta Shakin' Goin' On," Jerry Lee Lewis assured us, ecstatic as a dervish. Even the grill grew hotter, the fast food came faster. And when the whistling section of "The River Kwai March" penetrated us, we knew, knew in our bones, that we would win the Cold War. Freedom, like music, rolled straight through the heart. Oh Rose, my Secret Love and Queen of the Hop, my Sugarfoot Standing on the Corner amid Autumn Leaves, my Naughty Lady of Shady Lane, in this chronicle too crowded with vexed women yours is the unique aura of happiness, of the bubbling, deep-fat aroma of productive, contented labor, as hoped for by Adam Smith.

Ellelloû, known to his co-workers only as Flapjack, served as a short-order cook for three months, before grease burns compelled him to take employment as a parking attendant in the city's one multi-level garage. It was here, he imagined, that Mtesa had hidden the Mercedes at a crucial hour; but the car and the driver were gone, and the oil spots on cement were indistinguishable clues, and the girl in the apricot halter had vanished with Opuku. Yet one day, in a concrete nook at a turning of the third-tier ramp, he found, wrapped in a *tagilmust* like a baby in bunting, Sheba's *anzad*. The gift seemed a gentle enough irony. He smiled; like any believer, he was not affronted by the notion that he was being watched. He, who had always been chauffeured, became ruthlessly deft in the reverse-gear rearrangement of automobiles, mostly old chrome-heavy guzzlers from Detroit's Happy Times, well into the second revolution of their odometers and their dents beyond counting.

Meanwhile, through the two months of Jumādā, in this season the Tuareg term Akasa, rain continued to fall upon Kush, rain enough even for a namesake of Noah's grandson. Sweet grass grew tall in the vacant lots of Ellelloû and in the millions of hectares around; the cattle of the pastoralists fed so handsomely their weakened legs snapped, and the herdsmen toppled to the earth with excess of festival dancing and millet beer. The very bones strewn parched upon the sands put on flesh and gave milk; seeds dormant several millennia hurled toward the serried nimbus giant blossoms and bulbous fruit absent from even the most encyclopedic botanic handbooks. All this, Ellelloû thought sadly, I achieved by ceasing to exist. *I* was the curse upon the land.

National news was hard to come by in the Rift; the local paper was boastfully devoted to parochial concerns: oil prices, OPEC conferences, the end of the embargo, new shopping centers in the area, zoning regulations to control the housing boom. No report of any coup was heard in Ellelloû, where all civic projects, all literacy programs and health clinics, all paving, sewering, and dedication of parkland were carried forward in the name of the national leader who, with the grand elisions of historical myth, had singlehandedly and as it were simultaneously crushed the French, the king, and counter-revolutionary elements within SCRME. Events widely separated in time and causation, and some of them set in motion when I was a mere foot soldier and foreign student—the *loi-cadre* proclamation, de Gaulle's imperious withdrawal from *La France d'Outre-Mer*, the constitutional-monarchial interval, the revolt led by General Soba, the expulsion of the

neo-*colons,* the incineration of Gibbs, the execution of the
king—had been lumped and smoothed into one triumphant sequence whose signature was the green flag,
whose climax was the green grass swaying like an ocean
beneath the benevolent gray sky. Allah was mighty, immovable, and undiscernible; so was President Ellelloû;
praise him.

Anonymous within the bustling *polis* that had absorbed
my name, I searched the papers for news of myself. Page
two sometimes carried bulletins from the capital—as far
away, remember, as Rome from Amsterdam, as the
Crater Copernicus from the Lacus Somniorum. They
referred always to a vague "People's Government" as it
issued a vigorous barrage of new wage incentives, tax holidays for foreign investors, relaxations of import tariffs
and tourist visas, official welcomes extended to Israeli experts in drip irrigation and USAID malnutritionists, pre-
liminary plans for a cantilevered Braille Library to be
imposed on the center of Istiqlal, and other such political
promiscuities savoring much of the trusting nature and
unholy energy of Michaelis Ezana. Toward the end of my
tenure as burger chef, beneath an item hailing the arrival
of a team of Dutch specialists in flood control (I imagined
them with whitened, waterlogged thumbs), a snippet of
fine print said,

> Colonel Ellelloû, President-for-Life and Supreme
> Teacher, has been away from the capital on a
> fact-finding mission.

And so in a sense I was. Working by day, strolling the
streets by night, I spent much time contemplating my fel-
low-Kushites, as they had developed in this isolated oasis
of plenty. They had lost, make no mistake, the attractive
muscular lightness of alert predators, the leanness that
balanced them upon the land as airily as our maidens bal-

ance bundles of tamarisk faggots upon their heads. People
no longer looked carved, as they had in the village, in the
army, and even in those early days of independence and
monarchy in Istiqlal. These bodies sauntering along the
Avenue of the End of Woe, clothed in a decaled denim
that did for holidays as well as labor days, had been less
whittled than patted into shape. A loss of tension, of
handsome savagery, was declared also in their accents,
which had yielded the glottal explosiveness of their abo-
riginal tongues to a gliding language of genial implication
and sly nonchalance. There was no longer, with plenty,
the need to thrust one's personality into the face of the
person opposite. Eye-contact was hard to make along the
damp sidewalks of Ellelloû, where puddles took tints from
neon signs. The little hard-cornered challenges—to honor,
courage, manliness, womanliness—by which our lives
had been in poverty shaped were melting away, like our
clay shambas and mosques, rounded into an inner reserve
secret as a bank account; intercourse in Ellelloû moved to
a music of disavowal that new arrivals, prickly and hungry from the bush, mistook for weakness but that was in
fact the luxurious demur of strength. The business of oil,
of the businesses that clustered around the business of oil,
pre-empted the mental spaces formerly devoted to battle
and ritual, to death and God, so that these last two came
to loom (I suspected) as not only strangers but monsters,
unthinkables, like the abstruse formulae of science
whereby oil was lifted from its porous matrix and its
tangled molecules sorted into saleable essences. The
volume of mysteries upon which men float had been displaced, but the shimmer of small amusements and daily
poetries, the sly willingness of people to be pleased, appeared perennial. I, submerged in posthumous glory, immersed in the future I had pitted all my will against,
relaxed at last. Often I arose early, conveying my frame

with its clinging dreams to the luncheonette or to the concrete spiral of the parking garage; on my way I witnessed the droll earnest children being herded to school by the educational imperatives of the industrial state, dangling their schoolbags and clutching their books, solemn in their confidence that a grave thing was being asked of them, and that by obediently responding they were creating a nation. Their figures, uniformed, some of them, in green—our Kushite green, no longer an arid remembrance of Green Sahara but here, all around us, in the flourishing grass—seemed mute in the early morning, little figures silent as in a painting, collecting in clots at the bus stops. One does not know what it is to love a country until one has seen its children going off to school.

I was accumulating my earnings and assembling my shattered poise toward the inevitable return to Istiqlal. In the second month of my employment at the parking garage, when I had been promoted to the man who takes the ticket and the *lu* and releases the striped wooden arm at the bottom of the ramp, an idle task that leaves much time for reading, another item appeared on page two of the daily *Rift Report:*

> The Government today acknowledged official fears that Colonel Ellelloû, Chairman of SCRME, while seeking to negotiate the phasing-out of Soviet Russian missile sites within the Hulûl Depression, has been abducted by leftward-leaning terrorists.

So the ground for his official extinction was being prepared. The President decided the moment had come for his return. As he hitchhiked south with Sheba's *anzad* strapped to his back, the sky brightened, as if blanching in dread of his return to power. A truck carrying bales of last year's Parisian fashions—shantung hip-huggers, seethrough jumpsuits—from Algeria to the *souks* and bou-

tiques of Istiqlal picked him up. The driver was a young
Belgian seeking a better quality of life. The cab radio interrupted its playing of *La Plus Haute Quarantaine* to re-
peat a bulletin that the President, long missing, had been
presumed dead, and the Acting President with reluctance
and sorrow had taken up the reins of government. To
formalize his succession of Ellelloû, which of course is the
Berber word for "freedom," the new leader had assumed
the name Dorfû, an expressive Salu term with the double
meaning of "solidarity" and "consolidation." The national
anthem was played, followed by the theme song from
2001, by Richard Strauss.

Actually, the Salu *dorfû* has the root meaning of "croc-
odile-torpid-on-the-riverbank-but-far-from-dead," as dis-
tinguished from *durfo,* "crocodile-thrashing-around-with-
prey."

Michaelis Ezana and Angelica Gibbs were having dinner with Candy and Mr. Klipspringer. Candy had un-
wrapped herself and, out of purdah, looked, in a sensible
yet snug gray wool knit dress with a single strand of cul-
tured pearls, much what she was: an attractive woman
nearing forty who had survived an unfortunate first marriage. Mrs. Gibbs, on the other hand, was resplendent in a
crimson and mauve *boubou,* and she had hidden her
brass-blond hair in a matching headcloth. Her tan, acquired at the poolside of the reopened Club Sahare, where
the punctilious ghosts of colonial officers made way for
basking Dutch hydrologists and the brawny steel-workers
assembling the adventurous skeleton of the Braille Library, would never be mistaken for the complexion of an
African, though she now imitated the slit-eyed, careful,
side-long expression of native women. She was squatting
on a packing crate of self-help books and asking Candy,

"How can you bear to leave? The smells! The pace! For the first time in my life, I'm one with my blood. God, how I hated America, now that I think about it. Do this, do that. Turn right on red only. Rush, rush. Those dreadful slushy winters—they'll kill you."

"I'm only afraid when I see my first snowfall I'll die of bliss."

"Say, hasn't this rain been something?" Klipspringer exclaimed, rubbing his thighs to emphasize his enthusiasm, his tirelessness, his unflappability. "Right into August, wow!" The party was in farewell of him too. He had done his job here: established rapport, contacts, and a basis for expanded relations. His Arabic was now fluent, his Sara acceptable. He was wearing a dashiki purchased in Georgetown, D.C.

Ezana tilted his head, so his round cheeks gleamed in the light of Candy's candles, the sole illumination remaining in her stripped, fixtureless villa. "And yet," he said, "it has not rained for a week. I think it an uneasy omen, this return of the sun."

"Everything's mildewing," Candy said. "I tried to burn my furniture and it stank up the neighborhood."

"All the flowering shrubs the French planted have come back into bloom," Ezana said. "It is as when I was a boy, and the Jesuits taught us Pascal and his calculus."

Angelica laid a slender freckled hand on his tightly trousered thigh. "It's a beautiful city, dear," she said.

"Everything changes, everything heals," Klipspringer abruptly observed. He lifted a glass of *kaikai.* "Here's to 'er, Mother Change. A tough old bitch, but we love 'er."

The other three responded, Angelica with a glass of Perrier water; she was taking instruction in the Koran, and had already learned how to pound millet. Michaelis Ezana frowned down at her touch; in her African garb she seemed less giddying, less a radiant wind from Paradise.

An awkward baggage rather, her infatuation with him a heaviness. The present Mrs. Ezana was horrible—a bare-breasted Amazon, a blue-stocking—but with a horror totally familiar; he had grown pleasantly deaf in the range of her squawks, and could conduct his side of their quarrels in perfect absent-mindedness. Like dark planets, their relationship was exquisitely inertial. She gave him space. Her repulsiveness boosted him aloft. Ezana's lips parted thoughtfully and his gold tooth gleamed like a cufflink as he turned to Klipspringer and began to discuss his favorite subjects, irrigation, electricity, and indebtedness.

"The thing about indebtedness," Klipspringer told him, "is it's the best insurance policy you can buy. The deeper in debt the debtor gets, the more the creditor will invest to keep him from going under. You guys were taking an incredible risk, not owing us a thing all those years."

"Our Great Teacher," Ezana admitted, "was perhaps too inspired for our imperfect world."

"I don't feel I *know* you," Mrs. Gibbs impatiently blurted on his other side. She tugged at his hand with that fretful, proprietorial impatience of her wolvish race. "Michael, even in bed I feel it. Some secret you're withholding."

"Don't bug him," Candy advised her. "They love their secrets, they really can't help it. The African man hates to have his photograph taken. My husband of sixteen years, he was supposed to be the father of our country and nobody knew what he looked like."

"Sorry I never got to meet him," Klipspringer said. "He sounds like quite a character."

Sounds: amid the rustling of palm fronds on the roof, the rats scurrying in the empty rooms, and the late-night patter of their conversation, rustling their blood in hopeful torrents, the knock at the door was muffled.

"The male secret, of course," Ezana gallantly offered the ladies, "is our weakness, our need. But such a secret, like the symmetrically evolved ability of the female to nurture and soothe this need, becomes in exposure boring, monotonous, too—is this the word?—sempiternal. Life is like an overlong drama through which we sit being nagged by vague memories of having read the reviews."

Candace's big Songhai maid came into the room and said there was a beggar at the door. She had told him to go away, and he said he had oranges to sell. When she said they needed no oranges, he offered to dig a well or to sing a song. There was something autocratic about him, beyond her control, and would the mistress like to deal with him now?

The beggar, an *anzad* strapped to his back, had shadowed the maid into the room. "Holy Christ, look who it isn't," Candy said. The intruder, wearing tattered blue jeans and a T-shirt from which the stencilled legend had faded, looked small, pathetically frail, on the edge of their candlelight. Angelica and Klipspringer were politely puzzled, sensing an extraordinary impertinence and tension. Michaelis Ezana perched forward to study the stranger and, touching a reassuring hardness near his left armpit, sat back, returning his face to shadow. "You have your fucking nerve," Candy was continuing, and Ezana thought, Would that change, so bumptiously saluted by our American emissary, were all there were to the world. As well, there is a deadly sameness. The infant cries for suck; the mother heeds; the child grows; the man dies.

In his high-pitched nervous beggar's whine the interloper announced, "I have come not to disturb your feast, but to beguile it with a song." He removed the *anzad* from his back and with his bow of bent goa wood produced a wheedling of melody. He sang through his nose:

"A land without a conscience is an empty land,
a blasted land, a desert land
where the children have red hair and bloated bellies,
where the adults have covetous smiles and cruel
      laughs.

A conscience is more central to a land
than oil wells, foreign loans, and peanut co-operatives;
a conscience puts erectitude into the posture of the
      young men
and soft fire into the glances of the ladyfolk.

But nowhere in the bureaucracy of Kush
amid so many posts for stamp-lickers and boot-lickers
is there regular employment for such a presence.
I ask you, should not a national conscience have a
      pension?"

The musician gave himself over to a partially fumbled riff in minor thirds, and rested the bow at his side. His hostess said, "Oh my God, Happy. Don't you realize you can be shot now? They've gone on without you."

Ezana had taken an interest in the song and asked, "Is it not the essence of a conscience, that it be invisible and ignorable?"

The intruder nodded. "Visible only in its benign effects. As with Allah, to be nakedly present would be to institute tyranny."

"Then," Ezana ventured, "I would think a pension might be arranged, if the conscience in the past had performed services to the state. Unfortunately, I am in no official position to do more than speculate; for in the Dorfû administration Michaelis Ezana holds an emeritus position only. Which, however, is a promotion from his incarceration under the previous administration."

There comes a time in a man's life, the beggar thought, when he thinks of himself in the third person.

Angelica Gibbs, who had not yet mastered the African woman's sublime though deceptive attitude of subservience, asked irritably, "Who is this joker? Darling, why are we letting him ruin our party?"

"Kinda fun, I think," Klipspringer interposed tactfully, his smile doubled by the up-tilting two gray thorns of his fine mustache. "This is their style here, they just let things happen. I think it's great."

The beggar addressed the widow directly. "I bring you good news of the murderer of your husband. He like his victim is vanished in smoke. In time the two will become indistinguishable. Together their sacrifices have opened the sluices to American aid, whose triumph is signified by these twin jinn of the pragmatic, your lover and your escort. The Book says, *Each soul shall come attended by one who will testify against it and another who will drive it on.* Thus black and white, dry and wet, exert their rhythms. Your own pendulum, Madame, is swinging; I salute your costume, pure in its native authenticity. My own, I know, is a shabby mishmash. But you have long been in my mind's eye, and it rewards a life of wandering, that this beggar may gaze upon thee."

The lady was affronted. "Where did he pick up his English?" she asked Ezana and, with a quick switch of her vexed face, "What did he mean, about Don's murderer?"

"Our self-appointed conscience hopes to affirm," Ezana said, "for no doubt conscientious reasons of his own, that your husband willed his own passing, from which, however, much good has arisen."

"I think the fella's making a plea," Klipspringer amplified, "for continuity and orderly transition in government. I'm with him there, one hundred and ten per cent. If your people can't find it in their hearts to grant him this pension he's angling for, I wonder if the USIS couldn't rummage him up a travelling fellowship. Hey, here's an idea. Make him a Donald—what was his middle initial?"

"I've forgotten," Angelica said.

"Make him a Donald X. Gibbs Travelling Fellow," Klipspringer concluded, rubbing his thighs with brisk satisfaction. "We can free up a grant somewhere."

"I've forgotten a lot about Don," Mrs. Gibbs continued to confess. "I actually didn't see that much of him, he was always trying to help people. But he only liked to help people he didn't know. It kept us moving. I wonder if I hated him."

"Such selflessness," Ezana reassured her, "you will not find here in Africa. Here, ego and id are still yoked to pull the oxcart of simple survival."

Something sad in his tone, his assurance of an infinite Africa stretching before her, frightened the young widow, and she looked toward the other American woman for help; but Candy was leaving, not only Africa but leaving the room. With trembling hand she had taken the beggar aside, and moved him toward the front hall, suffused with the scent of *Petrea volubilis* come again in bloom.

Her trembling touched him, this wifely pulse beneath her skin, an amorous agitation superficially like anger, a sense of multiple percussions of blood chiming with his old impression of her as pouncing, as a predator that knows itself as a prey. "You really must get out of Kush," she told him sharply. "This new crowd in power doesn't have any of your irony. They're grim."

"Would you like to take me back with you, to the land of milk and honey?"

Her trembling increased. She gave him a little shove, as she had given the rack of sunglasses a shove. "No. I'm getting a divorce, Happy. This hasn't worked, and it would work even worse there. You *did* hate the States, you know, though you tend to remember the idyllic things. That's how Kush will be for me, I know, once I get out of it. But it's boring back home now. The Cold War is over, Nixon's over. All that's left is picking up the pieces and things like kissing OPEC's ass. You'd be depressed. It turns out the Fifties were when all the fun was, though nobody knew it at the time."

"I could become a professor of Black Studies. I could go into partnership with your father, and re-open the Chicago office, since I am a soul brother. They are looking now for tokens, are they not—your Establishment? We could create children, of a harmonious color. You could teach me to ice-skate."

"Happy, no. That could have been once, maybe; but not now. We'd just embarrass each other, like we always did. I know it's hard for you to believe, but we're through. Honest."

She was right, it is hard for a man to believe that his sexual power over a woman, however abused in its exercise, has diminished: as if we imagine that these our mysterious attractions travel in a frictionless ether, forever, instead of as they do, upon the rocky and obstructed ground of other human lives. The beggar said, "My best to your Dad," and, both of her white hands squeezed in one of his, whispered in the hollow hall, *"Tallaqtukī. Tallaqtukī. Tallaqtukī."*

Kadongolimi had said, "In this house you will be welcome when everything else crumbles." But as Ellelloû approached the villa in Les Jardins that had been transformed into a smoky, fragrant village compound, he saw that her other prophecy had already been fulfilled: weeds had sprung up. In the long rains rot had advanced through the thatch of the outbuildings and pulpy, hollow-stemmed vegetation had sprung up faster than footsteps could beat the ground bare. Without a word Ellelloû was recognized through his disguise of jeans and sun-glasses. The drunken bony man again met him; the naked girl again took his hand, but she led him to a grave. In the center of the courtyard where the flagstones had been pried up to make baking ovens, fresh earth, already adorned with a maidenhair of bright green grass, formed a mound of prodigious dimension. Kadongolimi then had sunk beneath her weight of flesh to displace this mass of forgetful earth. "Her heart was smothered, in the end she cried out for space, for the open skies," the girl told Ellelloû, and he looked at her with surprise, hearing in her voice his first wife's dancing accent, seeing in this slim body the continuum of women asserted, the form reborn he had taken, once, into his arms. I the lion, she the gazelle.

"Did she cry out for Bini?" I asked.

"For him among many. But there were many to attend her. Our touches were all one. She lived to see the ground watered again, and told us that our father had succeeded."

"I was going to ask her to take me back. Now I must ask you."

"We are being moved. Dorfû has his own blood-ties, his own people. Already, you can see, the huts are empty, the yam plots are overgrown. White men have come and bought our tools and *jujus* for their museums. Anu and I are staying until the earth settles a little more upon our mother, and there is nothing left to desecrate." Anu had also been my evil uncle's name; the thread of his lechery and menace had descended, tangled with the thread of beauty that had come into my hand, through the skein of blood-ties that was, after all, the one robe in which I would always be clothed, even in death, as long as the *griots* could sing my ancestry. The compound around me was returning to nature. The narrowest of footpaths, like the paths rabbits trace in the savanna, led diagonally across patios where the stringy bronzed wives of French administrators had laid aside their Bain-de-Soleil-spotted copies of de Beauvoir and loudly clapped for their servants to bring more *citron pressé,* more Campari-and-soda, more love disguised as servitude. Kadongolimi had lain on one of their abandoned chaise longues and then it had collapsed, heaving up this monstrous splash of earth at my feet. A miniature mountain, whereupon rain had begun to work erosion between the little weeds.

I asked the girl, "Will you go back to the village?"

"The village site is no longer ours. The land, they say, is zoned for agribusiness, subsidized by the new government. The government has plans, many plans."

"Do you hate the new government?"

"No," the girl said solemnly, in the dead tone of prudent words. "They are an aftermath, they are men with flat heads, who cannot be blamed. Kadongolimi talked with them, of our eviction, and was much amused. She forgave them. She told them there had been too much magic in Kush, that after a while magicians become evil men. She did not mind their flat heads. They offered her a pension."

Ellelloû was interested. "And did she accept it? Where is it? Did she fill out forms?"

"My mother refused. She said her youth had been sweet, and she had tasted it fully, and now she wished to taste unsweetened the bitterness of dying. She said her world was dying, her life had performed its circle; she asked them for a month undisturbed, that her body could be weighted to sink. For me she asked a scholarship. I think I will become an agronomist, or a pediatrician. Do I have your blessing?"

"Why ask? You have no need of it. The government proceeds without Ellelloû, his craziness got in the way, technology rules instead of craziness, man has resigned himself to being the animal of animals, the champ. Go farm your wombs, or whatever other microscopic deviltry the toubabs urge upon you. Their knowledge is nothing but Hell; they know this now, still they thrust it upon us, they drag us along, that were standing by the side of the march, they take from us all hope of Paradise. They look into the microscope and tell us there is no spirit. There is no way to imagine the next thousand years upon Earth without imagining Hell, life under one big microscope."

The girl said, "My mother told me you were my father and would not refuse a blessing. Even in the snake, each new skin is caressed by the old as it leaves." The words were no doubt Kadongolimi's, but pronounced softer, with no hint of teasing, of what in Salu we call having-it-both-ways.

"Where will your scholarship take you?"

"Some say Cairo. Some say Florida. It is a United State. Our government, with their oil revenues, are establishing a program there."

"I have heard the climate is oppressive. Be sure to take malaria pills. And your Uncle Anu—what will be happening to him?"

"I believe he has been hired by the Postal Department, as a sorter. He has merely to sit on a stool and toss envelopes into bags. The bags then are thrown into the Grionde. Since our ties with the revolutionary government in America have been strengthened, there has been a great influx of third-class mail. I have not heard your blessing."

"Why bless the unavoidable?"

"It is just that," she said, "which needs to be blessed. The impossible is self-sufficient."

I turned away. I thought if I listened, I could hear Kadongolimi speak, out of this mound of earth that was so
little different from her last manifestation to me. What we
most miss, of those that slip from us, is their wit, the wit
that attends those who know us—lovers, grandmothers,
children. The sparks in their eyes are kindled just once by
our passing. The girl waited with me for Kadongolimi to
speak, until we realized together that these flourishing
weeds, and these rivulets of erosion on the heaped mud,
were her words. There came now, from the dilapidated
thatch of the compounds, a scent reminiscent of the
stocked peanut fodder that served, for the young of the
village in their years of license, as cave and bed both; in
my mind the shadows of the foraging giraffes loped away,
incredible orb-eyed marauders fleeing, floating stiff-legged
away from the clacking of mortars and pestles brandished
by overexcited small boys. Kadongolimi had taken these
shadows into the earth with her, leaving me now no shelter save that which I could fabricate. Rain had started up
again, pecking at the grave, twitching the ticking leaves.
The naked girl beside me shivered. I put both hands on
her head, its hair set out in tight braided rows, and pronounced, in the disappearing accent of the Amazeg, my
blessing.

Kutunda was not easy to glimpse, let alone confront.
She still lived, with the simplicity the powerful sometimes
affect, to cloak their power, in the narrow slum building
in Hurriyah where she, an illiterate doxy, had been established by Ellelloû upon their return from the Sahel
border in the Mercedes. Now this same Mercedes, driven
still by Mtesa, whose mustache had flourished, carried her
back and forth along the steep sandy alleys between her

apartment and the Palais de l'Administration des Noirs;
but the windows had been replaced by a murky bulletproof
glass through which only the little tipped smudge of a
profile could be glimpsed. Photographs of her, by Dorfû's
side at this or that public ceremony, were frequently in
the now-official pages of *Les Nouvelles en Noir et Blanc;*
but the Kushite printing hands had not yet mastered
the newly imported American offset presses, and Kutunda's image was mottled or smeared beyond recognition.
(Before it had gone underground in 1968, as a subversive counter-revolutionary sheet, having degenerated
under the king's constitutional reign into a scandalous
tabloid dealing in the pornography of thalidomide freaks
and the astrology of the starlets, *Les Nouvelles* had been
handsomely produced on a flatbed letterpress by Frenchmen who, working with Didot fonts and scorning all pic-
tography, had printed the same hermetically inclusive and
symmetrical regulations over and over, along with medita-
tions upon Négritude from the latest masterpieces of
Gide, Sartre, and Genet.)

The basket shop beneath Kutunda's rooms still oper-
ated, and the hollow-cheeked young addicts still emerged
clutching their contraband wrapped in raffia, but the place
now was clearly manned by government bodyguards.
Indeed more than once Ellelloû spotted Opuku, his bald
head masked by a narrow-brimmed fedora and his great
shoulders clothed in an FBIish gray suit, running a security check on this outpost of the internal police. The
Mercedes came early in the morning and brought
Kutunda back rarely earlier than midnight. By then, a
single dull green light in the basket shop showed the
presence of a drowsy lone plainclothesman, and the agile
beggar skulking in the archway of the Koran school down
the alley dared move with his *anzad* to a position beneath

her narrow slatted window, which the slope of the hill here put so close above his head he hardly had to lift his voice, singing,

> *"Round and firm as the breasts of one's beloved's*
> *younger sister,*
> *she who exposes her gums when she laughs,*
> *and spies from her pallet wondering when her time*
> *will come,*
>
> *one final orange floats in the mind like a moon*
> *that has wrested itself free of the horizon*
> *but still is entangled in the branches of the baobab*
> *tree . . ."*

Kutunda's voice, at conversational pitch, said sharply, "Come up." A heavy tangle of keys was slithered through the slats and fell like a star at the beggar's feet. It was not easy, by moonlight, to distinguish the key that disconnected the alarm from the key that opened the door at the foot of the narrow stairs, and again to decipher, while the narrow pisé walls seemed to be leaning in, listening, the four keys needed for the two double locks on the two steel doors where once there had been a single great plank of mpafu he could open by tapping out the syllables of his name. Ellelloû manipulated the keys clumsily, taking the longest possible route: the first lock was opened by the fourth key he tried; of the three remaining, the third opened the second lock and the second of the two unused keys opened the third; then, in the last lock, the fourth key failed to turn! He tried the others, in reverse order, and found at last that the first key worked. This second door, reinforced with a lattice of riveted ribbing, bore a tiny brass plaque engraved in a script that would have been invisible but for the faint traces of brass polish left within the intaglio. He made out the inscription

> *Minister of the Interior*
> *Protector of Female Rights*

A space of clean brass below awaited further titles. As delicately as Ezana some months before had touched open his old office door, Elleloû touched this one. The door swung open upon a cube of light whose center held a shadow, a dim human core. His eyes, habituated to alley darkness, smarted.

She wore a silk bathrobe of queenly length and her eyes, once brown and flecked, were solid blue. Her posture, too, had changed; the heavy-haunched, cautious stoop of the woman as servant, reluctantly daring to lift herself from the earth, had become the slim erectitude of one who gives orders. At a light indication of her hand, he closed the door behind him. The intimate room he remembered had been expanded upwards, so that where there had been twisted rafters and falling plaster tufted with camel hair a hung dome held a grid of little round dressing-mirror bulbs adjustable to provide (he surmised) appropriate illumination for every situation, however confidential. For this occasion Kutunda had set the rheostat at full cold blaze. Her eyes unnaturally flashed. "You have run out of masks," she told him. "That was not a good song."

"It entranced my mistress once," the beggar said, hunched against the glare of her apartment, of her authority. Where the walls had been crowded with filing cabinets an executive bareness reigned, relieved only by silver abstractions ordered, he imagined, from Georg Jensen or the Franklin Mint. Her overstuffed armoires had vanished, her wardrobe and beautification equipment fled to another room—for this entire building and its neighbor, the hash shop downstairs reduced to a mere front, had been hollowed out to house Kutunda. Where her pot had been, a spiral iron staircase painted ivory led to the second floor of a bachelor-girl duplex. The dirty pallet from which her lover would contemplate the blank side, glowing rose at dawn, of the Palais de l'Administration des Noirs, had become a waterbed heaped with brocaded pillows, and her steel desk a rosewood escritoire exquisite in its fleur-de-lis pulls. Here, papers of state slipped from their pigeonholes and were, he imagined, initialled. She had vaulted from illiteracy into that altitude of power where reading and writing are a condescension.

"Sit down," she said, indicating a chair that was molded plastic as in an airport waiting-room, taking for herself an oval-backed, satin-covered Louis XVI armchair. "Tell me what you've been doing since the coup."

"I worked in that oil town in the Rift—"

"We call it Ellelloû," she said. "For lack of a better name."

"—and when I had a little stake I hitched back to Istiqlal."

"Have you seen the new library?"

"I've watched them pouring endless cement. I wonder if those wings suspended on the cables won't crack when the harmattan blows. Gravity, as you know, is a little extra near the equator. Or do you still doubt that the earth is round?"

She replied pompously, "We have experts to worry about that."

"When I was in power, I found that experts can't be trusted. For this simple reason: unlike tyrants, they are under no delusion that a country, a people, is their body. Under this delusion a tyrant takes everything personally. An expert takes nothing personally. Nothing is ever precisely his fault. If a bridge collapses, or a war miscarries, he has already walked away. He still has his expertise. Also, about the library, but applicable to many ventures—am I boring you? you, who told tales so amusingly in a ditch?—people imagine that because a thing is big, it has had a great deal of intelligent thought given to it. This is not true. A big idea is even more apt to be wrong than a small one, because the scale is inorganic. The Great Wall, for instance, is extremely stupid. The two biggest phenomena in the world right now are Maoism and American television, and both are extremely stupid."

"Then you will be pleased to know that the Braille Library is no longer to be named after your patron King Edumu. Michaelis Ezana has asked that the building be designated the Donald X. Gibbs Center for Trans-Visual Koranic Studies, as a wedding present to his new wife, Gibbs's rapidly acclimated widow."

The beggar said, "A beautiful gift, to crown a coupling so ill-fated. And a suitable monument for that insipid devil who in his racist blindness attempted to dump chemical pap and sorghum for cattle into the stomachs of our children."

"The gift she asked for, and has been refused, was your head in a basket. She wished to have you named as public enemy, found, and prosecuted. We have held back from that. We wish instead that your name be venerated, especially by schoolchildren."

"But there exists a venerable tradition of the criminal-king, from Nero to the sultans, from Ivan the Terrible to our own mischievous Edumu. A nation comes to take perverse pride in the evil it could support, the misgovernment it has survived. You scrupled too much, dear Kutunda, who for all your shimmering robes of high office retain the shifty-eyed timidity of a polluted, detribalized wench. Speaking of eyes, how have yours changed color?"

"Contact lenses, if you must know. They've been in sixteen hours, and they hurt."

"Take them out," he commanded. "And tell my successor, I forget his pseudonym, that in the annals of history moderation is invisible ink."

"I am not sure," she said, pausing to pry with the fingers of one hand her lids apart so that the lens fell into the cupped palm of the other, and then gazing at him bichromatically, "you should be talking to me like this." Picassoesque imbalances, he felt, radiated outwards through the room like the shatter of a windshield from the central asymmetry of her eyes. She bowed her head and removed the other lens, and gropingly removed from a pocket of her robe the curious capsule that held, one on each convex end, the lenses as hard to find, if dropped, as the obsolete Kushite coinage of mirrors.

Ellelloû asked, "Why have you made your eyes blue? Their beauty was brown."

"Dorfû has a penchant for Tuareg women, though the Tuareg are anachronistic, and will soon be settled, under government plans, in communities practicing a profitable mix of peanut cultivation and light industry."

"Dorfû. Are you aware that the word, in Salu, also signifies the torpor suffered by a reptile when it has swallowed too big a meal? Mothers putting their babies to sleep murmur *dorfû, dorfû* . . ."

Kutunda blinked away her tears and resumed the hauteur befitting a cabinet member. "It is true, he wastes no motion, unlike his predecessor. How have you enjoyed these months of vagabondage since your resignation?"

"I have been," Ellelloû told her, "indescribably happy. The wet weather delights me as it does every patriotic citizen of Kush. But beyond that I found, in that town of Ellelloûville, a middling happiness foreign, I fear, to both the mighty and the helpless of our continent. And in Istiqlal, to my surprise, I find that happiness intensified; indeed I now think that the natural condition of men is one of happiness, and that cities, being concentrations of men, are the happier in direct proportion to their size, and that the Koran was right to de-emphasize the tragic, except as it applies to non-believers, who are vermin and shadows in any case."

"If you are happy, why have you sought me out, risking death? My guards are trained to shoot to kill; that is the only technique for fanatic terrorists. Ordinary selfish criminals can be reasoned with, and merely maimed. Opuku's brother heads the new Ministry of Discipline. He has revived, from the days of the Foreign Legion, the *crapaudine*."

Her unreal blue lenses shed, Kutunda's face had softened—the sable irises flecked with gold or sand, the wide flat Sara face broadest across the jawbones, the mouth whose lips seemed the pod for many little white peas, the cinnamon freckles on her dusky cheeks, the wet-looking hair that wandered across her cheeks for all her crisp tailoring of power, her lovable look of being *besmirched*. I thought of her thighs and her buttocks wobbling with weight beneath the quick-silver folds of her queenly robe; my loins sweetened. I had too long been chaste. I said, "My dear Minister of the Interior and Protector of Female Rights, let me present three petitions. One, would you like, now, to marry me? Several vacancies have opened up in my sanctioned quartet of wives."

"This petition comes too late. I am betrothed to the state, and to the ideals of Islamic Marxism, stripped of irresponsible adventurism and romantic individualism. Dorfû has lovingly explained to me that we must never, he and I, marry. Thus we will each stand separate but equal, living exemplars to the men and women of Kush. We will be like the frontal heroic statues in limestone of the Pharaoh and his sister-bride, rather than one muddled image, as in Rodin's *The Kiss*."

"Or in the manner of Hitler and his Eva, rather than the amorously intertwined Roosevelts."

"My President's especial admiration, among statesmen of that period, is for Canada's Mackenzie King, who conferred with his mother in the hereafter. 'The Canada of Africa' is the motto we intend to put on our license plates." She yawned, my freckled foundling, her open mouth a cave of bliss pillowed by her powerful tongue. "My appointments at the Palais begin at nine a.m. sharp," she said. "What was your second petition?"

"For a pension, Madame. I am entitled to one, and with it I will leave the country forever, leaving it forever conscienceless. You will be free to do what you can with this hopeless, beautiful land."

"We feel free now, Dorfû and I."

"But you are not. You are now the actuality of Kush. Actuality breeds discontent, and if I were to reappear, as did Napoleon after Elba, the counter-counter-revolution would be launched. Already, my guess is, Michaelis Ezana chafes at the unofficial limbo in which he must operate, and he has acquired this toubab wife as a possible counter in the game you must, through your rash estrangement of my friends the Soviets, play with the Americans. Where their libraries come, Coca-Cola follows; as our thirst for Coca-Cola grows, our well of debt deepens, and the circle of sky above"—I drew one with my hands, beneath her dome of harsh lights—"is filled with Klipspringer's smile. The oil revenues will bring you dollars good for nothing but to buy what the makers of dollars also make."

Kutunda asked, "Why pay you to leave, when a bullet costs less than a *lu?*"

"The people know I am alive. I pass among them, and they do not need to name me. If I die, the dream of your rule will cease; it is built upon my safe sleep. Dorfû knows this, though you, who rashly advised me to kill the king, do not. Were the king still alive, attracting all blame to himself, I would still be President."

Her words were both clipped and bored. "Pensions are not my department."

Yawn as she would, her known warmth in this pillowed room, some olfactional echo of her tangy, short-legged, downward-tugged *volupté,* had deeply stirred me. My sitting position and loose beggar's robes concealed a club that had grown like a fungus in the dark of my lap.

"What was this third petition?" she asked.

I rose and presented it, my dusty old lust reborn like the desert and so swollen that those of my teeth less than perfectly sound ached at their roots. "Or tell me one of your stories," I begged. "Tell me a vile tale as you used to in the ditch, coming to me under the moon still moist from Wadal and the dwarf."

Kutunda too stood, her silk robe falling straight as armor from the tips of her breasts. "No. The time of fables is over for Africa. We must live among stern realities. You are arrested, as a traitor, an exhibitionist, and an indigent."

The men that came into the room, one through the double door and the other down the resounding iron spiral stairs, from a listening post wherein no doubt all our noises had been taped, including my scratchy struggles with the two double locks and Kutunda's sexy yawns, were not Opuku and Mtesa, they were Opuku and Mtesa's spiritual descendants. Along with their handcuffs and mandatory arm-twisting they brought the something detached (like energetic young actors going through the motions of a play composed by an old homosexual fogey

whose off-stage blandishments they have resisted and
whose political-religious opinions they despise) and chill-
ingly gentle that is their generation's contribution to the
evolution of humanity.

The king's cell had been only perfunctorily cleaned up.
His rubble of royalty—the broken stool, *les joujous,* the
rags once soaked in the blood of some poor shrieking
sacrifice of poultry or livestock and now caked the dullest
brown of earth—had been swept toward one corner, but
the sweeper had wandered away, perhaps to answer the
call to prayer, and had not returned. Michaelis Ezana's
all-too-brief (in my book) tenure had added a slippery
drift of magazines—*Paris Match, Der Spiegel, Tel Quel,
The Economist,* the Italian edition of *Playboy.* Also fil-
ter-stubs of low-tar-content cigarettes, empty Ovaltine
tins, and bedroom slippers of the softness of human genitals, the wool of unborn karakul lambs within and, without, the stitched hides of Greek lizards snared while
sunning on the marbles of the Acropolis. Foreign imports,
I thought, the Third World's ruination. Christendom and
whoredom, two for the price of one. Still, such were no
longer my problems; these had shrunk to the dimensions
of my own imperilled hide.

I dropped the slippers out the window, so they followed
at an interval of time that barefoot descent of Ezana
which my mind's eye has previously in these pages so vividly projected. The slippers plopped some seconds later,
not quite simultaneously, refuting Galileo, in the courtyard below. This was the little dank Cour de Justice; in
the courtyard beyond, over the tile roof of a kitchen pas-
sageway, I could see the schoolgirls of the Anti-Christian
High School forming the circles and parallelograms of
some after-school games. Their cries came like the calls of

blue-uniformed birds feasting on grasshoppers stirred up whirring by the passing of a herd of wildebeests. Light from the clay-colored sun slanted horizontally into the cell; the call to *salāt al-ʿasr* was sprung, with a twang, from the minaret of the Mosque of the Day of Disaster, and weakly echoed from the Mosque of the Clots of Blood. The supper smell of scorched feathers arose in the corridor, with the rustle and twitter of the soldiers' women. The brown shadows in the corners of my room turned blue; a pink blush seeped upwards into the sky, a delicate dye repelled, as by a dropping of wax, by a shadow-eyed three-quarters moon. The sun had set. The *salāt al-maghrib* was intoned. A meal was brought to me, of *fool* and boiled goat's knuckles. I leafed around in *Paris Match,* which had devoted its issue to American porn queens and West German terrorists, the daughters of clergymen and *Wirtschaftswunderarchitekten.* Both groups of young women looked drained by fatigue, the vampire shadow of the camera flash stark behind them on the empty walls. The rooms these photographs were taken in, and wherein these interviews were taped, appeared replications of the same room, a room hidden from the world yet, in effect, the world itself. Rooms, I thought— the world had become a ball of rooms, a hive, where once it had been a vast out-of-doors lightly dented by pockets of shelter. Our skulls are rooms, closeting each brain with its claustrophobic terror, and all Istiqlal, a mass of mud boxes, comprised a mosaic of inescapable privacies. The concealed cellars and apartments where the young celebrities of these wrinkled pages hatched their escapades and platitudes with an identical soul-dead fervor implied a fearful space beyond, and the word *room* seemed to contain some riddle without whose solution the world's sliding could not be halted, its sorrow capped. As night filled all the corners I waited for the spirit of the dead king to repossess his room and with rustling and tapping revive his dead toys and terrify me; but nothing happened save the curious chemical capture and release of sleep. I awoke to hear a soft rain steadily falling. The city was melting, the wet lights of the distant airfield glimmered, enlarged. My life hung in the balance, but I was utterly relaxed. Thus have I seen a leopard dangle all its four limbs from a high branch of a swaying acacia, murderous dreams now and then twitching its front paws.

Days passed in this rhythm; then at last Dorfû came to visit me, in the late afternoon, toward the end of the wet season. I was struck again by his beauty beyond gender, like that of polished wood, or of a supple vine whose graceful, gripping ascent into the light makes no mistakes. His smile within my cell was like the dab of sun that finds its way to the forest floor. His fez, his signature, was of a glossier plum, and his uniform, the color of a scrubbed winestain, harmonized without ostentation. In tailoring at least, Kush had found a leader to surpass Ellelloû. He had that fine Fula skin, that seems always freshly oiled. Tall, he moved with a certain stiff economy of motion, refuting any presumption that his administration would be frivolous. A toubab might have marvelled at Dorfû's regal ease, he having been so recently a lowly police spy; but we Africans have little difficulty in adjusting upwards to luxury and power. Indeed it may be true for all the sons of Adam that no good fortune, however extravagant, seems out of keeping with our proper, Edenic inheritance. He spoke in a courtly mix of English and Arabic. He carried a book bound in gold cloth.

"I believe," Dorfû smiled, "in some lands political prisoners are subjected to what is called re-education. Here, we prefer to think of it as entertainment. I thought I would read to you, as I once did to the pious Edumu." He settled cross-legged on his green cushion, opened the

Koran with curved thumb, and read, where he had left off nearly a year before, ". . . *and adorned with bracelets of silver. Their Lord will give them a pure beverage to drink.*" He looked up and asked, "What purer beverage than freedom?"

"None purer," answered Ellelloû. "I thirst for it."

Dorfû continued to read. "*The unbelievers love this fleeting life too well, and thus prepare for themselves a heavy day of doom. We created them, and endowed their limbs and joints with strength; but if We please We can replace them by other men.*"

Dorfû and Allah both, Ellelloû noticed, preferred to say *We*. A trick of leadership he himself had failed to master.

Dorfû concluded the sura. "*He is merciful to whom He will: but for the wrongdoers He has prepared a grievous punishment.*" The President lifted his eyes benignly from the glowing page. "A peculiar problem of African government," he said, "is the disposal of the bodies of the deposed. In Togo, the clever Sylvanus Olympio was inelegantly gunned down by the hand of his successor, Colonel Eyadema. In Mali and Niger, the ex-Presidents Keita and Diori are rather awkwardly incarcerated, awaiting their natural deaths. In this nation, our friend Edumu was manfully slain, but his body became a haunting marionette. Now you have suggested, in a taped interview with our sister Kutunda, that you be not only pardoned but assigned a pension in exile. A proposal as impudent as your ill-timed and obscene assault upon her chastity."

Ellelloû felt in his throat an odd constriction, overruling even thirst. "Like every citizen of Kush," he said, "I entrust myself to your mercy."

Dorfû's smile broadened. "You make a virtue of a necessity; that is the art of living. I have not forgotten who elevated me, albeit in haste, even with some scorn of my potential, to the rank of interim Minister. And I thought your reasoning, as expressed to Kutunda, not without all merit. She, I should inform you, has advised for you a variety of ingenious tortures, climaxed by cremation, that your lewdness no longer pollute the purity of Kush. I would hesitate to disregard her usually sound advice, but in this instance certain international and media considerations prevail. You died, as President, in the city that bears your name. Now the honor of the *Presidency* must be safeguarded. We must show our friends the Americans that we too value the office above the man."

"I do not wish to survive thanks to some American superstition."

"There is also the indigenous consideration that, on a continent where materialism has yet to cast its full spell, a live man far away is less of a presence than a dead man underfoot."

The constriction in Ellelloû's throat eased. "I would defer gladly to scruples authentically native. How much will my pension be, and when may I secure it?"

"We have decided that a colonel's pension would be appropriate, added to by half again as much for each wife who accompanies you, and a third again for each dependent child. Enough will be advanced for your passage abroad; when you have an address, the checks will arrive monthly. All this contingent, of course, upon your anonymity and silence."

"You will get off cheap. No wife will come with me."

"There is one, our intelligence-gathering arm reports, that you have not asked. But that is your *affaire,* as the French say." He bowed his head and read again the verses, *"Let him that will, take the right path to the Lord. Yet you cannot will except by the will of Allah."* Dorfû closed the Koran yet seemed in no hurry to go. Something lingered in the cell, with its jumbled relics and orange slant of late-afternoon sun, congenial to both men.

"Strange," Dorfû said. "You took the name Freedom, and have been captive, until now, of your demons. Our capital is called Independence, yet our polity is an interweave of dependencies. Even the purity of water is a paradox; for unless it be chemically impure, it cannot be drunk. To be free of hunger, men gave up something of themselves to the tribe. To fight against oppression, men must band in an army and become less free, some might say, than before. Freedom is like a blanket which, pulled up to the chin, uncovers the feet."

"You are saying, perhaps," ventured the prisoner, "that freedom is like all things directional. One of the magazines that Ezana abandoned, *Les Méchaniques Populaires* I believe, assures its credulous readers that all things move swiftly in some direction or other; even the universe by which we measure the separate motions of the earth and the sun itself moves, through some unimaginable medium, toward some unimaginable destination. How delicious it is, my President, to pause in movement, and to feel that divine momentum hurtling one forward!"

"It must have been the rushing of your blood you heard. The wind does not feel the wind. To be within the will of Allah is to know utter peace. Once, in the course of my training as a member of the coercive branch of government, I parachuted, expecting tumult; instead there was peace beyond understanding as the earth lifted beneath me, offering as on a platter its treetops, the branching patterns of its dried riverbeds, the starlike dots of its herds, and the thatched rooftops from whose cooking-fires smoke drifted as I did. This was near Sobaville, and I noticed how perilously slender the road between the barracks and the capital appeared. One of my first acts, as

Acting Minister of the Interior, was to have this highway made four-lane. In our infant governments, the connection between the head and the coercive arm must be close. Your wanderings as President perhaps should have included more visits to Sobaville."

"I had some taste for battle," Ellelloû allowed, "but none for the forced *camaraderie,* the latrine humor, of peacetime barracks. Men together generate unhealthy vapors. Am I free to leave, and, if so, when, Mr. President?"

With a little pragmatic shrug Dorfû lifted his hands from where they gracefully rested, wrists on knees. "When you are free within yourself, to terminate."

"I'd like to try it right now," I said. The main obstacle was my sensation that he needed me, and this, I saw, was a delusion.

Dorfû smiled. "Do not forget Sheba's *anzad.*" He added, "You should write some of your songs down."

"The pension—is it to be paid in *lu,* or a less chimerical currency?"

"On the strength of the projected peanut harvest, we are thinking of making the *lu* convertible and letting it float. However, if you would rather be paid in dollars—"

"Dollars!" Ellelloû cried, flaring up as when an evening breeze makes dark coals glow again. "That green scum which sits on the stagnant pond of capitalism, that graven pilfering of our sacred eagles and brooding pyramids, that paper bile the octopus spews forth! Pay me *en franc.*"

Dorfû nodded; the round top of his fez winked violet, floating like a momentary UFO in the horizontal, ebbing light. The four-color photograph Edumu had once upon a time framed, of a little girl and a presumed black man frozen in mid-tap on a make-believe staircase, had been removed from its sumptuous frame, the frame stolen for

its gold but the paper image reverently tacked back up. It
fluttered, as the evening call to prayer entered in at the
green-silled window.

Sittina's villa was one vast flower, all overgrown by the
oleander, bottlebrush, hibiscus, and plumbago that flourished in our hospitable climate. She herself was not at
home, though the sounds of her children squabbling and
playing nostalgia-rock records arose from within. I looked
through a window. Her *Well-Tempered Clavier* gathered
dust on the harpsichord, its pages open to a fugue whose
five sharps had stymied her. Our Chagall still hung on the
far wall. The Ife mask looked tatty and askew. As I
turned to leave, Sittina came along loping through the
morning mists, through the shade of the fully leafed chestnut trees, clad in a blue jogging suit, her hair no longer
held back by fish spines but cut close as a cap to her
head. As she ran, she looked bow-legged in the manner of
runners, the shins incurved so the resilient feet can keep
pace on an invisible straight line. "Félix," she said to me,
scarcely panting, and continuing to jog up and down as
she talked, "why—are you wearing—a three-piece
business suit?"

"It's what they give you when you leave prison," I told
her. "Also a beggar's disguise gets you arrested. Begging
has been declared non-existent by the government. Long
life to Dorfû! Death to extremists of both rightist and
leftist tendencies!"

"Don't make me—laugh," she said, "it throws—my
breathing off. It's ecstasy—once you hit—your stride. I've
lost—five pounds. Unfortunately—it's all come off my
ass—instead of my belly."

"That's middle age," I told her.

"I thought—you were—evaporated."

"Demoted," I said. "Can't we go inside? I'm getting a headache watching you jiggle."

"I've been offered a job—calisthenicist for the work teams—being organized in the refugee camps—over at Al-Abid."

"You want the job?"

"No. You know me. I hate being—tied down. But I need the *lu*—since you blew the dictatorship."

In addition to cropping her hair, she had minimized her wind-resistance by substituting for her great hoop earrings little sleepers of agate. Her narrow Tutsi skull offered to the air as compliant an edge as the prow of a yacht to the waves, as the profile of Nefertiti to the oceans of time. Sittina showed me this profile, saying over her shoulder, "Come on in"; she swept back a shaggy branch of feathery bamboo and tugged open her swollen front door. "The house's a mess," she apologized. "The last *au pair* I had took a cushy government job, in the Bureau of Detribalization. The Tuareg are all busy being house-guards for the people who got rich during the famine, and the government's trying to retrain the slum-dwellers to become nomadic herdsmen, because the nomads are good for the ecology. Mind if I take a quick shower? Otherwise the leg muscles cramp."

Her children had gathered around me curiously, solemn appraisers of a line of lovers. One child had orange hair—a sign, it relieved me to see, not of kwashiorkor but of Celtic sperm. "What is your name?" I asked him.

"Ellelloû."

"Do you know what that means?"

"It means solidarity."

"No, that is wrong. It means freedom."

"I don't *care*," the child told me, and turned on his

heel to hide a trembling lip. He was gleefully pounced upon by his siblings as he sought to control his humiliated sobbing. They jostled and tumbled him like hyenas at a hamstrung impala; but when they let him up, he was laughing. It was right, that I had not intervened. In the skirmish I had counted six heads, which totalled up, in welfare's new arithmetic, to two full pensions. My vest hugged my belly with premonitions of bourgeois comfort. A child slightly larger than the frizzy redhead, a girl in a Gucci pinafore, with a Nilotic slant to her eyes, asked me, "You love my mommy?"

"I admire her speed," I said.

"You going to take care of us?"

Before I could frame another evasion, Sittina raced through the living-room wet and nude. Her long tapered thighs, her bean-shaped buttocks. "Damn towels are in the dryer," she called over her shoulder. "Tell the kids it's time for the bus."

One of her children had been watching through a window, where the crowding flowers permitted a peephole; when he shouted, the others scrambled for their books, their slates, their hand-computers, their spiral-bound notebooks and supplementary cassettes. I helped them through the door, through the tangle of their rubber boots and clinging pet patas monkeys. The bus, imported yellow but overpainted with the national green, lurched to the shady corner and held its stop long enough to receive their noisy, needful bodies. Even the three-year-old was enrolled in a Montessori beadwork group. I breathed, in amplification of the *salāt as-subh* with which I had ceremonialized the dawn, a silent prayer of thanks for free public education, the cornerstone of participatory democracy and domestic bliss.

Sittina had returned to the living-room still naked. Her

sharp small breasts, her high central pocket of soft curls.
"Weren't in the dryer either," she said. "I remember I put
them out on the line to save electricity. But nothing dries
outdoors anymore. I'd go see, but some lousy American
tourist'd take my picture. Really, they're *so* awful. The
women in the *souk*, with those long red fingernails and
blue hair in bandanas and those cracked whiskey voices.
The West Germans are worse—all straps and fat and hik-
ing boots. Remember how I used to complain about the
Albanians? I'm sorry, you were right. I was wrong. We
should have stayed isolationist. There are nice things in
the shops now but who can afford them except the tourists? The boutiques up under the Gibbs Center are chic
but they're always full of lepers." Noticing my eyes upon
her body, she spun, in that room of incompleted curves,
and asked. "What do you think? Don't tell me. I know.
My ass is too skinny."

As usual, she had raced on ahead of me. Later, when,
with trembling legs, I went to the bathroom, there were
plenty of towels there, fluffily clean and shockingly white,
white as new snow, as raw salt. She, scenting the eschato-
logical drift of my call, had chosen to sustain her side of
our exchange in elemental, traditional costume. "Not too
skinny," I answered numbly. "Just right." The numbness
—Livingstone's in the mouth of the lion, the pious man's
in the grip of his fate—I had experienced before in the
course of this narrative, at most of its crucial turns.

"Still?" Sittina asked flirtatiously, in profile, the long
round brow of the Tutsi royal line as erotic, as meek and
glistening, as the twin bulges of her taut buttocks. Her
nipples were long and blue.

"Still," Ellelloû said, adding, "I must go away."

"To the Balak with Sheba again?"

"No."

"Back to the Bulub with Kutunda?"

"I think not."

"Down to the underworld with Kadongolimi?"

"This is a cruel litany."

"Off to the States with Candy?"

"She's left already. We're divorced. None of our friends was surprised; mixed marriages have a lot of extra stresses."

"Any marriage is mixed. Where will you go now, poor Félix, and who with?"

"With you? It's just a scenario. We could go somewhere where you could paint more seriously."

"Not sure seriously's my style," she said, striding on long legs into her long living-room, with harassed-looking waves of both arms indicating the fibrous brown masks and musty Somali camel saddles that overlooked like a baffled animal chorus her twinkling furniture of smudged glass and scratched aluminum. Among the Africana she had hung or propped canvases more or less eagerly begun but left with blank corners and unfilled outlines. "I can't bear to finish things, beyond a certain point they get heavy. There's something so dead about a finished painting. Or a finished anything, in this climate. Maybe it's palm trees and clay houses. You slave away, and what do you have in the end? A picture postcard from Timbuctoo."

"The South of France," Ellelloû said, "has very paintable trees." He had taken a step after her, she had grown so slender with distance, and Sittina answered his step by striding back to him, brown between her brown walls, and draping her long arms lightly on his shoulders. Tufts of armpit hair, still wet from the shower. Mustache traces above the corners of her smile, at the level of his eyes. "You smell like you want something," she said.

"I want to consolidate," Ellelloû confessed.

"Then we ought to try *us*, as a starter."

She did still coo, when she spread her legs. The mats on the floor, once they cleared away the children's toys, seemed in their marital haste soft enough. Beds are for toubabs, whose skins Mr. Yacub bred to lack the resilient top layer. Ellelloû was excited by the five-petalled faces of the audience of oleander at the windows. He in her—his pelvis cradled in her elegant thighs, his hand cupping the firm ellipses beneath—Sittina rolled her eyes in wild Watusi display of the bloodshot whites, taking in the furniture and wall ornaments upside-down. She moaned, "My God, think of the packing! And the children's dental appointments!!"

The good citizens of France no longer look up at the sight of *noirs* strolling down their avenues. Their African empire, which a passion for abstraction led them to carve from the most vacant sector of the continent, backed up on them a bit, like those other cartographic reservoirs for a century flooded with ink of European tints, and doused the home country with a sprinkling of dark diplomats, students, menial laborers, and political exiles. Even in Nice, along La Promenade des Anglais, which becomes Le Quai des États-Unis, amid the singing of the beach pebbles and the signing of autographs by topless young leftovers from the Cannes Film Festival, an ebony family, decently attired, draws only that flickering glance with which a Frenchman files another *aperçu* in the passionate cabinets of his *esprit*. Africa has been legitimized here by art. Delacroix skimmed the Maghrib and Picasso imported cubism from Gabon. Josephine Baker, Sidney Bechet . . . *noire est belle.*

The woman is extremely chic: tall as a model, with a
little haughtily tipped head and a stride that swings the
folds of her rainbow-dyed culottes. The man with her is
relatively unprepossessing, insignificant even, shorter than
she, half his face masked in NoIR sunglasses. He does not
appear to be the father of the variegated children who
march at their sides. From his carriage he might have
been a soldier. The boys from their look of well-fed felic-
ity will never be soldiers, or will make bad ones. The
girls, the girls will be many wonderful things—dancers,
mothers, strumpets, surgeons, stewardesses, acrobats,
agronomists, magicians' assistants, mistresses, *causes
célèbres,* sunbathers, fading photographs in mental al-
bums, goddesses glimpsed like cool black swans amid the
glitter of an opera house, caped in chinchilla, one gloved
hand resting on the gilded balcony rail as they turn to go.
The pagans pray to females. It gladdens the writer's heart,
to contemplate the future of his girls. The boys, he wor-
ries about. He fears they may fall, civilian casualties in
the war of muchness that is certain to overtake the planet.

The family lives, apparitions from a rumored continent,
beyond Carabacel, where the streets become steep and the
tile-topped garden walls bear a profusion of bougainvillea
and a forgotten rusting pair of scissors, in the Rue de
Ste.-Clément. Behind their walls they are assiduous,
economical, conjugal, temperate, optimistic, dynamic,
middling, and modern. The woman, it is rumored, paints.
The children, the neighbors attest, take violin, *anzad,*
clarinet, *kakaki,* piano, and *sanza* lessons. The small
black man can be seen sitting at round white tables along
the Quai, or a few blocks inland from the distracting,
sail-speckled Mediterranean, at open-air cafés beside the
river of traffic along the Esplanade de Général de Gaulle.
He has always a drink at his elbow, a Fanta, Campari-

and-soda, or *citron pressé* with a dash of anisette; he seems to be an eternally thirsty man. His other elbow pins down a sheaf of papers. He is writing something, dreaming behind his sunglasses, among the clouds of Vespa exhaust, trying to remember, to relive.

Little news of Kush comes here. France has become what China once was—an island of perfect civilization, self-satisfying, decaying, deaf. What does it care for the smoothly continuing coups in sandy lands where once its second sons in cerulean pillbox hats chased blue-skinned Tuareg deeper and deeper into the dunes? At an OPEC conference in Geneva, among the oil ministers taken hostage and harangued by an Austrian divinity-school dropout and his emaciated girl friend, was named one Michael Azena [misprint] of Couche. He survived the episode, though the revolutionaries smashed his wristwatch. Otherwise, Kush comes as a dusky whiff reminiscent of peanut fodder, or a green band of sunset sky toward Biot, or the taste of orange in a sip of Cointreau, or the shade of the Cinzano *parasol* overhead, faintly suggestive, when the sea breeze flaps its fringed edges, of the shade of a tent, the most erotic shelter in the world. Kush is around us in these hints, these airy coded bulletins, but the crush of present reality—the oblique temperate sun, the sensational proximity of the sea—renders these clues no more than fragile scraps of wreckage that float to the surface, fewer and fewer as the waves continue to break, to hiss, to slide, to percolate through the pebbles. All yesterdays are thus submerged, continental chunks sunk from sight that once were under our feet. How did he come here? the pink passersby perhaps ask, insulted by the *nègre*'s air of preoccupation, amid the beauties of their city, his face downcast to the *cahiers* in which he pens long tendrils like the tendrilous chains of contingency that have delivered us, each, to where we sit now on the skin of the world, water-lilies concealing our masses of root. *Those who have gone before them also plotted, but Allah is the master of every plot: He knows the deserts of every soul.* The man is happy, hidden. The sea breeze blows, the waiters ignore him. He is writing his memoirs. No, I should put it more precisely: Colonel Ellelloû is rumored to be working on his memoirs.

A Note About the Author

John Updike was born in 1932, in Shillington, Pennsylvania. He graduated from Harvard College in 1954, and spent a year in England on the Knox Fellowship, at the Ruskin School of Drawing and Fine Art in Oxford. From 1955 to 1957 he was a member of the staff of *The New Yorker,* to which he has contributed short stories, poems, and book reviews. He has published twenty books, including four collections of poetry and eight novels. In 1973 he traveled in Africa as a Fulbright Lecturer.